A DEATH ON
THE WOLF

Also by G. M. Frazier

Return to Innocence
Gerard
Brian's Wish
Summer Solstice

www.gmfrazier.com

A DEATH ON THE WOLF

G. M. FRAZIER

ISBN-10: 146625453X
ISBN-13: 978-1466254534

Epicea Books

For Daddy
1930 - 1984

A DEATH ON
THE WOLF

When I was a child, I spake as a child, I understood as a child, I thought as a child: but when I became a man, I put away childish things.

1 CORINTHIANS 13:11, KJV

PART ONE

Chapter 1
The Summer of 69

The summer I turned sixteen I shot a man. It was 1969. Neil Armstrong walked on the moon. Hurricane Camille destroyed our farm. And I shot a man.

I grew up near the town of Bells Ferry, Mississippi, on the Wolf River, about twenty miles north of Pass Christian. The farm house we lived in was a modest white frame structure built by my mother's parents. My father was an ex-Marine, a widower, and a millwright at the carbolineum plant in Bells Ferry. My mother died in 1963 giving birth to my sister, Sachet. I was supposed to be a junior—Patrick Lemuel Gody, Jr.—but my mother prevailed upon my father at the hospital to give me her maiden name, Nelson, so Patrick was relegated to second place on my birth certificate. As for the surname, our ancestors were French and came to this country in the eighteenth century. They settled around New Orleans, and our family name had originally been spelled "Godet" but got Anglicized sometime after the family migrated into southern Mississippi.

It was summertime, and from May until September my days would be marked by the routines only family farm living offers. There was always grass to mow, weeds in the garden, pine needles to rake, a cow to milk, peripatetic goats to round up, okra to pick, tomato vines to stick and tie, potatoes to dig, corn to shuck, beans to snap, and a hundred other chores. Add to all that the part time job I had taken at Dick's ESSO station in town, usually working three afternoons a week. But life wasn't all work, as there was always ample opportunity for a quick swim in the Wolf River, which was less than a mile down the road from our house. Frankie Thompson was my best friend, just four months younger than I, and because his family ran a small dairy farm, he was as busy as I was during the summer. But we usually managed to get away for an hour or two nearly every afternoon for a swim in the cool dark waters of the spring-fed Wolf. Our spot on the river was "secret," a pristine white sand beach not visible from the road and shaded by the trees where we swam and occasionally pitched a tent for campouts. Frankie and I had cut a path to it through the woods back in the fourth grade, and so far no one outside our circle of friends and family had discovered it—that we knew of.

With the exception of my job at the ESSO station, the summer of 1969 had begun like every other summer I could remember since starting school. Now that July had rolled around, and my routine was set, I assumed it would run its course and finish like all my summers that had come before it. I could not have been more wrong. This was to be my summer of endings and beginnings. A summer of life. A summer of love. A summer of loss. A summer of death.

— — —

On this first Monday in July, I was in charge of preparing dinner for Sachet and myself. Daddy rarely got home from work before six o'clock, so our Aunt Charity normally saw to our meals in the evenings—except on Tuesdays (her bridge night) and the first Monday of each month (her Eastern Star meeting). As I took the loaf of bread out of the pantry, I glanced at the clock on the kitchen wall by the ice box. It was almost 6:30. My sister was sitting over at the table, so I took the bread, grape jelly, and peanut butter over there and began making her sandwich.

As I began spreading the jelly on the bread, Sachet said, "I don't like it like that."

"Sash, this is a peanut butter and jelly sandwich. I'm putting the jelly on the bread. What is there not to like?"

"You're putting it on thick," she said. "I like the jelly to be thin and the peanut butter to be thick."

I looked at my sister. Our house was not air conditioned, and the big fan over in the corner was blowing her long blond hair around her face in soft swirls. Over the course of her five and a half years on this earth, I had made Sachet dozens, maybe hundreds, of peanut butter and jelly sandwiches. I had come to expect some complaint about this or that, but she had never made me aware of this requirement. I took the knife and scraped some of the jelly off. "Better?" I asked.

She nodded, then said, "Do you think they're really going to the moon?"

"Yes," I replied, "they're really going to the moon."

The launch of Apollo 11 was just a little over a week away, and given that every S-IC booster of the Saturn V rocket was assembled down at Michoud in New Orleans, and then test fired at NASA's Mississippi Test Facility outside of Picayune, the event was as big a deal around here as it was in Houston or Cape Kennedy. Daddy's brother, my Uncle Rick, worked at MTF. He was an engineer and worked for NASA, but I wasn't sure what he did. He was able to get us guest passes to the test firings, which were something to see, hear, and feel. Of course, everyone within fifty miles of MTF heard and felt the thunderous roar of those five F-1 engines when they would light off during a booster test. In fact, the last test left a crack in one of the windows in the principal's office at my school.

I was now spreading peanut butter on the other slice of bread. I watched my sister's green eyes as they followed the knife's every movement from the jar to the bread. She was carefully scrutinizing my culinary skills, ever ready to offer a criticism should I not perform to perfection.

"Aunt Charity says people were not meant to go to the moon," Sachet said. "She says God won't like it."

I finished the final assembly of Sachet's sandwich, placed it on a paper plate, and then slid it across the table to her. "Aunt Charity is an old fuddy-duddy," I said. I went over to the junk drawer in the kitchen and got a rubber band.

"How old is Aunt Charity?" my sister asked as I started pulling her hair back to get it out of her face.

I had to stop and think about her question. "She'll be forty in November," I said, and fastened the rubber band around the pony tail.

Aunt Charity was Mama's twin, and Mama was thirty-four when she died. Mama had two sisters: her twin, Charity, and their older sister, Faith. Mama's name was Hope, and she was the middle of the three sisters: Faith, Hope, and Charity. Even though Mama and Aunt Charity were twins, she was, by a few minutes, the oldest. Aunt Faith lived up north somewhere with her second husband. Mama's funeral was the last time I had seen her, and my only recollection of her almost six years later was the smell of cigarettes and stale White Shoulders.

"Do you want milk or tea to drink?" I asked Sachet.

"Milk," she said.

I went over to the ice box, got the pitcher of cold milk and poured Sachet a glass.

"Aren't you going to eat?" she asked me as I set the glass in front of her.

"I'm not hungry," I replied.

"You'd have to eat if Aunt Charity was here. She'd make you."

"She's not here. And if she were, you wouldn't be eating that." I pointed to the sandwich. The only time we could eat like this was when Aunt Charity was away. And heaven help us if she found out Daddy had taken us into town to eat at the Colonel Dixie, the only hamburger joint in Bells Ferry. The Bobby Dean Diner in town was fine, but the Colonel Dixie was off limits as far as our aunt was concerned.

Sachet took her first bite of the sandwich and I waited for the inevitable critique I knew would be forthcoming. But she just chewed and chewed and then took a gulp of milk. I replaced the pitcher of milk in the ice box and decided to leave well enough alone and not ask her how the sandwich was.

"Mama will be forty in November, too," Sachet said.

"If she were still alive," I said.

"So me and Mama and Aunt Charity have the same birth-day?"

"Yes."

"And I'll be six."

"Yes."

"So Mama died on my birthday and her birthday and Aunt Charity's birthday."

"Eat your sandwich," I said. This was an exchange my sister and I had had many times.

"If Mama and Aunt Charity were twins, how come Aunt Charity doesn't look like Mama in the pictures?"

I pulled out the chair at the table and sat down across from Sachet. This was a new inquiry that was taking this familiar conversation into uncharted territory. There was no way I could explain the genetics, which I wasn't even sure of myself, but I knew if I didn't give my sister an answer (and one she'd be satisfied with), I'd be dealing with this issue until bedtime. "Some twins are identical and some aren't," I offered.

"What's 'identical' mean?"

"That means they look exactly alike."

"Oh." She took another bite of her sandwich and chewed. "Do you still remember Mama?" she mumbled through the goo in her mouth.

"Yes."

"Do you miss her?"

"Yes."

"Me, too."

I could have easily pointed out the obvious to my sister, but I knew what Sachet meant. She didn't miss Mama; she missed having a mother. It's a terrible thing to lose your mother when you're ten years old—but maybe worse still to have to grow up without one at all. Aunt Charity had stepped in to fill the void from the day Daddy brought Sachet home from the hospital, but it wasn't the same. I knew it. Sachet knew it. And I suppose, most of all, Daddy knew it.

Aunt Charity was taller than I remember Mama being. She had brown hair. Mama's was blond like mine and my sister's. Our aunt lived next door to us in a big brick house that her husband had built in 1959. Jack Jackson, my Uncle Jack, had been a captain in the Marines, a decorated veteran of the Korean Conflict. Daddy eschewed college, enlisted in the Marines right at the end of World War II, and was discharged in 1950 with the rank of Sergeant. He got out before things really got going in Korea, so he never saw action. But he was in the Military Police, so he may not have been sent overseas anyway. He and Mama got married in '51 and I came along in '53. Mama had had two miscarriages before I was born.

Aunt Charity and Uncle Jack didn't have any children. Uncle Jack was a career Marine officer who took a commission when he graduated from Ole Miss in '52, the same year he and Aunt Charity got married. He was killed back in '66, in "Lyndon Johnson's infernal war" (to quote my father). Daddy had supported Barry Goldwater in '64 and he said the war in Vietnam would have long been over by '66 if Goldwater had been in the White House. Aunt Charity agreed with him. She said we all would have been dead by 1966 if Goldwater had been President. Listening to Daddy and Aunt Charity talk politics was entertaining, to say the least.

Before Mama died, Aunt Charity had been a school teacher, and she taught me and all my friends in the first grade. But she also "had money," which was a quaint way in Mississippi of describing someone you were fairly sure was financially well off, but unsure just how well off they were. There were people who were "rich," and those that "had money." Aunt Charity was of the latter: She didn't have to work. She lived in a nice house. She always drove a new Cadillac. And she had a white housekeeper. Aunt Charity paid me $20 each week during the summer to mow her lawn and keep the pine needles raked up. During the winter she always found something for me to do around her house so she could pay me $20 a week. Years later, I learned that Aunt Charity was very well off indeed from Uncle Jack's oil and gas leases from his family's land over in Louisiana—land and leases he'd left to her. Land and leases she subsequently bequeathed to my sister and me.

I heard the squeak of the screen door on the back porch, then: "You all home?" It was Parker Reeves, the colored man Daddy had hired back in January to help out on our small farm—a decision I was still trying to figure out since we didn't need any help, especially back in the dead of winter.

"We're in here," I hollered out the open kitchen door.

Parker appeared in the doorway, hat in hand. "Mr. Nels, them goats done got out again and are all over in Miss Charity's yard. I tried to get 'em up but they's too quick." I don't know why Parker insisted on calling me "Mister Nels." I suppose it was the remnants of the etiquette of the Old South, but it made me uncomfortable. I was fifteen-going-on-sixteen and he was old enough to be my great-grandfather. But to him I was "Mr. Nels" or "Mr. Nelson." Even Sachet, at five years old, was "Miss Sash."

I looked at Sachet. "When you finish, I want you to go wash your hands and face, brush your teeth, and put your pajamas on. You can watch some TV until I get back. I Dream of Jeannie comes on tonight. I'm going to help Parker get those goats up before Aunt Charity gets back and has a fit."

Sachet nodded and then gave me a little smile. She knew there would be hell to pay if Aunt Charity came home from her Eastern Star meeting and saw those goats in her yard, especially if they had been eating any of her flowers. "What about a bath?" she asked.

"No bath tonight," I said, getting up from the table. "You had one last night."

Chapter 2
Daddy's Way

It was after nine o'clock and Daddy had not gotten home. I had taken a bath and was in my pajamas, sitting in Daddy's recliner watching *The Carol Burnett Show* on the TV. Sachet was in bed asleep. I had finally gotten her down at 8:30, which was a half-hour past her bed time. She did not like to go to bed without seeing Daddy, but I knew if he was not home by eight, something was wrong at the plant and it was no telling what time he might get in. I had heard Bear, our collie, barking a few minutes ago when Aunt Charity got home from her meeting. The goats were back inside the fence behind the barn, and they hadn't done too much damage in her yard. With darkness fast approaching, I was hoping she would not notice.

I heard Bear bark again along with the sound of Daddy's pickup, with its tell-tale exhaust leak, pulling in behind the house. I got up and went to the kitchen.

As Daddy stepped through the kitchen door, the phone rang. Since the phone was on the wall right inside the door from the back porch, he caught it on the second ring. "Hello?"

I stood there watching him listen to whoever was on the other end of the line. It was unusual for us to get any phone calls this late at night.

"I don't know," Daddy said. "I just got home." He put his hand over the receiver and looked at me. "Did the goats get out again?" he asked.

"Yes," I said, and rolled my eyes to heaven. It was Aunt Charity on the phone.

Daddy smiled and I could tell he was trying not to laugh. "Yes, Charity…I'm sorry. It won't happen again…I know…I know. Yes…yes…soon as I get the lumber. Right. I promise. Yes…goodnight." He hung up the phone.

I walked over and took Daddy's lunch box from him as he hung his hardhat on the coat rack beside the door. He smelled of sweat and creosote and grease, a cocktail of scents I had grown up with and did not find objectionable at all. I took the thermos from the lunch box and went over to the sink to wash it and get it ready for tomorrow.

"Thank you, son," I heard Daddy say behind me as he sat down at the table.

"You had to work over tonight?" I asked rhetorically. I flicked the switch for the fluorescent light over the sink and poured out the bit of cold coffee still in the thermos while I waited for the running water to get hot.

"The number two boiler went down at three this afternoon and we spent five hours working on it," Daddy said.

The water was hot now and I started washing out the thermos. I looked in the dark glass of the window over the sink and I could see Daddy's reflection. He was watching me. "Do you want me to fix you something to eat?" I asked.

"I stopped down at the Colonel Dixie and got me a burger when I got off work. I ate it on the way home."

"Don't let Aunt Charity find out," I said, looking at Daddy's reflection in the window glass. He chuckled to himself.

"Nelson, we're going to have to rebuild the fence behind the barn this weekend," Daddy said. "Your Aunt Charity has reached her limit with the goats, and mending the fence every other day isn't working anymore. And Parker is too old to be chasing after the goats every time they get out."

"I know," I offered as I rinsed out the thermos and started drying it. "He and I had a time getting them back in. I'm glad Aunt Charity was at her meeting."

"Eastern Star tonight?" Daddy asked.

"Yes," I said, and popped the dish towel, then folded and hung it on the peg sticking out of the side of the cabinet over the sink. Daddy was a Mason, and he and Mama had belonged to the Eastern Star, too, but Daddy had not gone to any of the meetings since Mama died. He did try to make the Blue Lodge meetings on the second Thursday of each month, but work often prevented it. Looking back, and from what I know now of Freemasonry, I can honestly say my father took the central tenets of that ancient fraternity to heart and embodied them in everything he did. I was about to get a lesson in that fact as I went over and sat down at the table, looked at my father, and asked, "Why did you hire Parker? We don't need him and most of the time when he's here he's just sitting around out there at the barn."

Daddy leaned back in the chair and ran his hands through his hair. He was studying me. People said I looked like my father, but I couldn't see it. He had dark brown hair; mine was sandy blond. He had blue eyes; mine were green. Daddy was forty-two, tall and lean (that trait we did share), and his skin was tanned and weather-worn from twenty years of working in the Mississippi sun. "I know we don't need him, son," he finally said. "But he needs us."

"What do you mean?"

"The only family Parker had left around here was his grandson, Haywood. He worked down at the plant with me until back in January. He lived with Parker, paid the bills, bought groceries. He got in a bar fight on New Year 's Eve and stabbed a man and he's been in jail ever since. When he got arrested, Haywood asked me to go check on his grand-daddy, and I did for a couple of weeks. The last time I went to check on him there was no food in the house, so I tried to give him some money, but he wouldn't take it."

"How come?" I asked.

"Parker's a proud old gentleman. He didn't want a hand-out."

"But isn't that what his grandson was doing if he was paying the bills and all?"

"No. Haywood was paying the bills, but he wasn't pay-ing any rent to live there."

"Oh," I said. "I still don't see why you hired him."

"Because he wouldn't take my money but he would take a job, Nelson. Like I said, we didn't need him, he needed us. The twenty dollars a week I give him isn't going to break us, and I know he eats good when he's here. Charity sees to that. And he has helped out around here a lot, espe-cially since you started working down at Dick's."

"I guess so," I said.

"Speaking of you working down at Dick's, you going to have enough money by the fifth?"

"I think I'll have enough," I answered, sounding more sure than I really was.

We were now talking about the car I wanted to buy. I would turn sixteen on August 5th, and Daddy had promised to take off work that day and take me to get my license. And he knew I wanted to do the driving test in my own car; my first car, which I'd been saving for since April. Daddy had told me numerous times that I could drive our family car any time I wanted to. His old Dodge pickup was the primary vehicle for us, and the car was really only driven to church on Sunday and the few times we ventured out of the Bells Ferry area to go to the beach or shopping down at Biloxi or Gulfport, or if Daddy was feeling especially adventurous, the hour or so drive down to New Orleans. But our car was about the most un-cool vehicle around. Daddy loved it, but I thought it was hideous. It was a 1960 Chrysler Saratoga 2-door hardtop; a black behemoth with a red interior that had tail fins that were nearly chest high on me. I called it the Batmobile. Daddy bought it from a dentist down in Bay St. Louis the year before Sachet was born, the year before Mama died. The Batmobile had two redeeming qualities: it had air conditioning that would freeze your nuts off on the hottest day in August, and it had nifty swivel-out bucket seats that made getting in and out an adventure in itself.

As for the drivers license, it would be, quite frankly, a formality. I had been driving the back roads around here in the pickup since I was thirteen and people generally assumed I already had my license. I was also constantly riding the Honda 350 Scrambler Daddy had bought last summer. He was a motorcycle aficionado of sorts, and had bought and sold numerous old Harleys and Indians over the years. In fact, there was a '52 FLH Panhead in the barn now that he was rebuilding. The Honda was the first new bike he ever bought, and it had quickly become my main form of transportation; consequently, my old Schwinn had been gathering dust in the barn for nearly a year now. I think Daddy was secretly longing for me to get a car so he could have his motorcycle back.

The car I had been saving up to buy belonged to the estate of the late Mrs. Wendell Borcher, which had just come out of probate. Mrs. Borcher had left the car to a niece who lived over in Bogalusa and she didn't want it, so she asked the attorney handling the estate to sell it. As it happens, J. Preston Marks, Esq. and my father were high school classmates and fellow Masons, so through some "wink and nod" negotiations the sale was being delayed until I could save up enough money to close the deal. My sources of income were my $5 weekly allowance for doing chores and watching Sachet, the $20 a week I could count on from Aunt Charity for cutting her grass or whatever she needed doing, and my job at Dick's. The car was a pale blue '64 Impala 4-door hardtop with a 283 in it. What made it desirable, besides having that small block V8, was that Mrs. Borcher rarely drove it, which meant even though it was five years old, it spent most of its life in the garage, had less than four-thousand miles on it, and looked like brand new. And it would be mine for $500.

"How much have you got?" Daddy asked.

"About two-hundred."

"And what are you making a week pumping gas down at Dick's?"

"About twenty…maybe a little more when I get some good tips."

"I don't think you're going to have enough come your birthday, sport."

I knew he was right, but I was trying to remain optimistic. I think Daddy could see the fiscal worry in my face. "I'll tell you what," he said, leaning forward and placing his elbows on the table. "You help me rebuild the fence on Saturday and however much you're short come your birthday, I'll make up the difference. Deal?"

"Deal," I said with an enormous grin on my face. But it wasn't a deal at all. It was a gift. We both knew I would be helping to rebuild the fence on Saturday with or without this gesture from my father.

"Well, I'm going and take a shower and hit the hay," Daddy announced as he got up from the table. "Four o'clock comes around mighty early in the morning. How's my baby girl?"

I was wondering when he was going to ask about Sachet. "She got upset because I made her go to bed before you got home," I said.

I could see Daddy's expression drop. He loved my sister more than life itself, I believe. The mere thought that he'd done something to cause her distress bothered him. "Well...it couldn't be helped," he said, sounding more like he was reassuring himself than me. He turned for the hallway off from the kitchen.

"Dad?" I said.

He turned and looked back at me. "Yes?"

"Thanks."

"For what?

"About the car."

"Don't thank me yet, sport. It's supposed to be hot as hell on Saturday. You'll earn it."

Chapter 3
Breaking the Sabbath

Daddy was right: it was Saturday, and it was hot as hell. The lumber yard opened at eight, and we had taken the pickup and the long trailer to get all the posts and boards and wire we'd need. Then it was down to Dick's Hardware (the same Dick who owned the ESSO where I worked, but the hardware store was run by his brother) for the nails and paint. We would be replacing about three-hundred feet total of fencing, and I thought Daddy was being overly optimistic saying that we could get it all done before dark. But he said Parker was coming to help us after lunch. And then he told me the reason he wanted it completed today: I would be painting the new fence on Sunday after church. Daddy didn't share Aunt Charity's views about working on the Sabbath, and sometimes I wished he did.

It was a little before ten now and already nearly 90 degrees. Daddy had me digging out the old fence posts, repacking the dirt, and then digging new holes at eighty-inch intervals. He had been out before I even got out of bed and marked the spots where I was to dig. I had asked him why we just couldn't pull out the old posts and stick the new ones in. His answer was a curt, "Because I want this done right."

We had the goats shut up inside the barn, and they were making a racket. If it were up to me, I would have just turned them loose in the cow pasture and let them wander the nearly fifty acres with the cows. When I suggested that to Daddy, he asked who was going to help me scour those fifty acres and find all the goats when the new fence was done and it was time to put them back where they belonged. Suddenly my suggestion didn't sound too good.

Daddy was over by the barn cutting the boards to the correct length for the fence rails. He had set up the saw horses in the shade of the big pecan tree, and he was using the power saw, which was plugged into a long yellow extension cord coming from the barn. I was in the boiling sun using a claw hammer and a posthole digger. My tee shirt was damp with sweat and we weren't even into the heat of the day. I was beginning to see why Daddy had told me not to thank him prematurely for his offer to help me buy the car. He was right. I was earning it.

About an hour later I was soaked from head to toe. My eyes were burning from the perspiration that was continually pouring into them. And I was only about a third of the way done with my job of dismantling the old fence and digging new post holes.

Daddy had finished cutting the boards for the rails and was already constructing the new fence starting at the barn. He was working his way toward me and I was determined to stay ahead of him. The humidity was oppressive and there was not even the hint of a breeze blowing. The steamy air was filled with the sharp report of Daddy's hammer striking the nails and the racket of the cicadas. "Daddy," I hollered to him. "I'm about to die over here. Can I go to the house and get some water?"

He looked up and wiped his brow with the back of his gloved hand. "Yeah, and bring me some, too. See what Charity is fixing for lunch." I stuck the posthole digger in the ground and headed for the house. "You'll be a lot cooler out here if you get one of my caps and wear it," Daddy said as I walked by him. He pointed to the John Deere hat on his head. I hated wearing a hat, but I was willing to try anything for some relief.

As I opened the screen door on the back porch, the smell of Aunt Charity's cooking hit me in the face. Whatever she was fixing for lunch smelled fabulous. She was standing at the sink when I walked in the kitchen. No matter how hot it was, Aunt Charity always looked fresh and untouched by either the heat or the humidity. She was a trim woman, with ramrod straight posture, and she was always dressed like she was going to town. I don't think she owned any casual clothing. She took one look at me and started in: "Lord have mercy," she declared, "is Patrick Lemuel Gody trying to kill his only son? Just look at you."

"It's hot out there," I said.

"Sit down and cool off before you drop from heat stroke," Aunt Charity said.

It was probably 80 degrees in the house, but with the fans whirring away, it sure felt good to me. "I can't," I said. "I just came in to get some water and Daddy wants me to bring him some, too."

"Go over there and sit down," she ordered, pointing to the table. She went over to the ice box and got out a tray of ice and fixed me a glass of ice water.

I downed the cold glass of water in almost a single gulp when Aunt Charity handed it to me. She also had a cold wet dish towel, which she wiped my face with then said, "Hold this to the back of your neck and I'll get you some more water."

"I've got to take Daddy some water and get back to work," I said.

Aunt Charity gave me one of her stern looks. "You sit right there and cool off. I'll take your father some water." She went back over to the sink and refilled my glass, then fixed another glass of ice water. After she gave me mine, she left to take Daddy his.

Aunt Charity had only been gone about a minute when I heard the screen door on the back porch open. "That was quick," I said, expecting to see my aunt come in the kitchen, but instead Frankie Thompson appeared at the door. He had on his cut-offs, so I knew what he wanted even before he spoke. "Hey, man," I said. "I thought you were Aunt Charity. She just went out to take Daddy some water."

"Hey," Frankie said. "I'm going down to the river. Can you go?"

"I can't," I said. "I'm helping Dad build a new fence behind the barn."

"And y'all pick the hottest day of the year to do it?"

"I know," I said, and took another gulp of ice water.

Frankie came over and sat down at the table just as Aunt Charity got back. "How are you today, Francis?" she asked.

"I'm fine, thank you, Miss Charity." Frankie looked at me and smirked. His name was Francis John Thompson, Jr., and Aunt Charity was the only person who ever called him "Francis." She'd called him that since we were both her pupils in the first grade.

"Are you sure you can't go swimming?" Frankie asked.

"I can't, man. I've got to help Dad with the fence."

"Didn't he hire that nigger? Why can't he do it?"

I saw Aunt Charity go rigid over at the sink. I looked hard at Frankie. "Don't call him that."

"What?"

"You know what you said. Parker's not a nigger, he's a Negro."

"What's the difference?"

I was watching Aunt Charity out of the corner of my eye. She was about to go apoplectic. I was trying to think of a way to diffuse this situation before she exploded. I knew Frankie didn't mean anything by this. He was just a product of the way he'd been raised, as was I. The problem was, Aunt Charity believed every child in Mississippi should have been raised the way my sister and I had been, and she was ever ready to correct the deficiencies of those that weren't.

"Are you Caucasian?" I asked Frankie.

He looked at me. "Yeah, why?"

"Are you a whitey cracker?"

"No," he said sternly.

"Why not? What's the difference?" I asked.

Aunt Charity turned and gave me a big smile from over at the sink. Mission accomplished.

Frankie was just staring at me, so I decided to change the subject. "Does your dad need any help this summer? I need to make some extra money before my birthday."

"I don't know," Frankie said. "I can ask."

"Nelson Patrick Gody, you are not going to work at their dairy farm," Aunt Charity declared.

I looked up at her. "Why not?"

"Because you've got more than enough to do around here. And you've already got a job at Richard Tillman's filling station in town."

"But Aunt Charity, I need—"

She held up her hand, and I knew there was no need to say anything else. She'd already invoked my full name, which was fair warning. I would not be working at Thompson's Dairy Farm to earn the extra money I needed for the car.

"Where is Sash?" I asked.

"She is over at my house watching the color TV."

Aunt Charity's house had central air conditioning, and with the thermometer on the back porch approaching 100 degrees, I suspected that's why my sister was over there. I looked at Frankie. "I wish I could go to the river, man, but I've got to help with the fence." I lowered my voiced to keep Aunt Charity from hearing and said, "Maybe I can go tomorrow after I get done painting it."

Aunt Charity turned and glared at me. She had heard. "On the Sabbath?" she said with righteous indignation.

"I'm still going to church in the morning," I said. "I'll paint the fence when we get home."

"And you think going to church in the morning gives you leave to break the Fourth Commandment the rest of the Lord's Day?"

It was my turn to hold up my hand. "Talk to Daddy," I said, and got up from the table. This was a debate she and my father had had before, and I didn't want to get in the middle of it now. Daddy gave Aunt Charity virtual carte blanche when it came to co-parenting my sister and me. But on the subject of religion, especially Aunt Charity's legalism, Daddy was as unyielding as she was persistent. Thus, as for me painting the fence tomorrow, I knew who would win that argument. I never understood how two people could attend the same church every Sunday, listen to the same sermons, and have such disparate opinions on certain tenets of the Christian faith.

I walked over and kissed Aunt Charity on the cheek. "Thanks for the water," I said, and headed for the door. I turned back and motioned for Frankie to come on. "What's for lunch?" I asked Aunt Charity. "It smells good."

"I've got a pork roast in the oven cooking for dinner. That's what you're smelling. We're having fried chicken and biscuits for lunch." She stepped over to the cabinet and retrieved our well-seasoned iron skillet, turned and pointed it at me. "You and your father be in here at noon sharp." She looked at Frankie, who was now standing beside me. "Would you like to stay for lunch, Francis?"

Frankie eyed the skillet in her hand, no doubt wondering if Aunt Charity intended to club him with it if he said yes. "No, ma'am. I'm going swimming. But thanks."

"Well, be careful down there at the river. Watch out for snakes."

"Yes, ma'am. Bye, Miss Charity."

"Goodbye, Francis."

Once out the door, before either Frankie or I had a chance to say anything, we heard the roar echoing off the trees down by the bridge a half mile away. We both looked at each other and grinned, turned and ran for the front of the house.

As we made it to the front yard, the angry bark of the motorcycle was building, the sound like a great beast bearing down on us. We could hear the rider winding out each gear as he accelerated hard coming off the bridge over the Wolf River.

"What is that?" Frankie said.

"I don't know," I replied. "It doesn't sound like a Harley."

We stood there transfixed as the sound and the fury of this unknown machine got closer. Being nearly six-foot and about four inches taller than Frankie, I was the first to spot the bike and rider as they rounded the curve. "There it is," I said.

"Where?" Frankie said, suddenly on his tip-toes and holding onto my shoulder for balance.

Right about then the rider nailed the throttle again and the machine roared by us in a blur. He was doing 70, at least. The most I could tell about the bike was the color: it was black and chrome and sparkled like a gem in the mid-day sun.

"Nelson, we've got work to do."

Frankie and I turned to see Daddy standing there. "Did you see that?" I asked him.

"Yes, now come on. We can get a little more done before lunch."

Frankie and I followed my father back around the house. Frankie said, "I wonder what that was?"

"Daddy, do you know what kind of bike that was?" I said to my father.

He turned back and said over his shoulder, "I didn't get a good look at it. Get one of my hats like I told you, Nelson, and get back to work."

I stopped with Frankie at his bicycle, which was parked behind our car under the carport in the backyard. Bear was lying under the back of the car, panting. Normally he'd be up and jumping all over Frankie, but the day's heat had taken its toll on him.

"You sure you can't go?" Frankie asked.

I raised my eyebrows and cocked my head toward my father who was still walking toward the barn and the unfinished fence. "I can go tomorrow late if I get it painted," I offered.

Frankie was on his bike now and kicking up the stand. He looked up at me with a frown. "If we go tomorrow I'll have to bring Mark."

"So?" I said. Mark was Frankie's little brother. He was eleven and relished every minute he could spend with his brother and me.

"It's more fun when it's just me and you," Frankie said. "Why do you always want him to go with us?" he added.

"You're the one who just said Mark would have to go, not me," I said. I didn't know why Frankie thought I always wanted Mark to go with us. I couldn't think of a single time I'd ever suggested it.

"Mama and Daddy are going down to The Pass tomorrow after church to have dinner with some friends. They don't like me to leave him at the house alone for very long when they're gone."

"Well, I don't care if he goes with us. It's up to you."

With a wave and a "See ya," Frankie turned and pedaled off. I ran inside to get one of Daddy's caps.

Chapter 4

Frankie

It was Sunday, just after noon, and we were riding home from church. It wasn't quite as hot today as it had been yesterday, and the Batmobile's air conditioning was doing its job. It was just Daddy, Sachet, and me. Normally, Aunt Charity rode with us to Bells Ferry Presbyterian Church, but she drove her Cadillac today because it was the Sunday she and the other ladies in her Circle went to visit the orphans in the Masonic Home for Children over in Poplarville.

"Daddy, I'm cold," Sachet said from the back seat.

He looked at her in the rear view mirror. "Here, baby girl," he said, and tossed his suit coat back to her. "Cover up."

I could not help but smile. It was freezing in the car, and Daddy loved it. He worked in the sweltering heat down at the creosote plant five days a week. Our house was not air conditioned. His pickup truck was not air conditioned. But this car that he loved was, and as far as Daddy was concerned, its air conditioner had two settings: Off and Wide Open.

"What did you think of the sermon this morning?" Daddy asked.

"It was okay," I said.

Our pastor, the Reverend Douglas J. McMillan, D.D., had retired back in the spring and in June the church had begun in earnest the search for his replacement. The Pulpit Committee (the chairman of which was my father, who was also an elder and Clerk of the Session) had interviewed three candidates thus far. I would miss Rev. Doug. He was the only minister I'd ever known. He baptized me, taught me the Shorter Catechism, and served me my first Communion. He was Southern Presbyterian to the core and could make the most untenable tenets of Calvinism understandable, showing how each one flowed naturally from the Word of God. The young minister who preached this morning was competent, but we could all tell he was nervous. He had a pretty wife who sat in one of the front pews with their two rambunctious children. Daddy had offered to take them to children's church with Sachet after the offering, but the mother refused. Thus, the sermon was continually interrupted by their outbursts, which did not bode well for extending a call to this man.

"Dad?" I said, looking over at him.

He glanced over at me, careful to keep one eye on the road. "Yes?"

"What are we going to have for lunch?"

"Leftovers from last night, I guess." He looked over at me. "Why? What are you thinking?" I could tell from the expression on his face he was thinking the same thing I was.

"Aunt Charity is halfway to Poplarville by now," I said.

Daddy put his tongue in his cheek and let out a little laugh. He looked in the mirror at Sachet. "Baby girl, you want a hamburger for lunch?"

Suddenly Sachet appeared in the gap between the front bucket seats. I turned to look at her and started laughing. She had put on Daddy's suit coat and looked like a hobo's child.

"Don't laugh at me!" she demanded.

"Oh, will you relax, Sash," I said. "I swear, you get more like Grandma Gody every day."

Sachet stuck her tongue out at me and Daddy was giving me a frown. "So how about it?" he said, returning his attention to Sachet. "You want to eat at the Colonel Dixie?"

"Won't Aunt Charity be mad?" she asked.

"Yes," Daddy said, "but she'll get over it."

"Okay," Sachet said.

We were almost back home and Daddy was starting to slow down, looking for a place to turn around so we could drive the three miles back to town. I had a thought. "Daddy, Frankie's house is just up the road. Can we go by there and see if he wants to come with us?"

Daddy looked at the Bulova Accutron watch on his wrist that Sachet and I had given him for Christmas. "Don't you think they're probably already sitting down to Sunday dinner, sport?"

"Frankie told me yesterday his mom and dad were going down to Pass Christian to eat with some friends."

"All right, we'll see if he wants to go. But, Nelson, we got the fence done yesterday and I want it painted today, son. It shouldn't take you more than three or four hours and then you can have the rest of the day until dark to go and do whatever with Frankie. No play until the work is done."

"I know," I said.

We rounded the next curve and there was the entrance to the Thompson's farm a hundred yards up the road. Daddy reached over and punched the MAX button on the air conditioner to close off the outside air coming in because he knew we were about to be assaulted by the stench of the hundred or so cows that would be congregating near the barn.

"Look coming there," Daddy said, and pointed.

"That's the bike that went by the house yesterday," I said. It was headed straight for us. Daddy reached over and hit the electric switch to lower his window so we could hear the bike as it roared by. I sat up in the seat and watched it flash by us.

Daddy was watching it in the outside rear view mirror. "That's a Vincent," he said. "How about that. Don't see one of those everyday."

"What's a Vincent?" I asked.

"It's a British bike. Expensive. Fast. They don't make them anymore. Rollie Free hit a hundred and fifty miles an hour on a Vincent at Bonneville back in '48."

"Who around here would have a bike like that?"

"Probably one of the flyboys from down at Keesler just up here riding the back roads."

Suddenly, Daddy was hitting the brakes hard. Watching the motorcycle, he'd almost overshot the entrance to the Thompson farm. The "Fresh Eggs" and "Fresh Milk" signs were rapidly approaching and I wasn't sure if Daddy was going to be able to stop in time to make the turn. But with a deft flick of the wrist, he wheeled the Batmobile into the Thompson's drive, sending gravel and sand flying, and Sachet sliding across the backseat.

When we pulled up in front of Frankie's house, Daddy blew the horn just as I was opening my door to get out. Frankie came to the screen door that opened onto their front porch. Their house wasn't air conditioned, either.

"Hey, man," I said, walking up to the porch. Frankie still had on his church clothes: a white button-down shirt and navy dress slacks; we were dressed exactly alike.

"Hey," Frankie said. "What are you doing here?" He opened the screen door and stepped out onto the porch in his sock feet.

"We're going to eat lunch at the Colonel Dixie. You want to come with us?"

Just then, Frankie's little brother, Mark, came to the door. He was dressed just like Frankie and me, except he had on a tie. Frankie turned to him and said, "Go fix you a sandwich for lunch like Mama said. I'm going with them to eat in town."

Mark pushed the screen door open and looked at me. "Hey, Nels," he said.

I could see the disappointment in his face at the prospect of having to stay here alone and eat a sandwich. "Hey," I said. "You want to come, too?"

Mark's countenance immediately brightened and Frankie just glared at me. The moment was awkward, or at least as awkward as a moment like this could be between two boys who had been best friends since they could walk. I could hear the Batmobile idling twenty yards behind me and I knew Daddy was waiting.

"I don't want to go," Frankie finally said. He turned, pushed his brother out of the way, and went back in the house, the slamming of the screen door punctuating his retreat.

I bounded up the steps and went to the door. I peered through the screen, but couldn't see anything. "Frankie!" I hollered. "Don't be a jerk, man. Come on and go with us." I waited for an answer. Nothing.

Daddy gave a quick beep on the horn. I turned and looked down at Mark standing beside me. "Come on," I said and headed off the porch.

"You mean I can still go?" Mark asked.

"Yeah, come on," I said, waving for him to follow me.

Mark ran up beside me, and he was grinning from ear to ear. I was taking long strides to get back to the car quickly and Mark was having to near jog to keep up. "Frankie's going to be mad," he said, his voice bouncing in time with his every step.

"I don't care," I said.

I opened the door to the car and leaned the back of the front seat up so Mark could get in the backseat with Sachet. Daddy looked over at me as I slammed the seat back down and got in. "Where's Frankie?" he asked.

"He's not coming," I said, sounding more angry than I really was.

"Okay," Daddy said, raising his eyebrows. He turned to Mark in the back seat. "How are you, young fella?"

"Fine, Mr. Lem. Thanks for letting me go with y'all."

Daddy punched the D button on the dash to put the Batmobile in gear, did a wide U-turn in the Thompson's front yard, and we were headed back down their drive.

As we rode along, Mark said something about how good it felt in Daddy's air conditioned car, and the two of them were talking now, but I wasn't really listening I was thinking about Frankie. We had had disagreements and falling-outs before, as best friends are wont to do when they grow tired of each other and need some space. But this was different, this simmering animosity over his brother and me that had been on a slow boil for weeks now. It began one Saturday over a month ago when Mark went with us down to the river to swim.

Frankie and I would typically ride down to the river on our bikes, or both of us on "my" Honda, wearing nothing but our cut-offs and tee shirts. Once there, we'd shuck them off, along with our underwear, and hit the water. That Saturday, Mark wore his swimming trunks and, having the inherent modesty of a preteen boy on the cusp of puberty, would not strip down in front of us on the beach. He waited until he was in the river, where the dark water of the Wolf would ensure his privacy. He pulled off his trunks and then let them float along in the water with him until he got to playing around with us, not paying attention, and the current carried them away. None of us realized they were gone until we were ready to head back home nearly two hours later. Mark's trunks were probably halfway to Bay St. Louis by then.

Frankie thought this predicament was hilarious, and he could not stop laughing at his little brother, who was standing in waist-deep water, watching us on the sandy beach putting our clothes back on. I didn't laugh. I could see just how embarrassed Mark was as he looked at me with pleading eyes and said, "How am I going to get home?" That sent Frankie into another fit of laughter and I told him to shut up. I didn't fully understand Mark's embarrassment, but I wasn't going to make fun of it. Even if he rode his bike bucknaked the two miles back to his house, the chances of anyone seeing him were slim to none. I was about to pull my tee shirt over my head when I had a thought. "Mark," I called to him, "you can wrap my shirt around you and I'll take you home on the Honda."

Mark walked out of the river with his hands over his privates, his pale hips and butt a stark contrast to the rest of his tanned body—especially since he had the same dark olive skin that Frankie had: skin that soaked up the Mississippi sun and returned a tan any woman down on the beach at

Biloxi would die for—and many probably did. Frankie had told me there was Choctaw blood in the Thompson boys from their mama's side of the family, and their dark eyes, dark hair, and complexion showed it.

We left Mark's bike there on the beach and he rode on the back of the motorcycle with me to his house with my tee shirt wrapped around him. And unlike when we had ridden down there earlier, where I had putted along in second gear at 15 miles per hour so Mark and Frankie could keep up on their bikes, now when we pulled off the path from the river onto the road, I nailed the throttle and left Frankie behind. Mark and I were doing nearly 60 when we hit the bridge, and he was about to squeeze the breath out of me holding on for dear life. When we got back to his house, Mark climbed off the back of the Honda, and I watched him run for the porch with the sleeves of my tee shirt trailing behind him like a kite's tail. I never saw that shirt again.

After that day when I took Mark home and left his brother at the river, there was a change in Frankie, and the change seemed to intensify each time his little brother was forced by circumstance or providence to be in our company. And now, today, for the first time, I recognized the change for what it was in all its glory. It was jealousy. It was stupid and irrational, which was precisely why I knew now I could never reason with Frankie about it. And I sensed the resolution would either strengthen our friendship or destroy it. There would be no middle way.

Chapter 5
The Intruder

The next morning at breakfast, Aunt Charity dropped a bomb on me. After Sachet had finished her oatmeal and gone out to play, Aunt Charity told me she was bringing one of the children from the Masonic home to live with us for the rest of the summer. I didn't understand the "us" part so I made sure to ask if this stranger would be staying at Aunt Charity's house and not ours, and I was assured it was to be the former. I suppose it did not occur to me then that despite there being two houses on the Gody farm, separated by about fifty yards, Aunt Charity saw us as one family, and significant changes in one household were worthy of discussion in both. Seems she and Daddy had discussed this last night and he had given his blessing. My counsel was not sought—nor even desired, apparently—and the plan was presented to me as a *fait accompli* over eggs, bacon, grits and biscuits the next morning.

I was mulling this over now as I watched Aunt Charity at the sink washing Sachet's bowl. My sister was on the front porch, playing with her dolls and tea set, blissfully ignorant of this news I was sure would ruin the remainder of our summer. But, if there is one thing I had learned from my father, it was the futility of fretting over things you could not control. So, as I sat there swirling my fork in the remnants of my over easy eggs, I started trying to think of the bright side. It was hard, but I was trying. Maybe having another kid around for the summer wouldn't be such a bad thing.

Maybe having someone right next door to toss the ball with, or go down to the river with, or help out with milking the cow, or cutting the grass, maybe this was a good thing. My mood began to brighten. "So what's his name and how old is he?" I asked Aunt Charity.

She was drying the bowl she'd just washed. She spoke without turning to me. "Her name is Mary Alice Hadley and she is fourteen," she said.

So much for looking on the bright side. I just stared at Aunt Charity while I tried to find the words to express my frustration. Not only was a stranger, an intruder, coming to live with us, to encroach upon my summer, but it was a girl, and that was totally unacceptable. "How come nobody asked me what I thought about this?" I said with an angry timbre—a mistake, and I knew it the minute the last word left my mouth. I watched Aunt Charity slowly put the clean bowl in the cabinet. She turned to me, and instead of her patented gaze of stern indignation, I saw a softness there that was both familiar and strange. I saw a brief glimpse of my mother's face.

Aunt Charity came over and sat down at the table across from me. Normally, when I was about to get a verbal dressing down, I would be sitting with her towering over me. I could, of course, stand up at any time and reverse that, but I didn't dare. But now, here she was coming down to my level, meeting me as an equal. It was a totally unexpected move on her part and it had the effect of calming me. And again, I was seeing images of my mother from so long ago, and my heart ached because of it. My mother, who could melt the resolve of an obstinate boy with the sheer force of her gentle spirit; she had been the polar opposite of her twin sister. But, on rare occasions, like now, Aunt Charity would show that she and Mama had been cut from the same bolt, and that somewhere, deep beneath her unbending rectitude, lay the same pacific gifts that served my mother as a mother so well.

"Nelson," Aunt Charity began, "you are right. Your father and I should have talked with you about this, and I'm sorry we didn't. I think we both forget sometimes that you are a young man now and not a little boy."

"Yes, ma'am," I said, looking down at my plate. She had completely disarmed me. Sixty seconds ago I was cocked and locked and prepared for battle; now I was ready to wave a white flag.

"Nelson, look at me," she said.

I looked up at her. "Yes, ma'am?"

"Whatever misgivings you have about this, or any ill will you feel toward me for doing this without asking you first, let's get it out in the open now. Once Mary Alice is here, we will not speak of this again."

"You don't have to worry, Aunt Charity. I'll be nice to her."

"Oh, Nelson, I never thought for a minute that you wouldn't be nice to her."

"I just don't see why you're doing this," I said. "It's not like she doesn't already have a place to live."

"You'll understand better when you meet her."

"When is she coming?" I asked.

"I'm leaving in a few minutes to go pick her up." Aunt Charity got up from the table and took my plate and glass over to the sink.

"Are you taking Sash?" I asked.

"No, I'll need you to watch her until I get back."

"I have to be at work down at Dick's at two," I said.

"I should be back before noon. Marie is over at my house today. If I'm not back by the time you have to go to work, take your sister over there." Marie was Aunt Charity's housekeeper.

"Okay," I said. I looked at the clock on the wall. It was half past seven. What a way to start the day.

— — —

I was back at the barn, filling up the watering trough for the goats, when I heard the horn and looked over at Aunt Charity's house to see her gold Sedan de Ville pulling into the drive. Sachet was standing in the shade of the pecan tree watching me. She was tugging at her dress and holding one of her dolls. "Where's Aunt Charity been this morning?" she asked.

I rinsed my hands off in the stream of water coming from the spigot and then shut off the valve. "She had to go to Poplarville," I said, shaking the water from my hands. "Why do you keep pulling at your dress like that?"

"It itches," she said.

I walked over to her and pulled the back of her dress open. "It's the label," I said. "You want me to cut it out?" She nodded her head so I fished the knife out of my jeans pocket and opened the blade. "Hold still," I said. I moved her hair out of the way and started cutting the label.

"Don't cut me," Sachet said.

"Then be still." I finished cutting out the label and then smoothed the back of her dress down. "Is that better?"

My sister wiggled and worked her shoulders up and down to test the efficacy of my handiwork. "Why did Aunt Charity go to Poplarville?" she asked.

"She's bringing one of the kids from the home over there to stay with her this summer." I closed my knife and stuck it back in my pocket.

Sachet turned and looked up at me. "Why?" she said.

"I don't know." I took my sister's hand and we headed over to Aunt Charity's to meet the intruder.

As we got to the edge of my aunt's yard, the trunk lid on her Cadillac popped open. Aunt Charity was getting out of the car and she motioned to me. "Nelson," she called, "please get Mary Alice's suitcase out of the trunk." I waved acknowledgment.

As Sachet and I got closer to the car, I peered intently into the backseat to see what this girl looked like. But Aunt Charity's front yard was populated by tall, longleaf pines just as ours was, and she was parked in the shadow of one, thus, I could not see into the car well enough to tell if there was beast or girl or both in the backseat. Whichever, she had not gotten out yet and Aunt Charity was standing there, waiting for me to get the suitcase.

"I may need you to help me get Mary Alice in the house," Aunt Charity said in a hushed tone.

"Help you get her in the house?" I said, not sure I'd heard her correctly. I reached in the trunk for the large Samsonite bag. It was heavy, and I actually had to strain to lift it. "Good grief," I said as I lugged the thing out of the trunk. "What's she got in here, a load of bricks?"

"Mind your tongue," Aunt Charity said, again in a low voice.

I followed her around the car with Sachet right by my side. When Aunt Charity opened the back door, my first glimpse of this interloper was of a pink sundress with tiny blue flowers on it, so tiny they almost looked like blue dots.

She was wearing sandals and I watched as her legs slowly rotated out of the car and she put her feet on the gravel drive. Then the walking stick appeared, and the delicate hand that held it. When she leaned forward and I saw her face, my heart melted. She was the prettiest girl I had ever seen. Her complexion was fair; her eyes a deep blue. Her long brown hair fell on her bare, creamy shoulders with a little upturn curl. As she stood up and reached out for anything to hold to steady herself, I set the suitcase down and reached for her hand. When she felt me take it, she smiled, looked past me, to the unseen distance over my right shoulder, and said, "Thank you." And it was then I realized Mary Alice Hadley was blind.

Aunt Charity cleared her throat and said, "Mary Alice, this is my nephew, Nelson."

"Hello, Nelson," Mary Alice said. "I'm very pleased to meet you." Her voice was soft and clear, her diction clean and proper.

"I'm pleased to meet you, too, Miss Mary Alice," I said. And to this day I don't know why I called her Miss Mary Alice. It bubbled out of me just as instinctively as had the impulse to take her hand when she first stepped out of the car. I looked at Aunt Charity and said, "I'll help her in the house and come back for the suitcase." Aunt Charity smiled and stepped back, and with a little tug on Mary Alice's hand I led her from behind the open car door and up the drive toward the house. She had her walking stick in her left hand tapping away in front of us as we slowly made our way to the front porch.

It's difficult to put into words how I felt that day as I held Mary Alice's hand and helped her take her first steps into my world. No clichés or hackneyed phrases could possibly do justice to my emotions at that singular moment when it seemed time truly had stopped. I remember looking over at Aunt Charity as we walked along, and I think she had discerned what was happening even before it had registered with me as a conscious thought. I remember feeling ashamed of the things I had said to her at the breakfast table, as well as the unspoken thoughts that had filled my foolish mind that morning as I dreaded the arrival of this unwelcome visitor from the Masonic Home for Children. But, there I was, holding her hand, and totally smitten by her simple grace and charm. I was a boy in the throes of nascent love, and it thrilled me and terrified me and made my head swim. Recalling it now some four decades later, it still does.

— — —

Mary Alice Hadley almost cost me my job at Dick's ESSO later that same day. For the life of me, I could not keep my mind on anything that afternoon at the station—anything other than her. The extent of my distraction came to a head at four o'clock sharp when Mrs. Rosemary Routledge, the widow of the late Judge Walker T. Routledge of the Harrison County Chancery Court, arrived for her weekly fill-up. Miss Rosemary was about eighty years old and drove her late husband's '67 Buick Electra. She always came by the station on Mondays around four o'clock for gas. And, given that she only put about five miles every week on her car driving to Anne's Beauty Shop and to the IGA for groceries, I was usually lucky if I could get a gallon of Hi-Test in her tank. I didn't mind, however, because no matter the paltry amount of gasoline she purchased, Miss Rosemary always pulled a dollar bill from her purse and told me to keep the change. That was one tip I could count on every week, no matter what. Today's fill-up, however, cost me 37¢ and an oil change—and no tip.

When Miss Rosemary pulled up to the pumps, I was waiting there as usual. But, unusual for me, I did not immediately start pumping her gas. I don't know how long I stood there like a daydreaming dolt, but when Miss Rosemary said, "Young man, I'd like some gas, please," it snapped me back to reality.

"Yes, ma'am," I said, and grabbed the nozzle from the pump. I pulled the hose to the back of the car, flipped the license plate down, screwed off the cap, stuck the nozzle in, and started pumping. About ten seconds later Miss Rosemary let out the most god-awful scream, and it nearly scared me to death. I released the pump handle and ran around to see what was wrong.

Miss Rosemary was getting out of the car. Dick had heard the scream and left the brake job he was doing over in the bay to investigate. Before he could even get out to the pumps, Miss Rosemary was pointing at me. "Richard Tillman," she said to Dick as he walked up, "do you see what he has done?" Her bony finger was wagging up and down in my direction.

Dick pulled a red shop rag from his back pocket and started wiping his hands. He looked at Miss Rosemary, then me. I just shrugged. I didn't know what she was talking about. "What's he done?" Dick asked.

Miss Rosemary got an exasperated look on her face, like she was dealing with two nincompoops. She pointed to the gas pump, the Regular gas pump, the one from which I was filling her tank. I closed my eyes and shook my head because I knew what she was about to say. "He has put Regular gasoline in my car!" she exclaimed. "Regular! He knows I always get Hi-Test. This was the Judge's car and he said it must always have Hi-Test. He said it knocks on Regular."

Dick looked at me and I couldn't tell if he was mad or trying to keep from laughing. If it was the latter, I didn't think it was funny. If it was the former, which I was certain it was, I was scared I was about to get fired. "I'm sorry about that, Miss Rosemary," Dick said. "It was an honest mistake. It won't hurt the Judge's car, I promise."

Miss Rosemary turned a hard gaze on Dick, moving her head like a pigeon in full strut as she tried to get him focused in her tri-focals. "I want you to drain every bit of that inferior gasoline out of my tank and refill it with Hi-Test."

Now I was sure I was getting fired. Dick stepped over to the pump and looked at the numbers on the meter. I had put exactly seven tenths of a gallon in her tank. "Miss Rosemary," Dick said, "it didn't even take a whole gallon. I think your tank holds almost twenty-five gallons. I promise you with that little bit of Regular in there you won't notice a thing. And it won't hurt the engine. If it does, I'll buy you a new one."

I could see Miss Rosemary was thinking it over. To seal the deal, and get her on her way, Dick added, "I think you're about due for an oil change, so when you come by next week for your fill-up I'll do that for you, no charge."

Miss Rosemary's resolve was softening. "Well, if you say it won't harm anything, I suppose it will be all right…" she turned her octogenarian gaze on me and added "…this time."

"I'm really sorry, Miss Rosemary," I said. "It won't ever happen again."

"See that it doesn't, young man." She turned to get back in the car.

I quickly removed the nozzle and replaced her gas cap. As I was sticking the nozzle back in its holder on the pump, Miss Rosemary started up the car and pulled away. Dick looked at the meter on the pump and said, "You owe me thirty-seven cents." He pointed at me with the hand still holding the red shop rag and added, "That oil change is coming out of your goddamn pay next week." He turned and headed back to the bay and the brake job. "Get your head out of the clouds, boy," he said over his shoulder, "or you're gonna wind up owing me money come payday."

When I got home at 6:30, I was surprised to see Daddy's pickup sitting in the backyard. Evidently, this was one of those rare days for him when he actually got off work on time. As I motored the Honda into the empty side of the carport beside the Batmobile, Bear came running up from wherever he'd been napping. "Hey, boy," I said and petted him on the head as I climbed off the bike. "Have you had your supper?" I asked. I went over in front of the car and opened the big trash can where we kept the dog food and scooped some out and put it in Bear's bowl, which was on the ground beside it. His water bowl was full. Bear immediately began to devour the crunchy nuggets and I headed for the house and left him to it.

"I fed Bear," I said as I walked into the kitchen. Aunt Charity was at the stove, turning something in the iron skillet.

"I already fed him half an hour ago," she said without looking up.

I laughed. "Well, he's eating dessert, then. What are we having?" I walked over for a peek at what Aunt Charity was tending to on the stove.

"Pork chops, collards, and creamed potatoes," Aunt Charity said. "Go wash up, it's ready."

"Where's Daddy and Sash?"

"In the living room watching TV. Let them know that dinner is ready, please."

I went to the living room to find Daddy sitting in his recliner. My sister was in his lap and they were both asleep. The TV was not on and a copy of *The Little Engine That Could* was in my father's right hand. Under the expert tutelage of Aunt Charity, my sister could already read at the second grade level and she had long outgrown this book. But she loved it, and she loved for our father to read it to her. "Daddy?" I said, and reached down and touched his shoulder.

He opened his eyes and blinked and looked up at me. "Hey, sport. Guess I fell asleep." He looked down at Sachet in his lap. "I guess she did, too," he added.

"Aunt Charity says dinner is ready," I said.

"Okay." He nudged Sachet. "Come on, baby girl, it's time to eat."

I heard my sister's loud yawn as I headed to the bathroom to wash my hands.

When we all sat down to dinner, I noticed there were only four places set at the table. "Where is Mary Alice?" I asked.

Aunt Charity looked at my sister. "Sachet, would you say grace, please?"

We all bowed our heads as Sachet began to pray. "God is great, God is good. Let us thank Him…"

But I wasn't listening. I was wondering why Mary Alice wasn't here with us. As soon as I heard the "Amen," I repeated my question: "Where is Mary Alice?"

"I've already taken her dinner over to her," Aunt Charity said.

Daddy was handing me the platter with the pork chops on it. "You mean she's eating over at your house?" I asked. I took a pork chop and put it on my plate, then passed the platter past Sachet to Aunt Charity.

"I want one," my sister said, eyeing the platter as it went by her.

Aunt Charity looked at me as she took one of the smaller chops and put it on Sachet's plate. "Yes, Nelson, she is eating at my house. Why?"

I stood up and glowered down at my aunt. "She's over there by herself? Alone? She's eating alone?"

"Sit down, son," Daddy said sternly.

Aunt Charity was staring up at me with a look of bemusement. "Mary Alice is not an invalid, Nelson. She's fine. I'm going over and check on her shortly."

I was still standing, trying to keep my dismay at this breach of hospitality from rising to the level of genuine anger. Something was very wrong here. When words finally failed me, action set in. I reached for the bowl of mashed potatoes and doled out a double helping into my plate. I did the same with the collard greens. I grabbed a piece of cornbread, scooped up my napkin and flatware, picked up my plate, and headed for the door.

"Where are you going?" Daddy asked.

I stopped just as I went through the open door onto the back porch. I turned around to see all three of them staring at me from the table. "I'm going over there and eat with

Mary Alice," I said, and fixed my eyes on Aunt Charity. "I can't believe you would make her eat by herself."

As I walked over to my aunt's house, all sorts of things were going through my mind, not the least of which was how bad I would feel if I were in a strange place and left to have my evening meal by myself. But Mary Alice was blind, which, in my juvenile ignorance, made it doubly worse. What in the world could Aunt Charity be thinking? If she was going to treat the poor girl this way, she should have left her over at the Masonic Home in Poplarville. I was sure she didn't have to eat alone there.

The garage door was open, so I went in through the door from there that opened into Aunt Charity's kitchen. I expected to see Mary Alice sitting at the breakfast table in the kitchen, the last place I'd seen her earlier when I walked her into the house, but she wasn't. It was nice and cool inside, thanks to the central air conditioning. I stepped into the kitchen and closed the door behind me. "Mary Alice?" I called out.

"Yes?" she answered, her voice coming from the dining room.

I walked down the hall off from the kitchen and entered the dining room. The chandelier was ablaze over Aunt Charity's formal dining table, which would seat ten, and Mary Alice was sitting down at the far end. The room was quiet and still. I could faintly hear the fan from the central air conditioning and the tick of the grandfather clock in the hall.

Mary Alice was still wearing the pink sundress from earlier in the day. Again, I was dumbstruck by her quiet and simple beauty as I watched her slowly cut a sliver of meat from the pork chop on her plate then raise the fork to her mouth. Yes, she was alone. But it was obvious she was fine, fully capable of caring for herself in something so routine as eating a meal. She was, as Aunt Charity had said, no invalid.

"Hello, Nelson," she said as she felt for the plate in front of her so she could rest the fork there.

"How did you know it was me?" I asked.

She smiled, but her eyes did not come to me, to the sound of my voice. She continued to stare straight ahead. "I recognized your voice," she said.

"Oh. I came over to eat with you, if that's okay," I said.

"That would be nice," she said.

I went over to the table and sat down at the first place to her right, setting my plate and utensils in front of me. I watched Mary Alice's hand move across the highly polished cherry wood until it just touched her glass of iced tea resting on a coaster. She picked up the glass, slowly moved it to her lips, and took a sip. She went to place it back on the coaster and her memory of distance was almost perfect, but I could see she was about to set the glass askew on the coaster, which would cause it to spill over. I started to reach for it, but then she hesitated and made the necessary correction using her little finger as the guide. My help was totally unneeded.

"You're not eating," Mary Alice said as she picked up her fork and took it directly to the mashed potatoes. She took a bite, and I watched a repeat of the performance with the glass of tea, except this time no final correction was necessary; she set the glass back down squarely on the coaster. I was fascinated, and totally in awe of this delicate creature who seemed so poised and confident. She was a petite girl of fourteen, blind, and she had the manner and grace of a *grande dame* of the Old South.

I finally managed to begin eating my dinner, which was rapidly becoming cold in Aunt Charity's 68 degree house. "What did you do today?" I asked.

"I took a nap after you left and then I read most of the afternoon. Miss Charity took me around the house so I could get used to where everything is."

"How can you read?" I asked.

"Do you know what Braille is?"

I felt like an idiot. "Yes, I wasn't thinking about that."

Mary Alice smiled. "I brought several of my books with me."

"That explains why your suitcase was so heavy," I said.

Mary Alice laughed, and it was a magical, mythical, laugh; a Siren's call tugging at my heart. I was determined right then and there that she would never eat alone in this room again. "You know, you don't have to eat over here by yourself. Our house isn't as nice as this, and it's not air conditioned, but I'd like it if you ate with us...with me."

"Thank you, Nelson. I don't mind about the air conditioning, I'm not used to it and I'm freezing right now."

I looked at her bare shoulders covered just by the thin straps of her sundress, and what I presumed was a bra—though Mary Alice didn't have much in the way of breasts that I could see. I got up and went into the den where I knew Aunt Charity had a throw folded across the back of the rocker in front of the fireplace. I came back into the dining room, unfolded the throw, and draped it over Mary Alice's shoulders. She jumped a little. "Is that better?" I asked.

She reached up and put her hand on mine. "Yes, thank you. You are very sweet, Nelson."

I waited to see how long her touch would linger, but it was a fleeting encounter, and she went back to eating. I sat back at the table. "Are you really just fourteen?" I asked. I knew it was a dumb question, but this girl was unlike any female close to my age I'd ever met. Her accent told me she was from Mississippi; her mannerisms and diction told me she was from another time, another place, where girls were made of finer things.

"I'll be fifteen in December," she said with a smile. "How old are you?"

"I'll be sixteen next month. Can I ask you something?" I said, and started carving a piece off my pork chop.

"You mean something else?"

"What?"

Mary Alice laughed again, and I could tell she was playing with me. "You've already asked me something," she said. "Now you have to ask me something else."

I took a bite of pork chop and stared at Mary Alice. I swallowed and said, "How long have you been at the home over there in Poplarville?"

"Since last November."

"What happened to your parents?"

"They were killed in a plane crash when I was two. My grandmother up in Natchez raised me until she passed away last year."

"I'm sorry," I said.

"Your aunt reminds me of my grandmother," Mary Alice said. "She's been very good to me. I always look forward to her visits."

"I'm glad she invited you to spend the summer with us," I said.

"So am I. Your aunt said I would like you."

"She did?"

"Yes."

"And do you?"

"Yes."

I smiled, and it pained me that Mary Alice could not see that smile. "You can't see at all?" I asked.

"I'm totally blind now," she said and reached for the glass of tea again.

"Now? You mean you used to could see?"

"Yes, I started losing my sight when I was ten. By the time I was twelve it was totally gone. I have a genetic condition called Leber's Optic Atrophy."

I had never heard of that disease, but I later learned just how rare it was, especially in girls. What made Mary Alice's case rarer still was her total loss of vision. We ate the rest of our dinner in silence, me ever mesmerized as I watched her finish the plate of food in front of her with no more trouble than I had with mine.

"That was delicious," Mary Alice said as she took one of Aunt Charity's linen napkins from her lap and wiped her mouth.

"Aunt Charity is a good cook," I said just as the grandfather clock down the hall struck seven o'clock. "You met my sister when you got here. Have you met my dad yet?" I asked.

"No."

"Would you like to come over to my house and meet him?"

"Yes, I would." She pushed the chair back from the table and stood. The throw fell from her shoulders, and she stooped to pick it up.

"I'll get it," I said. I went over and picked up the throw and laid it across the back of the chair. "Do you want me to help you to the door?"

"No, I need to learn this house," she said. I watched as she touched the table with her left hand to get her bearings, then she turned to her right, almost a perfect ninety degrees. She reached over and put her right hand on my arm, I think just to see if I was still standing beside her. And then, slowly, she moved her hand up my arm. It sent chills through me. She continued until she had reached my shoulder, where she let her hand come to rest. "You're very tall," she said.

"Almost six feet," I affirmed.

Mary Alice walked forward slowly. I stayed by her side, and she kept her hand on my shoulder. I looked down at her face, and I could see the concentration there as she was calculating, remembering the distance and the steps. When we got to the doorway that led into the hall, she reached out and touched the facing. She knew right where it was supposed to be, and there it was. We stepped through and she started to turn to the right.

"Let's go out through the garage," I said. "It's the other way."

"I know, but I will need my walking stick."

"No, you won't," I said. "You've got me."

PART TWO

Chapter 6
Fly Me to the Moon

On the morning of July 16, 1969, I was sitting on the floor of Aunt Charity's den in front of her color TV. Sachet was sitting in the rocker and Mary Alice was on the couch. It was a little past seven o'clock and Walter Cronkite had just said good morning and announced that in just an hour and a half the Apollo 11 astronauts would lift off from Pad 39-A at Cape Kennedy and their next stop would be the moon. Sachet and I had come over to Aunt Charity's to eat breakfast so we could watch the launch in color.

I was trying to work up the nerve to go sit beside Mary Alice on the couch. I don't mean sit with Mary Alice on the couch; I mean actually sit beside her—right beside her. She had been a part of my summer for almost forty-eight hours now, and already I was dreading the end of August when she would have to return to her world. I had six weeks, and I intended to make every second count between now and then.

As it turns out, that whole episode Monday evening, with Mary Alice eating over at Aunt Charity's alone, was cooked up by my aunt and my father. Aunt Charity had given Daddy the rundown on my reaction to the news that Mary Alice would be staying with us, as well as my seemingly miraculous turnaround when I actually met her. Apparently, Daddy and Aunt Charity thought it would be great fun to see how I would react to our summer guest being forced to eat alone, since I'd made it quite clear that morning such arrangements would no doubt be my preference for this unwelcome visitor from the Masonic Home for Children. I was still unsure just how much prep work Aunt Charity had done in furthering my attempts to win this girl's heart, but I did learn that she had told Mary Alice that Monday evening to be expecting me to join her for dinner.

Just as Walter Cronkite was saying that Neil Armstrong would be the first human to touch the moon next Monday, take that first step, and that things would never be the same again, I got up and took my first step to initiate a relation-ship with Mary Alice Hadley. And somehow I knew, from then on, things for me would never be the same again.

Mary Alice was wearing pale green knee-length culottes and a white blouse. She had a pink sweater draped over her shoulders and the same sandals on her feet she was wearing the day I met her. She appeared to be listening intently to Walter Cronkite talk about the Apollo 11 mission, but I was-n't sure just how interested she really was. I was surprised that Sachet was glued to the TV because I knew she wasn't interested. The one time she went with Uncle Rick, Daddy, and me to a test firing down at MTF the noise scared her to death.

My moon walk had just begun and ended as I was now standing at the edge of the couch in front of Mary Alice. Rather than say anything, I just sat down. Close. Close enough that her bare leg was almost touching mine. (I was wearing shorts.)

"Hello, Nelson," Mary Alice said.

How the devil did she do that? I hadn't said anything, so I knew she couldn't say she recognized my voice. "Okay," I said, "how'd you know it was me this time?"

She smiled and said, "Well, you're awfully close. I rec-ognize your smell."

I was mortified and embarrassed. I had taken a bath the night before, and I had used my Right Guard. Without thinking, I lifted up my arm and sniffed.

Mary Alice burst out laughing. It startled Sachet over in the rocker and she turned to look at us. Mary Alice said, "I didn't mean that kind of smell, silly."

"Why are you sitting so close to Mary Alice?" Sachet asked me.

"Why don't you go outside and play?" I said.

"I don't want to."

I just rolled my eyes and pretended to be watching the TV. I was still trying to figure out what Mary Alice meant about my smell. When I was sure my sister's attention was back on the TV, I leaned over and whispered to Mary Alice, "Do I really smell?" She didn't say anything. She just held her hand over to me and I took it in mine. "I use deodorant," I said.

She laughed again, this time softly—that enchanting laugh that had bewitched me at the dinner table Monday night. "Nelson, I'm not talking about body odor. Everyone has their own smell. You have yours and that's what I meant."

"So I don't stink?"

"No, you smell nice. I like the way you smell."

"You do?" I said as I finally realized we were holding hands. I looked down at her small hand in mine. We sat there, me watching Walter Cronkite and various other reporters discuss the moon mission, while Mary Alice listened. I finally got tired of seeing my sister staring at us. "Let's go sit on the front porch," I said to Mary Alice.

"Don't you want to watch the launch?" she said.

"That's still half an hour away."

We got up, and I held Mary Alice's hand as we made our way to the front door of Aunt Charity's house and onto the front porch. It was a gray day, and much cooler than it had been for the past two weeks. There was the threat of rain in the air.

"Let's sit on the swing," I said, and led Mary Alice over to the big hanging bench swing. When we sat, we were still holding hands, and Mary Alice had resumed the same position she had on the couch: sitting next to me, very close.

"You know, you're the only person I've ever let lead me around like that," Mary Alice said.

"What do you mean?"

"I don't mind you doing it because you're not doing it because you feel sorry for me."

I thought about Mary Alice's comment. She was right, sort of. Except for how I felt when I thought Aunt Charity had abandoned her to eat alone, I had not felt sorry for her at all. My ministrations toward her were not grounded in pity, but rather courtly affection and I think she could sense that. It goes without saying that there was no self-pity on her part. She was the most poised and self-confident person of my age group that I'd ever met.

I had just launched us into a gentle back and forth swing when Sachet opened the front door and stepped out onto the porch. She was barefoot and carrying one of her dolls. "Go back inside," I said to her sternly.

"Why?"

"Because I want to be alone with Mary Alice."

"Why?"

I started to get up, but Mary Alice squeezed my hand. "It's all right, Nelson," she said.

Sachet stuck her tongue out and gave me a nana-nana-boo-boo look, then went over and sat in one of the chairs on the opposite end of the porch. She was wearing a short red sundress and when she picked her feet up and drew her knees to her chin, I said "Put your legs down, Sash."

"Why?"

"Because I can see your panties. You've got to learn to sit right when you're wearing a dress." I might as well have been talking to one of Aunt Charity's azalea bushes for all the good it did. My sister just ignored me, so I decided to do the same for her, and gave another push with my foot to keep the swing moving.

"You have a very pretty name," Mary Alice said to Sachet. "It's very unusual."

Sachet knew the story behind her name, so I waited to see if she would respond. When it appeared she was more interested in staring at me holding Mary Alice's hand, I said, "Our mother—"

"I'll tell it," Sachet said, cutting me off. She finally put her legs down.

"Well, tell it," I said. My sister was getting on my last nerve.

"Be nice," Mary Alice said.

"You don't know what it's like sometimes having a little sister."

"No, but I know what it's like having a big brother."

I turned to look at Mary Alice. "You have a brother?"

"Yes; now let your sister tell me about her name."

I got the nana-nana-boo-boo look from Sachet again and resigned myself to the fact that this morning was not going to go as I had hoped.

"Mama used to make lavender sachets to put in Daddy's closet with his clothes because of the creosote smell," Sachet said.

I knew that explanation was likely to confuse Mary Alice. "She used to put them in his pants pockets, too," I added. "Daddy works down at the creosote plant and the smell gets in his work clothes and it won't wash out. He used to say that those little sachets were like carrying Mama around with him all the time. She died when Sash was born and Daddy named my sister Sachet because she was the last sachet that Mama left him."

"That is so sweet," Mary Alice said.

"You don't know my sister," I said, and stuck my tongue out at Sachet. She stuck hers out at me in return.

Mary Alice let go of my hand and gave me a little slap on the leg. "I said be nice."

Sachet giggled and I let out an exasperated sigh.

"What's wrong?" Mary Alice asked.

"Nothing," I said, and took her hand again. "Tell me about your brother."

"He's ten years older than me, just like you are to your sister."

"How do you know how old Sash is?"

"Your aunt told me."

"Oh."

"My brother will graduate from law school up at Ole Miss next year."

"Where is he this summer?"

"Working for a law firm in Jackson. They have already offered him a job when he graduates."

"What's his name?"

"Robert James Beauregard Hadley. He goes by Beau." I later learned that Beauregard was Mary Alice's mother's maiden name and she was a direct descendent of the Confederate general, P. G. T. Beauregard.

"Do you get to see him much?" I asked.

"Yes, he comes to visit me every chance he gets. And we talk on the phone. He's driving down from Jackson in a couple of weeks."

"He's coming here?" There was a note of defensiveness in my question that I didn't really intend. Mary Alice picked up on it.

"Yes. Why did you ask it like that?"

I didn't really know the answer, other than I wanted Mary Alice all to myself, and another male in her life—even a brother—wasn't a pleasant thought. "I didn't mean that the way it sounded," I said. "I was just surprised when you said he was coming."

"You'll like Beau," she said.

Sitting in the swing, I had a clear view of Aunt Charity's side yard and our house beyond it. I looked up in time to see Frankie pulling into our driveway on his bicycle. "Hey!" I hollered. "I'm over here!" My shout startled Mary Alice and she jumped. "Sorry," I said. "My friend Frankie is over at the house."

I gave another push with my foot to keep the swing moving as I watched Frankie pedal his bike across the yard. "Hey," he said when he pulled up in front of the porch. He was staring at Mary Alice, and me holding her hand, with a bewildered expression on his face.

"Hey," I said to him. "Mary Alice, this is my best friend, Frankie Thompson. Frankie, this is Mary Alice Hadley."

"Hello, Frankie," Mary Alice said, looking straight ahead and not at him.

I waited for Frankie to respond in kind, but he just continued to stare at us sitting in the swing. Just then I saw Frankie's brother in our driveway on his bike. He had seen us, and turned to pedal across the yard. Given what had happened Sunday when I invited Mark to go to the Colonel Dixie with us, I knew this wasn't going to be good. I stopped the swing, let go of Mary Alice's hand, and stood up.

Frankie could see I was watching something off in the side yard, and he turned to look. As soon as he spotted his brother approaching, he kicked the stand down on his bike and got off. I stepped down off the porch onto the concrete walk that curved back around to Aunt Charity's gravel drive.

Mark pedaled up with a big smile on his face, totally oblivious to the danger zone he had just entered. Before Mark could get stopped, Frankie walked over and shoved him, sending him crashing into the grass with the bike falling on top of him. "I told you not to follow me up here!" Frankie yelled.

I ran over and lifted the bike off of Mark and helped him up. He was trying without much success to keep from crying. He was choking back the sobs as I brushed the grass clippings and pine needles off of him. He had scraped his left knee pretty good in the fall, but it wasn't bleeding. "Are you okay?" I asked him.

Mark nodded and said, "Yeah."

I turned to Frankie and said, "Have you gone crazy? What's the matter with you?"

"Me?!" Frankie yelled. "What's the matter with me? What's the matter with *you*?"

"What are you talking about?" I asked with dismay. Mark was still stifling his sobs and getting back on his bike.

Frankie put his hands on his hips. "I thought you were queer for Mark," he said and waved a hand at his brother. Then, pointing up at Mary Alice on the porch he said, "Now you've got a girlfriend?" The inflection he put on "girl-friend" was such that he clearly meant it as term of derision.

The comment about being queer for his brother came way out of left field and pissed me off. It was one thing to jokingly call each other a fag or queer, which we often did, but Frankie was dead serious. I was an easy going boy by nature and it took a lot to make me lose my temper, but Frankie had managed it. "Go home," I said, trying to sound calm, but my voice was trembling.

Frankie looked over at his brother, who was sitting on his bike watching us. "Let's go," he said and turned for his bike.

I glanced at Mark. "You stay here." Turning back to Frankie, I said, "You leave."

Before I had time to react, Frankie had lunged, tackling me hard and taking me down. We were rolling on the ground and Frankie was trying to punch me, but I was keep-ing him close, limiting his ability to land a fist on me. I heard Sachet scream from the porch just as Frankie broke free enough to push himself up and punch me in the face. Suddenly my sister was right there with us, beating Frankie over the head with her doll. "Leave him alone!" she screamed. Frankie turned and grabbed the doll from her and flung it into the trunk of the nearest pine tree. The head flew off the doll and went rolling across the yard.

Anger had me in its grip, and without thinking, I drew back my clenched right fist and just as Frankie turned back to me I punched him in the nose as hard as I could. It happened in the blink of an eye. He fell back on the ground and blood started pouring out of his nose as he groaned and put his hands to his face.

I got to my feet. My heart was beating so fast I thought my chest would explode. I couldn't seem to catch my breath. The knuckles of my right hand were stinging. Sachet was crying. She went over and picked up her headless doll and then ran up on the porch. Frankie got up and stumbled over to his bike. The front of his tee shirt was soaked in blood. As he got on his bike, he pointed to Mark and said, "I'm going to beat the shit out of you when we get home."

I stepped over to him, and I could see the fear in his eyes as he no doubt thought I was about to light into him again. "If you do anything to him I'll finish this fight."

Frankie didn't say anything but I could see he understood I meant business. He kicked up the stand on his bike, turned, and pedaled for the road. I turned to Mark. "You don't have to go," I said. "Stay here and let him cool off."

"I better go," he said.

It bothered me to think what might be awaiting Mark when he got home. "If he does anything to you, tell your mom and dad," I said. Mark was silent. He toed up the kickstand on his bike and started to pedal off. I reached out and grabbed his handlebars to stop him. "I meant what I said, Mark. If he hits you, and I find out, he'll regret it." Again, Mark didn't say anything. I let go of his handlebars and he pedaled off.

I stood there and watched Mark ride down the drive and felt my composure returning. I hated getting mad like this and was glad it rarely happened. I brushed myself off and walked over and picked up the head to Sachet's doll. When I got up on the porch, my sister was sitting in Mary Alice's lap. She was no longer crying, but her face was wet with tears. She had her eyes closed, and Mary Alice was gently stroking her hair and whispering something in her ear. The decapitated doll was lying in the swing next to her. I set the head beside it. I knelt down in front of them and said, "I'm sorry, Sachet. I'll buy you another doll."

Sachet opened her eyes and when she saw me she jumped out of Mary Alice's lap and threw her arms around my neck. She started crying again, and she was hugging me so tightly it nearly choked me. "Did he hurt you?" she said over my shoulder.

"I'm fine, Sash," I said. I stood up and picked her up with me. She was still hugging me tightly, and my arms were around her. "Sh-h. Don't cry, now. Frankie's gone and I'm fine."

She pushed herself back so she could look me in the face. "He didn't hurt you?" she said.

I smiled. "No, he didn't hurt me. Go inside and wash your face, okay? I need to talk to Mary Alice." I expected her to protest, but she didn't. My sister just nodded her head and I set her down on her bare feet and she scurried off into the house. I went over and moved the doll and its head and plopped down on the swing beside Mary Alice. "I wish I could go to the moon," I said and looked over at her. There was a tear leaving the corner of her eye. It hit me just how frightened she must have been, having listened to the fight erupt out of nowhere and not being able to see what was happening. "Mary Alice, I'm sorry." I reached over and took her hand.

She reached up and wiped away the tear with her other hand. "Are you all right?" she said.

"Yes, I'm fine. Were you worried about me? Is that why you're crying?"

She nodded. "Yes…and I felt so helpless. I thought you said he was your best friend? Why did he act like that? Why did he attack you?"

"Frankie is…was…my best friend. I don't know what's happened to him. He's gone crazy."

"Who was the other boy?" Mary Alice asked.

"His little brother. Frankie is jealous of him. I guess that's why he flipped out."

"Why is he jealous of him?"

"I don't know," I said.

"I heard what he said, Nelson."

"You mean about me being queer for Mark?"

"Yes."

I pushed off with my foot to start us swinging. "Frankie has never said anything like that to me before. I don't know why he thinks that. It's not true. He's been acting weird all summer every time Mark's been around us. He's jealous of you, too."

"Me?"

"Didn't you hear what else he said?" I asked. "About me having a girlfriend?"

"Yes, I heard that. Is that part true?"

I put my foot down to stop us from swinging. I raised Mary Alice's hand to my lips and kissed it softly. "If you want it to be," I said.

I had gotten used to conversing with Mary Alice without her looking at me, so I was surprised when she turned to face me. "I want it to be true," she said. She let go of my hand

and with both of hers she reached out and touched my face. She moved her fingers all over my face, exploring, seeing. "I knew you were handsome," she said as her fingers came to rest on my lips.

I was fully aroused and about to explode. I managed to push the thought of release to the back of my mind, then leaned forward and inexpertly touched my lips to hers. It was my first kiss—clumsy, probing, and inept. Mary Alice's lips tasted like cinnamon and I literally felt light headed as I allowed the tip of my tongue to briefly brush them. She had a dreamy smile on her face as our lips parted and I leaned up and looked at her.

The sound of Aunt Charity clearing her throat snapped me back to reality. I quickly leaned away from Mary Alice and turned around to see my aunt standing there with the open front door behind her and Sachet clinging to her. My aunt was clearly amused by what she'd just seen, which was a relief. I'd much rather she be amused than irritated at the thought her nephew was wooing her fourteen-year-old summer houseguest. "I thought you might like to know," she said, "you missed the launch."

I didn't care. I was already on the moon.

Chapter 7
Best Friends

Iturned the lamp on beside my bed when I heard Daddy in the bathroom shaving. My alarm clock said it was twenty minutes past four. I hadn't slept a wink last night. After I had gone to bed, it took me three sessions of frantic masturbation to relieve the sexual tension that had built up over the course of the day because of my romantic interlude yesterday morning with Mary Alice. But that wasn't the reason for my sleepless night. The fight I'd had with Frankie was the culprit, and the coming realization that our life-long friendship had come to an abrupt and unceremonious end yesterday in Aunt Charity's front yard. I was also bothered by Frankie's declaration that he thought I was queer for his brother. What had I ever done or said for him to draw that conclusion? I had spent a good part of the night reliving every moment that I could remember being around Mark and there was just nothing there. I'd always been nice to Mark, and that was it. When I heard Daddy finish in the bathroom, I got out of bed, put my slippers on, and headed in there to pee and wash my face.

"Good morning," I said as I entered the kitchen. My father was dressed in his work clothes and standing at the counter by the sink waiting for the coffee to finish. The kitchen was quiet and filled with the smell of Old Spice aftershave and perking JFG coffee. The windows were dark. Dawn was still over an hour away and the only light was the cool blue glow of the buzzing fluorescent tube over the sink.

"You're up awfully early," Daddy said as he turned to look at me.

I went over and sat at the table. "I've been up," I said. "I couldn't sleep last night."

The percolator was giving off its last sputters. Daddy got a mug out of the cupboard. When the pot had given its final gasp, he unplugged it, then filled the mug to the brim with steaming hot coffee. I watched as he poured the rest of the coffee into his thermos and screwed the top on. He went over to the ice box and got out the paper bag with his sandwich in it, which Aunt Charity had prepared last night. He put the bag and thermos in his lunch box and then set the lunch box on the floor beside the door. This was my father's morning routine, and he'd been doing it for nearly twenty years.

"How do you know when you're in love?" I said as Daddy sat at the table across from me with his mug of coffee.

He chuckled and took a sip. "I'd say not being able to sleep all night is a good sign. I assume we're talking about Mary Alice?"

"Yeah," I said.

"I'm proud of you, son—for the way you've treated her, I mean. You've made Mary Alice feel very special."

"She is special," I said. "How do you know how I've made her feel?"

"She talks to your aunt and your aunt talks to me." Daddy took another sip of coffee and stared at me. "Anything else keep you up all night? Like maybe the fight you had with Frankie yesterday?"

"How do you know about that? Did Mary Alice tell Aunt Charity?"

"No, your sister did. But I heard about it from Frank Thompson."

"Frankie's dad? When did you see him?"

"I stopped by there on the way home from work yesterday to get some eggs."

"And he knew about the fight?"

"Yes," Daddy said, and took another sip of coffee. "Mark had told him."

"What'd he say?"

"Let me hear your version first." So I gave him a blow-by-blow account of everything that happened yesterday morning from the time Mary Alice and I went out on the porch until the fight was over. "That's pretty much the story Mark told," Daddy said. "Except for the queer part. What's that all about?"

"I don't know, Daddy. Frankie's been acting jealous about Mark and me ever since that day at the river when Mark lost his trunks and I gave him a ride home. You remember me telling you about that?"

"I remember."

"And you saw how he acted Sunday just because I asked Mark if he wanted to go with us to the Colonel Dixie. It's like Frankie wants me all to himself. I think what really flipped him out yesterday was me sitting there with Mary Alice and holding her hand. I don't know why he thinks I'm queer for Mark since he said himself that I've got a girl-friend now."

We sat there in silence as Daddy finished off his coffee. He got up to take the empty mug over to the sink. When he came back and sat down at the table, he said, "Did you ever think what's really bothering Frankie is how he feels about you, not how he thinks you feel about his brother?"

It took several seconds for me to grasp the meaning of my father's question. "You mean you think Frankie likes me…I mean likes me like that?"

"I don't know, son. I'm just saying it's possible if he's been acting jealous, especially given what he said about you and Mark."

"Oh, man," I said, and looked down. I didn't want to admit it, but what Daddy had just said could be right. Was that it? Was Frankie mad at me because he thought I was queer for his little brother? Or was he mad because he knew I wasn't queer for him?

"Nelson, look at me," Daddy said. I looked up. "You and Frankie have been friends since you were both knee high to a grasshopper. Whatever's going on with him right now, he's clearly struggling with it. You need to remember he's still your friend as you work this out with him."

"I'm not queer, Daddy. I don't want to work it out with him."

"That's not what I meant, son. All I'm saying is don't be too quick to throw away this friendship until you've at least tried to understand what's going on with Frankie."

"And what if he is queer?" I said.

"Then you'll have to deal with it. But if it's true, son…don't you think it's bothering him, too? You all have never had a fist fight over anything that I know of. Why else would he be acting the way he is?"

"Because he's crazy," I said, dismissively.

Daddy chuckled. "I know you don't believe that. Anyway, I think you should go by there today on your way to work and apologize to him."

"Apologize?!" I was incredulous. "Why should I apologize to him? He started it."

"You broke his nose, Nelson. He spent most of the day yesterday at the doctor's office."

"Well, I didn't mean to. He shouldn't have started it."

"Are you glad you broke his nose?" Daddy asked.

His question hit me square in the gut. Of course I wasn't glad I'd hurt Frankie, and if I'd been honest with myself, the fact that I did was part of the reason I'd had a sleepless night. Now that I knew just how badly I had hurt him, I really felt terrible. I finally looked up at my father and said, "No, sir. I hate losing my temper like that."

"Think about how he must be feeling, Nelson. I'll bet you he's just as upset and confused about this fight as you are, just for different reasons. Do you want him wondering if his best friend hates him?"

I didn't say anything. I just glanced at Daddy and then looked back down at the red Formica of the table top. As usual, my father knew just what to say to put things in their proper perspective. I was going to have to go tell Frankie I was sorry, and not just because Daddy wanted me to, but because I really was sorry. I still couldn't get my mind around the possibility that my best friend was a homosexual, but Daddy was correct there, too. If he was, I'd just have to find a way to deal with it. My worry, especially after what happened yesterday, was whether Frankie could find a way to deal with it.

"Well, I've got to get to work," Daddy said as he got up from the table. He came over to me, ran his hand over my tousled hair, and then leaned down and kissed me on the forehead. "You remind me so much of your mother sometimes," he said looking down at me with his hand still resting on top of my head. "I love you, son." He turned and walked over to the door. He stooped and picked up his lunch box, then took his hardhat off the coat rack. He turned back to me and said, "You think about what we just talked about. Do what you know is right."

"I will, Daddy."

He put his hardhat on and opened the kitchen door.

"Daddy?" I called to him.

He turned back to look at me. "Hmm?"

"I love you, too."

He winked at me and headed out the door.

— — —

"What's wrong with you today?" Mary Alice asked me.

"Nothing," I answered.

We had just finished eating lunch and were sitting on the front porch at my house. Aunt Charity had taken Sachet into town with her. They were going to Anne's Beauty Shop for Aunt Charity's weekly hairdo and my sister was getting her hair cut. She had announced at breakfast that she wanted her hair short. Sachet had beautiful, long blond hair, so it was going to be interesting to see what "short" meant to her.

I had been distracted all morning, and Mary Alice had picked up on it. The conversation I'd had with my father before dawn was troubling, and while I had resolved to apologize to Frankie, I was not looking forward to facing him. My greatest fear was that our friendship was over, and I was heartsore because of it. Why couldn't things have just stayed the same?

"Tell me what's bothering you, Nelson," Mary Alice said. "And don't say 'nothing,' again," she added. I wanted to scream I was scared to death my best friend was queer and liked me, but instead I just told her I'd been thinking about Frankie. "You mean because of the fight?" she asked.

"Yes," I said, and it wasn't a lie. The fight was bothering me, too. "I'm going down to his house before I go to work and apologize to him. I found out from Daddy this morning that I broke his nose yesterday."

Mary Alice was sitting in one of the painted white chairs across from me. I was sitting in the only rocker on the porch. She had on light blue Bermuda shorts and a pink short sleeve shirt, but no sandals; today she was wearing pink slip on sneakers with white ankle socks. She started to get up, and when I saw her, I did too, out of habit. She didn't have her walking stick and I figured she wanted to go inside, maybe to the bathroom, and she was not familiar with our house yet. I asked her if she wanted me to help.

"No, no...you stay there," she said. "Keep talking so I can find you." Mary Alice was about ten feet away, across the pine slat floor of our porch. I sat back in the rocker and watched her take a tentative step forward. "Talk!" she commanded.

I laughed. "What do you want me to say?"

She turned toward the sound of my voice. "Keep talking," she said.

In a singsong, I intoned, "I'm—talk—ing—to—the—prett—i—est—girl—in—Miss—i—ssip—pi."

She chuckled and took two more steps toward me. Every instinct in me said get up and help her, but I kept my seat. "You're not talking," she said as she took another step.

"I'm—the—luck—i—est—guy—in—Miss—i—ssip—pi," I continued in a singsong.

She took two more steps. "Keep talking," she said.

"You're supposed to ask me why I'm the luckiest guy in Mississippi."

"Why are you the luckiest guy in Mississippi?" she said, and took another step.

"Be—cause—Ma—ry—A—lice—Had—ley—is—my—girl—friend." She laughed again, and I said, "Take three more steps and you'll be here."

When she stopped right in front of me, I reached out and took her left hand. She leaned down and with her other hand touched my leg. She turned and I let go of her hand and she sat down in my lap. She leaned back until her head was resting on my shoulder. I brushed her hair out of my face and inhaled deeply through my nose. There was a hint of Prell, but mostly it was just…her. She smelled divine.

Mary Alice laughed and said, "See, I told you…everyone has their own smell."

It was as if she could read my mind. I put my arms around her and then she rested hers on mine. She searched with her right hand until she found my hand and then we interlocked fingers. "I'm sorry you're hurting about your friend," she said. "That's nice that you want to apologize to him."

I didn't want to talk about Frankie right then. My only thoughts were on Mary Alice. "It's going to kill me when you have to leave next month," I whispered in her ear.

"Let's don't think about it," she said.

I started us to gently rocking. It was another gray day, like yesterday, and relatively cool—if the mid 80s could be considered cool. There was a breeze blowing through the tall pines in our front yard. I had asked my father earlier how you knew when you're in love. As I sat there rocking Mary Alice in my lap, I knew. I'd never felt like this before even though I'd had girlfriends ever since I was in the fifth grade. Bridget Wheaton and I had even "gone steady" through the first half of the tenth grade last year. Going steady with Bridget comprised two trips to the mall in Bay St. Louis holding hands in the back seat of Aunt Charity's Cadillac, and one movie (*Chitty Chitty Bang Bang*) at the Palladium Theater in Bells Ferry when we were out of school for Christmas break. That all seemed so trivial and childish now compared to what I felt with Mary Alice. I was in love, and the thought that in a few short weeks I would not be able to see her for weeks, maybe months, at a time was depressing beyond words.

— — —

An hour and a half later I was turning in to Frankie's drive on the Honda. The day had grown grayer, rain was imminent, so I was wearing a weatherproof windbreaker. I'd left early for work so I could get this apology out of the way, and I had butterflies in my stomach as I pulled up in front of the Thompson house and shut off the engine. Mark was sitting on the porch in his swim trunks and he was soaking wet.

"Hey," I said as I got off the bike.

"Hey," he replied and raised his hand from the arm of the chair in a slight wave.

"You been swimming?" I asked as I stepped up on the porch.

Mark shook his head. "Daddy set up the Slip 'N Slide in the backyard."

"Is Frankie in the house?"

"In his room."

"Where's your mom and dad?"

Mark crossed his legs and reached down to scratch his foot, which had grass clippings stuck all over it. "Mama went to town to get groceries. I don't know where Daddy is."

"How's Frankie doing?"

"You broke his nose," Mark said, and I detected a faint smile on his lips.

"I know," I said. "That's why I'm here. I want to tell him I'm sorry."

"He started it," Mark said. "That's what I told Daddy."

"He didn't hit you or anything, did he?"

"No, he told me he was sorry for knocking me off my bike when I got back here."

"Really? Why'd you tell your dad about the fight, then?"

"Had to," Mark said. "Frankie was bleedin' all over the place and wouldn't tell Daddy what happened so he asked me when we was on the way to the doctor's."

I stepped over to the screen door, opened it, and entered the house. I made my way through the living room and then down the hall to Frankie's room. His door was only open about six inches and I could hear the radio playing inside and a fan going. "Frankie?" I said, and knocked on the door.

"Yeah?" he said. I could tell it was Frankie's voice, but it sounded like he had a clothespin on his nose. I pushed the door open. Frankie was lying on his bed reading an Archie comic book. The first thing I saw was his bare feet. He had on his pajama bottoms and no top and the comic book was hiding his face. The Monkees' "I'm a Believer" was playing on the clock radio beside the bed.

"Hey," I said as I stepped into his room and closed the door behind me.

When Frankie lowered the comic to look at me, I literally did not recognize him. His nose was bandaged, and the gauze was held on by lateral pieces of tape attached to both cheeks. His face all around his eyes was a giant bruise, alternating in color from blue to black to deep purple. I just stared at him. I tried to say something, but couldn't find the words. My eyes started tearing up. This was my handiwork, and I had never been so ashamed of anything I'd done in my life. I wanted to die. Finally, I found my voice, and all I could choke out was, "Oh, Frankie."

I went over and sat down next to him at the foot of the bed. He leaned over and turned off the radio. Every time I looked at Frankie, it was like a knife going through me, and I could not hold back the tears any longer; they were streaming down my face. I reached up and wiped my eyes with both hands.

To my amazement, Frankie looked at me and said, "I'm sorry."

I let out a little laugh as I sniffed hard because my nose was running now. "That's what I came to say to you," I said, and wiped my nose with the back of my hand.

Frankie smiled as much as he could with all that gauze and tape on his face. "I deserved it," he said.

"You didn't deserve that," I said, and pointed to his face.

"I've been an asshole this summer, Nels. I don't know what's wrong with me."

"I'm sorry I hit you," I said.

Frankie shook his head. "Nah, it was my fault. I shouldn't have shoved Mark. I shouldn't have jumped you. And I shouldn't have said what I did."

I hesitated. This was the point I'd been dreading, and Frankie had brought us to it. Finally I said, "You shouldn't have said what?" Frankie took a minute to digest my question. I'd just given him the chance to take this conversation in one of two directions: he could either say that he should not have said that about me having a "girlfriend," or he could say—

"I shouldn't have said that you were queer for Mark."

I studied Frankie's face and let his comment hang. I finally said, "No, you shouldn't have. I'm not queer for your brother."

"I know that," he said, looking me square in the eyes.

"I'm not queer for anybody," I said. "I like girls." Our eyes were locked and I held Frankie's gaze as my words registered with him. He gave me a little nod, just barely. He knew that I knew what the unspoken truth was between us: that there was only one boy in this room who liked girls— and it wasn't him. Just as quickly as I'd seen his understanding, a look of trepidation replaced it. I remembered my father's admonition about my best friend wondering if I hated him.

"Are we still friends?" Frankie said, confirming Daddy's prescience.

I smiled and nodded my head. "Best friends…but just friends," I said.

Frankie laid the open comic book across his chest, then held his right hand out to me, not as you would to shake hands, but more, it seemed, as an impulse for some physical affirmation that our friendship had survived, would survive, would endure. I reached over enough that our fingertips touched. As Frankie looked at me, tears began to fill his eyes, and he repeated my words in a broken voice, "Best friends…but just friends." He blinked hard, gave me another slight nod of understanding, and then lowered his hand back to his side. We sat there for a few moments, silent, letting the reality of what had just taken place settle over us. There were a hundred questions bobbing around inside my head, but I had the good sense not to unload them on Frankie then.

"How long will you be like that?" I asked, pointing to his face.

"The bandage can come off next week. The doctor said the bruising should be gone in a couple of weeks."

"Does it still hurt?"

"A little."

"I'm really sorry," I said, sniffing hard the last bits of moisture back up my nose.

"Me, too. Thanks for coming by," Frankie said. He reached up and wiped his eyes with his fingers, and I saw him wince a little. No doubt his face was sore and the slightest touch hurt him. It hurt me, too.

"I gotta get to work," I said and stood up.

"Hey…" Frankie said.

"Yeah?"

"Go by the Five & Dime in town and get your sister a new doll. Tell her I'm sorry. I'll pay you back."

"Okay," I said and headed over to the door.

"Are you sure you don't like Mark?" Frankie said behind me. I cringed and turned around. I was surprised to see him lying there with a playful grin on his face. "I mean, he is kinda cute," he added, then did a Goucho Marx with his eyebrows.

It only took me a second to realize that Frankie was teasing me—and testing me. Testing me to see how I would handle the truth, which in his own way, cloaked in humor, he was admitting openly to me now. I broke into laughter and I knew then that things between Frankie and me would forevermore be different, that the new normal for us had just begun. But what mattered most would be the same; we were still friends—best friends. As I stared at Frankie lying there, I was laughing not only at how ridiculous he looked oscillating his eyebrows with his face all bruised and his nose bandaged, but at the relief I felt knowing I had not lost my friend, that he and I had dealt with this, and that he trusted me enough to share this part of himself. To let Frankie know we were on the same page I said, "Mark is a little young for me." Then I winked at him.

Frankie started laughing hard and he reached up and grabbed his face. "Oh, crap, that hurts! Don't make me laugh! Don't make me laugh!" he pleaded.

That just made me laugh harder. I looked at him writhing on the bed, holding his face, and said, "Just remember, incest is illegal in Mississippi, so your brother is jail bait."

Frankie nearly doubled up in pain he was laughing so hard. He picked up the Archie comic and threw it at me and yelled, "Get out of here and go to work before you kill me!"

Still laughing, I hurried out the door and closed it behind me.

Four days earlier, when Frankie had refused to go to town and eat lunch with us because I'd invited his brother to go too, I thought then that the resolution of this issue would either strengthen our friendship or destroy it—though at the time I didn't have a clue what the "issue" really was. As I was riding to work now, cruising along on the Honda at a leisurely pace with the misty rain stinging my face and eyes, I realized the resolution could have gone either way, that it had been up to me the entire time. My actions this day could have destroyed our friendship or strengthened it. My father's wise and sage counsel, and my abiding affection for my best friend, made the course I chose simple—inevitable, really. I loved Frankie, though I could no more have told him that then, or admitted it to myself, than I could have flown to the moon. I knew Frankie loved me, too—though certainly in ways I didn't comprehend. But, then again, maybe I did, somewhere in the back of my mind, and it was just too much for a fifteen-year-old Mississippi boy to bring to the forefront of conscious reflection. Whatever aversion I may have had to the thought that my best friend was a homosexual, it was that abiding affection—mine for him and his for me—that carried the day and ensured our friendship would endure come what may.

Chapter 8
The Black Shadow

Friday morning Aunt Charity set me to work cleaning out the flower beds in front of our house. She said the azaleas were looking "poorly" and needed fresh pine straw around them. Parker was in the garden picking corn, which Aunt Charity would be blanching for freezing later. That meant I would be shucking a couple of bushels, at least, before I went to work.

By ten o'clock, I had finished cleaning out the beds and had almost raked up enough fresh pine needles out of the yard to replenish them. Mary Alice was sitting on the front porch in the rocker keeping me company. This made my labors difficult because I could not make two swipes of the rake without stealing a look at her. She had one of her big Braille books lying open in her lap and it was fascinating to watch her fingers move across the pages as she read. I was to the point now that everything about Mary Alice fascinated me, and the parts of the day when my chores or my job kept me from being with her were like trying to function without air to breathe. The nights were worse as I would lie there for hours, not able to sleep, longing to be with her, impatient for the coming morning when I knew I'd see her at breakfast, and worrying about the end of August when she would be gone from my life altogether.

Finally, the last bit of pine straw was neatly packed around the last azalea bush at the far end of the house. I picked up the rake and headed for the front porch.

"What are you reading?" I asked as I sat down in a chair across from Mary Alice. I reached up and wiped the sweat from my brow with the back of my hand.

"*Great Expectations* by Charles Dickens," she said. "Have you read it?"

"In the ninth grade," I said. Her hand stopped moving on the pages and I watched as she felt for the ribbon marker that was sewn to the spine of the book. She pulled it out, placed it in the gutter to mark the page, then closed the book. "Don't stop because of me," I said.

Mary Alice smiled. "I'd rather talk with you. Are you finished with the flowerbeds?"

"Yes, finally. What do you want to talk about?"

"You pick."

I looked at her sitting there and just had to ask, "Is pink your favorite color?"

She laughed her magical laugh, tossing her head back and setting herself to rocking in the chair. "Yes, it is. Why?"

"You've had on something pink every day since you got here. Yesterday you had on a pink shirt and blue shorts. Today you're wearing pink shorts and a blue shirt. The day I met you, you had on a pink dress."

Mary Alice shrugged and smiled and said, "I like pink."

"Yeah, but how do you know what color your clothes are when you get dressed in the morning?" The words had no more left my mouth and I realized what an insensitive question it was. I felt like an idiot. "Mary Alice, I'm sorry. I shouldn't have said that."

"Come over here," she said.

I got up and tentatively stepped over in front of her. I figured she was going to stand up and, once she found my face, slap me—and I deserved it.

"Lean down," she said.

"You're going to hit me, aren't you?" I said sheepishly.

"No," she said with a giggle. "I want to show you something." She leaned forward and then pulled her hair to the side. "Look inside my shirt collar," she said.

I bent down and pulled open the back of her collar. "What?" I said.

"Look at the label."

I didn't notice a label. I was too busy studying the fine downy hair that started on the nape of her neck and then traveled the length of her spine, under her bra strap, and on until it was out of sight. It was silly, but at that moment it was the most sensuous (and arousing) thing I'd ever seen.

"See it?" she said.

"See what?"

"Are you looking at the label?" Mary Alice asked in an exasperated tone.

"I am now," I said. There was a Braille label either glued or sewn to the shirtmakers label inside the collar.

"Run your finger over it," she said. I complied and felt the bumps. "That's the word 'blue,'" Mary Alice said. "There's a label inside the waistband of my pants that says 'pink.'"

"Can I see that one, too?" I said, releasing her shirt collar.

"No, you may not," she said sternly as she leaned back in the chair.

I laughed. "I'm just kidding. Aunt Charity would have a stroke if she came out here and saw me looking down the back of your pants."

Blushing, Mary Alice put her hand to her mouth to stifle her laugh. I had succeeded in embarrassing her.

"You want to go for a ride?" I said.

"Where?"

"Nowhere…just a ride."

"Do you even have a license to drive?"

"I'm talking about on my bike."

"Oh…okay." She sounded a little unsure.

"Wait here." I bounded down the four steps off the porch and headed for the carport.

When I motored into the front yard on the Honda and stopped at the porch steps, I could see the look of confusion on Mary Alice's face. I shut off the engine, set the stand, and went up on the porch. "Is that a motorbike?" she asked.

"It's a motorcycle, a Honda Scrambler."

"I thought you meant a bicycle."

"I have a bicycle but I don't think we could both fit on it. We don't have to go if you don't want to."

Mary Alice stood up and said, "No, I'll ride with you." I could still hear some apprehension in her voice.

"Are you sure?" I asked as I took the big book from her hands.

"Yes," she said.

I set the book down in the chair, took her hand and started for the porch steps. "Oh, wait a minute," I said as I looked at the bike sitting in the yard, then looked down at Mary Alice's bare legs.

"What's the matter?" she asked.

"The pipes and mufflers have heat shields, but they still get pretty hot. You don't have any long pants you can wear, do you?" The last thing I wanted was for her to burn herself after reluctantly agreeing to go for a ride with me.

"I don't have any long pants," she said. "I mean I didn't bring any with me from Poplarville."

"Well...ah..." I was trying to decide if I wanted to risk it, and then I had a thought. "Come with me," I said as I turned us around and we headed back to the front door of the house.

"Where are we going now?" Mary Alice asked.

"Inside," I said.

I opened the front door and we stepped into the living room. No one was in there. I could hear Aunt Charity in the kitchen. She was canning tomatoes and fixing lunch. Sachet was in there helping her, so the coast was clear. Normally, Aunt Charity did not want Sachet underfoot when she was working in the kitchen, but my sister had been moping around ever since she got her hair cut yesterday. She had a severe case of buyer's remorse and our aunt was working her through it by coddling and cajoling her. I led Mary Alice to my bedroom.

"This is your room?" she said as we stepped through the doorway.

"Yeah." I left her standing by the door and went over to the closet. "How'd you know?"

"The smell," she said.

"The smell," I said under my breath. I shook my head and chuckled. I didn't smell a thing.

"Why are we in your room?"

"I'm looking for something." I was rummaging through the box of clothes on the closet floor that Aunt Charity had packed up to take over to the home for children the next time she went. Most of this was Sachet's clothes that she'd outgrown, but there was a few of my things in there, too. I thought there was a couple of pairs of my old jeans from when I was eleven or twelve down at the bottom.

"What are you looking for?"

"Ah…these," I said as I pulled the jeans from the box. I went over and held them up to Mary Alice. "I think these will fit you almost perfectly."

She touched my hand, then the denim jeans. "Are these yours?"

"Yes."

"Won't they be too big for me?"

"These were mine when I was about twelve. I'll go out and you can try them on."

"Wait," she said, "I don't know this room. I need to sit down to change."

I took her hand and led her over to the bed. "You can sit here on my bed," I said. Mary Alice leaned down and touched the bed spread, turned and sat. She started to unfasten her Bermuda shorts and I said, rather forcefully, "Wait a minute! Let me get out of here."

Mary Alice laughed. "You don't have to go out. Just turn around."

I went over and closed my bedroom door and stood facing it. "Okay," I said, "I'm turned around." I knew I could have watched her undress and seen things I'd only dreamed of, but she trusted me to protect her modesty and I wasn't about to betray that trust. However, that didn't keep me from listening. When I heard her slip her shorts off, I pictured Mary Alice in my mind's eye sitting there in her panties—sitting there almost naked where I would be sleeping tonight. It was an excruciatingly erotic mental picture that had a predictable effect on a certain part of my male anatomy. It didn't occur to me at the time how difficult it would have been to explain this to Aunt Charity if she had walked in on us: me standing there with a huge bulge in my jeans and Mary Alice over on my bed taking her pants off. Somehow I don't think my aunt would have found the scene amusing.

After what seemed an eternity Mary Alice finally said, "Okay, you can turn around."

I walked over to my bed and sized her up. "They fit you good," I said. My old jeans were just a little short in the legs for her, but the length was fine for a girl. "Let's go," I said and took her hand.

When we got back out to the front yard I folded down the rear footpegs on the Honda and then helped Mary Alice get situated on the rear part of the seat. I got her feet firmly planted on the pegs and told her to keep them there. I got on the bike and reached back and pulled Mary Alice's arms around me. I told her to scoot forward. "No matter what, Mary Alice, you hold onto me, okay?"

"Okay," she said.

I turned my head back to her. "Are you scared?"

"A little," she said.

"Don't be. You're going to love this, I promise." With Mary Alice holding tightly onto me, I reached down and turned the key and then hit the starter button. The engine spun to life and I blipped the throttle a couple of times, pulled in the clutch, and dropped the transmission into first. I toed up the kickstand, and leaned the bike up and balanced it between my legs to get the feel of Mary Alice's weight. She was definitely lighter than Frankie, the only other passenger I was used to carrying. I turned back to her and said, "Remember what I said. Hold onto me. And when you feel me lean into a turn, you lean with me. Don't fight it." Mary Alice said she'd had a bike when she was little and knew what I meant. I eased out the clutch, gave it a little throttle and we were off. I made a wide turn in the front yard, maneuvered in between the pine trees, and then headed down the drive to the road. When we got to the end, I stopped and asked Mary Alice if she was still okay. She did-n't say anything but I felt her nod her head. She was hold-ing me close and her chin was touching my back.

"All right, here we go," I said. I checked for any cars coming, turned right onto the road, and then twisted the throttle. I quickly shifted up into second and then third and kept the speed at about 25. "You still okay?" I hollered over the wind noise. Again I felt her nod, so I twisted the throt-tle a little more. I felt Mary Alice's embrace tighten as I shifted into fourth. I didn't want to scare her, so I kept the speed to about 35 as I started the lean for the turn that would lead to the straightaway down to the bridge over the Wolf River. I expected Mary Alice to resist the lean, but she did-n't and we negotiated the curve perfectly. I was still in fourth as we exited the curve and I had about a quarter-mile of straight road in front of me leading down to the bridge. I gave it a little more throttle and took us up to 50. Just as I was about to shift into fifth, I caught a glimpse in my left mirror of something coming up behind us. It was the Vincent.

We were still about a hundred yards from the bridge and the Vincent was coming up on us fast. Without thinking I yelled, "Hold on!" and downshifted into third and dumped the throttle. In a blink we were doing 60. The Honda's 325

CC engine was screaming as I shifted into fourth at 9000 RPM. We were doing 70 when we hit the bridge. I looked in the mirror again and the Vincent was right there, and then in a flash it roared by. I shifted into fifth and glanced down at the speedometer. I could barely see it because my eyes were watering so badly from the wind blast. The needle was approaching 80 MPH. The Vincent had passed us like were standing still.

When I realized just how fast we were going, it scared me. I rolled off the throttle and got into the brakes pretty good. The path down to the river was coming up and I wanted to take Mary Alice down there to show her where we could go swimming.

Mary Alice was still holding me tightly as I turned off the road onto the obscure path that led through the woods and down to the beach on the Wolf. Once I got to the white sand, I eased the bike to a stop and shut it off. The engine, the pipes, and the mufflers were all ticking loudly from the heat of that full-blast run. I told Mary Alice to let me get off the bike first so I could help her get off without burning herself. When she was safely off and we were standing there on the beach facing the water, I saw that she had tears streaming down her face. "Are you okay?" I said. She reached out to me and I took her in my arms and kissed the top of her head. "I'm sorry I scared you."

She said something and I didn't understand her because she had her face buried in my shirt. "What?" I said.

She let go of me and wiped the tears from her eyes. "I wasn't scared," she said. "That was the most fun I've had since…since I rode a rollercoaster when I was little."

"Seriously? That didn't scare you?"

She shook her head and smiled.

"Well…it scared me," I said. And it did, for two reasons: First, because it was the fastest I'd ever gone on the Honda. And, second, because I knew Daddy would take the bike away from me in a New York minute if he found out I was out here racing with it.

Mary Alice was taking in our surroundings: the wind in the trees, the feel of the sand beneath our shoes, the sound of the river twenty feet away. "Where are we?" she asked.

"This is the beach on the river where Frankie and I go swimming. I was thinking maybe you and I could come down here sometime and swim. You did bring a bathing suit with you from Poplarville, didn't you?"

"Two bathing suits, actually."

"And I bet one of 'em is pink."

Mary Alice laughed. "They both are," she said.

"We better be getting back. It's getting close to lunch time and Aunt Charity doesn't know we're gone. She'll start worrying if she misses us." I took Mary Alice's hand to help her back onto the bike, but she resisted.

"Wait a minute," she said.

"What is it?"

She reached out to me and her hands came to rest on my chest, then she moved them up until she was touching my face. I let her pull my face down to hers, and there on that white sand beach, the girl I loved kissed me. It was a soft and tender kiss, not clumsy and groping like when I kissed her on Aunt Charity's porch. It was the sort of kiss that could only be sublimely and uniquely hers. I knew in my heart that while she may have graced other boys with a smile, a laugh, even a held hand, Mary Alice had never bestowed this gift on another. Her first kiss for a boy she had saved for me. As I stood there holding her, it was easy to say a prayer of thanks to God for giving Mary Alice to me.

— — —

Aunt Charity had scolded me when we got back for taking Mary Alice on the motorcycle without telling her first. Lunch was interesting because it was the first time I'd really seen Mary Alice turn her charms on my sister. Despite Aunt Charity's best efforts, Sachet was nearly despondent over the loss of her hair. My aunt wouldn't admit it, but I think she was now regretting allowing Sachet's whim yesterday to become a reality at the beauty parlor. "I want my hair short," the declaration my sister had made at the breakfast table, resulted in Sachet looking like the kid on a can of Dutch Boy paint. I liked it, but no amount of my feeble compliments could assuage Sachet's remorse, especially since Daddy's reaction when he got home from work yesterday was, "Where has my baby girl gone?" Mary Alice, however, was making some headway, and by the time we'd finished eating, she had Sachet laughing and talking, and her mind off her short hair. After lunch, I spent an hour sitting under the big pecan tree in the backyard shucking corn. I had taken a chair out there, and Mary Alice sat with me reading her book.

When I got to the station that afternoon, Dick was working on a motorcycle in one of the service station bays. It was the Vincent. He had it up on the center stand with the front end held off the ground by a cinder block and a couple of two-by-fours under the engine. It looked like he had just finished putting the front wheel back on. "What's wrong with it?" I asked.

Dick muttered something and I didn't catch it. I started looking closely at this magnificent machine. Daddy had said they didn't make Vincents anymore, but this one looked like new. The engine was shiny black and a V-twin like on a Harley or Indian, but it looked different. Way different. More exotic. The whole bike was black except for the chrome pieces, which included the fenders. There was no tachometer and the speedometer was huge and sat bolt upright between the low-slung handlebars. It read all the way to 150 MPH. The one on my Honda tapped out at 110.

"Did he have a flat?" I asked.

"Almost," Dick said. "He came in here about an hour ago to get gas and I noticed his front tire was low on air. He asked me to look at it. He'd picked up a thumbtack. He was lucky."

"Did you get it fixed?"

"I patched it. You know we don't have any motorcycle tubes. I'm gonna tell him he needs to get that tube replaced. A patch on a bicycle tube is okay, but I wouldn't trust one on a motorcycle."

"Where is he?" I asked and looked around.

"How the hell do I know? He wandered off. Maybe he went down to the diner for some coffee. He's a strange one."

"I've seen him riding down around our house a few times," I said. "He passed me this morning when I was riding down by the river. I was doing nearly eighty and he went by me like I was standing still."

Dick looked at me. "What in the hell are you doin' goin' eighty miles per hour on that bike of yours? Your daddy know you ride that thing like that?"

"It's the only time I've ever gone that fast and it scared the crap out of me. I won't ever do it again. And Daddy would kill me if he knew."

"You damn right he would. You ain't got no business ridin' like that. You'll wind up gettin' yourself killed."

I knew for all his bluster, Dick wouldn't tell my father, so I changed the subject. I pointed to the Vincent and said, "Daddy figures this guy is a pilot from down at Keesler."

Dick started reattaching the front brake connections. "The guy that rides this thing ain't no pilot from Keesler."

"How do you know?" I asked.

"Look at that," Dick said, and pointed to the front brake drums. "It's got two front brakes." He finished attaching the brake and speedometer cables, then stood up and tested the brakes. "I reckon that's good enough," he mumbled. "Pull those boards out when I lift up on the front end." Dick leaned down and grabbed the front forks and grunted as he lifted the Vincent about an inch off the two-by-fours. I slid them out and held onto the handlebars as Dick let the bike down and I kept it balanced on the center stand. Dick used his foot to push the cinder block from under the bike.

I noticed a black leather duffle bag sitting on the bench over in the corner along with a black denim jacket and helmet. "Is that his stuff over there?" I asked.

"Yeah," Dick said.

"So how do you know he's not a pilot?"

Dick headed over to the tool box to replace his wrenches in the drawer. "Wait till you see him. He talks like a Limey and he's got a ponytail down to his ass. He ain't no pilot, he's one of them hippies you see down on the beach at Gulfport."

"What's a hippie doing in Bells Ferry?" I said.

"Beats the hell outta me," Dick said. "They're everywhere nowadays. Between the hippies, the fags, and the niggers, the whole goddamn country's goin' to hell."

I could count on one hand the number of times I'd heard Daddy use swear words over the last month, but I ran out of fingers and toes the first hour I worked for Dick Tillman. From him I got a full dose of profanity every time I came to work, and it was fun sometimes to prod him into getting wound up just to see what he'd come out with. He was always careful not to curse in front of customers, though. I, of course, had a small repertoire of vulgarities that I would use around my friends, especially Frankie, but they remained under lock and key when I was around adults, even Dick. This particular bit of cultural wisdom Dick had just offered up gave me pause. Normally, I would have shrugged it off as being just another "Dickism" to be ignored, but the reference to "fags" in the same sentence deriding niggers and hippies now had me thinking about Frankie. For the first time I began to contemplate just how bad things could get for him around here if people knew he was queer—or a fag, as Dick had put it. This was southern Mississippi, not California or New York or any of the other places where we assumed "alternative lifestyles" were tolerated or even openly accepted. The extent to which homosexuality was even acknowledged among my peers was to use the terms and behaviors associated with it as degrading predicatives while hurling what we perceived to be humorous insults at each other. Branding a friend "fag" or "queer" or "cock sucker" or inviting him to suck your dick was much more effective at putting him in his place than merely calling him an idiot or telling him to kiss your ass.

The bell announcing a car at the pumps dinged twice and my attention was forced back to my job. I went out and started filling Mr. Sonny Tanner's new Ford pickup with gas. Just as I was finishing up, I saw the rider of the Vincent walking down the sidewalk from up town. I could see what Dick meant. No pilot in the U. S. Air Force I'd ever seen looked like this guy. He was clad entirely in black from head to toe. His black jeans had silver studs down the out-side stitching of the legs. He was tall, maybe even as tall as my father, and his black tee shirt fit him snugly, revealing every ripple of his musculature. He had on black riding boots and a wide black leather belt with a big Bowie knife stuck in a sheath hanging from it. From a head-on view, his hair looked short, but when he turned to look at my Honda, which was parked off to the side of the station, I saw the ponytail. Dick hadn't exaggerated; the guy's dark brown hair was nearly down to his waist. Hippies were supposed to be all about peace and love, and if that were true, I was certain this man was no hippie.

As Mr. Sonny paid me for the gas, I watched the man in black enter the bay where his bike was parked. Dick started talking to him. The man asked him something, but I could-n't hear what was being said. Then Dick pointed to me, and the stranger turned to look at me. He had a cold stare that unnerved me.

"You gonna get my change?" Mr. Sonny said.

I looked down at the five dollar bill in my hand. "Yes, sir. I'll be right back." I glanced at the pump to see the amount and then sprinted into the office to ring up the pur-chase and get Mr. Sonny his 80¢ in change. He never gave me a tip when he stopped by for gas. I ran back out to the pumps and gave him the three quarters and a nickel. When I turned around, the man in black was standing there not six feet from me. I was startled and jumped back a bit and hit my elbow on the Hi-Test pump. This close, I could see he was not as tall as he had appeared at a distance. He had an olive complexion and there was an Oriental look to his dark brown eyes. Staring at me, he fished a cigarette out of the pack that was in his shirt pocket. It was a brown cigarette. I'd never seen a brown cigarette. He stuck it between his lips. When he pulled the lighter out of his left front jeans pocket, I said, "Can't smoke out here at the pumps." He ignored me, flicked open the lighter, and lit the cigarette. He clicked the lighter closed and stuck it back in his pocket. He took a long draw on the brown cigarette, then removed it from his lips and blew the smoke in my direction. The whole time his eyes never left me, and he never blinked. He was almost leering at me and it gave me the creeps. Finally, he spoke. "Is that your Scrambler over there, mate?" He did have an English sounding accent.

"Yes," I said.

The stranger put the brown cigarette back to his lips and took another draw. He blew out the smoke and said, "Was that you riding this morning outside of town with that pretty little Sheila on the back?"

"Her name's not Sheila," I said defensively, and there was an angry edge to my voice. The guy was pissing me off now that he'd mentioned Mary Alice.

He smiled and blinked for the first time. He put the cigarette back in his mouth and stuck his hand out to me. "Name's Bong," he said, "Peter Bong."

I reached out and shook the man's hand. "Nelson Gody," I said. "You're from England?"

He laughed and said, "Not a pom, mate. I'm from Australia." I guess he saw me eyeing that brown cigarette because he took the pack out of his pocket and held it over to me. "Want one?" he said. His voice was totally pleasant, and didn't seem to fit the way he looked.

"No," I said. "I don't smoke." The one and only time Frankie and I had tried a cigarette was back when we were fourteen. It made us both sick and I decided then smoking wasn't for me.

Peter Bong replaced the pack in his pocket. "You gave me a pretty good run this morning. You know what that is I'm riding?"

"It's a Vincent," I said.

"Not just a Vincent, mate. That's the Black Shadow. You yanks have never made a bike that can run with the Black Shadow, and the Japs never will."

"How fast were you going when you passed me?" I asked.

"About a hundred."

"How fast will it go?"

"I've had it to one-twenty and she still had some go in her."

"My dad said Rollie Free went a hundred and fifty on a Vincent at Bonneville."

I could see the surprise in the man's eyes. "Your old man knows his bikes. Free was riding a Black Lightning, a racing version of the Shadow. It was faster."

I could see Dick standing by the office door looking at me. "I gotta get back to work," I said to the stranger.

The man dropped the brown cigarette and crushed it with his boot. He walked back over to the office with me. "Does your dad ride, too?" he asked.

"Yeah, the Honda is really his bike. I just ride it all the time."

"Well, if you're serious about riding, mate, you should get you a crash hat."

"A what?"

"A helmet," he said and pointed to his head. He looked at Dick. "How much do I owe you?"

"Three dollars will cover it," Dick said.

The man pulled a black leather wallet, which was chained to his belt, from his back pocket. He opened it and took out three one dollar bills and handed them to Dick.

"Like I told you," Dick said, "I only patched that tube. You should go to a motorcycle shop down in Biloxi or Gulfport and get a new tube as soon as you can."

"Will do, mate," the man said. He looked at me. "Nice meeting you, Nelson."

I smiled and nodded. Dick and I watched Peter Bong bungee his leather bag to the back of the bike's seat. Then he put his jacket and helmet on and kick started the Black Shadow. It fired right off and had the same loping idle that a Harley does, but the sound of the Vincent's exhaust note had a harder edge to it. He rocked the bike off the center stand, put it in gear, and roared off.

"Hippie," Dick said in disgust.

"I don't think so. He's just different."

"Yeah, he's different all right. He said his name's Bong. What the hell kinda name is that?"

"I don't know," I said. "He said he's from Australia."

"Hippie," Dick said again and headed into the office.

Chapter 9
Sea of Tranquility

"Do you miss Uncle Jack?" I asked my aunt. I was sitting at the bar in her kitchen. It was Sunday morning, a little after ten, and I was dressed and ready for church. I even put on a tie since this would be my first time escorting Mary Alice to worship with me. She was in her room getting ready. Daddy and Sachet had already left since Daddy had to be there early to teach Sunday School, which Aunt Charity and I decided to forego since this was Mary Alice's first Sunday.

"I miss him every day," Aunt Charity said. "What in the world prompted that question?"

"I don't know," I said gloomily. But I did know. For the first time in my life I was grappling with the concept of a committed relationship and the dynamics of how two people in love managed their time when apart. The two adults that meant the most to me had both lost their life partners far too early, and yet they seemed to be getting along just fine. I, on the other hand, was reduced to near paralyzing melancholia at the mere thought of being away from Mary Alice.

Aunt Charity opened the oven and slid in the pot roast we would be eating later. She had decided to have us all over to her house for dinner today, especially since she knew we'd be over here anyway to watch the moon landing this afternoon on her color TV. "What's the matter with you?" she asked. "Your chin's been on the floor all morning."

I sighed and said, "I'm going to miss Mary Alice when she has to go back to Poplarville." I had not intended to admit that, but I'd let my guard down and the truth just spilled out of me.

Aunt Charity came over and sat on the barstool beside me. She smiled, and like before, I caught a glimpse of my mother in her face. "Why are you worrying about that now? She doesn't have to go back until next month."

"I wish you'd never brought her here," I said. There was movement behind me and to my left. I rotated around on the bar stool to see Mary Alice standing there. A quick look at Aunt Charity confirmed what I feared: Mary Alice had heard me.

The hurt in Mary Alice's face paralyzed me. I couldn't move. I couldn't speak. I watched her turn and walk slowly over to the door. She disappeared down the hallway and then I heard her bedroom door close. I turned to look at Aunt Charity. She just frowned and shook her head the way I'd seen her do a thousand times when she was displeased with something I or my sister had said or done.

My catatonia subsided and I got up and went straight to Mary Alice's bedroom door. I knocked softly and called her name. There was no response, so I turned the knob and opened the door. Mary Alice was sitting on the bed. She had on her Sunday dress, which was white, not pink. I went over and knelt down in front of her. Tears were running down her cheeks. "Mary Alice?" I said again.

"Please leave," she said.

"I didn't mean that…what I said in there to Aunt Charity. I was just trying to tell—"

"Please leave," she repeated, cutting me off. I didn't know what to do. What could I say to make her understand that I was dying inside? How could I tell her those words I'd said were nothing more than my frustration because she had taken up residence in my heart and I couldn't bear the thought of her leaving me in four short weeks? "Please leave," she said again, and this time her voice cracked as she choked back a sob.

I stood up and an overwhelming feeling of nausea seized me. I turned and ran from the room. I sprinted down to the bathroom where I vomited up my breakfast into the toilet.

Afterwards, I found Aunt Charity waiting for me in the den. She was standing at the sliding glass door looking out at her huge back yard. I walked over to her with my head down in total dejection. I felt so weak I could hardly move. She put her arms around me and I buried my face in her shoulder and began to cry.

"Oh, my baby boy," she said. "It's not easy, is it?"

Her words made me cry harder. Mama had always called me her "baby boy," and I couldn't remember the last time Aunt Charity had called me that. Maybe she never had. "What's not easy?" I asked as I released her and wiped my eyes.

She smiled and put her hand to my cheek. "Growing up," she said.

If what I'd been through so far this summer was growing up, I didn't want any part of it. Not easy? It was impossible. "She won't talk to me, Aunt Charity," I said. "I wanted to tell her I was sorry and didn't mean it, but she just asked me to leave."

"Her feelings are hurt, Nelson."

"I know," I said, and fresh tears welled up in my eyes.

"Go in the kitchen and get you some Coke to settle your stomach," she said. "I'll go talk to Mary Alice."

"What are you going to say to her?"

"You let me worry about that. Run on, now. Get you some Coke." She pointed toward the kitchen and left for Mary Alice's room.

After I finished a small glass of Coca-Cola, I went back in the den and sat down on the couch. There was a huge knot in my stomach. I leaned back and closed my eyes. I was trying unsuccessfully not to think about the possibility that my relationship with Mary Alice was over almost as quickly as it had begun. I don't know how long I'd sat there with my eyes closed when I felt someone sit down beside me. I opened my eyes and turned to see Mary Alice. Her eyes were red from crying, but otherwise she looked like nothing had happened.

"Hey, pretty girl," I said. I was surprised at my words, and at the serene way I spoke them. I'd never called Mary Alice "pretty girl" before, but the appellation surely fit. She looked like a picture in her white Sunday dress, and now I noticed the pink lace accents. "Will you let me explain, now?" I asked.

Mary Alice smiled. "You don't have to. Your aunt told me what you and she were talking about. I understand what you meant. But as much as it's going to hurt when I have to leave, I wouldn't trade this summer for anything. Don't you feel that way, too?"

"Yes," I said.

"Then will you promise me you will quit fretting over next month so much?"

"I'll try. It's hard, because I want to spend every minute with you. Knowing you won't be here…it hurts, Mary Alice. I can't help it."

She reached out until she found me, then put her arms around me and hugged me tightly. "Aren't you getting your license on your birthday next month?" she said over my shoulder.

"Yes."

"And aren't you getting a car?"

"Yes…how'd you know that?"

"If I promise to come here to your aunt's every weekend, will you promise to drive to Poplarville and pick me up and take me back?"

We released each other and I looked her in the face. "They'll let you do that?" I asked. "I mean, you can leave there on the weekends when you're in school?"

Mary Alice laughed. "I'm not in school. I have a tutor who comes four days a week. And it's not a prison, Nelson. Miss Charity said she would talk with them at the home. She thinks me coming here on the weekends will be fine. Will you promise to drive to Poplarville to get me?"

"Are you kidding? Of course I will." I was beaming and I had Aunt Charity to thank. She knew what the solution was to my depressed mood, and she'd set the wheels in motion to accomplish it. Come the end of August, Mary Alice might not be here day in and day out the way she was now, but with the promise of seeing her every weekend, I could survive. I hoped.

— — —

I was proud as a peacock to walk down the aisle at Bells Ferry Presbyterian Church with Mary Alice on my arm. We were a little late getting there, and the organist had already started playing when we entered the sanctuary. Whether or not everyone turned and stared at us because we were late, or because I was escorting an angel, I don't know. I'd like to think it was the latter. We took our places in our usual pew. Daddy was already here, and sitting down front. As the chairman of the Pulpit Committee, he would be introducing the minister who would be preaching and who was seeking to be our new pastor.

After Mr. Jake Harland, Chairman of the Board of Deacons, gave the announcements, then conducted us through the Apostles Creed and the opening hymn, Daddy ascended the pulpit to give the prayer in preparation for the morning offering. His supplication was heartfelt, simple and elegant. He asked for God's blessings on the service and the missionaries our church supported, he prayed for healing for the sick, and he gave thanks for the many blessings we all enjoyed and were usually too busy to acknowledge. When he gave the Amen, four of the deacons went up to the Lord's Table to retrieve the collection plates. The organ started to play as the deacons fanned out and started passing the plates. Daddy resumed his seat in one of the two chairs behind the pulpit on the rostrum.

After we sang the Doxology and the deacons returned the collection plates to the table, Daddy took the pulpit again to dismiss the smaller kids to children's church, and then he began his introduction of our guest preacher. As I watched my father up in the pulpit dressed in his dark blue suit, seemingly so at ease speaking before the hundred or so people who filled our small sanctuary, I thought what a fine minister he would make. Daddy had been an elder in the church since before I was born and he'd taught the men's Sunday School class for as long as I could remember. The few times when I'd grown bored in the boys' class and sat in on Daddy's teaching, I thought his expositions of scripture to be every bit as good as Rev. Doug's. Now, however, he was merely giving us a brief resume of the man who was about to deliver God's Word to us. His name was Rev. Kyle Petigru. He was a young, mousey looking man, with short hair slicked back with tonic. Daddy told us he was a 1968 graduate of Columbia Seminary, and an assistant pastor at a large church in Mobile. As my father talked, Rev. Petigru was sitting in the other chair behind the pulpit with an affected grin on his face. He was wearing a black Geneva gown, which we were used to because Rev. Doug would wear one on Communion Sundays and for baptisms and other special services. But Rev. Petigru was also sporting a collar and bands, something I'd only seen in photographs of eighteenth century ministers. It was a pretentious accoutrement that made me uneasy and made him look out of place. I didn't like this man, who hardly looked older than me, before he even spoke a word. When he did, my disdain became palpable.

The text Rev. Petigru chose for his sermon was John 9:1-41, the story of Jesus healing the man who was born blind. I'd heard Rev. Doug preach this story at least twice that I could remember, so when this guy started his exposition, it was all I could do to keep quiet. Rather than focusing on the true point of the passage, Rev. Petigru turned the story on its head and made it about how the spiritual aspects of one's life (namely, sin) can have physical consequences (for example, blindness). Jesus said the blind man's malady was not the result of sin, either his or his parents, because he was born that way. Such was not the case, according to Rev. Petigru, for those who were afflicted after having the gift of sight. The body was both spiritual and physical, and our sins could result in not just spiritual blindness, but actual blindness. Rev. Petigru told us that every physical ailment, every disease, every handicap, could be traced to some spiritual defect and this passage in John's Gospel proved it. I thought he was full of shit.

As this false prophet spewed his malarkey, I kept looking at Mary Alice beside me. I was hoping she wasn't paying attention, but she was, and clearly bewildered. A minister of God was telling the most innocent girl I'd ever known that she was blind because of her sins. I wanted to run up the aisle and strangle him with my bare hands. Instead, when I'd had all I could stand, I leaned over and whispered in Mary Alice's ear, "Come with me." I took her hand and we stood up. Aunt Charity looked at us. There was a big question mark on her face, but when I glanced up to the rostrum I could see Daddy understood. It was almost imperceptible, but there was a slight smile on his face. With everyone staring at us again, I led Mary Alice out of the sanctuary.

Two huge live oak trees graced the front yard of our church. The one to the right as you exited the front door had a concrete bench under it and Mary Alice and I went over and sat down. Before I could speak, Mary Alice told me she didn't think she liked my church.

"That guy is an idiot, Mary Alice. He's not our regular pastor. I wish you could hear Rev. Doug preach, but he retired and we're trying to find a new pastor."

"Do you believe what he said?" she asked.

"No."

"I've always tried to be a good person," Mary Alice said meekly.

For the second time in less than a week, I was losing my temper, and this time it was because of a sermon preached in my own church. "Mary Alice, please don't pay any attention to what he said. You are a good person. You're the kindest, sweetest girl I've ever met." I could hear the organ start up inside and the congregation began singing the final hymn, so I knew the front yard was about to be flooded with people. Daddy would be escorting Rev. Petigru to the front door after the benediction and then everyone would file past and shake their hands. There would be smiles and more than a few who had slept through the sermon would say how fine it was. "They'll be coming out in a minute," I said to Mary Alice.

She reached over to me and I took her hand. As the congregants exited the church, a few of them started making their way over to us. I introduced Mary Alice and several of the older ladies commented on how pretty she was and how they hoped to see her back next Sunday. The crowd thinned and I saw Daddy walking towards us with Rev. Petigru at his side. The noonday breeze blew the folds and pleats of the Geneva gown in a great swath of black around him. I said a silent prayer asking God to help me control my temper and not say something that would embarrass my father.

I stood up as they approached. Daddy looked at me and said, "Rev. Petigru, this is my son, Nelson."

Rev. Petigru still had that ridiculous grin on his face as he stuck his hand out to me. "Kyle Petigru," he said.

"It's nice to meet you, Rev. Petigru," I lied and shook his hand. I was a good five or six inches taller than him.

"And who's this pretty lady here?" he said. He let go of my hand and stuck his down to Mary Alice.

I waited and let him just stand there looking like a fool with his hand in front of Mary Alice while she stared off to his side. Normally, Daddy would have taken extra pains to quickly smooth over this awkward moment, but he was silent and I was relishing it. It briefly crossed my mind that if Rev. Petigru were correct, God would be striking me blind any minute for what I was thinking. I looked at Daddy and he gave me a little nod, as if to say, "Go ahead and reel him in."

"This is Mary Alice Hadley," I said. "She's blind."

Rev. Petigru's grin evaporated. There was a look of embarrassment on his face now as he glanced first at me, then Daddy, then slowly withdrew his hand from in front of Mary Alice. Whether his regret was grounded in the certainty that he had blown any chance of becoming our new pastor, or because he was actually sorry for preaching such a moronic sermon to a blind girl, I could not tell. Mary Alice remained stoic the whole time and never said a word, which I know had to be difficult since she had been raised just as I had been and you always spoke when spoken to by an adult.

Finally, my father broke the tension by announcing that Mr. and Mrs. Foxe were waiting to take Rev. Petigru to Sunday dinner at their home. As they turned and started walking toward the parking lot beside the church, I heard my father say, "That was an interesting sermon. You may want to preach on Isaiah 5:20 next time. Are you familiar with that passage, Reverend?"

"I don't believe I am off the top of my head," Rev. Petigru replied.

I gave a little chuckle as I took Mary Alice's hand and we followed behind them at a good distance. Rev. Petigru might not be able to recall Isaiah 5:20, but I could—at least the relevant parts: "Woe unto them that call good evil; that put darkness for light; that put bitter for sweet!" Amen, Daddy. Amen.

— — —

Uncle Rick drove up from Bay St. Louis to watch the moon landing with us. I always looked forward to his visits because he drove the nearest thing to an exotic car we were likely to see in these parts: a '67 Volkswagen Beetle. He would usually let me take it for a spin. It was a blast to drive, sort of like riding in an enclosed go-cart. Uncle Rick had already gotten official NASA photographs of the launch last week and he brought us two sets. One he said was for us to enjoy now, the other to put away as keepsakes. Daddy said he'd put that set in the safe deposit box next time he went to the bank. I called Frankie to see if he wanted to come to Aunt Charity's to watch the landing, but he said he was too embarrassed to be seen as the bruising hadn't gone down much. A fresh pang of remorse prompted another apology from me, but Frankie was gracious and told me not to worry about it. He seemed genuinely surprised that I'd called, which made me glad I had. I wanted him to know that I meant what I said in his room on Friday, that we were still friends.

At quarter past three we were all huddled around the color TV in Aunt Charity's den. I was disappointed that the only thing on the screen was the CBS News simulation of the Lunar Module in its decent toward the moon. We listened to the radio transmissions between Mission Control and the astronauts as they piloted the LEM toward the landing zone in the Sea of Tranquility.

"Uncle Rick, how come they don't have a camera showing the landing?" I asked.

"They're filming it. There won't be any live video transmissions until they do the walk later."

I leaned back on the couch and resumed holding Mary Alice's hand. Uncle Rick was on the floor in front of the TV with my sister in his lap. Daddy was in the rocker. Aunt Charity was in and out. I don't think this event impressed her too much. I caught myself holding my breath during the last minute of the decent to the moon. Finally, when one of the astronauts said "Contact light" over the radio, Uncle Rick let out a loud whoop, jumped up, and spun Sachet around in his arms. "They're on the moon!" he shouted. Sachet was squealing, Daddy was laughing, and I was trying to hear what was being said on the TV. Mary Alice had a big smile on her face and she was squeezing my hand. LUNAR MODULE HAS LANDED ON THE MOON appeared on the TV screen superimposed over a graphic of the LEM sitting on the moon's surface. Wally Schirra, who was commentating the landing with Walter Cronkite, said, "We're home," and Cronkite exclaimed, "Man on the Moon!" Then, confirming what we all knew, Neil Armstrong uttered the second most famous words he would speak on this mission: "Houston, Tranquility Base here. The Eagle has landed."

Aunt Charity came in the room just as I looked up at Uncle Rick who was still standing with my sister in his arms. He had tears in his eyes. He was one among thousands of engineers, technicians, and scientists who had worked long and hard for this moment and he was justifiably proud of what NASA had accomplished and the role he'd played in it.

This day had started off rocky for me. I had almost let my preoccupation with Mary Alice's departure next month ruin our relationship. After Aunt Charity rectified that problem, I had to deal with that idiot minister and his nonsensical sermon that seemed purpose-written to insult Mary Alice. But we navigated that shoal, too. Later that night, as

I sat there surrounded by my family and the girl I loved watching Neil Armstrong step out onto the surface of the moon, I was a happy and blessed boy. I was in the midst of my own Sea of Tranquility, and I knew it. But for some reason I had an uneasy feeling deep down that things were too good to be true, that this utopia could not last. Little did I know how perceptive my intuition would turn out to be.

Chapter 10
Lodge of Sorrow

When I got up Monday morning, Daddy had left a note scotch taped to the mirror in the bathroom. It simply read, *Nelson, your grandmother is coming for dinner this evening. Be nice. Love, Dad.*

Elizabeth LaFontaine Gody was the only grandparent I had ever known. My mother's parents both died young from cancer before I was born. My paternal grandfather was a banker, shot dead by a would-be bank robber in 1934, during the darkest days of the Great Depression when Daddy was seven and Uncle Rick was four. From the time I was old enough to grasp the concept, I determined that Grandma Gody was not all that fond of my father. By the age of twelve I had asked Aunt Charity about it. She said my grandmother had never gotten over Daddy enlisting in the Marines the week before he was to matriculate at the University of Mississippi. My grandmother was a graduate of Mississippi State College for Women and placed great emphasis on the value of higher education. She expected her two sons to graduate college and become professionals like their father. Uncle Rick was the only son who did. My father, in his mother's eyes, was little more than a day laborer who never lived up to his potential. That his annual income was actually more than Uncle Rick's, and he was considered one of the finest millwrights in Mississippi, meant nothing to my grandmother. I think Aunt Charity regretted apprising me of this bit of family history because she thought it permanently cemented the disrespect for Grandma Gody I struggled to hide whenever she came calling, or the few times each year (usually just Thanksgiving and Christmas) when Daddy would drive my sister and me to Picayune to visit our grandmother in the big old house where he was born. Now that I was old enough to understand that my grandmother thought her eldest son a failure, a failure not only in his choice of vocation, but a failure as a parent, my disrespect had blossomed into unfeeling dislike, and I would suffer her presence only because she was family—and for Daddy's sake.

"Why do you not like her?" Mary Alice asked me. I had just made her aware of this, and told her that Grandma Gody would be dining with us. We were sitting on Aunt Charity's front porch and it was almost time for me to leave for work.

"You'll see," I said. It was hard for Mary Alice to comprehend because she had been so close to her grandmother who had raised her. Unless Grandma Gody had been transformed by some sort of Damascus Road experience since I last saw her at Easter, I knew one meal with her would be enough for Mary Alice to understand.

— — —

When I got home from work, my grandmother's blue and white '57 DeSoto was parked in the driveway. There was also another car, a faded old Mercury that I'd never seen before, parked behind it. Just as I pulled up behind this strange car, Daddy came out on our front porch with three colored men. They were each dressed in dark suits and I could tell the conversation they were continuing from inside was serious. My father had a sad frown on his face as he shook these men's hands. I parked the Honda under the carport and went in the house.

Aunt Charity was at the stove as I came into the kitchen. Something smelled good. "Who were those men Daddy was talking to?" I asked.

"I don't know," she said, "but I suspect they were here about Parker."

"Parker? Why do you think they were here about him?" I looked over her shoulder to see what she was tending to on the stove. She was frying rib eye steaks in the skillet.

"He didn't come today," she said.

My aunt's intuition was sound because Parker was here five days a week, rain or shine. He had never missed a day since Daddy hired him. He might not do much when he got here, but he was always here. I looked over at the table, which was set for dinner. "Where's Grandma?"

"She took your sister in her room to read when those men came. Go wash your hands. Tell your father and grandmother that dinner will be ready in ten minutes; then you can go over and get Mary Alice."

"Sit up straight, Nelson," my grandmother said as soon as Daddy said "Amen" at the end of grace. "Elbows off the table, Sachet." Thus began our evening dinner with Grandma Gody.

"What were those men here for, Daddy?" I asked. The platter of steaks had already made its way around the table. Next came the dish with the baked potatoes. I took one for me and one for Mary Alice and then took the bottle of French dressing and doused my tossed salad.

"Could I have the ketchup, please," Mary Alice said.

"You put ketchup on steak?" I asked.

"No, on my salad."

I just stared at her. I'd never heard of anyone using ketchup for salad dressing. Aunt Charity started to get up, but I stopped her. "I'll get it," I said. I went over to the ice box and got the bottle of Hunt's and set it down by Mary Alice's plate. "One o'clock," I said as I sat back down. I waited to see if she realized I was giving her the coordinates of the ketchup bottle. She moved her hand over the red Formica of the table until she touched her plate, then her hand went directly to the bottle. "Daddy? What about those men?" I asked as I watched Mary Alice pour ketchup on her salad. It looked revolting.

"Sad news, I'm afraid," Daddy said. "Parker Reeves passed away yesterday...or maybe Saturday night. They found him yesterday morning when they went to get him for church. The funeral is tomorrow at two o'clock."

"Are you going?" Aunt Charity asked.

"Yes. Parker was a Brother. It will be a Masonic funeral."

"They let colored in the Lodge?" I asked. I'd never heard Daddy mention any colored members before.

He smiled. "No, the blacks have their own Lodge. You know that square brick building that sits off by itself on the other side of town like you're going to the lumber yard?"

"Yeah."

"Yes, sir," my grandmother corrected me. It was all I could do to keep from rolling my eyes.

"That's their Lodge building," Daddy said.

My grandmother cleared her throat and looked at Daddy. "Who is this Parker Reeves, Patrick? And why do you feel compelled to go to his funeral?"

"Parker worked for me, Mother. He helped out around here. And I'm going to the funeral for two reasons: Because I was invited and to pay my respects."

That answer seemed to satisfy her, so she drew a bead on Sachet, who was wrestling with the knife trying to cut her steak. "Let me cut that for you, sweetheart," she said. Her words said "Let me help you." Her tone said "You don't know what you're doing."

"I can do it," Sachet said.

"Young lady, you don't decline an offer of help that way. You say 'No, thank you, Grandma. I can cut it myself.'"

Sachet stopped cutting and looked at our father. He gave her a little wink to let her know she hadn't done anything wrong and she resumed cutting. "Mother," he said, "I'm sure your granddaughter appreciates it, but she's been cutting her own food up since she was four."

Still focusing on Sachet, our grandmother asked, "What happened to your beautiful hair?"

Aunt Charity literally winced. We had finally gotten Sachet settled on this issue by assuring her that this new short hair style was quite becoming, and now her grandmother was dredging up the ghost of goldilocks past. I was so proud of my sister when she just calmly looked at Grandma and said, "I wanted it short and I like it short." Sachet had finally managed to carve off a sliver of steak and she stuffed it in her mouth.

"You've put too much in your mouth, dear," Grandma said. My sister stopped chewing and pulled part of the wad of beef from her mouth. "Sachet, you don't take food from your mouth with your fingers," our grandmother proclaimed. My sister was totally confused and proceeded to spit the masticated beef onto her plate. "Oh, my Lord!" Grandma exclaimed.

And that's the way dinner went for the next twenty minutes. It was an exhausting meal. My grandmother was only content when she was presiding over carefully orchestrated crises that she was an expert at creating ex nihilo. After she had reduced my sister to tears, she tried twice to draw me into her sideshow, but I had become adept at deflecting her ambushes. At times like this I was sure my father, had we been Roman Catholic, would have been a prime candidate for sainthood. As unbearable as I found Grandma Gody, Daddy just took it all in stride. I never saw him lose his temper or say an untoward word to his mother. If he disagreed with something she said, or a directive she delivered to my sister or me, he could always find a way to express himself with diplomacy, mollifying her while at the same time letting his children know that everything was okay. It was fascinating to watch their interaction and I could not imagine what it would be like to have to deal with a parent in such a fashion.

— — —

It was a little past ten and I was lying in bed reading. The small fan over on my desk was humming away, but it wasn't loud enough to cover the sound of strange voices. I got up and turned the fan off. The voices belonged to men and they were coming from the living room. I switched off the lamp beside my bed and crept over to my bedroom door. I still could not make out what was being said, so I opened the door a few inches.

"...and this really isn't any of the Lodge's concern," Daddy was saying.

"How do you figure that? You're a Past Master; you know it is." I recognized this voice as coming from Mr. Jake Harland. He was Master of the Masonic Lodge in Bells Ferry.

"I'm only attending the graveside service," Daddy said.

"Don't matter," another voice said, which I didn't recognize.

"He's right," Mr. Jake said. "They've opened a Lodge of Sorrow and you know their graveside service is part of that."

"Worshipful Brother Harland, I know that," Daddy said. "But their public rituals are almost the same as ours. I won't be compromising my obligation in any way. I'll just be paying my respects to a fallen Brother."

"He ain't a Brother, he's a nigger." Dick Tillman's voice was unmistakable.

"Brother Dick," Daddy said in a very deliberate tone, "is there anything in our charter or constitution that says a black man can't be a Mason? And don't give me that nonsense about having to be freeborn. I doubt if there's a black man alive in Harrison County who was born a slave. Parker was old, but he wasn't that old."

"Since you're so fond of niggers," Dick continued, "maybe I'll just hire me one down at the station. Maybe I'll decide I don't need your son anymore."

I heard Daddy's recliner squeak and I knew he had stood up. "Dick, you can hire anyone you like. But let's get one thing straight: You fire Nelson over this and I'll come down to that station of yours and kick your ass." I was so shocked my mouth actually fell open. I'd never heard my father say such a thing to anyone. But what surprised me more than the words was his tone, which was hard and sure. This was no idle threat, it was a promise.

"Hold on, hold on," Mr. Jake said. "Nobody's going to fire anyone. Sit down, Lem. And you shut up, Dick. I didn't ask you to come along to make things worse." I heard Daddy's recliner squeak again as he sat back down. "Brother Lem," Mr. Jake continued, "you have to understand that if you clothe for labor and participate in that funeral you will be giving tacit recognition to a clandestine Lodge. We can bring you up on charges."

Daddy laughed. "Jake, that's a Stringer Lodge Parker belonged to. You know the Prince Hall Masons can trace their warrant all the way back to the Grand Lodge of England just like we can. The only reason they are clandestine is because we choose not to recognize them as regular, but that's our problem, not theirs."

"If you participate in that funeral service tomorrow, it's going to be your problem." This came from the man I did not recognize.

"Brothers," Daddy said, "you do what you feel you have to do. But know this: if you proffer charges against me, I'll demand trial before the Grand Lodge. As a Past Master, that's my privilege. The day is coming when white Masons and black Masons will work in the same Lodges. It probably won't happen in my lifetime, but if you want to give me the opportunity to get the ball rolling now, go ahead and make an issue of this. You know I'm not the only Freemason in this state who feels the way I do."

I didn't fully understand all that was being said, but from the silence that followed, I was confident that Daddy had just delivered a fatal blow to whatever case these men thought they had in the higher courts of the fraternity. Evidently, the possibility—however remote—that my father could force the issue of integrating the Lodges of

Mississippi, and actually prevail, was enough to give these men pause and lead them to reconsider their position on the funeral of Parker Reeves.

After the men had left, and I heard Daddy's chair squeak, I put my slippers on and walked down the hall to the living room. Daddy was in the recliner with his feet up, reading the newspaper.

"Hey," I said as I walked into the room.

He lowered the paper and looked up at me. "What are you still doing up?"

"I was reading. I heard those men and got up and listened."

"You shouldn't eavesdrop, Nelson," Daddy said. He folded the newspaper and laid it in his lap. "I'd rather you'd not heard all that."

"When I go to work tomorrow I'm gonna tell Dick I quit."

Daddy sat up in the recliner and lowered his feet. "Sit down, son." He gestured to the sofa. I went over and sat down. "I don't want you to do that," he said.

"Daddy, I don't want to work for someone who would talk to you like that."

He smiled at me. "Dick's a good man," he said.

"What? He all but called you a nigger lover and they all want to bring you up on charges or somethin'."

"Nelson...you caught the tail end of a conversation I started in our Lodge a long time ago. They are not going to bring me up on charges for anything. They were just doing what they knew they needed to do to protect our charter. I know you don't understand son, but one day, if you become a Mason, you will."

"If Dick's a good man, why'd you tell him you'd kick his as—you'd beat him up if he fired me?"

"Because when he brought you into this, he'd taken the conversation outside the Lodge. I was just letting him know what would happen if he did that."

"And you'd do that if he fired me?"

"He's not going to fire you, Nelson."

"But what if he did?" Daddy frowned at me and I could tell he was embarrassed I'd heard him say he would kick Dick's ass, so I just let it go. "How'd they find out you were going to Parker's funeral?" I asked.

"You know how news travels around here. They probably knew about it before I did." Daddy chuckled and I managed a smile. "As for Dick Tillman and your job," Daddy continued, "I want you to go to work tomorrow and act like nothing has happened."

"Can I go to the funeral with you?"

"You don't have to do that, son."

"I know. But I want to go."

"All right. But you'll have to call Dick in the morning and let him know you'll be in to work late."

"I will. Daddy…are you sure going to the funeral won't get you in trouble? I mean, it sounded like to me Mr. Jake and them were trying to warn you and get you not to go so you wouldn't get in trouble."

"They knew before they got here I'd go no matter what they said."

"Then why'd they come over here in the middle of the night to try to talk you out of it?"

"It was a formality, son. Like I said, you don't understand and I can't explain it to you. They are all good men and you don't need to think poorly of them for what you heard tonight."

I shook my head. Daddy was right. I didn't understand. "How can they be good men and talk to you that way? Threaten you for wanting to go to a colored man's funeral."

"We all do the best we can with the light we've been given, Nelson. That's what they're doing; that's what I'm doing. It's that simple."

"I don't get it," I said.

"I know," Daddy said. "But you will one day." He looked long at me, then said, "It's late. You should get to bed."

I glanced at the clock on the wall. It was ten after eleven: way past Daddy's bedtime, too. "Are you going to bed now?"

"In a little bit," he said, and leaned back in the recliner, putting his feet up. "I'm gonna finish reading the paper."

"Goodnight, Daddy," I said as I got up and headed for my room.

"Goodnight, son."

— — —

"I guess this still fits me," Daddy said. I was sitting at the kitchen table and I looked up to see my father standing there in a black tuxedo. I didn't even know he owned one. We were about to leave for Parker's funeral. I was wearing my church clothes: dress slacks, shirt, and tie.

"Holy cow," was all I could say. "When did you get that?"

"I've had this for ages. Last time I wore it was for Grand Lodge four years ago when I was Master of our Lodge. Does it look all right?"

"Yeah, it looks great." I'd never seen my father look so splendid. The tuxedo seemed to accentuate his six-foot, four-inch frame. He looked like a movie star. It was the first time I ever remember realizing what a handsome man my father was.

Daddy's leather case, containing his Mason's apron, was lying on the table. He picked it up and said, "Well, let's go."

During the ride to the little colored church way out in the country I asked Daddy what was up with the tuxedo. He explained that while not mandatory, some Masonic officers would wear a black tuxedo with white gloves for special occasions like funerals, or when the Grand Master would visit the Lodge, or for Grand Lodge every year. He said there were even some Lodges where all the members wore a tux to their regular monthly meetings.

"Don't you think everybody at the funeral is going to think you're trying to show off?"

Daddy laughed. "I'll fit right in, son. You'll see when we get there."

Ten minutes later, Daddy turned the Batmobile onto a narrow red clay drive that led up to a small white-washed church. The front yard was full of cars and I could see a large group of well-dressed people already gathered in the cemetery behind the church building. The men were all wearing suits, and quite a few were wearing Masonic aprons. The ladies all had brightly colored dresses.

When we got out of the car, Daddy took his apron from the case and tied it around his waist over the tuxedo jacket. His Past Master apron was white lambskin bordered in pale blue fringe. In the center field was the embroidered image of the Past Master's jewel: the compass, square, sun, and quadrant. Daddy put on his white cotton gloves as we walked back to the graveyard.

As we approached the crowd, we were warmly greeted by everyone, including the minister. He was a rotund black man with short white hair. He wore a gray Geneva gown with black velvet facings that had red embroidered crosses on each. The minister led us over to the grave site and I saw Parker's simple wood casket there, suspended over the hole dug in the earth. There was no vault that I could see. Standing in a semi-circle around the coffin were seven black men, all attired exactly as my father: black tuxedos, white aprons, and white gloves. Daddy told me to wait while he walked over and spoke to the men.

My father shook each of their hands. I knew there was something special about the handshake, and I watched to see if I could detect the mechanics of the grip that distinguished a Mason's handshake from an ordinary one. Whatever it was, it was so subtle I could not discern it. It looked like an ordinary handshake to me. As I scanned the crowd now gathering around the grave side, I noticed every face was black. Daddy and I were the only white people there.

An elderly lady came up to me and extended her hand. I took it and she said, "Your Daddy was mighty good to Parker. He's a good man."

"Yes, ma'am," I said. "Thank you."

As Daddy took his place with the other Masons around Parker's coffin, more people started coming up to me and thanking me for my father, telling me what a good man he was, and thanking me for coming. A tall black man wearing a Mason's apron approached me from the other side. When I shook his hand, he said, "I'm Haywood Reeves. Parker was my grandfather."

"I thought—" I caught myself before I finished my sentence. I'd almost said I thought he was in jail. "It's nice to meet you, Mr. Reeves," I said instead. "I'm sorry about your grandfather. He was a nice man."

"I used to work down at the plant with your Daddy," Haywood said. "He's a good man."

I'd heard my father called a "good man" so many times now I'd lost count. I knew he was a good man, but there was something about the respect, maybe even admiration, for my father being shown by these people that led me to think there was more to him than even I knew.

The Masons in the crowd, who were not conducting the funeral, had all gathered on the opposite side of the grave from us. The minister stepped out from the assembly where I was and said, "Brothers and Sisters, y'all know Brother Parker was a Mason and they will be conducting his funeral. Let's open with prayer." We all bowed and the minister prayed, and prayed, and prayed. It was a great, long, rhythmic prayer that meandered and included things totally unrelated to Parker. The minister seemed to be urged on by the auditory input of the mourners, especially when he would say something with which they agreed, and as a group they would all intone "Amen" in the midst of the prayer. After what seemed an eternity, he proclaimed the final Amen and the Master of Parker's Lodge began to speak:

"Brethren and Friends, it has been a custom among Free and Accepted Masons from time immemorial, at the request of a departed Brother or his family, to assemble in the character of Masons and, with the solemn formalities of the Craft, to offer up to his memory, before the world, the last tribute of our affection. Brother Parker has reached the end of his earthly toils." He hesitated and then pulled a few note cards from his jacket pocket. He glanced at them and then proceeded: "The thread which bound him to us has been severed and his spirit has winged its flight to heaven. The silver cord is loosed; the golden bowl is broken; the pitcher is broken at the fountain; and the wheel is broken at the cistern. The dust has returned to the earth as it was, and the spirit has returned to the Great Architect of the Universe, the Giver of all Life." The words themselves were beautiful, but the meanings were illusive and veiled—fully discernible, no doubt, only to the Masons listening. As I looked over at the half dozen men in aprons and dusty suits, I thought back to the ominous warning the Master of my father's lodge had delivered in our living room last night. It was clear to me now that Daddy could have come to this funeral and paid his respects and been standing with these men, Masons paying their respect but not taking a role in the service. But instead, he had chosen to participate in the funeral service itself, and it was this fact that had prompted the late-night visit from Daddy's fellow Masons.

Another officer of Parker's Lodge then read from a scroll. He gave Parker's full name, the dates he was entered an apprentice, passed to fellowcraft, and raised a Master Mason. Then the Master, referring to his note cards again, turned toward us and said the following:

"Our Brother has been raised in that blissful Lodge which no time can close, but which will remain open during the boundless ages of eternity. In that Heavenly Sanctuary, the Mystic Light, unmingled with darkness, will reign unbroken and perpetual. There, under the protection of the All-Seeing Eye, amid the smiles of Immutable Love, in that house not made with hands, eternal in the heavens, there, my brethren, may Almighty God in His infinite mercy, grant that we may meet again, to part no more. Almighty Father, into Thy hands we commend the soul of our beloved Brother."

In unison, all the Masons, including my father, intoned, "So mote it be," a curious phrase that I assumed meant, "so may it be."

The Master then picked up a white leather apron from the metal chair behind him, held it up, and said, "The lambskin apron is an emblem of innocence and the badge of a Mason; more ancient than the golden fleece or the Roman eagle, more honorable than the star or garter, or any distinction that can be conferred by king, prince, potentate or any other person. The apron continually reminds us of that purity of life and conduct so essentially necessary to gain admission into the Celestial Lodge above where the Supreme Grand Master of the Universe forever presides." He then placed the apron on top of Parker's casket.

The Master reached in his pocket and pulled out a sprig from a young pine. He held it up and said, "The evergreen, which once marked the temporary resting place of one illustrious in Masonic history, is an emblem of our enduring faith in the immortality of the soul. By it we are reminded that we have an imperishable part within us, which shall survive all earthly existence, and which will never, never die. Through the loving goodness of our Supreme Grand Master, we may confidently hope that, like this evergreen, our souls will hereafter flourish in eternal spring." He handed the sprig to my father who then placed it on Parker's casket.

The Master then gestured to Daddy, and then all the Masons crossed their arms over their chests. In the same clear voice I'd heard many times from the pulpit in our church, my father said, "We shall ever cherish in our hearts the memory of our departed Brother and, commending his spirit to Almighty God, we trustingly leave him in the hands of that Beneficent Being who is glorious in His Holiness, wondrous in His Power, and boundless in His Goodness; and it should always be our endeavor so to live that we too may be found worthy to inherit the kingdom prepared for us from the foundation of the world. So mote it be." All the Masons intoned "So mote it be."

And that was the end of the ceremony. It was simple and quite moving in and of itself, but my emotions at that moment were the product of the pride I felt for my father. It's natural for children to drift through their early childhood taking their parents for granted, then adolescence rears its ugly head and insouciance morphs into rebellion as they strive to define themselves by being as different from those who gave them life as possible. But for me, now on the eve of my sixteenth year, familial insurrection had yet to seize me—and in reality, it never would. I was my father's son. His moral compass was inexorably mine. I knew that day I would forever define myself not by contrasts to my father, but by emulation, striving to be a "good man" like him. But the term "good man" was not adequate to describe him. Daddy was a great man who charted his own course in life, guided by his own light, irrespective of the opinions of others, be they my grandmother's or those of his Brothers in the Lodge. He was the kind of man I wanted to be, the kind of man I was already becoming without fully realizing it.

Chapter 11

Beau

"Who is that?" Frankie asked me. It was Saturday just after lunch and we were sitting on my front porch. A red Mustang convertible with the top down had just pulled into Aunt Charity's drive. The radio was blaring Steppenwolf's "Magic Carpet Ride." The loud music ceased when the driver shut off the engine. Frankie and I watched him get out of the car and walk to Aunt Charity's front door. He had on a blue blazer, khaki slacks, and what looked like a pale blue button down shirt.

"I guess that's Mary Alice's brother," I said.

"Why's he dressed up?" Frankie said.

"I don't know."

Mary Alice had told me her brother was coming to visit today, so I'd determined to let her have the day with him. I thought it would be a good opportunity for me to spend some time with Frankie. I'd hardly seen him at all since our fight and my subsequent apology in his bedroom the next day. I was glad there did not seem to be any lasting artifacts on Frankie's face from our brawl. The bandage was gone, as was all of the bruising except for some slight discoloration at the bridge of his nose, which you really had to look closely to see. I could still detect a difference in his voice, though. When Frankie spoke, he sounded a little like he had a head cold.

"What do you want to do today?" I asked him. "Wanna go down to the river?"

"Can't."

"How come?" I asked.

"The doctor says I can't get in the water until my nose is completely healed. He said I might get an infection or something if I got water up my nose."

"How long's it gonna take to heal?"

"He said at least a couple of months."

"Geez," I said. "Wanna toss the football around?"

"Can't do that either."

"What? Why not?"

"He said I can't do anything where I might get hit in the face. He said if my nose gets hit while it's healing I'll have to have surgery." All the remorse I thought was gone over my breaking Frankie's nose came back in full force. Here I was thinking he was well, when in fact he was far from it. Not only had I broken his nose, but with one well-placed punch I'd effectively ruined the rest of his summer—and his fall. He couldn't do anything. Two months put us into football season and Frankie was on the team at school. Coach Underwood's notorious pre-season practice sessions would be starting up in a week, so clearly Frankie would not be playing. I looked over at him and I guess he could see from my expression what I was about to say. "Don't apologize again, Nels," he said. "I know you feel bad about it."

I smiled and nodded my head. "You want to sleep over tonight?" I asked. "We could camp out down at the river."

"When are we gonna build the cabin down there? We've been talking about it forever." That was true. Frankie and I had decided last summer that a small cabin for camping out down at the river was what we needed because my pup tent was getting too small to sleep the two of us. The problem was having funds to buy the materials to build the thing. I was saving every spare dime to buy a car and Frankie never seemed to have any money, spare or otherwise.

"Next summer, I guess," I said. "Maybe after I get my car I can start saving to buy the stuff to build it. Hey, we could go down there and throw a couple lines off the bridge, see what we can catch," I offered. I waited for him to tell me he couldn't go fishing with a broken nose.

"What's playin' at the movie in town?" Frankie asked.

"You want to go see a movie?"

"Yeah, let's check the paper and see what's playin'."

We got up and went inside to check the listing at the Palladium in town.

"*True Grit*," I said, pointing to the ad in the paper. "It's a John Wayne movie."

"What's it about?" Frankie said.

"I don't know, but who cares? It's John Wayne. Let's go see it."

"What time are the shows?"

I looked at the clock on the kitchen wall. "We've got plenty of time. The next show starts at two."

"You'll have to take me by the house to get some money," Frankie said. "I didn't bring my wallet. And if I'm spending the night I've got to get my stuff."

"So you do want to sleep over tonight?"

"Yeah, but here, not down at the river."

"Don't worry about your ticket for the movie," I said. "I'll get it."

"What about popcorn and a drink?"

"I'll pay for that, too."

"Wow...is this like our first real date?" Frankie said with a grin.

He was standing right next to me at the kitchen table so I shoved him. "Fag," I said in feigned contempt.

We both laughed.

— — —

True Grit had been playing at the Palladium since the middle of June, and judging from the number of people at the Saturday matinee, I figured this would be its last weekend. The theater was nearly empty.

"That's Glen Campbell singing," Frankie whispered as the lights dimmed and the credits started rolling on the screen. We were both munching on popcorn and were sharing a large Coke with two straws.

"He's in the movie, too," I said.

We settled down and didn't talk anymore until Frankie said, "Is that a girl?" He pointed to the screen where Mattie Ross was sitting at a desk giving her father cash money to take on his trip.

"Yeah," I whispered and stuffed some more popcorn in my mouth.

"Look at her hair. She looks like a boy," Frankie said.

"You wish," I mumbled with a mouthful of popcorn. Frankie started laughing and almost choked on his popcorn. "Shut up before they throw us outta here," I hissed.

— — —

When Frankie and I got back from the movie, Mary Alice and her brother were sitting on Aunt Charity's front porch so we decided to walk over there and meet him.

"Nelson?" her brother queried as he stood up and looked from Frankie to me as we stepped up onto the porch.

"I'm Nelson," I said and extended my hand.

"Beau Hadley," he said, and we shook hands. His shirt was not blue as I'd first thought. It was white with dark blue pinstripes. His double-breasted navy blazer had gold buttons. His hair was combed to perfection. You could slice bread with the crease in his slacks. He was as tall as me and exceedingly handsome. Had the word been part of my vocabulary at the time, I would have called him a fop. "My sister has told me all about you," Beau said.

"Nice to meet you," I said. "This is my friend, Frankie Thompson." I gestured to Frankie.

They shook hands and Frankie had a thunderstruck look on his face. His mouth was half open like he wanted to speak but couldn't. "Hi," he finally said.

I went over and sat down beside Mary Alice on the swing. Beau and Frankie sat in the two chairs facing us on the other side of the porch. I could read Mary Alice's gestures now, so when she moved her right hand in my direction ever so slightly, I met it with my left. Taking her hand, I leaned toward her and quietly said, "Hey."

She smiled, and still looking straight ahead, said, "Hey yourself."

I put my mouth to her ear and whispered, "If I kissed you right now what would your brother do?" Mary Alice didn't say anything. She didn't have to. Her blush said it all—and she was squeezing my hand so hard it hurt.

Beau was looking at us with a curious expression on his face. I couldn't quite decide if he was pleased or concerned. Maybe it was both. Surprisingly, it was Frankie who broke the tension when he looked at Beau and said, "That's a neat car you've got."

"Thanks," Beau said, looking at Frankie.

"Is it new?" Frankie asked. Something was up, but I couldn't put my finger on it. Frankie was somewhat into motorcycles, but he didn't give a hoot about cars and here he was trying to pursue a conversation with someone he'd just met based on one.

"It's a '67," Beau said. "I got it when I started my second year in law school."

"You're in law school!?" Frankie exclaimed in mock surprise. I had to roll my eyes and I'm glad Beau didn't see me. I'd already told Frankie earlier that Mary Alice's brother was in law school.

"I'll be starting my last year at Ole Miss this fall," Beau said as he studied the strange boy sitting three feet from him. He was clearly bemused.

"So what's it like?" Frankie asked.

"What?" Beau said, looking back at me and then Frankie.

"Law school," Frankie said. "Tell me about it."

I realized what was going on and I knew I had to do something before Frankie made a fool of himself. I stood up. "Frankie, I need to show you something inside," I said. It was a stupid thing to say, especially since we were sitting on Aunt Charity's porch.

Frankie looked up at me with pursed eyebrows. "What?"

I was already over at the front door with my hand on the knob. I had to think of an answer, and quickly. "Something Aunt Charity got the other day and I've been meaning to show you."

"What is it?" Frankie said as he got up out of the chair.

"Well, if you'll come on, I'll show you." I looked at Beau and said, "We'll be right back."

When I got Frankie inside and made sure Aunt Charity wasn't within ear shot, I looked at him and said in a whispered shout, "Are you nuts?!"

"What do you mean?"

"Frankie, you're hittin' on him."

"Who?" His question sounded seriously innocent. Maybe he wasn't even aware of what he was doing. Or maybe I'd completely misread the situation.

"Beau, you dummy," I said. "Your tongue practically fell out of your mouth when you were shaking his hand. And then you start asking him about his car and school with your eyes all bugged out."

A sly grin slowly appeared on Frankie's face. He knew exactly what I was talking about. "Are you mad?" he asked.

"Frankie...look...you and me joking around about you being queer is one thing, but you can't go making goo-goo eyes at guys you've just met. You're gonna get the crap beat out of you." Frankie's grin quickly faded, replaced by a blank emotionless stare. And then it dawned on me what I'd just said. We were not playing around. There was no pretext of humor to gloss over the truth this time. I'd just told my best friend explicitly, matter-of-factly, and to his face, that I knew he was queer. These were uncharted waters and I wasn't sure if either of us was prepared to navigate them. There was a long silence between us, and as uncomfortable as it was, I would not let myself look away. I held Frankie's stare.

"Do you think he noticed?" Frankie finally said, and I knew he was back with me and all was well.

"No, but if you'd kept it up, he would have."

"I should go out the back and go on home," Frankie said, sounding a little embarrassed now.

"No, you're not. Just go out there and be yourself."

Frankie looked down at the floor. "I was being myself," he said quietly.

"I didn't mean it that way," I said and put my hand on his shoulder. "If you like the guy, just don't be so obvious."

— — —

It was a little past eleven and Frankie and I had decided to go to bed and read. There wasn't anything good on the TV. We'd just finished brushing our teeth together in the bathroom and were getting undressed in my bedroom. The house was quiet. Daddy and Sachet had long ago gone to bed.

Whenever I slept over at Frankie's, I had to bunk on the floor in his sleeping bag because he had a twin bed. Mine was full-size and Frankie had always slept with me when he spent the night at my house. I was thinking about that now as I slipped my jeans off and laid them in the chair by my dresser. I wasn't sure if this arrangement was going to be awkward or not. I put on my pajama bottoms and looked over at Frankie. He had just pulled his shirt off and I watched him unfasten his jeans and let them fall to his ankles. He was wearing Fruit of the Loom briefs just like me. He stepped out of his jeans and then folded them over the back of my desk chair.

"Quit staring at my butt," he said as he pulled his socks off.

"Yeah, right," I said. I picked up one of Daddy's motorcycle magazines off my dresser. I went over and pulled back the covers on the bed and lay down.

Frankie dug around in his bag and pulled out his pajama bottoms and put them on. It was warm and muggy from the thunderstorms earlier and we were both going topless. The oscillating fan was blowing over on my dresser. With a comic book in hand, and like he had done countless times before, Frankie crawled over me to get to the other side of the bed rather than walking around and squeezing in beside the wall.

I let him get settled and didn't say anything. Several minutes went by as I was trying to read the road test on Honda's new 750 Four, but I kept thinking back to what had happened earlier, when Beau had taken Frankie, Mary Alice, and me for a ride in his Mustang. Mary Alice and I sat in the backseat and Frankie rode up front with her brother. Frankie had managed to get himself together after our little talk in Aunt Charity's foyer, and while not as obvious as before, it was still plain to me, every time he would steal a glance at Beau, that he was smitten to the core. The irony did not escape me as we rode along, me holding Mary Alice's hand and my best friend sitting up front wishing, I'm sure, he were holding her brother's hand. I probably should not have, but I leaned over and whispered in Mary Alice's ear (loud enough so she could hear me over the wind noise of the open car), "Does your brother have a girlfriend?" She got a puzzled look on her face and then whispered back that he had a fiancée and asked me why I wanted to know. I told her I was just wondering. But her answer made me think again, as I had done that day at work when Dick made his comment regarding "fags," about the difficulties that lay ahead for Frankie. Life wasn't going to be easy for him— that was for sure. He didn't have an effeminate bone in his body, so there was no question he could blend in anywhere and go unnoticed—or maybe *undiscovered* would be a better word. He just needed to be careful.

"Frankie?" I said, looking over at him lying beside me.

He was already deep into his comic book. He flipped it down onto his bare chest and looked at me. "Yeah?"

"How long have you known?"

"Known what?" The fan made its sweep by us and tossed Frankie's hair up in the front.

I hesitated because we were approaching those unchart-ed waters again. But I felt this was a conversation Frankie and I needed to have. Everything about our new normal couldn't always be sexually charged jokes, insults, and snide remarks.

"Known what?" Frankie repeated, his dark eyes narrow-ing as he stared at me.

"How long have you known you liked boys instead of girls?"

Frankie stared at me. There was a long pause before he said, "I don't know," and went back to reading his comic.

I closed the bike magazine and laid it on my stomach. "What do you mean you don't know?"

Still looking at the comic, he said, "It's not like I woke up one morning and said 'Oh wow, I like guys instead of girls.'" He looked over at me. "How long have you known you liked girls?"

"It's not the same thing," I said.

"It is the same thing if you're gonna ask a question like that. Can you answer it? How long have you known you liked girls?"

I thought Frankie was just trying to evade an answer until I actually attempted to formulate one for myself. How do you respond to a question like that? It's like being asked "How long have you known you were you?"

"See, you can't answer it either, can you?" Frankie asked. There was a hint of triumph in his voice.

"I guess not," I said. I looked at him again. "I meant what I said over at Aunt Charity's. You've got to be careful, Frankie."

"I know," he said. "But didn't you think he was good-lookin'?"

"Who? Beau?"

Frankie rolled his eyes. "Yes, Beau. Of course, Beau."

"Yeah, I thought he was good-lookin'. But not the way you thought it—and showed it."

"That was pretty pathetic, wasn't it?"

"It was pretty funny," I said. "Too bad Beau's not queer."

"How do you know he's not?"

"Mary Alice said he's got a fiancée."

Frankie sat up like he'd just lain in a bed of fire ants. He looked down at me and said, "You didn't tell her, did you?"

"Tell her what?"

"That I'm—" Frankie stopped in midsentence, no doubt realizing what he was about to say, what he was about to verbalize—probably for the first time.

"Don't worry," I said, "I didn't tell her anything. I just asked her when we were riding in Beau's car if he had a girl-friend. But Frankie…man, if she could see she would have figured it out for herself."

Frankie lay back down. "I think knowing that you knew made me feel like I didn't have to hide it anymore."

"Yeah well, you can't think like that. You know what's gonna happen if you don't hide it."

"I can tell you're serious about Mary Alice," Frankie said, changing the subject.

I reached up and ran my hands through my hair. "Yeah. I think I'm really in love." Frankie started laughing. I looked over at him. "What's so funny?"

"You are. What do you know about being in love?" he asked, still laughing.

"Nothing. And that's what scares me." There was no humor in my admission.

"Geez...you are serious," Frankie said and resumed reading his comic book. I did the same with the bike magazine, and now I could concentrate on the article. This new four cylinder 750 that Honda had come out with was amazing. It was obvious my father had already read this road test many times because he had marked it up extensively using two different color inks. I flipped back and looked at the cover. This was the March edition of *Cycle Guide*. I remembered what Peter Bong had said about us "Yanks" not having a bike that could run with his Vincent, and that the "Japs" never would. But it looked to me like they did now. The performance specifications listed at the end of the article were unreal: 67 horsepower and a top speed of 130 miles per hour.

As I read over those specs for the second time, my eyes were getting heavy so I closed the magazine and yawned. I looked over at Frankie and said, "Let's go to sleep. I'm tired."

Frankie turned to me. "So, are you okay sleeping in the same bed with me?" He did a Groucho Marx with his eyebrows just like he had done the day I apologized to him for breaking his nose.

"Just keep your hands to yourself," I said. Before I could react, Frankie leaned over and gave me a wet smooch on the cheek, then retreated back to his side of the bed with a big grin on his face. "Do that again," I said, "and I'll punch you in the nose again." I wiped his slobber off my cheek with the back of my hand.

"You said keep my hands to myself. You didn't say anything about my lips."

"Lips, hands, whatever...keep it all to yourself."

"You know I'm just teasing you, right?" he said.

"Yeah, I know."

Frankie handed me his comic book. "Okay, let's go to sleep," he said. "I'm tired, too."

I put his comic and the bike magazine on the table beside the bed and switched off the lamp. We lay there and my eyes gradually adjusted to the darkness. The sound of the fan was quickly lulling me to sleep.

"Nels?" Frankie said.

"Hmm?"

"Thanks for being my friend." He rolled over on his side facing the wall and pulled the sheet up over both of us.

"Best friend," I said. I rolled on my side facing away from Frankie and punched my pillow to get some more support.

Frankie gave a loud yawn and said, "Goodnight, Nels."

"Goodnight, fag," I said.

Frankie laughed and elbowed me in the back. I elbowed him back.

Chapter 12
Sweet Sixteen

I would be sixteen years old tomorrow. Had my past four weeks not been preoccupied with Mary Alice, I would have been obsessing over the approach of this milestone. As far back as I could remember sixteen seemed like the perfect age to attain. You were "grown up," but not an adult. You could drive (legally, in my case, once I got my license) and go where you wanted when you wanted. But August 5, 1969 would bring more to me than just this magic age: I would be getting my first car, which meant no more riding the bus to school. I had managed to save $382 toward the $500 purchase price for the late Mrs. Borcher's '64 Impala. Daddy had promised to kick in the additional amount, and tomorrow morning we would be picking up my car and taking it down to Gulfport for my driving test so I could get my license.

I'd spent the entire morning studying the driver's manual for the written test. I had it with me at work and when Dick didn't have me doing something, I was reviewing it, like I was doing now. The bell dinged twice to tell me someone was at the pumps wanting gas. It dinged two more times. I looked up from the manual to see Frankie out there on his bike stomping on the line stretched across the concrete. Ding-ding. Ding-ding. Ding-ding.

"Knock it off, goddamnit!" Dick yelled from the bay where he was doing a brake job. The dinging stopped and I heard Frankie laughing. Dick stuck his head in the office doorway and looked at me. "Go out there and tell that little son of a bitch I'm gonna kick his ass if he does that again."

Daddy's words to Dick from the other night immediately flashed through my mind. I laid the driving manual on the counter and went out to the pumps. "Are you trying to get me fired?" I said to Frankie.

"No," he said, still laughing. "I was just playing around. What's got his panties in a wad?" Frankie pointed to Dick in the bay.

"He's been pissed off ever since the parts store sent over the wrong brake shoes for that car. He had to drive down to The Pass and get the right ones."

"What kind of car is that?" Frankie asked. "It's weird lookin'."

"I don't know." I turned to look at it. "Dick had it up on the lift when I got here." I noticed he was pushing the oil receptacle from under the engine. "Looks like he's doing an oil change, too."

Just as I turned back to face Frankie I heard Dick yell, "I ain't payin' you to stand around and talk to your friends. Get in here and help me put the wheels back on this thing."

"I gotta go," I said to Frankie. "What are you doing in town?"

"My dad ran out of cigarettes." Frankie patted his shirt pocket and I noticed the pack of Camels stuffed in it. "You still gettin' your car tomorrow?" he asked.

"In the morning," I said. "Dad's taking off work the whole day."

"Party's at four, right?"

"Yep."

"Nelson! Goddamnit!" Dick yelled.

Frankie waved and took off and I sprinted into the bay. "Sorry about that," I said as I grabbed one of the wheels and lifted it up onto the hub of the rear axle. The rank smell of new rubber assaulted my nose and I noticed the blue coating still on the whitewalls. I started the lug nuts by hand. "Did you put new tires on this?"

"Yeah," Dick said as he started tightening the lug nuts with the air wrench. I was already putting the next wheel on.

After Dick had double-checked the lug nuts on all four wheels, I put the wheel covers back on it. Dick lowered the lift, which gave me my first good look at this car. It was solid white with a red interior and had a "Gran Turismo" script badge on each door. What Frankie called "weird," I thought was exotic. Whatever this car was, I'd never seen one before. It reminded me of an older Thunderbird, but the front with that huge grill was totally unique in a Rolls-Royce kind of way. There was even a grill of sorts on the back of the trunk. It had two gleaming chrome exhaust pipes sticking out under the bumper, indicating dual exhaust. "Whose car is this?" I asked.

Dick was around front opening the hood. "What do you care?" he said.

"I don't. I was just wondering. I've never seen it around here before."

"You think you know every car in Bells Ferry?" Dick was now over getting oil out of the cabinet.

"No." I went over and looked under the hood. I was surprised to see a big V8. It had bright gold valve covers.

"Here, make yourself useful," Dick said as he placed five blue and white cans of Havoline 30-weight HD on the bench in front of the car. We always used ESSO oil unless a customer specified something else. Daddy used Havoline in everything we had.

"Why are you using Havoline?" I asked.

"Quit asking so goddamn many questions and just put the oil in the engine."

"Okay, okay," I said. I filled the crankcase with oil, checked it on the dipstick, and then closed the long hood.

"The key's in it," Dick said. "Start it up and let it idle a minute and then park it out on the side by your bike."

I went around and opened the door and slid into the bucket seat. "Is this a four-speed?" I asked Dick, who was standing by the open car door.

"Yeah, this ain't a pussy's car." Dick said. "It's in neutral, start it up."

I pumped the gas, twisted the key, and the engine rumbled to life. It had a throaty exhaust note. I looked at the instrument panel. "This thing has a tach!" I said with surprise. "What is it?"

"A '62 Studebaker GT Hawk."

"This is a Studebaker?" My impression of Studebakers was forever cast in the shape of the old Lark that the principal of my school drove. That was a stodgy, boxy looking thing with nothing like the elegant lines of this car. "How big's the engine?" I asked.

"It's got a 289 with a four-barrel."

"A 289? It's got a Ford engine?"

Dick looked at me like I was an idiot. "Didn't I just tell you it's a Studebaker?"

"Yeah."

"Well, it's got a Studebaker engine in it."

Dick never could tell when I was yanking his chain just to get him wound up, so I decided to tug a little more. "But Ford makes a 289," I said.

"Just get the hell out," he said, waving me out of the car, "I'll park it."

I started laughing. "I'll park it."

"Then park the damn thing and quit pissing me off." Dick closed the door. "And be careful."

"I will," I said and punched the gas. The exhaust barked loudly in the confines of the bay as the tach needle swung up to 3000 RPM. I looked around the lipstick-red interior. It was clean. Someone had taken good care of this car. I pushed in the clutch with my left foot and put my hand on the white shifter ball. I tried to find reverse by moving the lever just as I would on Uncle Rick's VW Beetle. Nothing happened. "Where's reverse," I said.

"I told you this car ain't for pussies. You must be a pussy if you can't find reverse."

"Okay, you park it," I said and started to open the door.

Dick put his hand on my shoulder. "Keep your ass in there," he said. "Reverse is to the left of first and up. Look on the knob."

I looked at the shifter ball and saw a diagram embossed on it of the shift pattern. I wrestled with it a couple of times and finally found reverse. I eased out the clutch and the engine almost stalled.

"Give it a little gas," Dick said.

I feathered the clutch and touched the gas pedal and slowly backed out of the bay, careful to watch where I was going. I parked on the side of the building without incident. I went in the office and handed Dick the keys. "I really like that car," I said. "Are you gonna tell me whose is it?"

"Mine." Dick opened the cash register drawer and tossed the keys in it.

"Really? When did you get it?"

"When was the first time you seen it?" Dick slammed the drawer shut causing the register bell to ding.

"Today."

"Right."

"Can I take it for a spin?"

"Hell no. You don't even have your license yet."

"I will tomorrow," I said.

"And you'll have your own damn car tomorrow."

"How'd you know about that?" I didn't recall ever saying anything to Dick about me getting a car.

"You're gettin' old lady Borcher's Chevy. Your dad had me check it out to make sure everything was okay on it. It's been sittin' in her garage for six months."

"Was everything okay?" I asked.

"I had to put a battery in it," Dick said. "I told your dad it's gonna need tires soon. Still got the originals on it and they're gettin' dry rotted."

I looked up at the clock on the wall behind Dick's desk. It was fifteen minutes until six o'clock, closing time. "What do you want me to do now?" I asked.

"Nothin'. Get the hell out of here."

"It's not six yet," I said.

"I know what goddamn time it is."

"Okay," I said and headed for the door.

"Wait a minute," Dick said. He went over to the register and opened the drawer. He pulled out a twenty dollar bill and held it out to me. "Here, happy birthday."

This was a total surprise. I took the money from his hand. "Thanks, Dick."

"You ain't comin' in to work tomorrow are you?"

"I can if you need me to," I offered.

"I don't."

"My party's at four o'clock if you want to come."

"Sure, you come down here and tend to the station and I'll go to your house and eat cake and ice cream."

I rolled my eyes and Dick winked at me. "Enjoy your day, boy. You only turn sixteen once."

I headed home on the Honda with a big grin on my face. I now had $402 to put toward the purchase of my car. I was thinking, too, about how Daddy had said Dick was a good man, and yet he really wasn't anything like my father. He cursed like a sailor, was an unapologetic bigot, and had insulted Daddy to his face while threatening to fire me over something I had nothing to do with. But I was beginning to see what Daddy meant. Deep down, Dick was a good man. It's just that a good man in Dick's world was a distant cousin to a good man in ours. There was some family resemblance, but you had to look hard to see it.

— — —

"Dick bought a car today," I announced at the dinner table after Daddy had said grace. Aunt Charity was at her Eastern Star meeting and my father had dinner ready when I got home, which was an unexpected treat. He'd fixed crab cakes, hushpuppies, and French fries, which told me he'd been thinking about Mama today.

"What'd he get?" Daddy asked.

"May I have some hushpuppies, please?" Mary Alice said.

I put the dish of hushpuppies in her outstretched hand and looked over at Daddy. "He got a Studebaker. A GT something."

Daddy was about to take a sip of his iced tea. He stopped before the glass touched his lips. "A GT Hawk?" he said.

"Yeah, I think that's what he said it was. It had 'Gran Turismo' on the doors. You've heard of it?"

"Oh, yeah," Daddy said.

"It's a neat car," I said. "It's got a tach and four in the floor."

"What's four in the floor?" my sister asked.

I looked over at Sachet. "It's a four-speed transmission and the shifter's in the floor instead of on the steering column. Like on Uncle Rick's Bug."

"Oh," she said. I watched her cutting up her crab cake and thought about Grandma Gody.

"So you like that Studebaker?" Daddy said.

"Yeah, it's a nice car. Sounds good, too. It's got dual exhaust." I took a bite of crab cake. "This is pretty good, Daddy," I said with a mouth full.

"Your old man knows how to cook some things," he said with a smile. "That's your mother's recipe," he added. "Mary Alice, honey, you got everything you need?" he asked her.

"Yes sir, I'm fine," she said. "And Nelson is right, your crab cakes are delicious."

"Thank you, sweetie. I'm glad you like it."

"Where'd you get the crab meat?" I asked.

"Guy at work had some for sale today."

"What time are we going to get my car in the morning?"

"After breakfast," Daddy said.

"Dick gave me twenty dollars for my birthday, so now I've got four-hundred and two dollars."

"You almost made it to five-hundred, didn't you?" Daddy said.

"Almost."

Daddy looked at me and said, "How much have you got set aside for the tags and insurance?" I stopped chewing the food in my mouth and felt all the blood drain from my face. I hadn't even thought about insurance or a license plate for the car. "You forgot about that, didn't you?" Daddy said.

I nodded my head and swallowed. "I guess I did," I said, which really wasn't true. You can't forget something you never thought of in the first place. I was totally dejected. "Does this mean we can't get it tomorrow?" I asked.

"We can get the car tomorrow," Daddy said, "you just won't be able to drive it until you can put plates on it and get insurance. You'll have to do your driving test in the Chrysler."

Damn it. I almost said it out loud. I was finally going to get my first car tomorrow and I wouldn't even be able to drive it. I would have to take the test for my license in the Batmobile. I ate the rest of my dinner in abject silence.

— — —

I awoke at 6:45 the next morning to the smell of bacon frying. I would not officially be sixteen until 11:42 A.M., so maybe that was why I didn't feel any different. It was just another morning and I wouldn't be sixteen for another five hours.

I got dressed and went to the bathroom to pee and brush my teeth. As I looked in the mirror at myself, with the toothbrush hanging out of my mouth, I noticed a small red spot on my left cheek just beside my nose. I had managed to make it through to my mid-teens with a clear complexion. So now that I was turning the coveted sixteen, was this going to be my reward? My first zit? This day wasn't shaping up to be all that great. I would be getting my first car, but would not be able to drive it. And now acne appeared to be taking up residence on my face. At least I was not worried about getting my driver's license. I was prepared for the test, even if I had to use Daddy's car for the driving portion. No matter what, this day would end with me being a legal driver in the State of Mississippi.

"Whose car is that out there?" my sister was saying as I walked into the kitchen. She still had on her nightgown and was looking out the window in the dining area that faced our driveway and Aunt Charity's yard.

Aunt Charity was over at the stove taking the last pieces of bacon out of the skillet. "You'll have to ask your father," she said.

"Where's Mary Alice?" I asked and walked over to the window where my sister was standing.

"She's getting dressed. You want to go over there and get her?"

"Yeah," I said and looked out the window. Dick's new car was sitting in our driveway. "What's Dick doing here?"

"Who?" Aunt Charity said and placed a platter loaded with strips of crisp bacon on the table.

"Dick Tillman," I answered.

"Your father is out there somewhere, so maybe he came over to see him about something. The pancakes will be ready shortly so go on over to my house and get Mary Alice. And tell your father to come on. And if Richard Tillman is out there, see if he wants some breakfast." With spatula in hand, Aunt Charity walked over and kissed me on the cheek. "Happy Birthday," she said.

I smiled and said, "Thanks."

"I forgot, Nelson!" my sister screamed. She was bouncing on her toes and holding her hands up for me to take her.

I picked her up and she hugged me tightly. "Happy Birthday!" she said loudly over my shoulder.

"Thanks, Sachet." I carried her with me out into the back yard but I didn't see Dick or our father anywhere. The air was thick and humid. "Daddy!" I hollered and waited. There was no response, other than a couple of cows mooing out in the pasture. I set my sister down on her bare feet. "Go get dressed," I told her. I headed over to Aunt Charity's to get Mary Alice.

A heavy dew lay on the grass, so my sneakers were wet and covered in grass clippings as I stepped up on Aunt Charity's front porch. I took them off and went in the house. I went straight to Mary Alice's room, and since the door was open, I walked in without knocking. She was standing there wearing nothing but sandals and a pair of loose fitting, pale yellow pedal pushers. She was fumbling with her bra.

"I'm sorry," I said, "I thought you'd be dressed." I turned and retreated from the room.

"Wait, Nelson," Mary Alice called to me. "Will you help me with this?"

I stopped, and without turning around said, "Help you with what?"

"With my bra."

"Let me go get Aunt Charity," I said. After all, what did I know about a girl's bra?

"Quit being silly and help me. I can't get it fastened."

I turned and walked over to Mary Alice. She was facing away from me and I quickly sized up the problem. She had somehow managed to get the bra twisted when she slipped it on and the hooks in the back wouldn't line up. "You've got it twisted," I said. "I think you're going to have to take it off." Mary Alice reached up to slide the straps off her shoulders. "Let me go out," I said.

She turned to face me. "You can stay," she said as casually as if she'd just told me the time of day. She turned back to face the bed and I swallowed hard as I watched her remove the bra. She held it out to me over her shoulder and said, "Will you fix it?"

I took the undergarment from her hand and untwisted it. It was pink, of course. As much as I tried to avert my eyes, they were drawn to Mary Alice's near nakedness. The sight of her bare skin was driving me crazy, especially knowing what I could see if she were to turn around.

"Here, it's un-twisted," I said and put the bra back in her hand.

She slipped it back on, twist-free this time. "Will you fasten it?" she asked.

I fastened the hooks and then gently stroked my fingers across her shoulders and back. Her skin was soft and velvety. "Why'd you do that?" I asked.

"Do what?"

"Let me see you half naked."

Mary Alice turned back to face me. "I'm not half naked, Nelson."

"You don't have a shirt on," I said.

"Can you see anything you wouldn't see if I had a bathing suit on?"

"No, I guess not," I said.

Mary Alice stepped over to the bed and picked up her pink polo shirt and slipped it over her head. I watched her shake her hair and run her hands through it. I went over to stand beside her. She reached out and touched me, feeling my shirt, then pulled my face down to hers and kissed me gently. "Happy Birthday," she said when our lips parted.

I took her face in my hands and kissed her; it was my first attempt at a full-on, open-mouthed kiss and Mary Alice returned it in equal measure. Our tongues met in passion for the first time, and the taste was intoxicating. When this second kiss finally ended, I opened my eyes and looked at Mary Alice. Her lips were wet and puffy, and her eyes were closed too. She opened them, and for the briefest moment she appeared to be looking at me. "I love you, Mary Alice," I said, staring into her unseeing eyes.

She smiled and put her arms around me in a tight embrace. "I love you, too," she said.

"Hey, y'all!" Daddy's voice came booming from down the hall outside Mary Alice's room.

I turned to see if he was at the door. He wasn't. Mary Alice quickly moved away from me. My balls were aching and I was trying without much success to will the erection in my pants to disappear. "We're comin'," I hollered.

"Well, come on. Charity's got breakfast ready and she's havin' a fit. She said she sent you over here ten minutes ago to get Mary Alice."

Breakfast started off awkwardly—for me, not Mary Alice. I was quite certain I sat there eating my pancakes with the perfect "cat that ate the canary look" on my face. Mary Alice, on the other hand, looked as angelic and innocent as ever. Just a scant few minutes ago we had been passionately kissing in her bedroom and said openly that we loved each other.

"Where is Dick?" I asked as I helped myself to some more bacon off the platter.

"Down at his station, I expect," Daddy said. "Doesn't he open up at eight?"

I looked up at the clock. It was five to eight. "Yeah, so why is his new car sitting in our driveway?"

"It's not Dick's car," Daddy said. He looked over at Aunt Charity and I could see the two of them knew something I didn't. I looked at Sachet. She was oblivious to the conversation, lost in the world of pancakes, syrup, and bacon.

"Whose car is it?" I asked. "It looks like the one Dick got."

"It's the car you saw Dick working on yesterday," Daddy said.

"I don't understand," I said and took a sip of orange juice. "Dick said that car was his."

"It's not," Daddy said.

"Well, whose is it, then?"

"It's yours if you want it," Daddy said.

I looked at Daddy. What he was saying didn't make any sense. "Mine? I don't need two cars."

Daddy laughed and then explained what was going on. He had asked Dick to check out Mrs. Borcher's Impala, just as Dick had told me. And Dick had to put a battery in it to get it started and drive it over to the station, again essentially what Dick had told me. But what Dick didn't tell me was that the oil had never been changed in the engine. When he got it up on the rack he found the factory oil filter still on there and when he pulled the drain plug barely two quarts of thick black oil oozed out. He pulled the valve covers and found the engine full of jet-black sludge. He told Daddy he could try to flush it out, but after six years of running nothing but the factory fill, he felt the engine was probably shot. That was three weeks ago and Daddy had immediately started looking for another car for me. Uncle Rick to the rescue. He put Daddy in touch with an engineer down at MTF who was selling his '62 GT Hawk that had been babied since the day he bought it. He had just done a full tune-up and radiator flush; all it needed was brakes and tires. Me seeing the car at work yesterday, Dick letting me start it up and park it, that had all been orchestrated by Daddy and Dick to gauge my reaction to the car, to see if I liked it.

"So do you like it?" Daddy asked me.

"Yeah, I like it," I answered.

"You think you could be happy with that Studebaker rather than the Impala you thought you were getting?" For some reason Daddy seemed to think I had my heart set on getting an Impala. Why, I didn't know—there was nothing especially desirable about a '64 Impala, at least not the one Mrs. Borcher had owned, anyway.

"Daddy, I just want a car," I said. "I don't care what it is."

"Really?" My father's face brightened. He had actually been worried I would not want the Studebaker.

"That car is way cooler than any old Impala," I said. "Did you already buy it from the guy at MTF?"

"Yes."

"So how much cheaper was it than the Impala?" I asked. I was already reaching in my pocket for the $402 I'd saved. The Studebaker was two years older than the Impala, so I figured it would be less than $500.

"He wanted eight-hundred for it, son. I got him down to seven-fifty."

"Seven-hundred and fifty dollars?" I said in disbelief. So now, not only did I have a cool car that I couldn't drive because I couldn't afford to put tags and insurance on it, I was going to owe Daddy nearly $250—assuming he was still willing to kick in the $98 he would have on the Impala. It was looking like I'd be seventeen before I'd be driving my car. I fished the wad of twenties and two ones out of my pocket and put it on the table by Daddy's plate. "That's four-hundred and two dollars," I said. "I'll pay you the rest when I can. I'll see if I can work more at Dick's until school starts because I won't be able to work as much then."

Daddy picked up the money and thumbed the edges of the bills. "You forgot about the brake job, oil change, and new tires."

I shook my head and looked down at my half-eaten breakfast. "How much was all that?"

"Almost a hundred bucks," Daddy said. This was getting worse by the second.

"I'll pay you back for that, too," I said.

"You're awfully quiet, Charity," Daddy said. "Don't you have something to tell your nephew?"

I looked up at my aunt. She had a big grin on her face. She cleared her throat and said, "The car is my gift to you, Nelson."

"And the tires, brakes, and oil change are on me," Daddy said. "And the tags and insurance."

Now I was beaming. "So I can drive it today to get my license?"

"Yep."

I got up from the table and went over and gave my father a big hug. "Thank you, Daddy."

"You're welcome, son," he said and patted me on the arm.

"What about me?" Aunt Charity said.

I went over to her and said, "You have to stand up for this." She wiped her mouth properly with the napkin then stood up. I grabbed her in my arms and twirled her around the kitchen. Sachet was squealing and Mary Alice and Daddy were laughing.

"Oh, Nelson," Aunt Charity said in a pant, "put me down. Put me down."

I set her down and kissed her on the cheek. She was red-faced and flustered. "Thank you," I said. "That is the greatest birthday present ever."

"Do me now!" Sachet said.

"What did you get me for my birthday?" I asked her.

My sister stood up in her chair, held out her arms, and said, "Me!"

We all laughed as I went over and picked up Sachet and spun her around the kitchen so fast it made us both dizzy.

"You ready for your test?" Daddy asked me.

"You bet," I answered as I set Sachet back in her chair.

"Let's go," he said and got up from the table. He handed the wad of money back to me. "Take a hundred out of this for play money. The rest, we'll go by the bank and deposit in your college savings account."

— — —

I only missed one question on the written test and despite driving a totally unfamiliar car, I managed the road test with only one real issue: parallel parking. It took me three tries and I lost points for that. For everything else, the examiner said I drove like an old pro. Daddy had told Aunt Charity not to expect us back for lunch, so I figured he was taking me to McDonald's down in Gulfport. But he didn't. Once we got out of town and headed up 49, he pulled over at the Dixie Pearl Motel, which was right at the junction with 53, to let me drive the remaining fifteen miles back to Bells Ferry.

"You know this car is titled in my name, right?" Daddy asked as we drove along at a leisurely pace. I was keeping the speed around 45. I'd ridden on this road hundreds of times, but never driven it, so I was being extra cautious.

I looked over at him. "So it's—"

"Eyes on the road, son," he said, cutting me off.

I looked straight ahead and said, "So it isn't really mine?"

"It's yours. It was just easier to do it this way as far as putting tags on it and insurance. When you turn eighteen, I'll sign it over to you and you can title it in your name."

"Okay," I said. "What are we doing for lunch?"

"I thought I'd buy you a steak. But first, we're going by the bank and put your money in your college account." When Daddy said he was buying me a steak I knew we would be eating at Bobby Dean's in town, which had legendary Porterhouse steaks. People drove from as far away as Mobile and New Orleans to eat at the little Bobby Dean Diner.

"Daddy, why do I have to go to college?" I asked. "You didn't."

"I didn't and it broke my mother's heart. I was stupid when I was eighteen, Nelson. At sixteen, your head is screwed on your shoulders so much better than mine was then, it's not even funny."

"But you've done good," I offered. I did not like to hear my father being self-deprecating. "You joined the Marines and made sergeant."

Daddy chuckled. "All you have to do is stay in long enough and stay out of trouble to do that. But I've done well, overall, I guess. I just wonder sometimes what I could have been, what I could have done. There was just enough rebellion in me to do it, to enlist, just to spite my mother. I hope I've raised you to have more respect for me than that."

"Yes, sir," I said.

"You're college material, son."

"So were you."

"Not like you. I've got every report card of yours back to the first grade. I can count the number of Bs from all of them on one hand. The rest are As, and you know that. You can't waste your brain like I did, son."

"Daddy, don't say that," I pleaded. "You didn't waste your brain. You're..." I was searching for the right words when Parker's funeral popped into my head. "You're a good man," I finally said.

My father reached over and squeezed my shoulder. We rode the rest of the way to Bells Ferry in silence. I was wishing I'd not said anything about going to college, because I really didn't mean it. I'd always assumed I would go to college, but raising the subject the way I did forced Daddy to admit things to me I'd just as soon not heard.

We finished up at the bank and then headed down the street to Bobby Dean's. There was a parking space right in front of the diner and I negotiated my new car into it perfectly. When I shut off the engine and set the parking brake Daddy put his hand over to me. "What?" I said as we shook hands.

"Happy Birthday," he said and stuck his Bulova in my face. It was 11:50 A.M. I was sixteen years and eight minutes old.

When we walked in the Bobby Dean Diner, the first thing I saw was a hand-painted banner suspended from wall to wall in the back that said "Happy Birthday Nelson!" The place was noisy and packed with familiar faces. Daddy put his arm around my shoulder and shouted "Hey, everybody! My son just turned sixteen eight minutes ago!" Everyone looked up from their lunch plates and started clapping. Daddy steered me to the big table in the back that had a "Reserved" sign on it. Hands were stuck out for me to shake every inch of the way and I got several pats on the back.

Daddy and I sat at the oblong table that would seat six. "I wasn't expecting this," I said. "Are Aunt Charity, Sash, and Mary Alice coming?"

"No, this lunch is for men only."

Miss Darla, who had been a waitress at the diner for as long as I could remember, brought us iced tea. "Y'all haven't been in here in a coon's age," she said. She looked at me. "Baby doll, you're gettin' to be as handsome as your daddy."

"Yes, ma'am," I said. I was blushing, I'm sure.

"What y'all havin'," Miss Darla asked.

"Two of your twenty ounce Porterhouses," Daddy said. "But we'll wait to order until everyone gets here."

"Alrighty, hon," she said and went back up front to take care of a couple who had just come in for lunch and sat at the counter.

"Who else is coming?" I asked.

"Here's one now," Daddy said and pointed toward the door. It was Uncle Rick. One look at him and you knew he was an engineer: short sleeve white shirt, dark tie, and a pocket protector. His NASA badge was pinned prominently to it.

"Am I late?" he said as he sat at the opposite end from Daddy.

"Nope," Daddy said, "right on time, as usual."

My uncle took a small, gift-wrapped box from his pocket and slid it over to me. "Happy Birthday," he said.

"Can I open it now?"

"Of course," Uncle Rick said.

I tore the wrapping off and found a box with "Fisher Space Pen" embossed on the top. I opened it. The pen inside was gleaming and substantial looking. "Wow, thanks, Uncle Rick."

"That's the same pen the astronauts took to the moon—I mean they took one just like it, not that pen," he said and pulled one of the black, government issue, ball-point pens from his pocket protector and held it up. "You know why they can't use just a regular pen in space?"

"No, why?" I said and removed my new pen from the case. It was heavy.

"Because gravity is what makes the ink flow to the tip. No gravity, no flow. No flow, no write."

Daddy took the box my pen came in and looked at it. "So what'd they do with this Space Pen? Pressurize the ink cartridge?"

"Exactly," Uncle Rick said. "It's pressurized with nitrogen."

"Damn, they'll let anyone in here," a voice said. We looked up to see Dick Tillman standing at our table.

"Hey, Dick," Daddy said. "You want to have lunch with us?"

"Nah, I just ran down here to get me a sandwich and take it back to the station."

"You remember my brother," Daddy said and gestured to Uncle Rick.

"Sure." Dick and my uncle shook hands. "Good to see you, Rick."

"You, too."

Looking back at Daddy, Dick said, "So is everything square with the Studebaker?"

"He hates it. I guess I'll have to take you up on that offer to buy it."

Dick frowned at me. "You told me yesterday you liked that car."

"I do," I said. "Daddy's just pulling your leg."

"Good. You got a helluva lot more car than you would've with old lady Borcher's Chevy. Too bad they don't make 'em anymore."

Miss Darla walked up carrying a brown paper bag. "Here's your sandwich, hon," she said to Dick and handed him the bag.

"Thank you, sweetheart," Dick said. "Just put it on my tab."

Miss Darla looked at Uncle Rick. "You want some iced tea, baby?"

"A Coke, please."

"Fountain or bottle?"

"Fountain will be fine, thanks."

As Miss Darla strutted back to the counter, Dick turned back to us and said, "Boy, I'd like to have me some of that."

Daddy chuckled. "Word is, you already have." Dick feigned a look of surprise. The worst kept secret in Bells Ferry was the "affair" between Darla James and Dick Tillman. Neither of them was married, so why they insisted on keeping their relationship hush-hush was as much a mystery as it was a comedy.

"I'll catch y'all later," Dick said. "Happy birthday," he added and pointed to me.

"Thanks," I said.

Now that we were past the noon hour, the diner was at capacity and people were standing near the front door waiting for tables to clear out. I was surprised to see Frankie and his dad and brother come in the door.

"There's the rest of our crew," Daddy said. He waved at Frankie's dad and they headed back to our table.

I knew I was having a small birthday party at our house later, so this lunch gathering, arranged by my father, for just the guys was a nice surprise. Frankie sat beside me and his dad and brother sat across from us. We all ordered steaks, but Daddy and I were the only ones to get the big Porterhouses. When Miss Darla had brought everyone's drinks, Daddy surprised me again by holding up his red plastic glass of iced tea and saying, "To my son on his sixteenth birthday. No father could ask for a better son."

Everyone raised their glasses, including me, until Frankie elbowed me and said, "I don't think you're supposed to toast yourself, dummy." We all laughed and then drank the toast to the birthday boy—everyone except me.

Miss Darla had just brought our steaks and steaming baked potatoes the size of pee wee footballs when I saw Peter Bong, the man in black who rode the Black Shadow, come from the door to the back hall where the restrooms were. He had his helmet under his arm, so I figured he must have parked his bike in the rear and come in the back door. He stood there for a few seconds surveying the crowd, looking for an empty spot. There weren't any; every seat in the place, including the six at the lunch counter, was taken and there were five people waiting to be seated standing by the front door.

"Peter!" I called to him. Everyone at our table looked at me and then to the man whose name I'd just called.

The man in black turned to see who was calling his name. I waved to get his attention, then turned to Frankie and said "Scoot over and make room."

"For what?" Frankie said.

"For him," I said nodding in Peter's direction.

Peter stepped over to our table with a confused look on his face. When he got a good look at me he smiled in recognition. "The Honda Scrambler with the pretty Sheila on the back."

"Yeah," I said, "but her name's still not Sheila." Everyone at our table had stopped eating and was staring at this tall, dark, stranger with a ponytail halfway down his back.

Daddy stood up and offered his hand to Peter. "Lem Gody," he said. "You know my son?"

"I'm sorry," I said as I stood. "Daddy, this is Peter Bong. He's the guy we've seen riding the Vincent. I met him at the station the other day." Daddy and Peter shook hands and then I introduced him to the others.

"Remind me of your name, mate," Peter said to me.

"Nelson," I replied.

"I thought that's what it was." He pointed to the happy birthday banner hanging behind me on the wall. "You?"

"Yes. I'm sixteen today."

"Happy birthday," he said, then turned and looked around the diner again. "Looks like I'm going to have to wait awhile. It's was nice meeting you all."

"Why don't you sit with us," I offered. I looked at Daddy and said, "Is it okay?"

"It's your party," he said.

"Appreciate that, mate," Peter said. He went over to a table for two where a lone patron was sitting and asked to borrow the empty chair. Frankie and I scooted over to make room for him. He took his jacket off and sat down, then put his helmet on the floor and laid his jacket over it.

"New Zealand or Australia?" Uncle Rick asked.

"Australia," Peter said.

"Is Bong an Australian name?" I asked and started stirring the big mound of whipped butter that was melting on my baked potato.

"Malaysian," Peter answered. "My grandfather was from Kuala Lumpur."

Peter ordered an egg salad sandwich and we all enjoyed listening to him talk as we ate our steak dinners. Daddy asked him about the Vincent and Peter said that he had brought it with him from Australia. He suggested we all go riding sometime and, of course, Frankie and I eagerly agreed. When Uncle Rick asked him what he was doing in the U.S., Peter became evasive and changed the subject, asking me what I'd gotten for my birthday. Daddy and Uncle Rick exchanged looks that told me as friendly (though different) as Peter Bong seemed, they were uncomfortable with him. Evidently, Frankie's dad had the same impression. When lunch was over and Peter had thanked us, paid his bill, and left out the back door, Mr. Frank looked at his son and said, "You stay away from that man. He's trouble."

"I think he's cool," Frankie said. "You just don't like him 'cause he's got long hair."

"Got nothin' to do with his hair," his dad said. He looked at Daddy. "Lem?"

"I agree. Something isn't right there."

"Dick thinks he's a hippie," I said. "Is that why y'all don't like him?"

"Hippie or not," Daddy said, "I've learned to trust my first impressions when it comes to folks. I didn't get a good impression from Mr. Bong."

Miss Darla came over to the table. "Y'all need anything else?"

"Just the checks. Put my ugly brother's steak on my check." Daddy pulled his wallet from his back pocket.

"It's all taken care of," Miss Darla said.

Daddy looked up at the counter where Bobby Dean was standing behind the register. "He didn't have to do that," he said.

Miss Darla puffed. "That ol' tightwad? He didn't."

Daddy looked to Uncle Rick and Frankie's dad. They both shook their heads. He looked back at Miss Darla. "Who?"

"Mr. Ponytail who was sitting with y'all. Paid for the whole table and gave me a five dollar tip."

Daddy frowned. "Here's a couple more," he said. Uncle Rick gave her a dollar and Mr. Frank gave her two.

Miss Darla looked at me with a big grin and said, "I wish you had a sixteenth birthday every week, sugar. I could retire while I'm still young and beautiful."

We all laughed, except Daddy. He was still frowning.

PART THREE

Chapter 13
Sea of Heartbreak

In 1961, Don Gibson recorded a song entitled "Sea of Heartbreak." It reached the number two spot on Billboard's Hot Country Singles chart that year. On the day after my sixteenth birthday it was playing on the radio as I carried the love of my life for a ride in my new car. How prophetic that song's title would turn out to be for a day that had begun so sublime.

"So you liked my birthday gift?" Mary Alice asked just as we crossed over the Wolf River bridge.

"I still can't believe you got that for me," I said. "I was expecting to get it from Santa Claus for Christmas."

She laughed at me and said, "You still believe in Santa Claus?"

I rolled my eyes. "Of course not, but my sister does. It's a lot easier not to slip up if I just say that Daddy's presents are from Santa."

What Mary Alice had given me for my birthday was something I'd been drooling over since last winter in the sporting goods department at the Western Auto in town: a Browning Sweet Sixteen shotgun. Imagine my surprise yesterday when I unwrapped that oblong present to find a gleaming black and gold box with Browning Automatic Shotgun writ large on it. I knew the price of this magnificent gun was $185 and I could not believe Mary Alice had that kind of money to spend on a birthday present for someone, even if it was her boyfriend.

"So, why did you get me the gun?" I asked. Even though I was driving, I could not help but steal a glance over at Mary Alice. She was gorgeous with the wind blowing her hair as we cruised along at 35 miles per hour.

"I asked your dad if there was anything you really, really wanted other than a car and he said the only thing he could think of was that shotgun."

"And you had the money to buy it?"

"No, Nelson, I got your Aunt to carry me down there and I shoplifted it." Mary Alice giggled at her own sarcasm. "Sorry about not having any bullets for it," she added.

"Shells, not bullets," I said. The Western Auto was out of 16 gauge shells, and it was the only store in town that sold ammunition of any kind. Earlier, I had called down to the store and spoken to Mr. Tooley, the owner, and he told me they'd be getting some in with the next shipment in a week or so.

"Are we going into town?" Mary Alice asked.

"We're going away from town," I said. "Why? Do you need something from town?"

"Let's go down to the Colonel Dixie and get a milkshake."

That was a great idea and I wished I'd thought of it. There was a tractor path coming up that led into one of Ben May's pastures, so I pulled in there and turned around. Once I'd backed out onto the road, I slipped the transmission from reverse into first, dumped the throttle and popped the clutch. The rear tires chirped and we roared off back down the road. When the tach needle hit 4000 RPM, I shifted into second. When we hit 50 miles per hour, I shifted into third and then let off the gas and dropped it into fourth. I was grinning from ear to ear. Yes, I loved this car. Mrs. Borcher's '64 Impala was a distant memory soon to be forgotten.

We had to go by the house on the way to town and as we approached my driveway I saw Frankie turning into it on his bike. I stopped at the end of the drive and blew the horn.

"Hey!" he shouted, turning to look at me over his shoulder.

I looked over at Mary Alice. "Do you care if Frankie goes with us?" I asked.

"No," she said.

Frankie had ridden back down the drive and was at the car now. "We're going into town and get a shake," I told him. "Go park your bike and ride with us." Frankie grinned and pedaled back up into the edge of the yard, dropped his bike, and then ran back to the car. I opened the door and leaned the seatback forward so he could crawl in.

"Hey, Mary Alice," he said as he slid into the backseat.

"Hello, Frankie," she replied.

I looked at Frankie in the rear view mirror and hit the gas. I laughed out loud as he was thrown back in the seat and we roared off as I wound out the Hawk's V8 in first gear then shifted into second. "Man, I love this car," Frankie said.

When we got to the Colonel Dixie, I went in to get our shakes while Mary Alice and Frankie waited in the car. When I came out, Peter Bong was parked beside us sitting on his Vincent motorcycle. He was talking to Frankie, who was leaning out the back window on the passenger side of the car. I spoke to Peter as he got off his bike and went in the restaurant.

"Where is he from?" Mary Alice said as I handed her the vanilla milkshake through her open window.

"Australia," I answered. I stuck Frankie's chocolate shake back to him and he took it.

"Thanks, man," he said, "I'll pay you back."

"How come you never have any money with you?" I asked as I got back in the car.

"Hey, I wasn't planning on going anywhere I'd need money. I was just coming up to your house and then you asked me to come along, remember?"

"Yeah, yeah," I said.

"I gotta hurry up and finish this," he said.

I took a sip of my shake and looked at him in the rearview mirror. "Why?"

"Peter said he'd take me for a ride on his Vincent."

I turned around to face Frankie, who was now sprawled out lengthwise and taking up the whole back seat. "When?" I asked. He was sucking hard on the red straw in his shake and had Mary Alice not been sitting beside me I would have made a totally appropriate—and crude—wise crack.

"When he gets done eating," Frankie said and pointed to the glass wall of the Colonel Dixie dining area in front of us.

"I don't think you should," I said—a little more sternly than I had intended.

Frankie frowned, and still sucking on his shake, sat up. "Why not?" he asked, the straw clenched between his front teeth.

"You heard what my dad and your dad said yesterday," I reminded him.

"So what?"

"Your dad told you to stay away from him."

Frankie had reached the bottom of the cup and was slurping up the remnants of his shake. "Don't worry about it."

He pushed on the back of my seat. "Let me out," he said. "I've got to go to the bathroom."

I let Frankie out and watched him go inside. "How's your shake?" I asked Mary Alice.

"Very good," she said. "Thank you."

I asked her if I could taste it, so she held the cup over to me. "I'd rather taste it like this," I said. I leaned over and kissed her long on the mouth.

"Are you trying to embarrass me?" Mary Alice asked.

"What do you mean?" I said, licking the vanilla taste on my lips.

"We're sitting in public."

"We're sitting in my car," I retorted.

When Frankie and Peter Bong came out of the restaurant, Frankie announced he was going for a ride with Peter. I started to issue another protest, but decided against it. As they climbed on the Vincent, Peter leaned down and looked in the car at me. "Why don't you go back home and get your bike and we can all go riding?" he said.

"Maybe next time," I said. "I promised Mary Alice I'd take her for a ride in my new car."

"Okay, mate," Peter said. He kicked the big V-twin to life and I watched as he and Frankie roared off on the Vincent.

Mary Alice and I rode around Bells Ferry for about half an hour before heading back to the house. When we got there, Frankie's bicycle was still lying in my front yard. As I was helping Mary Alice out of the car, Aunt Charity stepped out onto her front porch and hollered for me to get the mail out of the boxes. "Just wait here in the car," I told Mary Alice. I walked down to the end of our drive where both our mailbox and Aunt Charity's was. Our box was empty, but I got my aunt's mail and then Mary Alice and I walked over to Aunt Charity's. I gave her the mail and Mary Alice and I sat in the swing where we'd first kissed nearly a month ago.

Not five minutes had gone by when Aunt Charity appeared at her front door with a foreboding look on her face. "Nelson, I need to see you a minute," she said. I got up and followed her into the house. She led me to the kitchen and motioned for me to sit at the bar. She picked up an envelope that had been a part of the day's mail and handed it to me. "Read that," she said.

I took the envelope and looked at the imprinted name and address on the flap. It was from Mary Alice's brother. I removed the letter and read it. As my eyes scanned the neatly written script I could not believe what I was reading. When I came to the end I looked up at Aunt Charity in total shock. "Are you going to tell her?" I asked.

"You should do it," she said. "And just read the letter to her, Nelson. Don't editorialize."

"Let's just burn it and say you never got it," I proffered.

My aunt frowned at me. She didn't have to tell me we could not do that. I got up with the letter in hand. That pain in my stomach had returned—the same pain I got that Sunday morning when Mary Alice heard me tell Aunt Charity that I wished she'd never brought Mary Alice here for the summer. I went out on the porch and sat in one of the chairs facing the swing where Mary Alice was sitting. "Mary Alice," I said and cleared my throat. "Aunt Charity got a letter today from Beau."

Her face brightened. "Really?" she said.

"She wants me to read it to you. I don't think you're going to like what it says."

Now Mary Alice was picking up on my forlorn tone. "What's wrong, Nelson?" she said with a hint of worry. "Is Beau all right?"

Hell no he's not all right! I wanted to scream. He's lost his cotton picking mind. But instead I unfolded her brother's letter and read it to her:

August 3, 1969
Dear Mrs. Jackson,

Thank you for your gracious hospitality this past Saturday during my visit to see my sister. I also want to express my appreciation for how kind and generous you have been to Mary Alice since she has been at the Masonic Home. She has told me numerous times how much you remind her of our grandmother, and after meeting you, I concur. That fact makes the writing of this letter all the more difficult, so I'll get right to the point. I believe the relationship between my sister and your nephew is inappropriate. I realize that Mary Alice will be fifteen in a few months and that Nelson is himself just fifteen, but about to turn sixteen. Nevertheless, it was clear from meeting him that he is considerably more mature than his age would otherwise dictate. I do not feel my sister is ready to be in any sort of serious relationship with a boy like Nelson. I do not want this to jeopardize the relationship you have with my sister, but I must insist that you cut short her stay with you and return her immediately to the Masonic Home in Poplarville. Should you choose not to accede to my wishes, you will leave me no other choice but to exert whatever pressure I can on the administration at the home for their assistance in this matter. If necessary, I am prepared to petition the Chancery Court in Pearl River County for emergency guardianship of my sister and remove the Masonic Home from the situation altogether. I sincerely hope this will not be necessary. Please feel free to share as much of this letter with my sister as you deem appropriate.

Sincerely yours,
Beau Hadley

I was so angry I knew I had to be careful what I said as I folded the letter and stuffed it back into the envelope. What right did Beau Hadley have to dictate whom his sister could or could not date? And what did he know about me to make such a harsh judgment of my fitness to be in a relationship with her? He'd met me once and spent a scant hour or so in my presence. He thought I was too mature? What kind of screwed up thinking was that? It was outrageous, but Aunt Charity seemed resigned just to go along with what Beau wanted, which deep down inside I knew we'd have to do in the end.

I finally got my emotions under control enough to turn my attention to Mary Alice. She was sitting in the swing silent and composed. "Are you going to say something?" I asked, my voice cracking.

"You don't need to worry about this," she said calmly. "This is just Beau...being Beau. You have a license now, which means you can drive anywhere, right?"

"Yeah," I said and wiped my nose with the back of my hand. "Why?"

"Will you take me to Jackson in the morning? I need to see my brother about this."

The prospect of driving all the way to Jackson in my new car was exiting in and of itself, no matter the circumstances, but I knew we couldn't go without my father's permission, and somehow I didn't think he would give it. "I'll have to ask Daddy," I said.

"Will you ask him?" Mary Alice said.

"Yes."

"And if he says you can, will you take me?"

"Yes."

Chapter 14
The Dixie Pearl

At dinner, Daddy reluctantly gave me permission to drive Mary Alice to Jackson the next day. He seemed to be as flummoxed over Beau Hadley's letter as I was, and not a little irritated, too. Daddy didn't like it that someone was calling his son's character into question, and neither did I. Normally never one to withhold her opinions on anything, Aunt Charity was unusually quiet on the whole situation. I figured she would be totally against my taking Mary Alice to confront her brother over this, but Aunt Charity made no comment about it at all. Daddy warned me that I was going to be a fish out of water driving in Jackson traffic. He told me the route to take (53 from Bells Ferry over to 49, then stay on 49 north all the way to Jackson) and suggested I get Dick to give me a road map when I went by there to get gas and tell him I wouldn't be in to work. Daddy told me to expect the trip to take at least three hours if we didn't stop too much.

After dinner, Mary Alice called her brother to tell him to be expecting us between eleven and noon. When he found out I was bringing her, he got angry and forbade it. Mary Alice remained calm and just told him again to be expecting us at the law firm around lunch and then she hung up. I really could not figure out what she hoped to accomplish. It seemed Beau's mind was made up, and he certainly was in a position to be calling the shots when it came to his little sister. I thought about Sachet and tried to put myself in

Beau's shoes, but I still could not get past the fact that he was judging me without really knowing me. If he really knew me, knew my heart, he would know he didn't have to worry about his sister being with me.

It was almost ten o'clock and I was thinking on these things now as I sat in Daddy's recliner watching *The Jonathan Winters Show* on TV. I'd had my bath and was in my pajamas. Daddy had gone to bed an hour ago. The house was quiet except for the fans and the TV…and the phone, which was ringing now in the kitchen.

I jumped up and sprinted into the kitchen and caught it on the second ring. "Hello?" I said. No one said anything, but I could hear breathing on the other end. "Hello?" I repeated.

"Nelson?" a shaky voice said back to me.

"This is Nelson," I said, still unsure who was calling us this late at night.

"I'm glad you answered." I recognized the voice now. It was Frankie, and I could tell he'd been crying.

"Frankie? What's wrong?"

"Nothing," he said. "Can you come get me?"

I didn't say anything because his question didn't make any sense. Finally, I asked, "What do you mean? Are you okay?"

"I need you to come get me," he said.

"Tell me what's wrong, Frankie—let me talk to your dad."

"I'm not at home," he said.

"What?" And then I gave an audible groan when I remembered the last time I'd seen Frankie was that afternoon on the back of Peter Bong's Vincent motorcycle as they left the Colonel Dixie. And Frankie's bike was still lying in our front yard the last time I'd looked out there after dinner. "Where are you?" I asked him.

"I'm at the Dixie Pearl Motel. You know where it is? Out on 49 close to Lyman?"

"Is Peter Bong with you?" I asked. Frankie didn't say anything. "Frankie, are you with Peter?"

"No, I'm by myself," Frankie finally said.

I was trying to control my temper and not let Frankie know how mad I was at him for being so stupid. "Did he hurt you?" I asked him.

"Who?"

"Peter Bong. Did he hurt you?"

"No," Frankie said. "Just…please come get me. And, Nelson…"

I waited and finally said, "What is it?"

"I need some clothes."

"What happened to your clothes?"

"He took 'em."

I groaned again. "Frankie, man…what have you gotten yourself into?"

"Just come get me, please," Frankie pleaded. "I'm in room fourteen."

"All right," I said. "I'll be there in about twenty minutes. I've got to get dressed."

"Okay. Bye."

I hung up the phone and wondered how in the devil I was going to explain this to Daddy. I was sure the phone ringing had waked him. I went back in the living room fully expecting to see him sitting there, but he wasn't. I turned off the TV and then the lamp beside Daddy's recliner. I stood there and let my eyes adjust to the darkness, then went down the hall past my room, then past Sachet's. I stepped back and looked in her room and could see by the night light that her bed was empty. Daddy's door was cracked enough for me to stick my head in. I could see him lying there with my sister cuddled up beside him, both sound asleep.

Quietly, I crept back down to my room and closed the door. I got dressed and was about to leave when I remembered what Frankie had said about his clothes. I went over to my dresser and got out a pair of jeans and a tee shirt. Frankie was a lot shorter than me, but I was slim, so we were about the same size in the waist. I put the jeans back and grabbed a pair of khaki Bermuda shorts. I turned the light out and closed the door behind me. In the darkness, I made my way down the hall to the kitchen and got a paper grocery bag out of the pantry and put the shorts and tee shirt in it. I hesitated and then reached up on the top shelf behind the flour tin and got Daddy's Colt Detective Special that he kept there. I opened the cylinder to make sure it was loaded, which I already knew it was. Whenever he would have to go out into the back portion of the cow pasture, or when we went down to the river fishing, Daddy would stick this .38 Special inside his waistband for snakes. I put it in the bag with the clothes.

When I got out into the back yard, Bear came running up and scared me so bad I almost dropped the bag, but at least he didn't bark. I got in my car and started it up. The rumbling exhaust of that Studebaker V8 sounded deafening in the still night air and I was sure if that didn't wake Daddy it would be a miracle. I waited to see the back porch light come on, and when it didn't, I turned the headlights on and slowly backed up, turned the car around, and headed out our drive to the road.

I only met one car on the way to get Frankie, and that was when I went through the little community of Lyman. When I came to a stop at the intersection of 53 and 49, I looked to my right and could see the sign for the Dixie Pearl Motel about 200 yards down on the north bound side of the four-lane road. The sign was a huge Confederate flag with an open oyster shell in the middle of it holding a gleaming white pearl. At night, all the details on the sign were outlined in red, white, and blue neon tubes. The blinking green neon "Color TV" sign suspended underneath the main sign looked out of place. I turned right and slowly drove toward the motel. As I got to the crossover turn, I looked closely at the cars and trucks in the parking lot. There wasn't a motorcycle among them.

I crossed over the north bound lanes of 49 and pulled into the motel parking lot. All the parking spaces directly in front of the rooms were taken, so I parked out in the lot. I got out with the paper bag containing the clothes I'd brought, and the gun, under my arm. I looked around to see if there was anyone around. There wasn't. All was quiet in the thick, humid night air. The entire parking lot and the front of the motel were aglow in red, white, and blue from the big sign towering over me. Slowly, I made my way to the row of rooms to look for number 14.

As I got closer to the rooms I could hear TVs going in a few of them. I walked quietly past room 18, then 17 and 16. I had to step over the metal cover from the air conditioner of room 15, which was off and partially obstructing the walkway. I stopped at the door to room 14. The curtains in the window were dark and there were no sounds on the other side of the door. I knocked and waited. Nothing. I knocked again and put my mouth close to the door and said,

"Frankie?" I heard the lock on the door turn and then it opened about four inches, held fast by the security chain. Through the partially open door I could just make out Frankie's face in the darkness of the room. "It's me," I said in a whispered shout. Frankie unhooked the security chain and I pushed open the door and stepped into the pitch black room. Frankie closed the door behind me and relocked it and I stood there waiting for my eyes to adjust to the darkness.

The room was stuffy and humid, like someone had just come out of the shower. But there was also an underlying smell of body odor, beer, and cigarettes. When my eyes adjusted enough that I could see from the light coming in around the drapes on the window, I noticed the room had one big bed that was a mess. I went over and turned on the lamp that was affixed to the wall over the bedside table. That almost blinded me and I had to squint to allow my eyes to adjust again. I turned around to look at Frankie. He was standing there with a white bath towel wrapped around his waist. His hair was damp and all messed up. He was trembling and looked like a frightened little boy. "Did you bring me some clothes?" he asked. I reached in the bag and handed him the folded Bermuda shorts and tee shirt. "Did you bring any underwear?"

"He took your underwear, too?" I said.

"He took everything," Frankie said, pulling the tee shirt on. "Even my socks and shoes." He let the towel fall to the floor and then slipped my shorts on.

I looked around the room. There were three empty beer cans on the table beside the bed, another four on the table where Frankie was sitting, and a near empty fifth of Jack Daniel's sitting on the dresser beside the TV. The ashtray on the table beside the bed was full of brown cigarette butts. For the first time I was coming to realize what had happened in this room and it was making me sick.

Frankie ran his fingers through his hair trying to comb it down. When he turned toward the light I could see a long scratch on his neck, more a cut really, just not very deep, that had bled a little. And there were finger marks on his throat. "Frankie, man, what the heck happened?" I asked. "What'd he do to you?"

"Let's go," Frankie said, his voice shaky. "I'll tell you about it later."

The ride back to my house was silent. I kept the paper bag with the revolver in it stuck between my legs. I was halfway expecting at any minute to see the single headlight of a motorcycle come up behind us. Nevertheless, we made it back without seeing another vehicle of any kind.

As I pulled up behind Daddy's Chrysler parked under the carport I shut the engine off and coasted the last few feet. I switched off the headlights, set the parking brake, and looked over at Frankie. "What are we gonna do if my dad is up and waiting for me?"

Frankie started to say something, then turned and opened the door. The dome light came on as Frankie leaned out of the car and vomited. It was painful to listen to. He retched over and over. It sounded like his insides were coming out. I opened my door and the cross breeze brought the smell through the car and it almost made me heave. Peter Bong hadn't been the only one drinking in room 14 of the Dixie Pearl Motel that night.

Whether or not Daddy was awake now was immaterial. Frankie was sick, and I needed to get him in the house. I got out of the car and by the time I made it around to the passenger side, Frankie had stumbled out and fallen to his knees and was dry heaving. When he finally stopped, I stuck the crumpled paper bag containing the gun under my arm and leaned down to help him to his feet. I held onto him as we walked to the house, and sure enough when we entered the kitchen, Daddy was sitting at the table in his pajamas.

I can only imagine what a sight we were, Frankie barefoot, holding on to me looking like death warmed over with fresh vomit on his chin. Judging from the look on Daddy's face, it wasn't a pretty picture. As soon as Frankie could focus and saw my father sitting there, he started retching again.

Daddy jumped up from the table and said, "Take him to the bathroom." I set the bag with the gun in it on the counter and Daddy helped me half carry Frankie down the hall to the bathroom. We just did make it in time for Frankie to get to the toilet and let go with another round of dry heaving. When he was done, we sat him on the edge of the bathtub and Daddy was already running warm water in the sink. Frankie's face was drenched in sweat and he was shaking. Daddy took a wash cloth, wet it, and wiped Frankie's face, cleaning off the disgusting vomit that reeked of beer and whiskey. He got another clean wash cloth, wet it, and sponged Frankie's face. He handed me the cloth and then took Frankie's face in both his hands. He forced open Frankie's eyes with his thumbs. "He's had way too much to drink," Daddy said grimly. He looked over at me. "How much did he throw up outside?"

"Tons."

"Good. What the hell happened?"

"Did the phone wake you up?" I asked him.

"No, your car did when you left out of here. Where'd you go?"

"To get him. He called about ten o'clock and asked me to come pick him up."

Daddy pursed his brow and looked back at Frankie. "Did you get into your daddy's liquor, son?"

"He wasn't at home," I said.

Daddy looked at me. "Where was he?"

"Nelson," Frankie said. His eyes narrowed on me as he shook his head no.

I had never lied to my father and I wasn't going to start now. "He was with Peter Bong," I finally said.

Frankie closed his eyes and started sobbing. I closed the toilet lid and sat down. How much worse could this day get?

"That jackass with the ponytail from yesterday?" Daddy asked.

"Yeah," I said, looking up.

Daddy motioned for me to hand him the wash cloth, which I did. He wiped Frankie's face again and then put the cloth in Frankie's hand. "Where were they?" he asked me.

"At that motel out on 49 like you're going to Gulfport."

"Did you see Bong?"

"No, he was already gone when Frankie called me to come get him. Daddy, he took all of Frankie's clothes, even his underwear and shoes. Why would he do that?"

"Probably to make sure he could be long gone before Frankie would get up the nerve to call the police."

Frankie had stopped crying and was nodding his head. "That's what scared him off, I think. I told him I was gonna call the cops."

"Did he do something to you?" Daddy asked. "Is that why you told him you were going to call the police?"

Frankie nodded and then looked down, clearly embarrassed.

Daddy sighed. "So he kidnapped you, took you to the motel, got you drunk, and then tried to force you to do things?"

Frankie looked at me. "Tell him the truth," I said.

Frankie's eyes were filling with tears again. He looked at my father and shook his head. "He didn't kidnap me," he said.

Daddy took the wash cloth from Frankie and put it back in the sink. He then traced the long red cut on Frankie's neck with his finger and asked, "What's this?"

Frankie reached up and touched the cut on his neck. "He put a knife to my throat and told me he'd kill me if I ever told anyone."

"Did he choke you?"

Frankie hesitated. He seemed surprised by my father's question. "How'd you know that?" he asked.

Daddy put his hand to Frankie's chin and lifted it up. "You've got finger marks around your throat, son."

"Yeah, he choked me."

Daddy had been kneeling in front of Frankie this whole time and now he stood up. "Do you still feel sick?" he asked Frankie.

"Yeah," Frankie said, "but I don't think I'm gonna puke anymore."

"Okay, let's go in the living room," Daddy said.

Frankie stood up and he was a little unsteady at first but he made it down the hall without any help from me or Daddy. He sat on the sofa and I sat beside him. Daddy sat in his recliner. I looked at the clock on the wall. It was quarter past eleven.

Daddy looked at Frankie. "Tell me how you wound up in a motel room with that man if he didn't kidnap you."

Frankie leaned forward and put his face in hands and shook his head over and over. It didn't look as though he was going to offer an answer, so I told Daddy about going to the Colonel Dixie and Frankie leaving there on the back of Peter Bong's motorcycle.

"What time was that?" Daddy asked me.

"I don't know—around three o'clock I think."

"So he hasn't been home since before three this afternoon?" He pointed to Frankie.

"I don't know," I said.

"I called Mom from the motel when we got there and told her I was spending the night here," Frankie said.

"Frankie," Daddy said, "are you telling me you went to that motel room willingly?"

Frankie nodded but didn't say anything.

"Damn, son," Daddy said, shaking his head. "What in the world were you thinking?" Frankie was silent. He was embarrassed and I was embarrassed for him. Daddy stood up and scratched his brow. "I need to call the sheriff…and your father, Frankie."

Frankie looked up at Daddy with pleading eyes. "Mr. Lem, please don't do that. Dad said—" Frankie stopped.

Daddy sat back on the edge of his recliner and looked long at Frankie. "Your dad said what?" Frankie didn't respond; he just looked down. "Your father already knows about this, doesn't he?" Daddy said.

Frankie nodded without looking up.

"Did you call him first?" Daddy asked. "I mean before you called here?"

"Yes, sir," he said. And then he started crying like his heart was broken. I reached over and put my arm around his shoulders and he leaned into me and cried and cried. Daddy went to the kitchen and got a clean dish towel and handed it to him. Frankie wiped his eyes with it.

"Tell me what happened when your dad got there," Daddy said. "Is he still drinking?"

"Yes, sir," Frankie replied matter-of-factly. I was dumfounded. Drinking? I didn't know Frankie's father drank.

"Was he drunk when he got there?"

Frankie nodded. "He was drunk. He started cussin' and slappin' me around."

"Has he hit you before when he's been drinking?"

"Sometimes."

"What about your brother?"

"No, he doesn't hit Mark. He likes him."

"So what happened after your dad got there and started cussing?"

Frankie's eyes filled with tears again, but he remained calm. "He yelled at me and called me a faggot. Then he threw me down on the bed and started choking me. He choked me so hard I passed out. When I woke up, he was gone."

"Your dad choked you? It wasn't Bong?" my father said angrily, showing emotion for the first time since Frankie started spilling his story.

"It was my dad."

"Son of a bitch," Daddy said under his breath. It wasn't often when I saw my father on the verge of losing his temper, but he was clearly struggling to hold it in check now. "Is your stomach burning yet?" he asked Frankie.

Frankie blinked at the sudden change in subject. "Yes, sir," he said.

Daddy got up and headed into the kitchen. I could see him in there getting something out of the ice box.

"Is he going to call my dad?" Frankie asked me.

"I don't think so."

Daddy came back with a glass of iced milk and handed it to Frankie. "Drink this," he said, "it'll make you feel better."

Frankie took a couple of tentative sips and when it appeared he wasn't going to throw it up, he downed the rest of the glass in three big gulps leaving nothing behind but four ice cubes. He set the glass on the end table.

"Frankie," Daddy said, "I have to call your parents. Your dad's probably passed out drunk by now, but your mother needs to know you're okay and will be staying here tonight. And tomorrow, I've got to call the sheriff. You understand why, don't you?"

"I guess so," Frankie said, resigned to the inevitable. "Are you gonna tell him what my dad did to me?"

"I think we have to, son. If we don't put a stop to this now, it's just going to get worse. Your dad needs help. Drunk or sober, no man should hit his kids."

"Don't you know the sheriff?" I asked Daddy. Joe Posey was the sheriff of Harrison County and he lived in Bells Ferry.

"I know him," Daddy said. "He's a member of the Lodge."

Frankie and I sat there in silence as Daddy went to the kitchen to use the phone. I was more or less in a mild state of shock. How could I not have known all this about the boy I called my best friend? The times I'd slept over at

Frankie's, and every other time I'd been around his dad, things seemed fine. Frankie had never said much about his father one way or the other. I suppose I'd naively assumed Frankie enjoyed the same sort of relationship with his father that I had with mine. I was finding out in short order how wrong I'd been. Frankie's dad was not only a drunk, he was abusive, and it had been happening right under my nose. I reached out and put my arm around Frankie and hugged him to me. "How come you never told me about your dad drinking and hitting you?"

Frankie rested his head on my shoulder. "I don't know. It was just easier to pretend it didn't happen. You don't know how lucky you are."

"What do you mean?"

"To have a dad like that," Frankie said, pointing to my father standing over in the kitchen talking on the phone.

Daddy was keeping his voice low so we could not hear what he was saying, but his animated hand gestures showed how upset he was getting. When he hung up, he slammed the phone down so hard it made the bell inside ding.

"What did Mom say?" Frankie asked when Daddy came back in the living room and sat down.

"That was your dad," he said.

"What'd you tell him?" Frankie asked.

Daddy sighed. "I told him you were okay, and I'd let you spend the night here. I also told him if he ever laid a hand on you again he'd have to deal with me." He ran his fingers through his hair and leaned back in the recliner.

"What'd he say?" Frankie asked.

I could tell Daddy didn't want to answer. "He told me I better get used to you staying here because you'd never set foot in his house again."

Frankie took that declaration stoically. "That's what he told me back at the motel," he said quietly.

"Don't worry about it tonight, son," Daddy said. "You boys need to get to bed," he added.

"Are you going too?" I asked.

"In a bit. I need to cool off. You two go on."

Frankie and I stood up and told Daddy goodnight then headed to the bathroom. I brushed my teeth while Frankie stood over the toilet and peed. Just as he was finishing up, I was examining my face for that pre-zit that had appeared on my birthday. It was gone, thankfully.

"You don't have an extra toothbrush, do you?" Frankie asked. "My mouth tastes like crap." I had just opened the medicine cabinet to look when Frankie said, "Ouch! Damn!"

I closed the cabinet door and looked at him in the mirror. He was fumbling with the zipper on my shorts he was wearing. "What'd you do?" I asked.

"I pinched my dick in the zipper. I forgot I didn't have any underwear on."

I laughed at him and then rinsed my mouth and my toothbrush. I held it out to him. "We don't have any extra toothbrushes. You can use mine if you want."

Frankie took the brush from my hand. "You don't mind?"

"Not if you don't. Flush the toilet," I said and left him to finish up.

I was already in bed when Frankie came in the bedroom and closed the door behind him. He pulled off the tee shirt. "You got some PJs I can sleep in?" he asked.

I pointed to my dresser. "Second drawer on the left."

Frankie took my Bermuda shorts off and laid them over the chair and then slipped my spare pajama bottoms on. He came over to the bed, crawled over me, and got settled. I reached over and turned out the light.

"Nels?" Frankie said.

"Hmm?"

"I really fucked up, didn't I?"

I was surprised at Frankie's use of the F-word. It was always there in our respective arsenals of profanity, but we rarely pulled it out and used it. "What'd you let him do to you?" I asked. I didn't really want to know, but the question just came out anyway.

"I don't want to talk about it."

"What'd he want to do that made you tell him you would call the cops?"

"Didn't you hear me say I don't want to talk about it?"

"Yeah, sorry."

"That's okay," Frankie said. "Thanks for coming to get me. I don't know what I would have done if you'd said no."

I turned to Frankie, but in the darkness I could not see his face. "There's no way I would have not come and got you, man."

I felt Frankie moving his hand under the sheet until he found mine beside him. He grasped it and squeezed. "Still best friends?" he asked, his voice breaking as he started to cry.

I squeezed his hand back. "Still best friends," I affirmed.

I fell asleep that night with my best friend holding my hand and crying beside me.

Chapter 15
Jackson

I awoke to the early morning sun streaming in my window. Frankie was right up against me with his arm around me and I could feel him breathing on my neck. I lifted his arm and moved it off me and then sat up in the bed. I rubbed the sleep from my eyes and thought about what had happened last night, wishing it had just been a bad dream, but knowing it wasn't. It was all too real, and Frankie sleeping in the bed beside me confirmed it.

As I threw back the sheet and put my feet on the floor, Frankie stirred and then rolled on his side facing the wall. I got up and dressed quietly and then went down the hall and peeked in my sister's room. Her bed was still empty, so I looked in Daddy's room. She was asleep in his bed. I went to the bathroom and found a note there from him taped to the mirror along with a ten dollar bill:

> *Nelson, Be careful today and remember what I told you about traffic in Jackson. Take Frankie with you. I don't want him around his dad until he's talked to the sheriff. Give him this $10 so he'll have his own money and won't have to ask you if wants to buy something. Love, Dad.*

I was surprised that Daddy wanted me to take Frankie, and not a little disappointed. Despite the reason we were going to Jackson, I was looking forward to it just being

Mary Alice and me taking the trip. I tore the note off the mirror and put the ten dollars in my wallet.

I finished up in the bathroom then went down to the kitchen and poured me a glass of orange juice. Daddy had left the morning paper on the table so I turned back to the funny pages as I sipped the juice, which tasted bitter because of the lingering toothpaste in my mouth. It was half past six and I knew Aunt Charity would be coming over any minute to fix breakfast. I wanted to get on the road to Jackson by eight, so I hoped Mary Alice was up and getting ready.

I had just taken another sip of juice when the most blood-curdling scream came from down the hall. It was Sachet. I jumped up and ran down the hall past my room and looked in Daddy's room. Nothing. "Nelson!" my sister called and I stepped back and looked in my room. Sachet was on my bed on all fours looking at Frankie. He was sitting up with a confused look on his face. I knew what had happened. My sister had waked up and come to my room to get in bed with me, only to find Frankie instead. It must have startled her, and clearly her scream had scared poor Frankie half to death.

"It's just Frankie," I said. I went over and sat down on the bed. She crawled in my lap and put her head under my chin. "You okay?" I asked her. She nodded her head and rubbed her eyes. "Go in the bathroom and wash your face and brush your teeth. Aunt Charity will be over here in a minute to fix breakfast."

"Okay," Sachet said. She slid off my lap and scurried off to the bathroom.

I turned around and looked at Frankie. "What about you? Are you okay?"

Frankie blinked several times like he was trying to focus on me. "No," he said. "My head feels like it's gonna explode."

"How much did you drink last night?"

"I don't remember."

"Do you remember how sick you were?"

"Yeah," he said, reaching up to rub his eyes. "I'm never gonna drink again as long as I live. I'd rather die than be that sick. I learned my lesson."

"Did you learn another lesson?"

"What do you mean?"

"You don't go off with a pervert on a motorcycle."

"Yeah," Frankie said with a slight smile. "I learned that lesson, too. I guess that means I won't be riding with you on your Honda anymore." He laughed and poked me in the back.

"It's not funny, Frankie. I'm serious. He could have killed you."

"I know," Frankie said, his levity passing. "Is your dad still here?"

"Nope. He leaves for work about five. He left me a note and said to take you with me and Mary Alice to Jackson."

"Why?"

"I don't know," I lied. Since Frankie hadn't seen Daddy's note, I didn't see any reason to bring up the issue of his father and the sheriff.

"Why are you going to Jackson?" Frankie asked.

"It's got something to do with Mary Alice's brother," I said. "I'll let her tell you about it. Go on and get dressed. I want to leave right after breakfast."

"What am I gonna wear? I don't have any clothes."

I told Frankie to wear the Bermuda shorts I'd brought him last night. I got him one of my Izod polo shirts out of the closet and some socks and underwear from my dresser. When he asked me about shoes and stuck his freshly socked feet up in the air I went back over to the closet and got him an older pair of my sneakers that would have eventually found their way to the Masonic Home in Poplarville. My feet were bigger than Frankie's, but I was glad to see these old shoes fit him. Just as he finished dressing, we heard Aunt Charity calling my name from the kitchen.

"There's Aunt Charity," I said. "Hurry up in the bath-room so we can eat breakfast and hit the road."

— — —

"Is somebody gonna tell me why we're going to Jackson?" Frankie said loudly over the wind noise. Like yesterday, he was sprawled across the back seat of my car, leaning against the passenger side armrest, the humid morning air blowing his dark hair through his open window. After eating a huge breakfast, he seemed strangely back to normal after his drunken sexual escapade last night with the man in black, not to mention being attacked by his father. I couldn't help but think it was just a front and I wondered how long he would be able to maintain it.

It was twenty past eight and we'd just left Dick's ESSO and were headed out of town on 53 at a steady 50 miles per hour. I had a full tank of gas and a map of Mississippi with the entire route to Jackson highlighted in yellow. I was nervous and excited about the long drive ahead and the only part I was even remotely apprehensive about was navigating downtown Jackson and trying to find the law office where Beau Hadley was clerking. Mary Alice was holding my hand across the center console and for one brief moment before Frankie asked that question, I had forgotten about why we were going and why my best friend was in the back-seat with us.

"Hello?" Frankie said. "Is somebody gonna answer me? Why are we going to Jackson?"

"Do you care if I tell him?" I asked Mary Alice.

She released my hand and opened the small pink purse in her lap. From it she took the envelope containing her broth-er's letter. "Let him read it," she said and held the envelope over to me.

I took the envelope and held it back to Frankie. "Read this," I said to him.

When Frankie finished reading the letter, he leaned up between the front bucket seats and held out the envelope. "I liked your brother when I met him, Mary Alice," he said, "but now I think he's an idiot." I smiled and put the enve-lope in Mary Alice's hand. Leave it to Frankie to put into words what I'd been thinking ever since I read it. "If we're going to Jackson so you can beat him up," Frankie added, punching me in the arm, "I'll help you."

I laughed. "I'm not going to Jackson to get in a fight," I said.

"So why are you going, then?"

"Mary Alice wants to talk to him about that letter."

Frankie puffed and resumed his recline in the back seat. "Let me talk to him," he said. "I'll set him straight."

"And what would you say to my brother, Frankie—after you beat him up?" Mary Alice asked with a giggle. I looked over at her, at the wind tossing her hair, at how her face seemed to glow in the soft morning light made shadowless by the patches of fog we were encountering at regular inter-vals along the way.

Frankie was back up between the front seat backs. "I'd tell him he doesn't know how lucky his sister is to have met my best friend. I'd tell him he ought to be thankful Nelson Gody is your boyfriend."

Mary Alice was squeezing my hand and I glanced over to see a satisfied smile on her face.

We got to Jackson around 11:40, having only stopped once for a restroom break outside of Hattiesburg. While we were at that service station, Frankie asked me to buy him a Coke, and I remembered what my father had told me about giving Frankie $10 so he would not have to ask me for money. I gave him the ten dollar bill out of my wallet and when he came back with a Coke and a Slim Jim, he tried to hand me the change. I told him to keep it in case he wanted to get something else while we were in Jackson. Frankie told me he'd pay me back. I smiled because I knew he wouldn't; he'd never paid me back in his life.

Traffic was pretty heavy in Hattiesburg, but it was nothing compared to what we encountered in downtown Jackson as the noon hour approached. I'd been to Jackson before, but that was with Daddy driving and I didn't pay any attention then to cars, trucks, buses, and people, which were everywhere today. For the first time since we left that morning I was wondering if I'd bitten off more than I could chew. That feeling intensified when we finally made it onto Capitol Street, lined down both sides with its tall buildings intimidating me every inch of the way as I searched for a place to park. The address Mary Alice had for Beau's law firm was about two blocks from the old capitol building, and all the parking on Capitol was parallel—the one portion of my driving test I'd not done well on—and all the spaces appeared to be taken.

"There's an empty one!" Frankie yelled. He pointed up ahead. "That car's pulling out."

An old Buick was leaving a space right in front of the Paramount Theater. I checked my rear view mirror and the car behind us was quite a ways back so I pulled up to the empty space, mentally crossed my fingers, and started the backing maneuver to get the car into the space. I only had to make one stop and correction before I got us into the slot perfectly and I breathed an audible sigh of relief when it was done.

We got out and Frankie said, "Gotta pay for parking here." He pointed to the meter standing watch beside the right front fender of my GT Hawk. I reached in my pocket but Frankie said, "I got it." He went over and stuffed a dime in the meter and turned the handle. "An hour?" he said, looking over at me.

"Put another dime in," I said. "I don't want to get a ticket."

Frankie fed the meter another dime while I helped Mary Alice out of the car. She had her walking stick with her and she unfolded it. She opened her purse and handed me the piece of paper Aunt Charity had written the address on.

"I think you should lock your car, man," Frankie said. "We're not in Bells Ferry." He waved his arm at the hustle and bustle of people passing by us on the sidewalk.

I looked back at the car sitting there with all four windows rolled down. "Yeah," I concurred. I rolled the windows up, made sure the keys were in my pocket, and then locked the doors. With Mary Alice on my arm and her walking stick tapping in front of us, we made our way up Capitol Street to her brother's law office.

"It's hot," Frankie announced, as if we didn't already know it. It was well over 90 degrees, the humidity was high, and there was next to no breeze. The drive up hadn't been too bad at highway speed with the windows down and the floor vents open. I'd often heard Daddy refer to Jackson as the hottest place in the state, and I could see why. We hadn't gone half a block and I was sweating profusely.

"I guess this is it," I said when we got to the four-story red brick building that stood almost directly across the street from the towering Deposit Guaranty building. The brass placard affixed to the wall by the front door read

Prosser, Wallace, Shane & Thompson
Attorneys at Law

Frankie tapped his finger on the name *Thompson* and said, "My uncle."

"Really?" I said.

Frankie just rolled his eyes and opened the door for Mary Alice and me.

We entered a huge reception area chilled to the temperature of a meat locker. The oak parquet floor was covered with several elaborate Oriental carpets, all mostly in deep shades of red. The walls were done up in heavy oak paneling and there were several portraits of what I assumed were past and present lawyers of the firm all along the wall to our right. There was a sitting area in the middle with a couch and two big wing-back chairs arranged around a coffee table that had a few magazines on it. In the far back corner sat a nice-looking lady at a desk. There was soft music coming from somewhere. I looked around but I didn't see any speakers.

"Is there a receptionist?" Mary Alice asked.

"Yes," I said and led her over to the lady at the desk. Frankie stayed behind and plopped himself into one of the wing-backs.

"May I help you?" the lady said with a smile. She was eyeing Mary Alice's walking stick. "Oh, are you Mary Alice?" she said, as if recognizing the girl standing before her.

"Yes, ma'am," Mary Alice responded. "My brother is Beau Hadley. He's clerking here this summer for Mr. Shane."

"Beau told me to be expecting you. I'll let him know you're here. If y'all will just have a seat back over there it shouldn't be too long."

"Thank you," Mary Alice said. I smiled at the lady and Mary Alice and I walked back over to join Frankie in the sitting area. We sat on the sofa and Frankie was already reading a *National Geographic*. He held the magazine over to me open to a picture of some African woman with no top on and huge brown tits hanging nearly down to her belly button.

I pushed the magazine away and shook my head. "Grow up," I said dismissively. Frankie flipped me a bird and resumed reading. I looked at Mary Alice sitting beside me. "I still don't know what good you think this is gonna do, Mary Alice. Your brother has made his decision. He doesn't want me and you together."

"And you're okay with that?" she said, picking up on the resignation in my voice.

I guess over the past 24 hours I had allowed myself to accept what appeared to be the inevitable. "No, I'm not okay with it," I said. "But—"

"There's no but," Mary Alice retorted. "I'm not a little girl anymore and my brother needs to learn that right now. He's not going to make me lose you."

With that declaration, Mary Alice revealed for the first time that she saw what we had together as something more permanent than merely the girlfriend-boyfriend relationship of two fickle teenagers. I felt the same way, and I was now angry with myself (and not a little ashamed) that I'd been so willing to just let Beau have his way without putting up a fight. Unlike her feckless boyfriend, from the moment I had read Beau's letter to her, Mary Alice had formed a plan of action to deal with it. Frankie's first reaction after reading the letter was to assume I was driving to Jackson to beat her brother up. As immature and unrealistic as it may have been, it was a plan, and one Frankie assumed I had in mind. But I had no plan, just acquiescence.

"So you all made it."

I looked up out of my thoughts to see Beau Hadley standing there. He had on an impeccably tailored dark gray suit, white shirt, and a red and white striped bow tie. He held out his hand and I stood up and shook it. "Hi, Beau," I said coolly. I looked at Frankie, who still had his nose buried in the *National Geographic*. Whether he was ignoring Beau because he was mad about his letter, or because he was remembering how close he came to making a fool of himself when he first met the man, I didn't know.

"I don't have much of an office," Beau said, "but we can talk in the conference room." He gestured toward the double doors that were over by the receptionist's desk.

Mary Alice stood up beside me. "I want to talk to you alone, Beau," she said.

"All right," he said with a frown. "Can I get you something to drink?" he asked, looking at me.

"No, thanks," I said.

Beau turned to Frankie, who still hadn't looked up from the magazine. "Would you like something?" he said.

I kicked Frankie in the leg when it seemed he wasn't going to respond. "What?" he said, looking up at me.

"Beau wants to know if you want something to drink."

"No," Frankie said and went back to the magazine.

Beau looked at me with raised eyebrows and then led his sister over to the conference room doors. After he closed the doors behind them I sat down on the sofa and looked at Frankie. "What's the matter with you?" I asked.

"What do you mean?"

"Why were you rude like that?"

"Because he's an asshole. Is that why you drove all the way up here? To kiss his ass and be nice to him?"

"Frankie..." I sighed and just decided to let it go. I didn't feel like getting into a discussion with him about civil comportment.

Twenty minutes later Mary Alice and her brother emerged from the conference room. Mary Alice's eyes were red and I could tell she'd been crying. It was looking like this trip was a big waste of time, just as I'd feared it would be.

"I want to thank you for bringing Mary Alice up today," Beau said. His tone was sounding strangely conciliatory. He stuck his hand out to me and said, "I owe you an apology for that letter to your aunt."

This time Frankie did look up from his magazine. And I didn't know what to say as I shook Beau's hand. "I...uh...thanks. I wasn't expecting that," I stammered.

"I can be overly protective of my little sister sometimes, Nelson. But she's not so little now and I trust her judgment."

"So you're okay with me being Mary Alice's boyfriend?"

"Yes," Beau said without hesitation. "As long as she is, I am."

I almost forgot all those comportment thoughts that had been running through my head earlier. I wanted to grab Mary Alice and dance around that big oak-paneled room with her in my arms. I wanted to jump and shout.

Evidently, Beau could see all that pent up emotion in my face, for he gave me a wink and a grin, pointed to his sister, and said "Give her a hug; she deserves it."

I reached out and embraced Mary Alice and then took her face in my hands and kissed her full on the lips. She was laughing. I was laughing. And for a split second, there was no one else in that room.

Beau cleared his throat. "Mary Alice tells me you all haven't eaten." He reached in his jacket pocket and pulled out a card and handed it to me. "Lunch is on me today." I looked at the card. It had *The Magnolia Club* printed on it with an address on Congress Street. "The maître d's name is Vincent," Beau said. "I'll call and tell him to be expecting you. Now, if you all will excuse me, I've got to get back to work." He leaned down and kissed Mary Alice on the cheek. "Goodbye, little sister."

"Goodbye, brother," she replied.

And with a quick wave Beau left us and disappeared through a door on the opposite side of the room from the receptionist's desk. It had all happened so quickly I was still trying to catch up. "So that's it?" I asked and tugged on Mary's Alice's hand.

"What do you mean?" she said.

"I mean he was hell-bent on splitting us up and Aunt Charity taking you back to the home in Poplarville, then we come up here and you spend a few minutes talking to him and now everything is just fine, back just like it was?"

"Yes, I told you yesterday not to worry about that letter."

"What in the world did you say to him?" I asked.

"That's between me and him," Mary Alice said with a sly smile.

"Let's go eat," Frankie interjected. "I'm hungry."

The Magnolia Club was on the top floor of a twelve-story building that had a relatively modest looking exterior. However, the décor of the main dining room was strikingly similar to that of the law firm where Beau Hadley worked. The walls were clad in dark oak paneling; the floor was covered in sumptuous dark red carpet. Heavy linen cloth covered every table. Vincent, the maître d', escorted us to a round corner table and left us with three huge menus bound in fragrant leather with *Lunch* embossed on the cover in gold. The view of downtown Jackson out the wall of glass surrounding the outer edge of the dining room was breathtaking: Over my right shoulder was the old capitol building and if I looked over Mary Alice's right shoulder I could see the tall Deposit Guaranty building. I had never been in a restaurant like this, but then I remembered this was a private club. And judging from the way everyone else here was dressed, the three of us looked totally out of place.

"Why are the plates already on the table," Frankie asked. "And what do I need three forks for?"

Mary Alice chuckled. "That's a formal place setting, Frankie. You've got a fish fork, a salad fork, and a dinner fork."

"I'm not gonna order fish or a salad."

"Just shut up and look at the menu," I said.

Frankie opened the menu and I did the same. I could not believe the prices. And even though I'd had one year of French, most of the stuff listed I couldn't even pronounce, let alone figure out what it was. I looked up at Frankie and he had a big "Can you believe this?" look on his face.

"Ah…Mary Alice, I don't know what to order. I mean, I don't even know what any of this is. And the cheapest thing on here is twelve dollars."

Mary Alice ran her hand over the menu lying on the table in front of her. "I don't think the two of you are going to want anything from this menu. Get Vincent's attention. I should have had him seat us in the Jeff Davis room. That's informal and they have a more traditional lunch menu."

"The Jeff Davis room? Have you been here before?" I asked.

"Yes. My grandmother was a member."

Just then our waiter came up to take our drink orders. We all ordered iced tea and Mary Alice asked him to bring us menus from the Jeff Davis room. He filled our water glasses and took the huge leather tomes away. Frankie took a long gulp of ice water. "I bet that's the most expensive drink of water I've ever had," he said as he set the glass back down on the white linen.

I was thinking about how at ease Mary Alice seemed to be in this place. Since she said her grandmother had been a member, I was coming to realize that my initial impression of Mary Alice being from another time and another place wasn't too far off the mark. She was clearly used to a lifestyle that was totally alien to me.

The waiter was back with our glasses of tea and the menus from the Jeff Davis room, which were smaller than the others, but still bound in the same leather. I opened my menu and found fare that I did recognize, even though the prices were totally unfamiliar. The cheapest entrée was the "Jeff Davis Burger with French Fries" for $9.95, the price of the biggest Porterhouse at Bobby Dean's in Bells Ferry. We all three ordered the Jeff Davis Burger. Twenty minutes later when those burgers were set before us, Frankie and I could not keep from laughing. We had never seen hamburgers like these. They were gigantic. The bun was the size of a soup bowl. The beef patty looked like one of Aunt Charity's meat loafs and was topped with two thick slices of beefsteak tomato, lettuce, onion, and pickles. Even the French fries were oversized. The waiter set three small containers of mustard, ketchup, and mayonnaise on the table for us to prep our burgers as we pleased. Mary Alice found our reactions amusing, and I figured she'd never dined in The Magnolia Club with a couple of teenage rubes from southern Mississippi.

It was ten after two when we got back to the car, and I had totally forgotten about the parking meter. It had expired, but there was no ticket on the car so I was relieved. Traffic downtown didn't seem to have abated any, but I managed to get us back on 49 going south without incident. Frankie napped most of the way home after we stopped at the same station we had going up for a restroom break. He was asleep when we pulled into our driveway at 5:30. When I saw his dad's pickup sitting there, along with the sheriff's cruiser, I didn't want to wake him. Our day in Jackson had turned out to be a great escape, and a success from the standpoint of its mission. But now we had returned to Bells Ferry and the cold hard reality of Frankie's escapades last night was waiting for us.

Chapter 16
Combat Pay

I made Frankie stay in the car until I took Mary Alice over to Aunt Charity's and ascertained whether she knew what was going on. She did. Daddy had told her when he got home earlier and called the sheriff, which was why she was fixing dinner at her house and had Sachet there with her.

When Frankie and I went in the house, Sheriff Posey, Frank Thompson, and Daddy were all sitting in the living room waiting for us. Daddy had told the sheriff what he knew of the previous night's events, and Frankie's dad had given his version. But the sheriff wanted to hear it straight from Frankie, which he did. He took Frankie for a walk and left the rest of us waiting in the living room. That was the longest half-hour I think I've ever spent, sitting there in the stony silence, the tension between my father and Frank Thompson so thick you could feel it in the air. Daddy would not look at the man; his contempt was that palpable. As for Frank Thompson, he sat there the entire time leaned back on the sofa with his eyes closed, appearing to be as affected by the situation as a man waiting for a bus down at the Trailways depot.

I don't believe my father had shared my quiet hope that once Frankie's dad sobered up things would be more or less back to normal. To the extent I had thought about it, I knew Frank Thompson would have some fences to mend: harsh, nearly unforgivable, words had been spoken to his son in a drunken rage. But I had allowed myself to forget the biggest obstacle to a return to normalcy: the physical assault. Throttling your son into unconsciousness is not normal by any standard under any circumstances and was an unforgivable act of brutality in Daddy's eyes. When the sheriff returned with Frankie, that was the first thing Frank Thompson was confronted with, and he vehemently denied it.

"I never laid a hand on him," Frankie's dad announced. "That goddamn pervert did it." Frankie just sat there beside me emotionless (we were both jammed together in the only sitting chair in our living room) as his father lied through his teeth.

Sheriff Posey was standing in the middle of the room. When he pulled the front of his suit jacket open to put his hands on his hips, I noticed the shoulder holster, and the grip of a cocked and locked Colt .45 automatic. Joe Posey was heavyset, a few inches less than six foot, with a big beer belly that hung over his belt. You could tell he tried to look neat and presentable, his body just didn't cooperate. "Frank," he said, "your son told me exactly what you did to him, and I believe him. You're just lucky he's refusing to cooperate as a witness, else I'd arrest your sorry ass right now and put you under the jail. You need to get some help with your drinking so that you can be the kind of father that boy deserves." He jerked a thumb in Frankie's direction.

Frank Thompson stood up. "I've said all I'm gonna say on the matter. I didn't touch him. If he says I did, he's a lying little faggot." He looked over at Daddy. "You can come get his clothes in about an hour. I'll have 'em packed up and ready."

"Wait a minute," Sheriff Posey said, holding up his hand. "You were serious about not letting Frankie come home?"

"You got that right."

"Why the hell not?" the sheriff asked. "Where's he supposed to go?"

"I don't give a shit. I didn't raise no faggot so he's not comin' home with me. Call his grandma over in Saucier, maybe she'll take him."

"Doesn't your wife have a say in this?" Daddy asked, his voice calm, masking a rage bubbling under the surface.

"She sure as shit don't have a damn thing to say about it, Lem Gody. I'm not henpecked and nobody tells me how to run my house."

"I thought I'd seen it all," Sheriff Posey said, "but you take the cake, Frank." He looked over at Frankie. "Do you know your grandmother's phone number, son?"

Frankie nodded his head yes. He was trying to stifle his sobs and the tears were rolling down his face. Daddy was so mad I just knew at any minute he was going to leap out of his recliner and knock Frank Thompson into next week.

The sheriff looked back at Frankie's dad. "Get the hell out of here," he said dismissively.

Frankie's dad went to the front door then turned back to Daddy. "Remember what I said, Lem. You come get his things in an hour or I'll burn 'em, I swear to God I will."

And that's all it took. Daddy was up and after Frankie's dad so fast that the sheriff literally had to jump in his way to stop him. Frank Thompson hurried out the door like the coward he was.

Frankie jumped up and ran to the bathroom. I followed him and got there just as he slammed the door and locked it. I jiggled the door knob and Frankie yelled, "Leave me alone!" I could hear him sobbing so I decided to let him be and went back to the living room.

"Is he okay?" Sheriff Posey asked me as I sat back down.

"He locked himself in the bathroom and he's crying," I said.

"Well, as soon as he gets out of there we need to get in touch with his grandmother because if she won't take him I've got to call in a social worker."

"Hold on, Joe," Daddy said. He'd sat back in his recliner and his eyes were closed and he was pinching his brow like he had a splitting headache. He probably did. Finally, he opened his eyes and looked at the sheriff. "His grandmother in Saucier is Frank's mother, and she's as big a drunk as he is. If Frank is serious and you let that boy go live with her, you might as well write him off right now."

Again, I was being blindsided by another open secret about Frankie's family of which I knew nothing. Had I been walking around unconscious for the last fourteen or so years, ever since Frankie and I first met? How come I didn't know these things? How come I didn't know my best friend's dad was a drunk who hit him? How come I didn't know his grandmother was a drunk, too?

"What about his mama's parents?" the sheriff asked.

"They live up around Philadelphia somewhere," Daddy said. "I don't think they were ever too pleased about their daughter marrying Frank."

"Well, it's either his grandma or the State of Mississippi, so we got to figure out who to call."

Daddy looked over at me. "How would you feel about Frankie living with us for awhile?" he asked.

The question took me by surprise but I didn't have to think about my answer. "It's okay with me," I replied. So many thoughts were racing around in my head at the prospect of Frankie moving in I couldn't keep it all straight.

"Think about it a minute, son, before you jump in with both feet. If Frank Thompson starts going around town running his mouth about his son being a faggot, that talk is going to come right back to this house, right back to you. It won't be nice and it could get ugly."

"He won't say anything, Daddy," I said.

"Why do you think that, son?" Sheriff Posey asked.

"Because he's ashamed of Frankie. The last thing he'd do is go around telling everybody that his son is queer."

The sheriff looked at Daddy and jerked his thumb in my direction. "He's got a point," he said. "So, is he queer?" he asked my father. "I mean he told me he went to the motel willingly with that jaybird and it wasn't until things started getting rough that he wanted out."

"Hell, Joe...I don't know what's going on with Frankie. But it doesn't matter. You don't strangle your kid just because you find out he might be queer."

"Yeah, you're right about that. So, you're okay with him staying here?"

"Yes," Daddy said. "And what about this Peter Bong character? He threatened to kill Frankie. Are you gonna pick him up?"

"If I can find him. I'll put out a bulletin on him. Based on what you and the boy told me, I've got a good description: Five-ten, one-hundred sixty pounds, olive complexion, long hair, ponytail, Australian, rides a Vincent motorcycle. And get this: when I asked Frankie if the guy had any tattoos or other distinguishing features he told me there was a mermaid tattooed on his ass." Sheriff Posey shook his head. "Think I should put that in the bulletin?" he asked with a cockeyed grin.

"Sheriff Posey, do you think he'll come back here after Frankie?" I asked.

"I don't know, son. Y'all should start locking your doors at night if you don't already. But I got a feeling that if Bong wanted to make sure Frankie never talked he would've killed him right there in that motel room. That boy doesn't know how lucky he is."

"Joe," Daddy said, "can you hang around here, eat some dinner, and then go with us down there to get Frankie's things? An hour is just enough time for Frank to get all liquored up and I don't want to have to kill that man if he starts something."

"Not a problem," the sheriff replied. "I'll stay here as long as you need me. What's for dinner?"

Forty-five minutes later, after a hasty meal of pot roast over at Aunt Charity's, we turned into Frankie's driveway behind Sheriff Posey's cruiser. There was a bonfire in the front yard sending a plume of dark smoke straight up into the early evening sky.

"I don't believe this," Daddy said as we got close enough to the house to see what was happening.

"Is that my stuff?" Frankie asked from the backseat of Daddy's car. He moved from the middle of the seat to up behind Daddy to get a good look.

As Daddy came to a stop behind the sheriff's car, I looked at the mess in the yard. Frank Thompson had gutted Frankie's bedroom and dragged everything, including the furniture, out into the yard. He had piled most of Frankie's clothes on the bed, along with what looked like his sleeping bag, and set it ablaze, mattress and all. It was burning wild-ly, no doubt fueled by the contents of the discarded can of

charcoal starter fluid lying on the ground beside it.
Frankie's dresser was just a few feet away with all the drawers pulled out and there were a few pieces of clothing in a
pile beside it. Old toys, GI Joes, cars, tanks, and trucks were
scattered everywhere. All of Frankie's board games were in
a pile, no doubt waiting to be burned. The Monopoly box
top had come off and the money was blowing all over the
place. Frankie's dad was sitting on the porch smoking a
Camel with a beer in his hand looking rather proud of his
handiwork. It was a heartbreakingly surreal scene that left
me speechless.

Daddy got out of the car and adjusted his trousers, which
revealed a flash of bright metal. The nickel plated Smith &
Wesson Model 27 he kept in the drawer of his bedside table
was stuck in his waistband under his shirttail. "You boys
stay in the car," he said to us.

When Frank Thompson saw my dad, he did an exaggerated check of his wrist watch and said, "You're late." Then
he waved his arm toward the fire and grinned.

Sheriff Posey got out of his cruiser and pointed at him.
"Frank, get a hose and put that damn fire out right now or
I'm gonna arrest you."

Frankie's dad didn't move. "Arrest me for what?" he
said. "This is my property. I can have a fire if I want to. I
can burn the whole goddamn house down if I want to."

I looked back at Frankie. "Your dad's crazy," I said.

"He's just drunk," Frankie replied. He seemed strangely
calm to think he was watching his bed and clothes burn to
cinders in his front yard.

"Lem," the sheriff shouted, "help me get this hose over
there and put that fire out before it spreads and does burn his

damn house down." He pointed to the rolled up garden hose attached to the faucet in the flower bed.

As Daddy and Sheriff Posey started for the hose, Frankie's dad stood up. He had Frankie's old little league baseball bat in his hand. "You leave that goddamn hose alone, you fat sonofabitch!" he yelled, pointing the bat at the sheriff.

"Sit your drunk ass back down," Daddy said. He was pointing the .357 Magnum at him. Frankie's dad saw the gun about the same time I did and put his butt back in the chair and dropped the bat.

Sheriff Posey turned the faucet on and he and Daddy dragged the hose over to the fire and showered it with water until it was just a steaming, stinking, smoldering, smoking mass of burnt wood and charred clothing and foam rubber. It smelled horrible. Daddy came back over to the car. He leaned down and looked in at me. "You and Frankie go back to the house and get the pickup. We'll never get all this stuff in the car."

I jumped out and ran around and got behind the wheel. Frankie got out and took my place in the front passenger seat. I adjusted the driver's seat, started the engine, got us turned around, and then we headed down the drive.

As we pulled out onto the road and I hit the gas, Frankie pointed to the clock on the dash and said, "I wish I'd said no."

I looked at the clock. It was 7:20. "What are you talking about?" I said.

"This was about the time yesterday when me and Peter got to the motel and he asked me if I really wanted to do this."

"You mean he gave you a chance to back out and you didn't take it?"

I waited for an answer, but there was none coming. Frankie was just staring out the open window at the pine trees flashing by. I put my foot in the four-barrel and that big Chrysler 383 roared as we raced back to the house.

— — —

We got all of Frankie's stuff hauled back to the house by eight o'clock. We brought Frankie's dresser and mirror back too, and the only reason Daddy had us load that in the back of the pickup was because Frankie's dad said he would burn it if we didn't. We put it under the carport, along with Frankie's other stuff, except for the few pieces of his clothing we salvaged, which we brought into my room and piled in the middle of the floor. Frankie and I were now going through that pile to see what he had left to wear. I had just finished giving Sachet her bath and she was sitting at my desk, wearing one of my tee shirts for a nightgown, dividing her time between coloring and watching us.

"You don't have much left," I said to Frankie as we finished folding and sorting everything.

Frankie was sitting on the floor across from me folding the last pair of socks. "Yeah," he said.

"Are you living here now, Frankie?" my sister asked without looking up from her coloring book.

I could tell Frankie didn't know what to say, so I answered. "For awhile," I told her.

"Baby girl," Daddy said from the doorway, "it's past your bedtime. Go brush your teeth and get ready for bed."

"Will you read me a story, Daddy?" my sister asked.

"Yes, if you hurry. Run along, now."

In a flash my sister was out of the room and Daddy came over and took her place at my desk. "This is a mess, isn't it?" he said and motioned to the clothes on the floor. "So what's he got there?"

I gave Daddy a quick inventory: Three undershirts (Frankie wore the sleeveless kind), two pair of underwear, five pair of socks, one pair of jeans, two tee shirts (one red, one green), and his dress shoes. When this was all in a heap on the floor it looked like a lot; once folded and counted, it didn't. Most of Frankie's clothes were now a pile of ashes in his front yard.

"Don't you think it's all gonna need washing?" my father asked.

"It didn't get dirty," Frankie said.

"Smell it," Daddy said.

I picked up one of the folded tee shirts and held it to my nose. It had the foul smell of that fire. "It smells like smoke," I said.

"You might as well take it all in the laundry room to be washed," Daddy said to me. "And tomorrow, I want you and Frankie to clean out your mother's sewing room. We'll make that Frankie's bedroom."

"There's no bed in there," I said.

"I know that. You two just get it cleaned out. I'll worry about the bed." The room Daddy was talking about was originally intended to serve as a child's nursery when this house was built by my grandparents in the 1920s. It had been my mother's sewing room as long as I could remember, and when she died, it more or less became a catch-all junk room. It had a small closet and was just large enough for a twin bed and maybe Frankie's dresser.

"What do you want us to do with all that stuff in there?" I asked.

"Most of it can be thrown away, but anything you're unsure of, put it in the living room and I'll go through it."

"Do you think I'm gonna be here long enough to need my own room?" Frankie asked.

Daddy sighed and rubbed his hand over his face. "Yes, son, I do. When we went to get your clothes and I saw that fire and your things strewn over the front yard, that settled it, and the sheriff agrees with me. Your father needs help, Frankie, and until he gets it, I don't think you're safe around him. I'm going to meet with Preston Marks tomorrow to see what I need to do to get legal custody of you."

"Oh, man," Frankie said, but his voice was devoid of any emotion. "Daddy's never been like this before," he added. "I mean, he gets drunk almost every night and he hits me sometimes, but he's never flipped out like this. It's my fault."

"Whoa," Daddy said, holding up his hand. "What you did yesterday was beyond stupid, but your dad reacting the way he did was not your fault, so just get that out of your head right now. What he did to you last night, and what he did today—that's his fault. Period. Understand?"

Frankie gave a slight smile. "Yes, sir. Thanks, Mr. Lem. And thanks for letting me stay here."

"You're welcome, son. Let's get one of the ground rules out of the way while I'm thinking about it: we all work around here, and it'll be the same for you. I'll give you five dollars a week allowance, but you've got to earn it. I know that's probably less than what your dad was paying you to work on the dairy farm, but it's what Nelson gets. Does that sound fair?"

"Yes, sir," Frankie said. "More than fair. Daddy never paid me anything."

I looked at Frankie. "You told me your dad pays you twenty-five dollars a week for working on the farm."

"That's what he told me he was paying me, but he never gives me any money. He always says he's putting it in the bank for me. I always have to go to Mama when I want some money, and she hardly ever has any except for groceries because that's all Daddy will give her."

Now I knew why Frankie never had any money and was always mooching off me and never paying me back.

Daddy pulled out his wallet and handed Frankie and me each a five dollar bill. "This week's allowance," he said.

Frankie tried to give his back. "Nelson already gave me ten dollars this morning, Mr. Lem."

"That was combat pay," Daddy said with a wink.

"Well, I haven't earned this yet," Frankie said, still holding the money out to my father.

Daddy stood up. "Yes you have, son," he said. "You've got a good heart, Frankie. Just don't do anything to make me regret letting you live with us."

"I won't," Frankie said.

"Good. And I guess you all need to go clothes shopping tomorrow." Daddy pointed to the clothes in the floor then looked at me. "Take him to Peterson's in town, Nelson. We've got an account there. You want Charity to go with you?"

"We can handle it," I answered.

"Okay. I'm going and put Sash to bed and then get a shower. You guys need to do the same when I'm done. Somebody in here forgot to put deodorant on this morning."

I quickly pointed to Frankie because I knew it wasn't me. He just shot me a cold stare which made Daddy chuckle as he left the room.

"What do you think your dad meant?" Frankie asked.

"Maybe he meant you earned it for helping us move your stuff—I don't know."

"No, I'm talking about what he said about me doing something to make him regret letting me live here."

I stood up and picked up the clothes I'd folded and set them on the bed. "Daddy said you've got a good heart. What he didn't say is that it's your head that needs some work."

Frankie got up off the floor and brought his stack of folded clothes over to the bed. "What the heck is that supposed to mean?"

"It means if you keep doing stupid things like you did yesterday, he's gonna regret letting you live here."

"Oh."

— — —

The next morning Frankie and I went to Peterson's department store in town and spent over $50 on clothes for him. We got just the basic stuff: undershirts, underwear, pajamas, socks, some new sneakers, two pair of jeans, two pair of khaki shorts, plus dress slacks and shirt for church. The one item we splurged on was a blue Izod Lacoste polo shirt. I knew Frankie liked my Izod shirts and when I saw him eyeing the Izod display at the store I figured Daddy wouldn't mind. We also went to the drugstore and got Frankie a toothbrush and other toiletries. When we got back to the house just before lunch, a delivery van from Wheaton's Furniture and Appliance was in our driveway.

"Are y'all getting some new furniture?" Frankie asked as I pulled up beside the van.

I set the handbrake and shut off the engine. "Not that I know of," I replied.

Frankie grabbed the bags from the backseat and we headed for the house. Just as we got to the back porch, the delivery man came out along with Aunt Charity.

"What'd we get?" I asked my aunt.

"It's a bed for Francis," she replied. "The two of you need to get that room cleaned out before you leave for work, Nelson."

"We will," I said. "Where do you want him to put the bed until we do?"

"Just have him take it in through the front door and put it in the living room."

Frankie put the bags from Peterson's on the back porch and then he and I watched the delivery man pull a long, tall cardboard box from the back of the van. He asked if Frankie and I would carry it in, which we did. Next came the mattress and box springs, which were individually wrapped in heavy plastic. Frankie helped him carry those in.

Aunt Charity had fixed roast beef sandwiches (from leftovers) for lunch and Frankie and I wolfed those down so we could tackle the sewing room and get it converted into his bedroom before I had to leave for work at two o'clock. Daddy had said to throw everything away except what I was unsure of, but once I started going through the boxes and saw Mama's things, I was sure he'd forgotten some of what was in that room. All those boxes went in the living room for him to go through. The old broken GE vacuum and a bunch of my old toys that were in the closet went in a pile in the backyard to be hauled to the dump, but Aunt Charity intervened and told me to box up the toys for her to take to the Masonic home for kids. Mama's Singer sewing machine went in the living room. When we finished, between the big box containing the bed, the mattress and box springs, and all the stuff from the sewing room, our living room was nearly impassible.

"It's not a very big room," I said, looking at Frankie's new bedroom, now spic and span from a top to bottom cleaning.

Frankie had just finished mopping the hardwood floor and was standing there leaning on the mop handle. "It's not that much smaller than my room at home," he said.

"Wait until we get the bed in here and your dresser," I said.

"I'm not complaining, man. I still can't believe your dad is doing all this for me—letting me live here, buying me clothes, a new bed. Who is Preston Marks?"

"Who?"

"Preston Marks. Your dad said last night he was going to see Preston Marks about getting custody of me."

"Oh. He's a lawyer. You've seen his office in town. It's right there beside the bank."

"So what's your dad gonna do, sue my dad to get custody of me?"

"I don't know how it works," I said. "Don't worry about it."

"I don't want my dad to get in trouble."

I gave Frankie a look of incredulity. "Your dad practically killed you, then he burned all your stuff, and now you don't want him to get in any trouble? Are you kidding me?" Frankie looked down and I could see I'd hurt him with my cold recitation of the chain of events that had brought us to this point. "I'm sorry," I said and put my hand on his shoulder. "I shouldn't have said it like that."

"It's okay," he said, his eyes heavy with tears. He sniffed and wiped his nose with the back of his hand. "So what's that mean if your dad gets custody of me?"

"I don't know. But I've always wondered what it would be like to have a brother," I offered. "Guess I'll find out now."

Chapter 17
My Brother's Keeper

I heard the bell ding and looked up to see Daddy's old Dodge pickup sitting out at the pumps. The Coca-Cola clock hanging over the door to the office said it was five after three, and if my father wasn't at work, something was up. I had been sweeping up oil-dry in the service bay, so I set the push broom aside and went out there.

"Where is Frankie?" Daddy asked me as I walked up to the pickup.

"At the house, I guess. Why?"

Daddy reached over and picked up some papers off the seat and handed them to me. I scanned the legal wording at the top: *In the Chancery Court of Harrison County Mississippi... Second Judicial District...In re Francis John Thompson, Jr....Ex Parte Emergency Order.*

"What is this?" I asked.

"It's an emergency order granting me legal and physical custody of Frankie. Sheriff Posey is supposed to meet me here in a minute and then he's going and serve this on Frank Thompson."

"So does this mean you're adopting Frankie?" I asked.

Daddy laughed. "No, this is just an order of custody. If Frankie's dad ever gets his act together, it can be rescinded. I want you to go home and get Frankie and bring him back here. I don't know how his dad is going to react to this, but if he comes to the house looking for his son, I don't want Frankie there. I've told Charity to take Sachet and Mary

Alice shopping and to be at the diner at six. We'll eat there, so you and Frankie meet us there when you get off work."

"If you're not buying gas, Lem," Dick yelled from the office door, "get the hell out of here and quit bothering my employee!"

I turned around to look at Dick. He had a big grin on his face. He could see, however, that Daddy wasn't laughing, so it didn't last long. Daddy waved him out to the pumps.

"What's up?" Dick asked as he stepped up beside me.

"I need you to let Nelson run home and get Frankie and then I need you to let him stay here out of sight until closing time."

"Let who stay here out of sight?"

"Frankie."

"Frankie Thompson?"

"Yes," Daddy said.

"All right," Dick said, sounding both curious and worried at the same time. "What's this all about?"

"Brother to Brother?" Daddy said.

"And no further," Dick replied.

"Frank Thompson got drunk the other night and nearly killed his son. Yesterday he pulled all of Frankie's things into their front yard and set fire to 'em. Frankie has been staying with us and today Preston Marks got me emergency custody of Frankie. Joe Posey is gonna serve the order on Frank in a few minutes and I want Frankie out of the way."

Dick turned and looked at me. "What are you waiting for? Go get him."

"I appreciate it, Dick," Daddy said. "Keep an eye out for Frank. He'll be trouble."

"If he brings his ass around here he's liable to get a load of buckshot in it."

Daddy cracked a brief smile. "You still got that old Fox double behind the counter in there?" he asked.

"Yep. And it's loaded with double-ought."

"Run on and get him, son," Daddy said to me. So I trotted over to my car and headed home to get Frankie.

When I got to the house, Aunt Charity was pulling out of her driveway with my sister and Mary Alice in the backseat of her Cadillac. I waved, but Aunt Charity didn't see me, or maybe she just wasn't used to my new car and didn't recognize it. Frankie was sitting on the front porch, apparently waiting for me. He'd changed out of my clothes and into his new Izod polo shirt and a pair of the khaki shorts we'd purchased earlier. And he had on his new sneakers.

"Hey," I said as I walked up on the porch.

"Miss Charity said your dad was coming to get me," Frankie said.

"He sent me. Do you know what's going on?"

"No."

"Daddy got the court order giving him custody of you. I think he's going with the sheriff to give a copy of the order to your dad. He wants you to come down to the station with me in case your dad flips out again and comes looking for you."

Frankie stood up. "How do I look in my new clothes?"

"You look fine. Did you hear what I just said?"

"I heard you."

"And?"

"And what? I'm tired of thinking about my dad and I don't want to talk about it, okay?"

"Okay."

"Let's go then," Frankie said as he brushed by me and down the porch steps.

— — —

The rest of that afternoon at the station was uneventful. When Dick closed up at six o'clock, I just left my car parked there and Frankie and I walked down the street to the Bobby Dean Diner. Aunt Charity's Cadillac was parked on the street, so I knew they were there. But I didn't see Daddy's pickup anywhere, which worried me.

"Where's Daddy?" I asked as I sat down at the table beside Mary Alice. We were at the same big table in the back where Daddy had had my birthday lunch. Before Aunt Charity could answer we both saw him come through the front door.

"Everybody hungry?" Daddy said as he sat down.

"How'd it go?" I asked.

"We'll talk about it later," he answered.

"I'm hungry," Frankie declared, no doubt grateful for my father's deferment of any conversation about the situation that had brought us all to the diner.

"You're always hungry," I said.

Dinner was pleasant enough as we all tried to act normal for Frankie's sake. He seemed to be the most unaffected as he consumed two hamburgers and a pile of French fries over Aunt Charity's protests. I got the chicken and dumplings and some of Bobby Dean's famous cornbread.

Even though we were surrounded by family and the patrons of the diner, I was happy to be spending some time with Mary Alice. We held hands under the table as we ate. I felt like I'd been neglecting her ever since we got back from Jackson. Though she had not been privy to any of it firsthand, Mary Alice was now fully aware of the situation with Frankie, but she and I had yet to discuss it privately.

When we got home, Daddy said he wanted to talk to Frankie alone and since Frankie's bed still needed to be assembled, the two of them were doing that now, and talking, in Frankie's room. Sachet was over at Aunt Charity's where she was going to spend the night. Mary Alice and I were on the front porch. I was in the rocker and she was in my lap.

"You know what two weeks from today is, don't you?" I whispered in her ear as we rocked back and forth.

"Yes," she replied and then added, "You're not going to start that again, are you?"

August 22 was the day Aunt Charity was supposed to return Mary Alice to the Masonic home in Poplarville. For nearly two weeks I'd managed to keep thoughts of her departure at bay, not counting the brief but nerve-racking episode with her brother. But now with that date nearly upon us, it was becoming more and more difficult to keep from thinking about it. "Did you mean what you said about coming here every weekend if I'll come get you?" I asked.

"Of course. And you know, us being away from each other during the week will be good—especially after you start back to school."

"How do you figure that?" I asked.

"It will give you a chance to meet other girls to date without having to worry about me. And on those weekends when you want to be with other girls, you can just call and let me know that you won't be picking me up that weekend."

Up until that point I'd been rocking us gently in the warmth of the early evening sunshine. But with these strange words coming from Mary Alice's mouth, I stopped the rocker. "What are you talking about?" I said in disbelief. "I don't want to be with any other girls."

"You know that's not true, Nelson."

"It is true…wait a minute. Do you want to date other boys?"

"Yes, of course. I have two boyfriends at the home in Poplarville."

"Two?" I croaked.

"Yes, and one of them is my fiancé." Mary Alice started giggling and I knew I'd been had. This was a devilishly mischievous side of her I'd not encountered before.

"That was mean," I said. I set the rocker back in motion and resumed breathing. She slapped my hand, which was resting on her lap. "Ouch," I said in a feigned whine. "That hurt."

"Want me to kiss it and make it better?" Mary Alice asked.

I didn't have to answer. She had already taken my hand in hers and moved it to her lips. Since Mary Alice had broached the topic, I decided to pursue it with a question that had more or less been in the back of my mind since the drive back from Jackson. "If we could get married, Mary Alice, would you marry me?"

I waited for an answer. Mary Alice was still holding my hand to her lips. Finally she said, "Your fingers smell like cornbread."

I let out an exasperated puff. "How romantic," I said. "Just what a guy wants to hear when he asks a girl to marry him."

Mary Alice was giggling again, teasing me, while I was trying to be serious. "Yes," she finally said, "I'll marry you."

"I'm serious," I protested.

"So am I. That's why I told Beau you would be my husband one day."

Whoa. She'd switched out of humor mode and blindsided me again. "You told him that?" I asked.

"I did."

"Why?"

"You can be so silly sometimes, Nelson."

"What do you mean?"

"You asked me why. You're being silly because you know why."

She was right. I did know why. It was the very reason I'd brought up the subject of marriage in a serious way, albeit as seriously as a sixteen-year-old could. "Because we love each other," I said.

"That's right," she said, leaning back, melting into me with her affirmation. I could only assume Mary Alice was being truthful in saying she had told her brother that we would one day be married. Evidently, he had taken her seriously, for why else would he have done such a quick turnaround regarding her relationship with me? Whatever the reason, I knew I loved her and the thought of Mary Alice as my wife made me smile inside.

These pleasant thoughts were suddenly interrupted when I saw the blue '65 Galaxie 500 belonging to Frank Thompson pull into our drive. I nudged Mary Alice. "Let me up," I said. I wanted to get her in the house quickly and tell Daddy, but then I noticed it was Frankie's mother driving the car as it came to a stop. Frankie's little brother was in the passenger seat. Mary Alice and I stood up as I watched Judy Thompson and her son get out of the car and walk up to the porch.

"Hi Miss Judy," I said to Frankie's mother. She'd been crying, and I wished I knew what had transpired earlier when Sheriff Posey took that custody order to Frankie's dad. I could only assume that was what Daddy had wanted to speak about in private with Frankie.

"Hey Nelson," Miss Judy said. Mark was at her side and he looked at me with a smile but didn't say anything.

This was an awkward moment because I was actually unsure if I should invite her in without telling Daddy first. Common courtesy finally directed my decision and I introduced her to Mary Alice and then showed her and Mark into the living room. They both sat on the sofa and I took Mary Alice to my room and asked her to wait there. I went down the hall to Frankie's room to find him and Daddy putting sheets on his new bed. I told them that Frankie's mom was here and, as I expected, Frankie ran to the living room. When Daddy and I got there, we found Judy Thompson hugging her son and crying. What I learned next surprised me, but I don't know why. Frankie's dad was in jail. When Joe Posey had served a copy of the custody order on him, he took a swing at the sheriff and got himself arrested. Now Frankie's mom was here to take him home.

"I can't let you do that," Daddy said to her.

"He's my son, Lem. He belongs at home. Frank is in jail now and Frankie needs to be at home."

"I don't want to go home, Mama," Frankie said. As he was the day his father had been sitting on the sofa where his mother was now, Frankie was jammed in beside me in the sitting chair adjacent to Daddy's recliner. Since he had lived for so long with an abusive father, it occurred to me that maybe for the first time in his life Frankie felt safe.

Miss Judy's eyes filled with tears as she digested her son's declaration. "Your daddy's not there now, Frankie," she said. "You can come home."

"Judy," my father said, "Frank will be out of jail later tonight or in the morning on bail."

"Bail?" she asked, her voice trailing off to almost a whisper. Frankie's mother had never struck me as being particularly bright, and I could see from the look of surprise on her face that she had assumed her husband was in jail and gone for good. I felt sorry for her because my father had just shattered her illusion of safety.

Daddy plucked two tissues from the box of Kleenex on the table beside his recliner. He handed those to Frankie's mom and she wiped her eyes and nose. "So what does that order mean that the sheriff left at our house?" she asked. "Are you going to keep my son from me?"

"Of course not, Judy. I'm not doing this to hurt you and you're welcome to come visit Frankie whenever you want. But your husband has to stay away from Frankie. That's part of the order. He almost strangled your son to death, Judy. Frank needs—"

"Frankie should not have gone to that motel with that man," she interrupted.

"True," Daddy said. "But you can't sit there and tell me Frank Thompson was right to choke your son over it and then just leave him there. And then he refused to let Frankie come home. And then he set fire to all of Frankie's things in your front yard. Your husband needs help, Judy."

"Frank said he didn't choke Frankie. He said that man did it."

"He did choke me, Mama," Frankie said. "He slapped me and I kept putting my hands over my face so he wouldn't hit my broke nose and then he threw me down on the bed and started choking me."

I didn't know about Daddy, but I was getting a little put out with Frankie's mom. Rather than being grateful for what my father was doing for her son, she seemed to be defending the actions of her husband. Evidently, Frankie was tired of this conversation too, because he stood up and said, "Come see my room, Mark." Frankie motioned for me to follow him and his brother down the hall.

"It's little," Mark said as we entered the room.

Frankie went over and stretched out on his new bed. "I like it," he said. Daddy and he had gotten Frankie's dresser in there and while everything was a little snug, it worked and I think Frankie really did like it.

"So you're not coming home?" Mark said.

"No," Frankie said.

"Ever?"

"I don't know."

PART FOUR

Chapter 18
A Cabin in the Woods

```
NATIONAL HURRICANE CENTER    MIAMI

ADVISORY NO. 1    1 PM EDT    THURSDAY  AUGUST 14, 1969
...TROPICAL STORM CAMILLE FORMS RAPIDLY NEAR GRAND CAYMAN IN
THE CARIBBEAN...

A NAVY RECON PLANE RECONNOITERING A TROPICAL WAVE IN THE
CARIBBEAN THIS MORNING ENCOUNTERED A RAPIDLY DEVELOPING
DEPRESSION WHICH REACHED STORM INTENSITY WHILE THE AIRCRAFT
WAS STILL IN THE AREA.

AT 1 PM EDT...1700Z...THE NEW STORM...TO BE KNOWN AS CAMILLE...WAS
LOCATED NEAR LATITUDE 19.3 NORTH...LONGITUDE 82.3 WEST. THIS
IS ABOUT 60 MILES WEST OF GRAND CAYMAN OR 480 MILES SOUTH
OF MIAMI.

CAMILLE IS MOVING WEST NORTHWESTWARD 12 TO 14 MPH WITH
STRONGEST WINDS ABOUT 60 MPH OVER A VERY SMALL AREA NEAR
THE CENTER.

CAMILLE IS EXPECTED TO MOVE ON A CURVING PATH TO THE NORTH-
WEST REACHING THE VICINITY OF THE WEST TIP OF CUBA EARLY
FRIDAY MORNING. CONDITIONS FAVOR RAPID INTENSIFICATION OF
THIS YOUNG STORM.

GALE FORCE WINDS IN SQUALLS WILL AFFECT THE ISLE OF PINES
BY MIDNIGHT AND EXTREME WEST CUBA BEFORE DAYBREAK TOMORROW.
TIDES ON THE SOUTH COAST OF CUBA WILL RANGE 3 TO 5 FEET
ABOVE NORMAL...AND HEAVY RAINS MAY AFFECT MUCH OF WEST CUBA.
THE FUTURE COURSE AND DEVELOPMENT OF CAMILLE WILL NOT BECOME
CLEAR UNTIL FURTHER RECONNAISSANCE IS COMPLETED LATER THIS
AFTERNOON. HOWEVER ALL INTERESTS IN SOUTH FLORIDA AND THE
KEYS SHOULD BE ALERT TO ADVICES LATER TODAY WHICH MAY
REQUIRE RAPID PROTECTIVE ACTION IN SOME AREAS.

REPEATING THE 1 PM EDT POSITION...19.3 NORTH...82.3 WEST.

THE NEXT ADVISORY WILL BE ISSUED BY THE NATIONAL HURRICANE
CENTER AT 6 PM EDT TODAY.

SIMPSON
```

— — —

Things had settled down and Frankie had settled in. Having a new person suddenly in your household can be quite an adjustment, but Frankie surprised us all by really trying to fit in. Rather than waiting around for someone to tell him what chores to do, he took the initiative and was always asking. He made his bed every morning and kept his room clean and picked up—things I sometimes neglected to do. I learned something else about my best friend that I never knew: he liked to cook, and he was good at it. Consequently, Aunt Charity had taken him under her wing and was routinely putting him to work in the kitchen. Daddy was pleased that Frankie seemed genuinely appreciative for being allowed to live with us. And despite Judy Thompson being assured by my father that she could come visit Frankie any time, we hadn't seen her since Friday. I figured it was because Frankie's dad wouldn't let her come see her son.

Frankie and I had begun working on the cabin in the woods down by the river we had been planning since last summer. I still had over $70 left out of the $100 I was allowed to keep as "play money" from my birthday money, so the Saturday morning after Daddy got custody of Frankie, we took the pickup down to the lumber yard and got the two-by-fours, siding, shingles, paint and other items we'd need for the construction. Based on a sketch done by Frankie (which Daddy commented was quite good), we began the construction Sunday afternoon, Aunt Charity's Sabbath objections notwithstanding. The land abutting the river there was owned by Ben May, and Daddy secured permission from him for us to build. We cleared out a spot in the woods far enough from the river bank so that, even when the Wolf was at its highest during the spring rains, our cabin would be safe. Our white sand beach would just be a short twenty yard walk through the woods from the cabin's door. Daddy helped us do the measuring and lining off to get the foundation square and level, but after that, Frankie and I owned the labor. By Thursday, we had the cabin framed up, and, with luck, we planned to have the roof and siding on it Friday, and have our first camp-out Saturday night. Thursday evening was the first time I remember hearing of a tropical storm named Camille gaining strength in the Caribbean. Daddy said he'd seen it on the news.

— — —

"Did y'all get the mail today?" Daddy asked as he walked in the back door, hung his hardhat on the coat rack, and set his lunch box on the counter. It was Friday about ten minutes before seven o'clock. Frankie was at the stove cutting up an onion into a hot iron skillet full of melting butter. Aunt Charity and I were at the table heading the shrimp that would soon be sautéed in that skillet. Mary Alice was in the living room with my sister, who was watching TV. It had been a normal day and was winding down toward a normal family dinner of shrimp, boiled new potatoes, and tossed salad. That was about to change.

"I got the mail," I said.

Daddy frowned. "What was in the box?"

"It's on the table by your recliner," I said. "Just bills it looked like."

Daddy walked over, picked up the phone, and dialed a number. We knew something was up when he asked to speak to the sheriff. "Have him call me as soon as possible," Daddy said into the receiver. "Yes, it's an emergency," he said in response to a question none of us could hear. He hung up the phone and looked at Aunt Charity. "Can you take care of this and let me talk to him?" He pointed to

Frankie who was still at the stove, cutting up the onion. After she washed the shrimp juice from her hands, Aunt Charity took Frankie's place at the stove and he and Daddy came over and sat at the table. "Do you remember what you were wearing that day you went to the motel with Bong?" he asked Frankie.

I started thinking back to that day when Frankie got in the car with Mary Alice and me to go to the Colonel Dixie. I couldn't remember what he had on. But why did Daddy want to know?

"I don't remember, Mr. Lem," Frankie said.

"Was your shirt red?" Daddy asked.

"Yes," I blurted out. Daddy's question had jarred my memory. I looked over at Frankie. "You had on that red button-down shirt that's got the black stripe over the shoulder, remember?"

"Yeah," Frankie said. "I remember now. I liked that shirt."

"Why, Daddy?" I asked.

My father frowned again and pinched his brow. "I think Frankie's clothes from that night are out there stuffed in our mail box."

Thirty minutes later dinner was on hold and Sheriff Posey was sitting at our table. Frankie's crumpled up clothes from the Dixie Pearl Motel were in an evidence bag in front of him. It was just the shirt and gray denim shorts, however. Frankie's undershirt, underwear, socks, and shoes were not in our mail box.

"What time did you get the mail out of the box today, Nelson?" the sheriff asked me.

"It was right after lunch...maybe one o'clock?"

"And the only thing in the box then was the mail?"

"Yes, sir."

"That means he was here this afternoon between one and when you got home, Lem," he said to Daddy.

Frankie, smelling of garlic and white onion, was sitting beside me. "I don't get it," he said. "Why would he bring my clothes back now?"

"Why would who bring your clothes back now?" the sheriff asked.

"Peter Bong."

"So you think Bong did this?" Sheriff Posey pointed to the bag on the table with the clothes in it.

"You don't?" Daddy asked.

The Sheriff looked at Daddy. "Why would he put this in your mail box, Lem? How would he know Frankie is staying here?"

"Good question," Daddy said.

"Has Frank Thompson been up here since he got out of jail Monday?" the sheriff asked.

"Not that I know of," Daddy said. "I'd have called you if he had. You think he put Frankie's clothes in our box?"

"I hope he did. Did either of you boys see him drive by today?"

Frankie and I both shook our heads. Neither of us had seen Frankie's dad since last Thursday at the bonfire in their front yard.

"Why do you hope it was Frank that did this?" Daddy asked.

"Because if that jaybird that took Frankie to the motel did it, things just got a whole lot more serious. I was hoping Mr. Bong would be a smart boy and be halfway back to Australia by now. No, let's hope Frank Thompson did this, because if he didn't, it means Bong is here, and he knows where Frankie is, and he's letting us know he knows."

We all sat there in silence, absorbing the import of what Sheriff Posey had just said. I glanced over at Aunt Charity in the kitchen. She was frozen in place with a wood spoon in her hand, like a mannequin display down at Peterson's. Sheriff Posey got up from the table and said he was going to talk with Frankie's dad. I could hear the theme music from *Gomer Pyle, U.S.M.C.* coming from the TV in the living room.

— — —

NATIONAL HURRICANE CENTER   MIAMI

ADVISORY NO. 6   6 PM   EDT   FRIDAY   AUGUST 15, 1969

...CAMILLE LASHING EXTREME WESTERN CUBA...

GALE WARNINGS ARE IN EFFECT AT 6 PM EDT FOR MARQUESAS KEYS AND DRY TORTUGAS.

SMALL CRAFT IN THE FLORIDA KEYS SHOULD REMAIN IN SAFE HAR-BOR AND THOSE ALONG THE FLORIDA WEST COAST FROM TAMPA SOUTH-WARD SHOULD NOT VENTURE FAR FROM SAFE HARBOR. SMALL CRAFT ON THE FLORIDA SOUTHEAST COAST SHOULD EXERCISE CAUTION.

AT 6 PM EDT HURRICANE CAMILLE WAS CENTERED NEAR LATITUDE 21.5 NORTH...LONGITUDE 84.4 WEST OR ABOUT 270 MILES SOUTH-WEST OF KEY WEST. THIS POSITION IS BASED UPON AIR FORCE RECONNAISSANCE...LAND BASED RADAR...SHIP AND ISLAND REPORTS.

CAMILLE IS MOVING TOWARD THE NORTH NORTHWEST AT 7 MPH. HIGH-EST WINDS ARE ESTIMATED 115 MPH NEAR THE CENTER WITH GALES EXTENDING OUT 125 TO 150 MILES TO THE NORTH OF THE CENTER AND 50 MILES TO THE SOUTH.

HURRICANE CONDITIONS ARE EXPECTED SHORTLY OVER THE EXTREME WESTERN TIP OF CUBA AS TIDES RANGE UP TO 8 FEET AND HEAVY PRECIPITATION EXPECTED TO CAUSE LOCAL FLOODING. ALTHOUGH GALE WINDS IN SQUALLS MAY OCCUR OVER PORTIONS OF EXTREME SOUTH FLORIDA TONIGHT...SUSTAINED GALES IN THE EXTREME WESTERN KEYS ARE NOT EXPECTED UNTIL EARLY SATURDAY.

IT IS EXPECTED THAT CAMILLE WILL ENTER THE GULF OF MEXICO EARLY SATURDAY MORNING AND PROCEED ON A NORTHERLY COURSE OVER THE EASTERN GULF AT A SLIGHTLY INCREASED FORWARD SPEED. WHILE A LITTLE DECREASE IN INTENSITY IS EXPECTED AS THE HUR-

RICANE CROSSES CUBA...CAMILLE SHOULD REGAIN MAXIMUM WINDS
OF 115 MPH IN THE GULF OF MEXICO.

ALL INTERESTS ALONG THE EASTERN GULF OF MEXICO SHOULD REMAIN
IN CLOSE TOUCH WITH ALL FUTURE ADVISORIES AND BULLETINS.
REPEATING   THE   6   PM   EDT   POSITION...LATITUDE   21.5
NORTH...LONGITUDE 84.4 WEST.

THE NEXT ADVISORY WILL BE ISSUED BY THE NATIONAL HURRICANE
CENTER AT MIDNIGHT EDT WITH AN INTERMEDIATE BULLETIN AT 9
PM.

HOPE

— — —

At ten o'clock that Friday night, the tension level was high
in our house.   Sheriff Posey had confronted Frank
Thompson earlier about the clothes in our mail box and, as
expected, he said he didn't know what the sheriff was talking about. This left two possibilities: Frankie's dad was a
liar (which we already knew to be true) and was just playing
mind games with his son, or Peter Bong had returned to
Bells Ferry to terrorize Frankie and, we feared, exact
revenge for Frankie's reporting of what had transpired in
that motel room.

I was lying in bed, reading the owner's manual for my
new Browning Sweet Sixteen, and thinking on these things.
The house was quiet except for the fan going on my dresser
and the muted music I could hear coming from Frankie's
room. He'd bought a transistor radio earlier in the week
using some of his allowance money. Daddy had asked Aunt
Charity to keep Sachet at her house tonight. Nothing was
said openly about the reason, but I suspected it was because
my father was worried Bong would pay us a visit in the middle of the night.

I thought Daddy was in bed asleep until I heard the soft
knock on my door and he opened it.

"What's up?" I asked as I laid the booklet on my chest.

Daddy was standing there in his pajamas and slippers. "I'm glad you're still up. I want to talk to you and Frankie. Let me go get him."

I sat up in the bed and waited until Daddy appeared back at the door with Frankie behind him. Frankie was shirtless, in his pajama bottoms, and had a scolded puppy dog look on his face. Daddy sat down at my desk and Frankie just stood by the door with his head down. I glanced at Daddy, then nodded my head in Frankie's direction with a questioning furrow on my brow.

Daddy shrugged and said, "Sit down, Frankie." He pointed to the chair over by my dresser.

Frankie didn't move. Still looking down, he said, "I'm sorry, Mr. Lem. I won't play it loud like that again."

"What?" Daddy asked. He looked at me and it was my turn to shrug.

"I didn't mean to have my radio that loud," Frankie said.

Daddy cracked a little smile and shook his head. "Is that why you think I called you in here, son?"

Frankie looked up. "Yes, sir."

"Frankie, I wasn't paying one bit of attention to your radio. I didn't call you in here to fuss at you. I think Nelson will tell you, I don't do much fussing. If you're doing something I'm not happy with, I'll tell you about it and that's that."

The relief sweeping Frankie's face was clear. Instead of sitting in the chair by my dresser, he made a beeline for my bed, climbed over me, and took the spot that used to be his when he'd spend the night.

"What'd you want to talk about, Daddy?" I asked.

"I'm thinking about sending you boys, and your aunt, your sister, and Mary Alice, to stay with your grandma over in Picayune until they catch this Bong guy."

"Daddy, don't do that," I protested.

"I know you don't get along with your grandmother, son, but I have to think about everyone's safety here."

I was about to say something else when we heard a crack, then another, from outside my window in the front yard. It sounded like M80s going off. Then there was shouting.

"What was that?" Frankie said.

"Gunshots," Daddy replied. He immediately jumped up and switched off the lamp beside my bed. "Stay here," he ordered and then ran to his room, to get his gun I was sure.

"You think it's Peter Bong?" Frankie asked. I could hear the fear in his voice. Just enough light came through my door from the hallway for me to see how scared he was. I heard Daddy coming back down the hall from his room, and sure enough, as he passed my doorway, I saw the glint of the nickel plated Smith & Wesson in his hand. Then there was loud banging at the front door.

"If that's Peter Bong," I said, "he's about to get shot." The words had no more left my mouth when I heard some-one hollering Daddy's name from the front porch.

"I don't think that's Peter," Frankie said. Then we heard voices coming from the living room.

"Nelson," Daddy said loudly from down the hall, "you and Frankie come here."

Frankie and I scrambled out of the bed and sprinted down the hall to the living room. Daddy was standing there with Sheriff Posey who had his .45 in one hand and a pair of white briefs in the other.

"Are these yours?" he asked, holding the underwear out to Frankie.

Frankie took the briefs and looked at them. "They look like mine. Did you shoot him?"

"Who?" the sheriff said.

"Peter Bong."

Sheriff Posey motioned for Frankie to hand him back the underwear, which he did. "It wasn't Bong out there, son, it was your father."

"Daddy?" Frankie said, bewildered. "Did you shoot him?"

"No, but I scared the shit out of him. He's handcuffed in the backseat of my car now."

"So it was Frank who put the clothes in the mail box?" Daddy asked.

"Looks that way," the sheriff said. "I decided to come up here after it got dark and watch and see if Bong would show up. I parked over yonder in Charity's driveway and then, about ten minutes ago, I see a pickup go by with just the parking lights on. It stopped just past y'all's drive and that's when I got out and made my way over here. I waited, and, sure enough, here comes someone straight up to the house carrying these drawers." He held up the underwear for emphasis. "It looked like he was gonna put 'em on the front porch, so I pulled out my gun and let off a round into the air. He took off running, so I let off another, and hollered for him to hit the ground. Imagine my surprise when I get over to him with my flashlight and see it ain't Bong but Frank Thompson."

"So how did Frank wind up with his son's clothes from that night?" Daddy asked.

"He hasn't told me yet, but I suspect it's just like I thought: he found 'em laying outside the room and picked 'em up."

"And what about Bong? You still think he's long gone?"

"I do, Lem. I think he wised up that night, hit the road on that motorbike, and never looked back. He knew what we'd do to him around here if we caught him."

I felt relieved at the thought that this whole deal had been Frankie's dad playing a sick prank, rather than a pervert seeking revenge on Frankie. Judging from the look on Frankie's face, he did too—though I couldn't imagine what he must have been thinking after finding out it was his own father trying to terrorize him with memories of that night. No wonder he didn't want to go home.

"I appreciate you lookin' out for us, Joe," Daddy said and stuck his hand out.

The sheriff holstered his .45 and then shook Daddy's hand. "Well, let me haul Frank down to the station and see if I can't get some kind of statement out of him. He's drunk off his ass, so it probably won't be much tonight."

"Are you gonna keep him in jail?" Frankie asked.

"Just tonight, until he sobers up. I'll let him out in the morning." Frankie frowned and Sheriff Posey said, "Don't worry, son. I think your daddy learned his lesson tonight. I wasn't joking when I said I scared the shit out of him. The first thing he's gonna have to do when I get him to the jail is take a shower and put an inmate jumpsuit on. And I'll have to leave the windows down on my car for the next few days to get the stink out." With a wink and a grin, the sheriff headed for the door, then turned back. "Have y'all heard about that hurricane...Camille?"

"I saw something about it on the ten o'clock news," Daddy said, pointing to the TV. "It's down by Cuba."

"Yeah, but I heard some talk around the station earlier that it might be coming up this way. Anyhow, y'all can get a good night's sleep now."

— — —

NEW ORLEANS

ADVISORY NO. 10   11 AM CDT   SATURDAY AUGUST 16, 1969
...CAMILLE...SMALL BUT DANGEROUS...THREATENS THE NORTHWEST FLORI-
DA COAST...

THE WEATHER BUREAU HAS ISSUED HURRICANE WARNINGS ON THE
NORTHWEST FLORIDA COAST FROM FORT WALTON TO ST. MARKS AND
GALE WARNINGS ELSEWHERE FROM PENSACOLA TO CEDAR KEY EFFEC-
TIVE AT 11 AM CDT. PREPARATION FOR HURRICANE FORCE WINDS
AND 5 TO 10 FOOT TIDES IN THE AREA FROM FORT WALTON TO ST.
MARKS SHOULD BE STARTED IMMEDIATELY AND COMPLETED TONIGHT.

ALL INTERESTS ALONG THE NORTHEASTERN GULF COAST ARE URGED
TO LISTEN FOR FURTHER RELEASES.

GALE WARNING WILL REMAIN IN EFFECT AT DRY TORTUGAS UNTIL
WINDS AND SEAS SUBSIDE LATER TODAY.

AT 1100 CDT...1600Z...HURRICANE CAMILLE WAS CENTERED NEAR LAT-
ITUDE 24.5 NORTH...LONGITUDE 86.0 WEST...OR ABOUT 380 MILES
SOUTH OF PANAMA CITY FLORIDA AND IT IS MOVING NORTH NORTH-
WEST ABOUT 10 MPH.

CAMILLE IS EXPECTED TO CONTINUE THIS MOVEMENT TODAY WITH A
GRADUAL TURN TO THE NORTH TONIGHT. A SLIGHT INCREASE IN
SPEED IS LIKELY TONIGHT AND SUNDAY.

HIGHEST WINDS ARE ESTIMATED 115 MPH NEAR THE CENTER. HUR-
RICANE FORCE WINDS EXTEND OUT ABOUT 40 MILES FROM THE CEN-
TER AND GALES EXTEND OUT ABOUT 150 MILES FROM THE CENTER.
CONDITIONS ARE FAVORABLE FOR SOME FURTHER INCREASE IN
INTENSITY TODAY.

REPEATING THE 11 AM POSITION...24.5 NORTH...86.0 WEST.

THE NEXT ADVISORY WILL BE ISSUED BY THE NEW ORLEANS WEATH-
ER BUREAU AT 5 PM CDT AND BULLETINS AT 1 AND 3 PM CDT.

CONNER

— — —

Saturday morning after breakfast, Frankie and I worked hard to finish up the cabin down at the river. Daddy bought a door for us and helped us frame and square it and get it installed. We used sheets of Plexiglas, framed, to cover the two small windows on the sides. When completed, the cabin was ten by twelve, roughly equivalent to a good-sized camping tent. And, with a proper door, we could keep it closed up without worry about snakes getting in it. We planned to paint the outside after lunch and then camp out in it that night.

When we got back to the house for lunch, I was surprised to see Aunt Charity had the charcoal grill going in the back yard under the big pecan tree. It was to be an outdoor lunch, for she had the picnic table covered with a red and white check table cloth. While hamburgers from the Colonel Dixie or McDonalds were anathema to my aunt (she did, however, tolerate us eating the ones at Bobby Dean's Diner), she would occasionally have the butcher down at the IGA grind up a sirloin tip, and treat us to what she considered "wholesome" hamburgers. Today was such an occasion. As I watched my aunt place her carefully formed patties on the grill, I thought back to those giant Jeff Davis burgers at The Magnolia Club up in Jackson and wondered what her assessment of those $10 monsters would have been.

Since Frankie had become our Junior Chef in Residence, he immediately took over the tending of the burgers once Aunt Charity got them on the grill. With a can of Coke in hand, I sidled up beside him at the grill and said, "I never knew you liked to cook so much. How come I never saw you doing any of this at your house?"

"Because my dad would never let me," Frankie said, turning one of the burgers that was over a hot spot. "He says cooking is women's work."

I bit my tongue and resisted telling Frankie the opinion of his dad I'd come to form over the past ten days.

"Nelson," Aunt Charity called to me from the back porch. "Come get these buns and put them on the table and help Mary Alice out there."

I went and got the platter of steaming hot buns, walked Mary Alice over to the picnic table, and got her situated. I had to stop and stare at her for a moment because she just looked so good sitting there, the sun streaming through the canopy of pecan leaves above us, making her hair and skin radiant. I leaned down and kissed her on the cheek, inhaled the scent of her hair and skin, and said, "Hey, pretty girl."

"If y'all are gonna make out, do it somewhere else," Frankie hollered from over at the grill.

Mary Alice blushed, but I heard her giggle a little too. I shot Frankie a bird and he laughed as he started scooping the burgers off the grill and onto a platter. "These are done," he declared.

When we all sat down to eat, a breeze picked up and was whipping the corners of the table cloth. Daddy asked Sachet to say grace, but Frankie surprised us all by asking if he could say the prayer, something he had not done since moving in.

"Of course," Daddy said. My sister immediately went into pout mode but she didn't say anything. We all bowed our heads and Frankie prayed:

"Dear God, thank you for the Godys and giving me a new home. Thank you for my best friend. Thank you for this food. Please watch over my mom and brother and help my dad. Amen."

That Frankie was a Baptist was easily apparent from his first person prayer in the company of others, but his simple supplication touched us all, especially Aunt Charity. When I looked up, I could see her eyes moist with tears. She reached over, put her hand on Frankie's, and smiled at him. Daddy even seemed to be a little choked up. Sachet just sat there pouting, but Daddy gave her a little poke in the ribs which elicited a flinch and a reluctant giggle.

— — —

NEW ORLEANS

ADVISORY NO. 12   11 PM CDT   SATURDAY   AUGUST 16, 1969
...CAMILLE...EXTREMELY DANGEROUS...THREATENS THE NORTHWEST FLORI-
DA COAST...

HURRICANE WARNINGS ARE IN EFFECT ON THE NORTHWEST FLORIDA
COAST FROM FORT WALTON TO ST. MARKS AND GALE WARNINGS ELSE-
WHERE FROM PENSACOLA TO CEDAR KEY.   PREPARATIONS AGAINST
THIS DANGEROUS HURRICANE SHOULD BE COMPLETED SUNDAY MORN-
ING.   A HURRICANE WATCH IS IN EFFECT WEST OF FORT WALTON TO
BILOXI.

WINDS WILL INCREASE AND TIDES WILL START TO RISE ALONG THE
NORTHEASTERN GULF COAST SUNDAY.   GALES SHOULD BEGIN IN THE
WARNING AREA SUNDAY AND REACH HURRICANE FORCE IN THE FORT
WALTON ST. MARKS AREAS SUNDAY AFTERNOON OR SUNDAY NIGHT.
TIDES UP TO 15 FEET ARE EXPECTED IN THE AREA WHERE THE CEN-
TER CROSSES THE COAST.   ALL INTERESTS ALONG THE NORTHEAST-
ERN GULF COAST ARE URGED TO LISTEN FOR LATER RELEASES.

AT 11 PM CDT...0400Z...HURRICANE CAMILLE WAS LOCATED NEAR LAT-
ITUDE 25.8 NORTH...LONGITUDE 87.4 WEST...OR ABOUT 325 MILES
SOUTH OF PENSACOLA FLORIDA.   CAMILLE WAS MOVING NORTH NORTH-
WESTWARD ABOUT 12 MPH.   A CHANGE TO A MORE NORTHERLY COURSE
IS INDICATED WITH LITTLE CHANGE IN FORWARD SPEED.

HIGHEST WINDS ARE ESTIMATED 160 MPH NEAR THE CENTER.   HUR-
RICANE FORCE WINDS EXTEND OUTWARD 50 MILES AND GALES EXTEND
OUTWARD 150 MILES FROM THE CENTER.   CAMILLE IS EXPECTED TO
CHANGE LITTLE IN INTENSITY DURING THE NEXT 12 HOURS.

SMALL CRAFT FROM PENSACOLA TO CEDAR KEY SHOULD SEEK HAR-
BOR...AND SMALL CRAFT ON THE ALABAMA...MISSISSIPPI AND SOUTH-
EAST LOUISIANA COASTS SHOULD NOT VENTURE FAR FROM SHORE.

REPEATING THE 11 PM POSITION…25.8 NORTH…87.4 WEST.

THE NEXT ADVISORY WILL BE ISSUED BY THE NEW ORLEANS WEATH-
ER BUREAU AT 5 AM AND BULLETINS AT 1 AND 3 AM CDT.

SLOAN

— — —

At eleven o'clock that night, Frankie and I were lying on my fully opened sleeping bag on the floor of our new cabin. It was hot and muggy, so we'd both stripped down to just our underwear, and I was beginning to wonder if this had been such a good idea. At least we hadn't been plagued by mosquitoes—yet. The gas-fired camping lantern was hissing over in the corner filling the single room with its brilliant white light. The smell of the fresh brown paint on the outside had been overwhelming on the inside at first, but we'd gotten used to it. Frankie had brought his transistor radio, and we were listening to that and talking. We stopped talking when the bulletin about Hurricane Camille broke into the middle of "Sugar Sugar" by The Archies.

"One hundred sixty mile an hour winds," Frankie said, echoing the voice coming from the tiny speaker of his radio.

"Yeah, but it's gonna hit Florida," I offered.

"Then why is there a hurricane watch all the way to Biloxi?"

"I don't know, but he said it was gonna hit around Ft. Walton."

"Do you remember Betsy, when we were little?" Frankie asked.

"It was four years ago, Frankie. We were twelve. We weren't little."

"Whatever. I don't think Betsy had winds that high."

"Betsy hit Louisiana," I said. "We just got a lot of rain and a little wind here. If this hurricane hits all the way over in Florida, it'll be the same thing this time."

"They don't know where it's gonna hit. They're just guessing."

I didn't want to keep talking about this hurricane. "Guess what Mary Alice and I have talked about doing," I said.

Frankie leaned up on his elbow and looked at me. "Having sex," he said with a lascivious grin.

"Oh, good grief, Frankie. Is that all you think about?"

"Don't tell me you haven't thought about doing it with her. I bet you beat your meat every night thinking about it."

Frankie had me there, but discussing my intimate thoughts and actions regarding Mary Alice with him seemed to violate some unspoken commitment that lay inside me somewhere. "We talked about getting married," I said.

"Married?" Frankie scoffed. "You just turned sixteen. And how old is she? Fourteen? Fifteen? Y'all can't get married."

"I'm not talking about getting married tomorrow, idiot." I looked over at Frankie. He had a strange look on his face. "What is it?" I asked.

"Did you hear something?"

"Don't even try that," I said. I hadn't heard a thing and I wasn't going to fall for Frankie's attempt to bait me into getting scared.

"I'm not kidding. I heard—" He stopped because we both heard the noise from outside. Frankie reached over and switched off the radio. There was no breeze blowing. The insects were noisy, but this sounded like something crunching the undergrowth as it moved around outside the cabin. I looked up at the Plexiglas windows, but because the camping lantern was so bright, the windows just looked black; I couldn't see anything outside. Frankie pointed over to my old knapsack. "You didn't bring a gun, did you?" he whispered.

"No," I whispered back.

The door knob rattling made us both jump and I felt a surge in my chest as my breathing increased. The door was locked, but it wouldn't take much to just kick it open. I knew Frankie was thinking the same thing I was: Peter Bong. We waited, hoping that whoever was out there would just go away, but the door knob rattled again. I reached over for my khaki shorts to get my pocket knife. It was the only weapon I had. Just as my hand went into the pocket, we heard the voice from the other side of the door: "Nelson, let me in."

It was Daddy. Frankie and I both fell on our backs and started breathing again. After a couple of seconds I leaned up and twisted the lock on the door knob and opened the door. I hadn't realized just how hot and stuffy it had gotten in the small cabin until the rush of night air swept in around us. Daddy was standing there with a flashlight in his hand—and his Smith & Wesson revolver tucked inside the waistband of his trousers.

"You boys get dressed," he ordered.

I started slipping my shorts on as Frankie reached for his tee shirt. "What's wrong?" I asked.

"Just get dressed. I'll tell you on the way back to the house."

Chapter 19
Something Wicked This Way Comes

What my father had to tell us was Uncle Rick had called him at ten o'clock that night to say that one of the NASA meteorologists at MTF was convinced the northerly turn the National Hurricane Center had been expecting for Camille was not going to happen, and the hurricane was going to hit much further west than they were predicting. Not Florida at all. Probably not even Alabama. He thought it was going to hit Mississippi. And with 160 mile per hour winds and an expected 15 foot storm surge, the destruction along the coast was going to be extensive.

The people at MTF were taking this man's predictions seriously enough that they had told everyone to report in at 6 A.M. to secure the facility for the incoming hurricane. Uncle Rick said all the main buildings on the site had been constructed to withstand 200 mile per hour winds. After he got my grandmother squared away at her house in Picayune, he intended to ride out the storm at his office. His recommendation to Daddy was we should start preparing for the worst, come first light.

When Daddy woke Frankie and me a little before six Sunday morning, we found out just how good a forecaster the guy at NASA really was. The 5 A.M. advisory on Camille had stated the storm had shifted "a little westward," and the hurricane warnings had been extended all the way to Biloxi and watches all the way to New Orleans. It was a little before seven now. Frankie was over at the stove scrambling eggs, I was sitting at the table, and Daddy was on the phone with Aunt Charity. He told her we would not be going to church today and for her to stay at her house and fix breakfast for herself, Mary Alice, and my sister. He filled her in on what Uncle Rick had to say about Camille and told her she should start getting her potted plants off the porch and the patio. He said we would take care of the big things like her patio furniture and lawn chairs. After he hung up with my aunt, Daddy called Dale Pitts, the guy that ran the lumber yard, and persuaded him to open up on a Sunday morning. "Trust me," Daddy said, "you will sell every piece of plywood you've got today and I'll be your first customer." Next, Daddy called the Chairman of the Board of Deacons at church and told him to get the other deacons together with pickups and trailers and be at the lumber yard by eight to get plywood to board up all the windows at the church, especially the stained glass ones in the sanctuary. As the Clerk of the Session, and the senior elder, he also told Mr. Jake he was canceling services today, and the deacons should call all the families on their respective diaconate lists and let them know.

After breakfast, we headed to the lumber yard. Frankie and I were now sitting beside Daddy in the cab of his pickup as we bounced down the road. Daddy's truck really needed new shocks. I looked out the window at the gray morning sky. It wasn't very ominous looking and there was hardly any wind at all—certainly nothing to portend the storm of the century bearing down on us. We had the trailer in tow too because Daddy was intent on getting enough plywood to board up every window in our house as well as Aunt Charity's.

"What about nails?" I asked. "Is the hardware store gonna be open today?"

"I don't know," Daddy said. "But I checked before we left and we've got plenty of nails."

"Why do we need to board up the windows?" Frankie asked. "We're a long way from the coast."

"We're not as far as you think," Daddy said. "As the crow flies, we're no more than fifteen miles inland. If that thing hits the coast with 160 mile an hour winds, we could see 130 here."

"I want to go down to the cabin when we get back and get my radio," Frankie said. In our rush to get dressed and leave the cabin last night with Daddy, Frankie had left his new transistor radio behind and I had left my sleeping bag.

"You can worry about getting that later," Daddy said. "Right now, I need you helping us get ready for this storm."

"Yes, sir," Frankie said, a little dejected.

Main Street in Bells Ferry was deserted, as was to be expected at eight o'clock on a Sunday morning. Mr. Pitts had just opened up the gate at the lumber yard outside of town when we got there. We loaded up the bed of the pick-up and the trailer with plywood and headed back to the house. Once there, Daddy set me to work with a tape meas-ure, pencil, and pad. My job was to measure every window in our house and my aunt's house. Daddy set the saw hors-es up by the barn and was cutting the plywood to my meas-urements. He told me to measure twice before writing any-thing down because we didn't have any wood to spare. He had Frankie over at Aunt Charity's carrying her patio furni-ture, and the chairs on the front porch, into her garage.

— — —

NEW ORLEANS

ADVISORY NO. 14   9 AM CDT   SUNDAY   AUGUST 17, 1969

...CAMILLE...EXTREMELY DANGEROUS...CONTINUES TO MOVE TOWARD THE MOUTH OF THE MISSISSIPPI RIVER...WARNINGS EXTENDED TO NEW ORLEANS AND GRAND ISLE...

HURRICANE WARNINGS HAVE BEEN EXTENDED WESTWARD TO INCLUDE ALL OF THE MISSISSIPPI COAST AND SOUTHEASTERN LOUISIANA AS FAR WEST AS NEW ORLEANS AND GRAND ISLE.

GALE WARNINGS HAVE BEEN EXTENDED WESTWARD TO MORGAN CITY LOUISIANA. HURRICANE WARNINGS ARE NOW IN EFFECT FROM NEW ORLEANS AND GRAND ISLE LOUISIANA EASTWARD ACROSS THE MIS-SISSIPPI...ALABAMA...AND...NORTHWEST FLORIDA COAST TO ST. MARKS. GALE WARNINGS ARE NOW IN EFFECT ELSEWHERE FROM MORGAN CITY TO CEDAR KEYS FLORIDA. PREPARATIONS AGAINST THIS EXTREME-LY DANGEROUS HURRICANE SHOULD BE COMPLETED WITHIN THE NEXT FEW HOURS.

WINDS ARE INCREASING AND TIDES ARE RISING ALONG THE NORTH-ERN GULF COAST FROM GRAND ISLE EASTWARD. GALES HAVE BEGUN A SHORT DISTANCE OFF SHORE AND WILL BE SPREADING INLAND OVER THE WARNING AREA TODAY AND WILL REACH HURRICANE FORCE FROM SOUTHEAST LOUISIANA ACROSS COASTAL MISSISSIPPI...ALABAMA...AND EXTREME NORTHWEST FLORIDA BY LATE THIS AFTERNOON OR EARLY TONIGHT. TIDES UP TO 15 FEET ARE EXPECTED IN THE AREA WHERE THE CENTER CROSSES THE COAST AND TIDES OF 5 TO 12 FEET ELSE-WHERE IN THE HURRICANE WARNING AREA. EVACUATION OF THE LOW LYING AREA THAT WOULD BE AFFECTED BY THESE TIDES SHOULD BE DONE AS EARLY AS POSSIBLE TODAY BEFORE ESCAPE ROUTES ARE CLOSED. PRESENT INDICATIONS ARE THAT THE CENTER OF CAMILLE WILL PASS CLOSE TO THE MOUTH OF THE MISSISSIPPI RIVER LATE THIS AFTERNOON AND MOVE INLAND ON THE MISSISSIPPI COAST TONIGHT.

ALL INTERESTS ALONG THE NORTHEASTERN GULF COAST ARE URGED TO LISTEN FOR LATER RELEASES AND TAKE ALL NECESSARY HURRI-CANE PRECAUTIONS IMMEDIATELY.

AT 9 AM CDT...HURRICANE CAMILLE WAS LOCATED NEAR LATITUDE 27.4 NORTH...LONGITUDE 88.4 WEST...OR ABOUT 200 MILES SOUTHEAST OF NEW ORLEANS. CAMILLE WAS MOVING ON NORTH NORTHWEST COURSE AT ABOUT 12 MPH. A CHANGE TO A SLIGHTLY MORE NORTHERLY COURSE IS LIKELY AS THE CENTER APPROACHES THE COAST.

HIGHEST WINDS ARE ESTIMATED 160 MPH NEAR THE CENTER. HUR-RICANE FORCE WINDS EXTEND OUTWARD 50 MILES AND GALES EXTEND OUTWARD 150 MILES FROM THE CENTER. CAMILLE IS EXPECTED TO CHANGE LITTLE IN INTENSITY DURING THE NEXT 12 HOURS.

SMALL CRAFT ON THE LOUISIANA...MISSISSIPPI...ALABAMA...FLORIDA COAST NORTH OF CEDAR KEYS SHOULD REMAIN IN PORT.

THE THREAT TO THE FLORIDA COAST IS DECREASING AND WARNINGS
WILL PROBABLY BE DISCONTINUED FOR PART OF THAT AREA LATER
TODAY.

CAMILLE IS NOW UNDER THE SURVEILLANCE OF RADARS AT NEW
ORLEANS...PENSACOLA AND APALACHICOLA.

REPEATING THE 9 AM POSITION...27.4 NORTH...88.4 WEST.

THE NEXT ADVISORY WILL BE ISSUED BY THE NEW ORLEANS WEATH-
ER BUREAU AT 11 AM AND BULLETINS AT 1 AND 3 PM CDT.

HILL

— — —

By 10:30 we had finished boarding up all the windows on our house and were working on the front windows at Aunt Charity's when she came out on the front porch and brought us all glasses of iced tea. She also brought the news from the nine o'clock advisory from the weather bureau: Hurricane Camille was just 200 miles from New Orleans and hurricane warnings had been extended all the way to that city. They were now calling for the storm to come ashore on the Mississippi coast.

Daddy took a sip of tea and said, "The hurricane center in Miami ought to hire that guy from NASA and double his salary."

"Why?" Frankie asked.

"Because, according to my brother, this is exactly what he was predicting last night when the official forecasts were still calling for the storm to hit Florida." Daddy took another long sip of tea and then looked up at the tall pine trees that filled Aunt Charity's front yard. "I'm glad these are all on the west side of the house," he said.

"How come?" I said, looking up at the trees. For the first time I noticed the breeze had picked up a little and the overcast sky was growing darker.

"If Camille hits anywhere from Pascagoula to New Orleans, the winds are going to be out of the east or southeast. If these trees go on the front side of the storm, they'll be falling away from the house instead of on it." Daddy turned to look at the big pecan tree in our back yard. "That one worries me," he said, holding out his glass of tea toward the tree.

"I thought that tree was over sixty years old," I said. "Don't you think it'll be all right?"

"Pecan trees don't take wind too good. If that one goes from easterly winds, it will fall right on our house. The back side of the storm will bring the winds in out of the west, and that's when we will have to worry about these pines— though the winds won't be as strong on the back side."

We finished our iced tea and got back to work. About 11:30, the smells coming from Aunt Charity's kitchen were getting our attention and we knew she was preparing something good for lunch.

"What about the sliding glass doors?" I asked as we finished nailing the plywood to the last window on the back of Aunt Charity's house.

"That's double-paned, tempered glass," Daddy said. "We'll just tape that up good."

"Are we gonna put the cars in the barn?"

"I haven't decided yet."

A little after one o'clock we had finished lunch (spaghetti and meat balls), and were taking a short break before heading back over to our house to get all of the loose yard items up and into the barn. When my father had earlier pointed out various things that needed securing, it made me realize how your perspective has to change when it comes to simple things, like a dog food bowl or a trash can, when there is the threat of 130 mile an hour winds approaching. I think Bear could sense the coming storm because he was unusually clingy the whole time we were boarding up the windows. He'd stay right with us, lying at our feet and getting in the way until Daddy would make him move; then he would only go a few feet and plop back down.

I was about to get up from the sofa, where I was sitting beside Mary Alice, to turn the TV on when the phone rang. Daddy was leaning back in the recliner in Aunt Charity's den with his eyes closed. He looked asleep. As I stared out the sliding glass doors into the back yard, the sky for the first time was beginning to look stormy. And the wind was definitely picking up.

"Lem, it's your brother on the phone," Aunt Charity said from the doorway. Unlike at our house, where we only had the one phone on the wall in the kitchen, Aunt Charity had a phone in the kitchen, in the den, and in her bedroom.

Daddy reached over and picked up the gold Trimline phone on the table beside him. "Hey, Rick," he said into the receiver. "Yeah, we've got all the windows boarded up...yep." There was a long pause while he listened to what Uncle Rick was saying. I didn't like the look on his face. "How low?" he asked. Another long pause. "That's unbelievable...right...I don't know, we'll have to decide...right. If you hear anything else, let us know...right. You're gonna check on Mother...good. Okay, Rick. Thanks for calling. I guess we'll see you when this is all over...I love you too, brother. Bye." Daddy hung up the phone and told me to go in the kitchen and get Aunt Charity and Frankie.

"What is it?" I asked. "What'd Uncle Rick say?"

"Just go get them and I'll tell you all."

So I got up and went to the kitchen and brought my aunt and Frankie back to the den.

"Where is Sachet?" Daddy asked as I sat back on the sofa with Mary Alice. Aunt Charity sat in her rocker by the fire place and Frankie fell on the sofa beside me.

"She's in my room taking a nap," Aunt Charity answered.

"Good," Daddy said. "I don't want her to hear this and get scared."

"Hear what, Lem?" Aunt Charity said, her voice laced with worry.

Mary Alice reached over for me to take her hand, which I did. My father may have been worried about scaring my sister when he should have been worried about scarring us, too.

Daddy cleared his throat. "This hurricane is a lot worse than what anyone knows right now. Rick just got a briefing from their meteorologist at MTF, who had just gotten the latest data in from the last recon flight into Camille. They are analyzing the data now and it won't be public until the next advisory at three o'clock. The hurricane is about 150 miles from shore and is making straight for Mississippi. Rick said the official report at three is going to say the wind speed is now up to 190 miles per hour, but their guy thinks that's a conservative estimate based on how low the central pressure of the storm is. The recon plane measured the pressure at 26.61 inches. He said they've never measured a hurricane with pressure that low in the eye."

Daddy said all this as if he understood what it meant. I didn't, and judging from the look on Aunt Charity's face, neither did she.

"So, the lower the pressure, the more strong the storm?" Frankie asked.

"That's right," Daddy said.

"So what does that mean, Lem?" my aunt asked.

"You remember how bad southeast Louisiana looked after Betsy went through?"

"Yes."

"Rick said the lowest central pressure recorded in Betsy was 27.8 inches. Camille is at 26.6 and they don't expect it to weaken. The NASA guy thinks Camille will be packing 200 mile per hour winds and 230 mile per hour gusts. We could be looking at 160 mile per hour winds here easy. We've got to decide if we're going to ride it out, or pack up and head north."

— — —

NEW ORLEANS

SPECIAL ADVISORY NO. 16   3 PM CDT   SUNDAY   AUGUST 17, 1969

...CAMILLE...EXTREMELY DANGEROUS...CENTER NEAR THE MOUTH OF THE MISSISSIPPI RIVER...BEARING DOWN ON MISSISSIPPI ALABAMA COAST...

HURRICANE WARNINGS ARE IN EFFECT FROM NEW ORLEANS AND GRAND ISLE LOUISIANA EASTWARD ACROSS THE MISSISSIPPI...ALABAMA...AND NORTHWEST FLORIDA COAST TO APALACHICOLA. GALE WARNINGS ARE IN EFFECT FROM MORGAN CITY TO GRAND ISLE. PREPARATIONS AGAINST THIS EXTREMELY DANGEROUS HURRICANE SHOULD BE COMPLETED BEFORE DARK. DISCONTINUE WARNINGS EAST OF APALACHICOLA.

WINDS ARE INCREASING AND TIDES ARE RISING ALONG THE NORTHERN GULF COAST FROM GRAND ISLE EASTWARD. WINDS AT THE MOUTH OF THE MISSISSIPPI RIVER ARE NOW NEAR HURRICANE FORCE. GALES IN SQUALLS ARE SPREADING INLAND OVER THE WARNING AREA AND WINDS WILL REACH HURRICANE STRENGTH FOR OVER MUCH OF THE AREA FROM SOUTHEAST LOUISIANA ACROSS COASTAL MISSISSIPPI...ALABAMA...AND INTO EXTREME NORTHWEST FLORIDA LATER THIS AFTERNOON OR BY EARLY TONIGHT. THE FOLLOWING TIDES ARE EXPECTED TONIGHT AS CAMILLE MOVES INLAND...MISSISSIPPI COAST GULFPORT TO PASCAGOULA 15 TO 20 FEET...PASCAGOULA TO MOBILE 10 TO 15 FEET...EAST OF MOBILE TO PENSACOLA 6 TO 10 FEET. ELSEWHERE IN THE AREA OF HURRICANE DISPLAY EAST OF THE MIS-

SISSIPPI RIVER 5 TO 8 FEET. IMMEDIATE EVACUATION OF AREAS THAT WILL BE AFFECTED BY THESE TIDES IS ADVISED.

THE CENTER OF CAMILLE IS EXPECTED TO PASS CLOSE TO THE MOUTH OF THE MISSISSIPPI RIVER LATE THIS AFTERNOON AND MOVE INLAND ON THE MISSISSIPPI COAST NEAR GULFPORT EARLY TONIGHT.

SEVERAL TORNADOES ARE LIKELY OVER EXTREME SOUTHEAST LOUISIANA EASTWARD TO FORT WALTON FLORIDA AND UP TO 100 MILES INLAND THIS AFTERNOON AND TONIGHT.

HEAVY RAIN WITH LOCAL AMOUNTS 8 TO 10 INCHES WILL SPREAD INTO SOUTHEASTERN MISSISSIPPI...SOUTHWEST ALABAMA...AND THE FLORIDA PANHANDLE THIS AFTERNOON AND TONIGHT. ANY FLOOD STATEMENTS NEEDED WILL BE ISSUED BY THE LOCAL WEATHER BUREAU OFFICES.

ALL INTERESTS ALONG THE NORTHEASTERN GULF COAST ARE URGED TO LISTEN FOR LATER RELEASES AND TAKE ALL NECESSARY HURRI-CANE PRECAUTIONS IMMEDIATELY.

AT 3 PM CDT...2000Z...HURRICANE CAMILLE WAS LOCATED NEAR LATI-TUDE 28.6 NORTH...LONGITUDE 88.8 WEST...OR ABOUT 120 MILES SOUTHEAST OF NEW ORLEANS. CAMILLE WAS MOVING NORTH NORTH-WEST 15 TO 18 MPH.

AN AIR FORCE RECON FLIGHT INTO CAMILLE THIS AFTERNOON ESTI-MATED THE WINDS 190 MPH NEAR THE CENTER. THE CENTRAL PRES-SURE WAS 26.61 INCHES. HURRICANE FORCE WINDS EXTEND OUT-WARD 60 MILES AND GALES EXTEND OUTWARD 180 MILES FROM THE CENTER.

REPEATING THE 3 PM POSITION...28.6 NORTH...88.8 WEST.

THE NEXT ADVISORY WILL BE ISSUED BY THE NEW ORLEANS WEATH-ER BUREAU AT 5 PM AND BULLETINS AT 7 AND 9 PM CDT.

CONNER

— — —

The three o'clock advisory confirmed everything Uncle Rick had told Daddy. There was no doubt in anyone's mind now that Camille was going to slam into the Gulf Coast of Mississippi somewhere between Bay St. Louis and Biloxi. Full evacuation orders had been issued by Civil Defense for the coastal areas. No evacuation was mandated for inland Harrison County where we were, so for better or worse, Daddy and Aunt Charity had decided we would ride out the storm in my aunt's house. It was brick, built on a concrete slab, and Daddy felt it would be able to hold up to the winds we were expecting. Our old frame house he wasn't so sure of. I was in my bedroom now packing up most of my clothes, as well as my sister's, to carry over to Aunt Charity's.

Daddy stuck his head in my door and asked, "Where is Frankie?"

"I don't know," I answered. "I guess he's over at Aunt Charity's."

"Well, go in his room and pack up some of his clothes too."

We only had two suitcases; Daddy had already used one for his things, and the one I had was already stuffed full with mine and my sister's clothes. Then I remembered the box with my old clothes in it in the bottom of my closet. I got that, dumped its contents on my bed, and went to Frankie's room to pack up most of his clothes. The last thing I put in the box were the three comic books that were on Frankie's dresser.

"I think we should put all the cars in Charity's back yard," Daddy said as we were walking back over to her house. I was carrying the two suitcases and he had the box with Frankie's stuff in it. I noticed Daddy had his Smith & Wesson stuck inside his waistband.

"Wouldn't they be better off in the barn?" I asked.

"That barn will never take the kind of winds this storm is going to hit us with. The back yard is best for the cars."

"Why?"

"Because it's big and there are no trees in it." Aunt Charity's back yard was devoid of trees and was the size of a football field. In fact, many a game of touch had been played in it.

It was nearly 3:30 now and the wind was really starting to pick up. The sky overhead looked angry and you could feel that rain was imminent. We took the things inside and Daddy asked Aunt Charity to start filling all her clean Mason jars with water, and all her pitchers, too. He was thinking ahead, anticipating that we were going to be without electricity for quite some time. We had a well that supplied fresh water to both our houses, but the pump was electric. No power meant no water. Daddy suggested we all take baths or showers before six o'clock and then fill the tub to the brim with water.

After Daddy and I got all the cars and his pickup parked in the middle of Aunt Charity's backyard, we realized Frankie was missing. Aunt Charity said she thought he had been with us. She hadn't seen him in over an hour.

"Let's go look for him," Daddy said.

"Lem," Aunt Charity said, "you need to stay here and tend to your daughter."

"Sash? What's wrong with her?"

"She's scared, Lem. She doesn't know what's going on with all this. I've talked to her, but she needs her father right now."

Daddy looked at me. "Go see if Frankie's at the house, son."

"We were just at the house. He wasn't there."

"Well, he's got to be somewhere. Check the barn and the work room off of the carport. And go ahead and round up Bear and get him in the garage over here. It's gonna start getting nasty out there in short order."

I went back over to our house and searched every room. Frankie wasn't there. On my way out of the kitchen, I grabbed Daddy's old Marine Corps messenger bag off the coat rack, got the spare flashlight out of the pantry, and stuck it in the bag. I was about to go out the door when I had a thought and stepped back into the pantry. I reached up on the top shelf to see if Daddy had remembered to take the Colt revolver—the one I'd taken to the Dixie Pearl that night to get Frankie. I felt around behind the flour tin and, sure enough, it was there. I stuck it in the messenger bag and slung the bag over my shoulder.

I went out to the barn and looked for Frankie. I even checked up in the hay loft. He was nowhere to be found. I called Bear until he came running up and I was about to lead him by the collar back over to Aunt Charity's when I noticed Frankie's bicycle was not under the carport. "His radio," I said aloud.

After I got Bear settled in the garage, I went in the house and found Daddy sitting in the den with Sachet in his lap. He was reading her a story. "Daddy, Frankie's bike is gone. I think he went down to the cabin to get his radio."

"That boy," Daddy said exasperatedly. He started to get up, but my sister would have none of that.

"No, Daddy," she pleaded. "You have to finish the story."

Daddy fell back in the chair and looked at me. "Take the Honda and go get him and y'all get right back here."

"I've already got Bear in the garage, so you're gonna have to come hold him for me to get the bike out," I said. "Soon as I open that door he'll be gone."

"Let me up, baby girl, so I can help your brother," Daddy said. "I'll be right back." Reluctantly, Sachet slid out of Daddy's lap so he could get up.

"The wind is really kicking up," Daddy said as he held Bear by the collar and I rolled the Honda out into the driveway. "The rain is gonna be starting any time now, so just leave Frankie's bike in the cabin and you two get back here fast, understand?"

"Yes, sir," I said and hit the starter button. The engine spun to life. I blipped the throttle a couple of times and then took off.

I kept my speed down to about 30 because the wind gusts were blowing me all over the place. I'd forgotten I still had the messenger bag slung over my shoulder until it started beating against me from the wind buffeting. When I got to the head of the trail leading down to the cabin and our spot on the river, I decided just to leave the Honda parked on the side of the road. The way the wind was blowing, I didn't want to take a chance on riding down to the beach and have a branch, or even a tree, fall across the path where I couldn't get back out.

The sound of the wind whipping through the trees as I walked down the semi-dark path was kind of eerie and I began to wonder if Frankie had come down here to get his radio why he was still here. He knew a hurricane was coming. When I rounded the last bend in the path before it opened up onto the white sand beach, I froze. Frankie's bike was lying in the sand at the edge of the woods. Parked out on the beach by itself was the Vincent Black Shadow.

Working against my catatonic neck muscles, I forced myself to scan the woods on either side of me. Because the sky had grown so dark, and the woods were so thick, it was really hard to see, but I was satisfied that Bong was not lurking in the shadows waiting to jump me. I could see our cabin through the trees and undergrowth about a hundred feet to my right. No one was around it, and I could not see the door from this angle. I had two choices: I could turn around and run back to the Honda and get the hell out of there, or I could try to find Frankie, who was no doubt in trouble. I quickly realized there was no time to go home and get the sheriff to help Frankie; I was his only hope. Tentatively, I made my way down the path right to the edge of the sand beach. I knew once I stepped out into the open, anyone down either side of the beach would be able to see me and whatever element of surprise I was foolish enough to think I had would be gone.

I wasn't worried about trying to be quiet because the wind was making enough noise in the trees to mask any sounds I was making. This worked to my disadvantage too because I couldn't hear any sounds Bong might be making if he was trying to sneak up on me. As I began to make my way along the edge of the sand over to the path we'd cut to the cabin, I said a little prayer that the Lord would be with me and that Frankie would be all right.

The gusts of wind were picking up sand and it was stinging my bare legs and getting in my eyes, but I pressed on. Finally, I made it to the path leading to the cabin. Now I could see the door and it was closed. I did another quick survey all around and still I didn't see anyone. Back in the other direction, and around a slight cove in the river, was a section of our beach that was hidden from view. Frankie and I called it our "private beach" because it's where we could come out of the water naked and lie on the sand without having to worry about being seen, should someone happen to wander down our path to the main beach. If Bong had Frankie over on that part of the beach, I'd practically have to get in the water to get over there.

Rather than back tracking to check that out, I decided to go on up to the cabin. I slowly made my way up the freshly cut path. As I got closer, I could see the door on the cabin wasn't really closed; it was pushed to, but not closed all the way. My heart was racing so fast it gave me the jitters and I had to stop and mentally force myself to calm down. I had never been so scared in my life. I still had about twenty feet to go to the cabin, and it was only by sheer will power that I was able to overcome my fear enough to make my legs carry me that remaining distance.

After what seemed an eternity, I was finally standing in front of the cabin door. Try as I might, I could hear nothing coming from inside because of the wind whipping through the trees. It was strong enough that smaller dead branches were falling all around the cabin, and the sound of those breaking was loud enough to be heard over the wind. With my hand trembling, I reached out and pushed the door open. What I saw will be seared into my memory forever.

Peter Bong didn't hear me; it was only the added light entering the cabin from my opening the door that let him know I was there behind him. When he leaned up off of Frankie and turned to look at me, it was as if Satan himself were staring a hole right through me. There was pure evil in his eyes. I gasped as I stumbled backwards, away from the door. In what seemed like slow motion, Peter Bong got to his feet and pulled his black jeans up in one seamless move. When I saw the glint of that Bowie knife on his belt, I knew I had to run but my legs felt like two lead pipes. That all changed when I saw his hand go for the hilt. I turned and ran as hard as I could.

I made it out onto the beach just as Peter Bong tackled me and knocked me to the sand right by his motorcycle. I rolled onto my back and kicked to try to scramble away, but he had latched onto my belt with his left hand and the harder I pushed away from him, the closer he pulled himself to me until, finally, he was on top of me. The wind was blowing the sand in our eyes and, even with the gusts, I could smell the alcohol on his breath as he put his face close to mine and said something. To this day I cannot recall what it was. It may have been so horrific that my young mind simply would not process the words and allow them into my memory. Out of the corner of my left eye I saw the blade of that big knife come up to my face and I knew I was about to die. Once I had accepted that fact, I quit struggling to get away. There was a small pocket knife in my right pocket, but with Peter Bong right on top of me there was no way I could get it out and unfold it. He could cut my throat before I could even get my hand in my pocket. I closed my eyes and after saying one more prayer for Frankie, I uttered the words Christ spoke on the cross at the moment of his death: "Father, into thy hands I commit my spirit."

I expected right then to feel the blade of Peter Bong's knife on my throat, and I held my breath in anticipation of that cold steel slicing through me. But then the strangest thing happened. As I had quit struggling and relaxed every muscle in my body, I'd gone limp and I realized my right hand was under me and something was jabbing me in the back. I moved my hand in the sand under me until I touched the object and suddenly my resolve to die at the hands of this madman was gone. I was lying on the messenger bag. The bag I'd put a flashlight in just a little while ago. The bag I'd put my father's Colt .38 Special in just a little while ago.

I kept my eyes closed as my hand found the flap on the bag. I tried not to move too much so Peter Bong would not figure out what I was doing. Whatever the reason he was delaying my demise, I didn't want to change the status quo. If he was having second thoughts about killing me, that was fine. Once I got the gun out of the bag, I knew I would have none. My hand found the pistol in the bag just as the first heavy drops of rain began to strike my face. I had my fingers around the grip and I leaned up enough to relieve the pressure on the bag. I opened my eyes to see Peter Bong still over me, but with his head turned to look up at the dark sky and the huge rain drops that were starting to fall. That was the opening I needed. I pulled the Colt from the bag and stuck the muzzle to his chest. And, just as he turned those devil eyes back to me, I pulled the trigger.

That close to my face, the blast from the gun shut down my ear drums and suddenly there was no more wind noise. There was no more sound of any kind except a squealing ring in my ears as I watched Peter Bong move back, his face contorting in surprise and pain. His eyes were squinted shut. When he opened them to look at me again I pulled the trigger again. The gunshot this time sounded like a little puff as Peter Bong fell back and rolled off me.

I scrambled to my feet and looked at the gun in my hand. It had blood on it. I could not believe I'd just shot a man. It took a few seconds, but the stinging cold rain drops forced me out of my daze and I remembered where I was and why I'd come here. Frankie. I stuffed the revolver back in the messenger bag and ran up the path to the cabin. Frankie was still lying face down on my sleeping bag that we'd left there the night before. His Bermuda shorts and underwear were down around his ankles, which Bong had tied together with some of the old string left over from our lining off the foundation of the cabin. Frankie's wrists were tied together with more string and his mouth was gagged with Bong's black bandana. I pulled it from his mouth, got out my pocket knife, and cut the strings tying him up. When Frankie finally opened his eyes and saw it was me he started screaming something, but my ears were ringing so badly I couldn't hear him well enough to understand what he was saying. I helped him get his underwear and shorts pulled up and then he threw his arms around me and hugged me and started crying. I could barely hear his sobs but I didn't need to; I could feel them. I knew we had to get out of there. The rain was coming down harder, the wind was getting stronger, and I didn't know if Peter Bong was dead or not. For all I knew he could be coming for us with that knife right then.

"Come on Frankie," I said. "We've got to get home." I could hardly hear my own words; they sounded like they were echoing in my head instead of coming out my mouth. I helped Frankie to his feet, and with him holding on to me, we stumbled down the path and out onto the beach. Peter Bong was still lying where he'd fallen and the white sand around him was covered in dark red blood. Frankie and I made our way back up the path. We got on the Honda, and with the rain coming down steady now, I started the engine and we headed for home.

Chapter 20
A Night to Remember

The rain was coming down hard as Frankie and I pulled into Aunt Charity's driveway. We had just gotten off the Honda when Daddy's pickup came around the house, the windshield wipers flapping away. He was coming to look for us. When he saw us through his fogged over windshield, he waved and turned around to return the truck to the relative safety of the back yard.

I left the Honda sitting in the rain and took Frankie in through the front door since the garage was closed. We went straight to the bathroom and when I caught a glimpse of myself in the huge vanity mirror over the double sinks I was shocked to see blood all over my shirt. The rain had diluted it to a deep pink. Frankie was a mess. He was shivering so badly his teeth were chattering as he sat on the edge of the bath tub. I was cold from the rain too, but my adrenaline rush was keeping my nerves and body temperature in check. My ears were still ringing but my hearing was almost back to normal.

"What's wrong with Frankie?" Sachet said from the doorway.

I turned to her. "Get out!" I yelled. The look of surprise on her face only lasted a second before she burst into tears and went running back down the hall.

I focused my attention back on Frankie. He was shaking and had a spaced out look on his face. I didn't know what to do. I put my hands on his face to force him to look at me and that's when I saw his eyes were no longer brown, they were all black. His pupils were so dilated they had completely crowded out the iris of each eye leaving just black holes. Frankie tried to say something.

"What?" I said.

"Pills," Frankie said in a hoarse whisper between chattering teeth. "He made me swallow some pills." I jumped up and sprinted for the door and ran squarely into my father.

"What's going on? Why'd you yell at your sister?" he said.

"Daddy, Peter Bong had Frankie down at the cabin. He made him take some pills. We need to make him throw up."

"What?!"

I didn't have time for Daddy to comprehend what I'd just said. I pushed by him and ran down the hall and to the kitchen. Aunt Charity was standing at the sink. "I need to give Frankie something to make him throw up," I said, panting.

My aunt turned to me. "What do you mean?" she asked.

"Aunt Charity, please...I don't have time to explain. What can I give him to make him throw up?"

"Nelson, tell me what is going on right now."

"Frankie swallowed some pills. We need to make him throw up."

A flash of understanding swept my aunt's face, though I'm sure she thought I meant Frankie had intentionally taken some pills. She went to the spice cabinet and pulled out the canister of table salt. She grabbed a glass from the dish drainer and filled it half full of salt. She filled the glass the rest of the way with hot water from the tap and stirred it until most of the salt had dissolved. "Where is he?" she asked.

"In the bathroom," I said, and motioned for her to follow me.

When we got to the bathroom, Daddy was sitting on the edge of the tub holding Frankie. It was clear my best friend was rapidly drifting out of consciousness. "Make sure he's awake, Lem, or he'll choke on this," Aunt Charity said.

"What is it?" Daddy asked.

"It's hot salt water. It'll make him vomit, so be ready. But he's got to be alert before we try to make him drink it."

"Frankie!" Daddy said loudly. He shook him and slapped his face a couple of times until he opened his eyes.

"Don't hit his nose," I said.

"Frankie, tell me my name," Daddy demanded. He shook Frankie again. "Tell me my name."

"Mr. Lem…" Frankie said in a whisper.

"Good, son," Daddy said. "I need you to drink this." Daddy took the glass of thick steaming salt water from my aunt and held it to Frankie's lips. "Drink it right down."

Frankie nodded his head and said, "Okay."

Daddy turned the glass up and Frankie gulped the mixture down until all that was left in the glass was a glob of salt goo in the bottom. Frankie's face was all twisted up from the foul taste. As soon as Daddy saw him start to gag, he moved Frankie over to the toilet and they just made it before Frankie let go with projectile vomit into the bowl.

Daddy and I left the bathroom with Aunt Charity running a hot bath for Frankie, who was sitting on the toilet lid like a little boy as Aunt Charity pulled his tee shirt off of him. I knew he was really out of it if he was going to sit there and let my aunt undress him and get him in the bathtub.

"Daddy, we need to call the sheriff," I said to my father as we walked down the hall.

"Why?"

"Let's go in the living room," I said and pointed to the doorway off from the hall.

The living room was dark because of the boarded up windows so Daddy switched on the lamp on one of the end tables. My hearing had recovered to the point I could hear the rain beating down on the roof. After Daddy and I sat down on the sofa, in a strangely calm manner, I recited to him what had transpired over the past forty minutes. When I finished, he looked confused.

"Wait a minute," he said, scratching his brow, "you shot Peter Bong down at the river?"

"Yes, Daddy. He tried to kill me. I had to shoot him."

"Where did you get a gun?"

"I had your Colt Detective Special. I'd put it in your old Marine Corps bag…" I realized I still had the bag hanging off my shoulder so I held it up. "I'd put it in the bag when I was over at the house looking for Frankie. I still had the bag with me when I rode down to the river to get him."

"And that's blood all over your shirt?" He pointed to me.

"Yes, sir."

"You're right. We need to call the sheriff." Daddy got up and headed to the kitchen and I went to the bathroom to check on Frankie.

I found him in a steaming hot bath full of sudsy foam from Aunt Charity's perfumed bubble bath. He was more alert now and nearly back to his old self. "Hey," he said as I sat down on the toilet lid.

"You feeling better?" I asked.

"Yeah."

"Do you remember what happened?"

"Yeah. What did you do to Peter Bong? I remember seeing him on the beach."

"I shot him. I think I killed him. Daddy's calling the sheriff right now, so I guess I'm going to jail."

Frankie's eyes narrowed. "Why would you have to go to jail? You were saving me. He was gonna kill me."

"I was saving me too," I said. "When I opened the cabin door and he saw me, he came after me with that knife. If I hadn't shot him he would have killed me."

"It's good you thought to bring a gun with you."

"I didn't. That was providence."

"Is that his blood on your shirt?"

I looked down at the front of my tee shirt. "Yes. I'm going and take a shower in Aunt Charity's bathroom." I got up and headed for the door.

"Nels?" Frankie called to me. I turned and looked back at him. "I didn't let him do anything to me this time."

"I know," I said.

Normally, I could be in and out of the shower in fifteen minutes. My shower that evening took a half-hour. I knew when I got out I'd be facing Sheriff Posey. I'd killed a man and I was not a little surprised at how I was reacting to it. Maybe the shock and remorse were still to come, but so far I had no regrets. The man I killed had done unspeakable things to my best friend and was no doubt intent on killing him this time around. And he would have, without any doubt, killed me there on the beach beside that Black Shadow motorcycle. These were not rationalizing thoughts racing around in my head. These were cold hard facts supporting the justified killing of an evil man.

Aunt Charity's bedroom was quite large, and she had a big roll-top desk over in one corner. When I came out of the bathroom with a towel wrapped around me, Daddy was sitting in the desk chair waiting for me.

"Is Sheriff Posey going to arrest me?" I asked.

"No…at least not tonight. He's not even coming out here. He said he's got bigger problems with this hurricane than dealing with you shooting a pervert who deserved it."

"He said that?"

"That's pretty much a direct quote."

"He's not even going down to the river to see if he's dead, or call an ambulance or anything?"

"I don't think so."

I went over and sat down on the edge of my aunt's bed and ran my hand through my damp hair. Now a tinge of remorse was setting in. If I'd killed Peter Bong, that was one thing. But if I hadn't, that meant he was lying on that beach suffering. I looked up at my father and said, "What if I didn't kill him?"

"I know what you're thinking, son. Whether you killed him or not, Peter Bong put himself where he is right now. If he's dead, he's dead. If he's on that beach bleeding to death, then so be it. He's got no one to blame but himself. If we didn't have this hurricane about to hit us, I'm sure Joe would be heading down there right now with medics. It's his choice not to and you don't have any control over that."

"I know, but…"

Daddy got up from the chair and walked over to me. He motioned for me to stand up and when I did he embraced me. As soon as I felt his strong arms around me, I began to cry. I put my arms around him and squeezed as hard as I could. All the emotion that I'd managed to keep at bay, from the moment I saw Peter Bong's motorcycle there on the beach until just now, came welling up as I sobbed into Daddy's shoulder.

Aunt Charity went all out for dinner, even after having cooked a full meal for lunch. She'd fixed a pot roast with potatoes, carrots, and onions, and a big pot of string beans. When we sat down to eat in her dining room, it was a little after six o'clock and the wind was now blowing hard enough that we could hear it in the trees outside.

"How hard do you think it's blowing?" I said as I carved my first bite of roast from the slab on my plate.

"Forty miles an hour, at least," Daddy replied. I could see from his expression he didn't want to talk about the storm, probably to keep from scaring my sister.

Sachet was still eyeing me warily. I had hurt her feelings deeply when I yelled at her earlier. As aggravating as she could be at times, I had never raised my voice in anger to my sister and that's why my words had cut her to the quick. After my cry in Daddy's arms earlier, I'd done my best to make amends with her, but my sister, even at the tender age of five and half, was a master at nursing a grudge.

Mary Alice was her usual composed self, calmly sitting there eating her dinner as the wind and rain raged outside. I had yet to tell her the full story of what had happened with Frankie down at the river. She just knew he wasn't feeling well and had been sick to his stomach.

Frankie looked pale and I could tell he was forcing himself to eat, largely at Aunt Charity's urging. She'd said he needed food in his system to help counteract what was left of those pills he'd been forced to swallow. Taking one last bite of roast, Frankie looked at Aunt Charity and said, "I'd really like to go lay down."

My aunt excused herself and got up from the table. "Come on Francis," she said, "let's get you to bed." Aunt Charity's house had four bedrooms, so Frankie and I would be sharing one of her guest rooms, the one that had two twin beds. Daddy and Sachet would be in the one that had a full-size bed. Mary Alice had been using the other room, which had a single twin bed, all summer.

After dinner, I went out to the garage to check on Bear. He didn't like being cooped up, but at least he had room to move around since Aunt Charity's Cadillac was in the back yard with all our other vehicles—except the Honda, which was sitting over by the door with a big puddle of water under it, still dripping from the ride home in the rain. So far there were no puddles on the floor from Bear. I refilled his water bowl and put a couple of scoops of dog food in his food bowl, which he commenced to devouring. I walked over and looked out the narrow rectangular windows in the garage door. The rain was coming down so hard I could barely see all the way to the road and the wind was whipping it around in sheets. There were a few limbs down in the front yard, but so far things didn't look too bad.

— — —

BULLETIN 7 PM CDT   SUNDAY AUGUST 17, 1969

...CAMILLE...EXTREMELY DANGEROUS...CENTER SKIRTED MOUTH OF THE MISSISSIPPI RIVER...TAKES AIM ON THE MISSISSIPPI ALABAMA COAST...

HURRICANE WARNINGS ARE IN EFFECT FROM NEW ORLEANS AND GRAND ISLE LOUISIANA EASTWARD ACROSS THE MISSISSIPPI...ALABAMA...AND NORTH WEST FLORIDA COAST TO APALACHICOLA. GALE WARNINGS ARE IN EFFECT FROM MORGAN CITY TO GRAND ISLE. PREPARATIONS AGAINST THIS EXTREMELY DANGEROUS HURRICANE SHOULD BE COMPLETE IMMEDIATELY.

WINDS ARE INCREASING AND TIDES ARE RISING ALONG THE NORTHERN GULF COAST FROM GRAND ISLE EASTWARD. HURRICANE FORCE WINDS ARE NOW OCCURRING AT THE MOUTH OF THE MISSISSIPPI RIVER. GALES IN SQUALLS ARE SPREADING INLAND OVER THE WARNING AREA AND WINDS WILL REACH HURRICANE FORCE OVER MUCH OF THE AREA FROM SOUTHEAST LOUISIANA ACROSS COASTAL MISSISSIPPI...COASTAL ALABAMA...AND INTO EXTREME NORTHWEST FLORIDA EARLY TONIGHT. THE FOLLOWING TIDES ARE EXPECTED TONIGHT AS CAMILLE MOVES INLAND...MISSISSIPPI COAST GULFPORT TO PASCAGOULA 15 TO 20 FEET...PASCAGOULA TO MOBILE 10 TO 15 FEET...EAST OF MOBILE TO PEN-SACOLA 6 TO 10 FEET. ELSEWHERE IN THE AREA OF HURRICANE WARNING EAST OF THE MISSISSIPPI RIVER 5 TO 8 FEET. IMMEDIATE EVACUATION OF AREAS THAT WILL BE AFFECTED BY THESE TIDES IS URGED.

THE CENTER OF CAMILLE IS EXPECTED TO MOVE INLAND ON THE MISSIS-SIPPI COAST NEAR GULFPORT EARLY TONIGHT.

SEVERAL TORNADOES ARE LIKELY OVER EXTREME SOUTHEAST LOUISIANA EASTWARD TO FORT WALTON FLORIDA AND UP TO 100 MILES INLAND THROUGH TONIGHT.

HEAVY RAINS WITH LOCAL AMOUNTS 8 TO 10 INCHES WILL SPREAD INTO SOUTHEAST MISSISSIPPI...SOUTHWEST ALABAMA...AND THE FLORIDA PANHANDLE TONIGHT. AND FLOOD STATEMENTS NEEDED WILL BE ISSUED BY THE LOCAL WEATHER BUREAU OFFICES.

ALL INTERESTS ALONG THE NORTHEASTERN GULF COAST ARE URGED TO LISTEN FOR LATER RELEASES AND CONTINUE ALL NECESSARY HURRI-CANE PRECAUTIONS.

AT 7 PM CDT...THE CENTER OF HURRICANE CAMILLE WAS LOCATED BY NEW ORLEANS AND OTHER LAND BASED RADARS NEAR LATITUDE 29.5 NORTH...LONGITUDE 89.1 WEST...OR ABOUT 70 MILES EAST SOUTHEAST OF NEW ORLEANS AND 60 MILES SOUTH OF GULFPORT MISSISSIPPI. CAMILLE WAS MOVING NORTH NORTHWEST ABOUT 15 MPH.

HIGHEST WINDS ARE ESTIMATED 190 MPH NEAR THE CENTER. HURRI-CANE FORCE WINDS EXTEND OUTWARD 60 MILES AND GALES EXTEND OUTWARD 180 MILES FROM THE CENTER. THE AIR FORCE RECON FLIGHT INTO CAMILLE THIS AFTERNOON REPORTED A CENTRAL PRESSURE OF 26.61 INCHES.

WIND GUSTING TO NEAR 80 MPH AT BOOTHVILLE AND TO NEAR 60 MPH AT NEW ORLEANS WEATHER BUREAU OFFICE AT 6 PM.

REPEATING THE 7PM POSITION...29.5 NORTH...89.1 WEST.

THE NEXT ADVISORY WILL BE ISSUED BY THE NEW ORLEANS WEATHER BUREAU AT 11 PM AND A BULLETIN AT 9 PM CDT.

SLOAN

— — —

The seven o'clock bulletin confirmed that Camille was coming ashore somewhere around Gulfport which meant we were going to be directly in its path. At quarter to eight the lights blinked and Aunt Charity started going around lighting all the oil lamps she'd set out and Daddy started taping up the sliding glass door in the den with masking tape. The winds, as he had predicted, were coming out of the east which meant they were slamming directly into the back of the house and hitting the sliding glass doors hard. During the stronger gusts, we could even see the glass in the doors bow a little. Daddy still maintained that the tempered glass would hold and the tape was just an extra measure of protection.

"Charity," Daddy said, "you better get some towels. The wind is forcing the rain in around these doors." I went over and looked and sure enough the tracks were full of water and the carpeting was wet.

Daddy finished taping the door and then put Sachet to bed. She had fallen asleep over in the recliner. Aunt Charity came in the den with three bath towels and started rolling them up and putting them at the base of the sliding glass doors. I decided to go down the hall and check on Frankie.

The lights blinked again just as I stepped into the bedroom. The lamp on the table in between my bed and Frankie's was on. He'd gone to sleep reading one of his comic books and it had fallen from his hand and was lying on the floor. I reached down and picked it up and put it on the table. Frankie seemed to be sleeping peacefully. He'd been through so much over the past ten days and yet his spirit seemed indomitable. As I watched my best friend lying there, thoughts of what I'd done earlier to ensure that he and I both could be in this room right now crept forward from the back of my mind where I'd forced them. I'd shot a man, and even if I hadn't killed him he was surely dead by now from his wounds and the weather. I knew I did what I had to do, and intellectually I had no doubts or regrets. But you can't take a life and not have it affect you deep inside where the intellect is not the gate keeper. I reached for the lamp to turn it out, but before my hand made it to the switch it went dark. The electricity was gone.

I stood there for a minute with my eyes closed to get used to the darkness. Without the sound of the air conditioning or the TV from the den, the wind noise from outside was really striking. With every gust there was a little roar and at times I could actually hear and feel the house shudder. When I opened my eyes there was quite a bit of light coming from the doorway to the hall from all the oil lamps and candles Aunt Charity had burning throughout the house. I made my way back to the den and sat on the sofa beside Mary Alice. Daddy was leaned back in the recliner and my aunt was in her rocker in front of the fire place. The wind was making a howling noise in the chimney.

"Daddy, is the flue closed in the chimney?" I asked. For the first time I noticed the wind roar from outside was getting to the point that conversation across the room required me to raise my voice.

"Yes, I checked it."

"How fast do you think the winds are now?"

"Sixty, seventy maybe."

I reached over and took Mary Alice's hand and it was trembling a little. I leaned over and said into her ear, "Are you scared?" She squeezed my hand and nodded her head. I pulled her over to me and put my arms around her.

For the next two hours we all sat there like that: Daddy in the recliner, Aunt Charity in the rocker, me on the sofa with Mary Alice in my arms. We listened to the fury of Camille build until the roar was so loud that conversation was impossible. I'd never been in a tornado, but I'd heard people who had say it sounds like a freight train, and this did. And it just seemed to keep getting louder as the night went on.

I finally just had to get up. I stepped over to Daddy and pointed to my wrist, indicating I wanted to know the time. He looked at his watch and said something and I literally could not hear him—that's how loud the wind roar was. I finally just took his wrist in my hand and looked at the watch myself. It was ten after ten.

I decided to go to the garage and see how Bear was doing. Aunt Charity had a candle burning on the bar in the kitchen, so I took that with me so I could see. I expected Bear to jump all over me as soon as I opened the door, but he didn't. He was lying over in the corner and when he saw me he wagged his tail a few times but didn't move. I figured the storm had him confused. I looked to see if he'd gone to the bathroom anywhere and he hadn't.

When I got back to the den and sat down beside Mary Alice, she put her mouth right to my ear and said, "I want to go lie down. Will you come with me?"

I told her I would. We both stood up and I motioned to Daddy that I was going to Mary Alice's room with her. He nodded. I looked over at Aunt Charity. She had her eyes closed and was rocking slowly in her rocker.

Once we got to Mary Alice's room, she said she wanted me to lie down with her. Aunt Charity had put a small oil lamp on the nightstand and it was burning at a low flame, just enough to illuminate the room with a soft yellow glow. Mary Alice and I lay down on her bed, she on her side and me behind her, front to back, with my arms around her— "spooning" as they used to call it. My nose was buried in her hair and it smelled wonderful. The house was getting warmer now that the air conditioning wasn't running. And I didn't think it was possible, but the wind roar from the hurricane was actually getting louder. It was unnerving and for the first time I began to wonder what was actually happening outside and if the house could hold up to this relentless assault. Lying there with Mary Alice in my arms, inhaling her essence, feeling her gentle breathing against my embrace, was relaxing even in the midst of this storm and I found myself slipping into the edge of sleep.

Daddy gently shaking my shoulder awakened me. I opened my eyes and as I looked around the room it took a few seconds for me to remember where I was. Mary Alice was there beside me asleep and the oil lamp was still burning dimly on the night stand. But the house was dead quiet. I looked up at Daddy and asked, "Is it over?"

"We're in the eye," he said. "We don't have much time. I want you to take Bear out and let him use the bathroom."

I worked my way off the narrow bed without disturbing Mary Alice. "What time is it?" I asked as I rubbed my eyes.

"Quarter past one," Daddy said.

I followed him down the hall. He had a flashlight and he reached in his back pocket and pulled out another one and handed it to me. "Put the leash on Bear. I don't want him loose because once the winds start back up it will be quick."

"I didn't bring his leash," I said.

"I did. It's hanging on the wall in the garage where Charity has all her gardening tools. And don't open the garage door. Bring him in the house and take him out the front door."

"Why can't I take him out the garage door?"

"Because the wind could have warped it and I don't want to open it and then not be able to get it closed. Just do like I said, please."

I got Bear hooked up to his leash and Daddy followed us out onto the front porch. Normally, in the middle of the night, you'd expect to hear crickets and frogs and all manner of insects making a racket, but everything was still and silent. We stood there on the porch and shined our flashlights out in the front yard. Limbs of all sizes were everywhere. "Are you going over and check on our house?" I asked Daddy.

"No, and I don't want you going any further than right out there in the front yard. Take him on out there and let him do his business before this thing gets going again."

As soon as I stepped off the porch with Bear I let out some of the leash I'd had wound up in my hand to give him some walking room. As I expected, he immediately went over to one of Aunt Charity's azalea bushes and peed on it. I looked up and was shocked to see a star-filled night sky, clear and beautiful. "Look at that," I said and pointed my flashlight upward.

"Yep," Daddy said, "there're no clouds in the eye of a hurricane. No clouds, no wind, no rain."

I walked around a little further out in the yard. Bear was tugging on the leash the entire time. The beam of my flash light fell on one of the huge pine trees lying across the yard. I did a quick pan with the light to see which one it was, but they were all still standing—or so I thought. Once I shined the light up the trunk of the tree I was beside, I saw that the wind had snapped it off about twelve feet up. This was an old pine, nearly two feet in diameter and seventy feet tall. "One of the trees is down over here," I hollered to Daddy. I caught a whiff of dog poop so I knew Bear was indeed "doing his business," as Daddy had put it. I moved the flash light around until I spotted him finishing up about ten feet away.

Daddy stepped over beside me and shined his flashlight on the downed pine. "The tap root held," he said. "I'll bet you anything that pecan tree over there is on top of our house."

"You don't want to go look?"

"No, we don't know what may be in the yard between here and there. We can see what's happened in the morning. Judging by how long it took the eye to get here, we'll have another four hours or so of winds from the opposite direction when it starts up again."

"When's it gonna start up again?"

"I don't know—depends on how wide the eye is and how fast the storm's traveling. But it won't be like before when the winds started up gradually. If you'd been awake you would have seen how quickly the winds died when the edge of the eye passed. It'll be the same way on the backside. It will be calm like this one minute and then boom—hundred and fifty mile an hour winds."

"You think that's how fast the winds got? A hundred and fifty?"

"At least. Look at how cleanly that big pine is snapped off." Daddy put his flashlight beam on the break point of the tree.

Bear was sticking his cold nose against my hand so I knew he was finished. "I think he's done," I said.

"Okay, let's get back inside."

Chapter 21
Gone with the Wind

About thirty minutes after Daddy and I went back inside the house, Camille returned in full force. It was just as my father had said it would be. In a matter of minutes we went from calm and silence to the deafening fury of 150 mile per hour winds, this time coming from the west and blasting the front side of the house. The risk was greater now, if for no other reason than all those big tall pines in the front yard that could come crashing down on us as the winds thrashed them mercilessly.

By five o'clock we could tell the storm was starting to subside and by six the battering we'd endured for nearly ten hours was over. At first light I opened the draperies over the sliding glass doors and peered through the spaces in the tape into the back yard. It was full of limbs up close to the house, but the cars and pickup out in the middle appeared to be fine. The wind and rain had plastered them with leaves and pine needles, but Daddy had been smart to put them back there.

I went out into the garage and this time Bear did jump all over me as I made my way to the garage door and looked out the windows. The angle was such that I could not see our yard or house, but what I saw in Aunt Charity's front yard was enough to make me think the worst. The downed pine tree I had encountered during the brief respite of the passing eye was only one of five that I could see now. Three other pines had been snapped off by the easterly winds and two by the westerly winds on the backside of the storm.

Fortunately, neither of those had hit the house, but they had come close. The front yard itself was littered with limbs, leaves, and unrecognizable debris.

At seven o'clock, while everyone else was still sleeping, Daddy and I took our first venture out to see what was left of our world—and it wasn't much. Bear was happy to be free of the garage and he immediately took off running and exploring. Our house was still standing, but as I stood there on Aunt Charity's front porch staring at it, something didn't look right. It almost looked like it was sitting in a different position. The big pecan tree in the backyard had gone down, but not as Daddy had predicted. It had somehow withstood the full brunt of the initial pounding of Camille only to be felled by the winds on the backside of the storm. Hence, it was not lying on top of our house, but neither was it up against the barn, which is where its final resting place would have been had the barn been there. The barn was gone—literally. The only indication it had ever existed was the rough outline left in the wet clay soil. Daddy's workbench, all his tools, the old Harley he was restoring, everything that had been in the barn was gone. Our vegetable garden was a disaster area.

"That's amazing," Daddy said, pointing to our carport. It was still standing, but the small workshop that had been attached to the back of it was gone. The arbitrary nature of how the winds had wreaked havoc on our farm was bewildering. The barn was gone, while a hundred feet away the house was still standing. The new fence we'd built back in July was still standing. In preparation for the storm, Daddy had released the goats into the cow pasture, but as I peered out into the open field I didn't see any cows or goats.

Daddy and I walked over into our yard and as we got closer it was easy to see why our house looked like it was in a different position. It was. Built by my maternal grandparents over forty years earlier, this was a frame house sitting on a skirted brick pier foundation. The easterly winds on the front side of the storm had ripped a corner of the skirting on the backside of the house, which let the fierce gusts whip underneath, eventually lifting the house and moving it in a skewed fashion about three feet off the foundation piers on the north end. This caused the floor to buckle right at the point of the wall separating my bedroom from the living room. The roof, however, remained intact, and when Daddy and I went inside there were no signs of water leakage anywhere.

At eight o'clock, Daddy broke out our gas-fired camping stove on the patio and Aunt Charity began fixing bacon and eggs for breakfast. Mary Alice woke up a little after eight; my sister, a few minutes later. I finally had to wake Frankie when breakfast was ready at eight thirty. He was no doubt still suffering the aftereffects of those pills Peter Bong had made him swallow.

Peter Bong. Somehow I'd gone half the night and most of the morning without thinking about him and what had happened yesterday. That all changed a few minutes before ten o'clock when Sheriff Posey arrived. He wanted Frankie and me to go with him down to the river and tell him the whole story. Daddy went too. He rode up front and Frankie and I sat in the back of the sheriff's cruiser, behind that steel grate that prevented prisoners in transport from getting to the sheriff or a deputy in the front seat.

Once we got to the bridge over the river I knew there was no chance we were going to find Peter Bong alive—or dead, for that matter. Sheriff Posey stopped on the bridge and we all got out. The waters of the Wolf were higher than I'd ever seen them and flowing in a tumultuous rush southward to Bay St. Louis. Even though we could not see the beach where I'd shot Peter Bong, I could tell from the swollen torrent twenty feet below us that it was completely submerged under the muddy water.

"Where'd it happen?" the sheriff asked.

I pointed to the bend in the river. "Our beach is about twenty yards the other side of that bend."

"Take me down there," Sheriff Posey said.

We left his cruiser on the bridge and walked down the side of the road until we got to the path down to our beach. We made it about ten yards into the woods, stepping over downed branches and small trees, before we could see there was no point in going any further. The Wolf had completely engulfed our beach and was well up into the woods.

"Our cabin is still there!" Frankie exclaimed and pointed.

I looked and sure enough, there it was. "That's where he had Frankie tied up," I said to the sheriff. I figured he'd want us to cut across and try to get to the cabin through the undergrowth, but he didn't.

Sheriff Posey pointed down the path in the direction where our beach had been. "So down yonder is where you shot that jaybird?"

"Yes, sir," I said.

"And he was trying to kill you with a knife?"

"Yes, sir."

"And he was still laying there when you and Frankie left out of here?"

"Yes, sir."

The sheriff rubbed his hand over his chin. "You boys go on back up to the car," he said. "I want to talk to Lem a minute."

Frankie and I went back to the car and waited. As we stood there leaning on the bridge railing staring down at the angry water, Frankie said, "What do you think he's gonna do?"

"I don't know," I said. I was contemplating how they were going to drag the river with the water this high and moving this fast.

When Daddy and the sheriff got back to the car, Frankie and I were in for a not unwelcome surprise. The sheriff said he was not going to file any sort of report on this "incident." He said, glancing sidelong at Daddy, that there was no evidence here of a shooting and, as far as he was concerned, none had occurred. Looking at Frankie and me, he added that if he ever got wind again of this "prank" that we had played on him by calling and making a false report, we'd be in big trouble. He pointed first to me and then to Frankie and said, "You don't make false reports about something as serious as shooting somebody, you got that?" We both looked at each other and nodded our heads. "Good," the sheriff said. "We'll just consider this matter closed. And I mean closed, understand? I don't ever want to hear anything about this again."

"Yes, sir," Frankie and I said in unison. We watched as Sheriff Posey and Daddy shook hands.

"I appreciate this, Brother Posey," Daddy said.

The sheriff smiled and said, "You've got a good son, Lem...and his sidekick ain't too bad, either." He looked at Frankie and winked.

When we got back to Aunt Charity's, there was another sheriff's car in the driveway and a uniformed deputy was standing beside it. "Is your radio working, sir?" the deputy asked the sheriff as we got out of the car.

Sheriff Posey leaned back in the car and said, "Damn. I forgot to turn it on." He stepped over to the deputy and said, "What's up?"

"We got a mess down at the Thompson farm," the deputy replied.

Frankie insisted on going with the sheriff to see what the situation was at his family's home, but Sheriff Posey would not let him. He promised Frankie that as soon as he could, he would come back here and let us know what was going on. "Keep him here until I get back," he told Daddy. At one o'clock the sheriff kept his promise and informed us that the Thompson Dairy Farm had been virtually destroyed by Camille and there was little of the house left standing. Evidently, Frank Thompson had not heeded any of the warnings and had not taken any precautions, like boarding up the windows to protect the house. As a result, Frankie's mother and father, as well as his little brother, had all been severely injured in the storm and were en route by ambulance to the hospital up in Hattiesburg. Frankie took the news stoically, showing the same resiliency of spirit in a crisis I'd learned now was uniquely his.

The first task on Monday afternoon was to get all the plywood off the windows so we could get them open and get some ventilation in the house. Removing the boarding proved to be a lot more difficult and time consuming than nailing it up, and we didn't finish until dinner time.

— — —

Tuesday morning Uncle Rick showed up in a big white four wheel drive truck with NASA emblems on the doors. He had brought us a portable generator and two five gallon cans of gasoline to fuel it. The phones were still out, so Daddy had not been able to contact him or my grandmother. Uncle Rick had already been to Picayune and gotten Grandma Gody set up with a generator. He said her house was fine, and except for frazzled nerves, she had weathered the storm unscathed.

The generator was a blessing because Daddy had planned to drive to Hattiesburg that afternoon to buy dry ice for the chest freezer on our back porch in an attempt to save all the frozen meat and vegetables in it. The problem was the generator could only be hooked up to one house, and that clearly needed to be Aunt Charity's since that's where we were living. So we loaded the freezer into the back of Daddy's pickup and brought it next door and put it in Aunt Charity's garage. Uncle Rick said the generator wasn't powerful enough to run the central air conditioning, but at least we could have fans, lights, and running water.

As a mechanical engineer, Uncle Rick took particular interest in the way Camille had merely moved our house off the foundation piers rather than completely obliterating it. He concluded that what saved the structure itself was Daddy boarding up all the windows. He said had the windows been unprotected, once they were broken, it would have allowed the wind to get inside the house, ripping it apart. Uncle Rick surmised that was exactly what had happened to Frankie's house, based on what we told him about the damage there. My uncle told us one thing about his experience with Camille that we found amusing: He had stayed at MTF during the storm and Monday morning when he went outside in the parking lot of his office building, he found the wind had blown his Volkswagen over sixty feet and turned it upside down in the grass yard bordering the lot. He got a couple of the other guys who had weathered the storm there to help him roll the Bug back onto its wheels. Uncle Rick said it started right up and except for a dent in the roof was good as new.

My uncle was the first to bring us the news of the utter devastation along the coast. It was evident now the eye of Camille had come ashore at Pass Christian, and the destruction there was absolute. Estimates were coming in that the storm surge had been nearly 30 feet in places and the sustained winds at the eyewall were tornado strength: at least 200 miles per hour. Uncle Rick said, based on the damage he had seen in the Bells Ferry area, and the destruction of our farm, we had faced 165 mile an hour winds at the peak of the storm just before the eye passed over us.

Wednesday brought news from Sheriff Posey that Frankie's father had died from the head injuries he sustained when their house was destroyed. Daddy drove Frankie up to the hospital in Hattiesburg to see his mother and brother. I didn't really want to go, but Frankie asked me to, so I went. Given all that had transpired over the past few weeks with Frankie's family, what we encountered should not have surprised us, but it did. It was a cold lesson in just how cruel people can be.

Frankie's little brother was still in a coma, and we visited his room first. As we stood by Mark's bed, I saw the first hint of emotion in Frankie since he had learned two days earlier of the tragedy that had befallen his family. Despite appearances to the contrary, I knew Frankie loved his little brother, and while I hadn't given it much thought at the time,

I suppose the weeks of being away from him, not being able to see him, had been difficult, though Frankie hadn't said anything. Now, seeing him lying in that bed unconscious, his head bandaged and I.V. lines running into his veins, brought Frankie to tears. He kissed his brother on the forehead and said something in his ear before we left the room.

Frankie's mother had a broken arm and a lot of cuts and bruises, but she was fully conscious and in possession of her faculties. Whatever hopes or illusions that I had regarding her love for her son, especially after she had come to our house that day with her entreaties to allow Frankie to return home, were forever laid to rest fifteen seconds after we set foot in her room. From the moment Frankie uttered the words "Hey, Mama," she cut loose with such vitriol that it pretty much left us all shell-shocked. She blamed Frankie for his father's death because he had not been home to help the family prepare for the storm. She blamed Daddy for keeping Frankie away from his family. She blamed me for her son being a "faggot," which was my first clue that she shared her late husband's sentiments about their son's sexuality. My father had intended to ask her if she would like him to handle the funeral arrangements for Frankie's dad, but after we had endured roughly three minutes of her unbridled wrath, Daddy motioned for us to leave, which we did without saying another word to Judy Thompson. Frankie did not attend his father's funeral because no one bothered to tell us when or where it was.

Chapter 22
The Long Goodbye

Thursday we were in full recovery mode. Daddy had procured a chainsaw from a Brother at the Lodge (ours had disappeared with everything else in the barn) and we had begun the arduous task of cleaning up the front yards. Uncle Rick and Daddy had determined our house could not be saved; the damage to the framing and flooring was just too extensive. It would have to be demolished and a new house built.

By lunch time, after Frankie and I had carried more fifty pound pine logs than we could count to a pile in the yard on the south side of Aunt Charity's house, Frankie finally asked me, "What's the matter with you?"

"Mary Alice has to go back to Poplarville tomorrow," I answered. With everything else that had befallen us, her imminent departure still managed to occupy my thoughts and affect my mood in the same way it had all summer when I had allowed it to consume me.

After lunch, Frankie told me to take Mary Alice for a ride. He said he and Daddy could handle the clean up for a while without me. Daddy was listening, since the three of us were sitting on the front porch, and I knew I needed his approval because there was still a lot of work to be done. With a single nod he gave it, so I headed back into the house to get Mary Alice.

As we rode down the road toward Bells Ferry, it felt good to be driving the GT Hawk again since I'd not been behind the wheel in nearly a week. I'd given all our vehicles a quick wash yesterday—even Daddy's pickup—to get the leaves and wind-blown mud off, but now in the full glare of unshaded sunshine I could see my car needed a more thorough scrubbing. The day was hot and muggy, so we had all the windows down and the floor vents open. Mary Alice was wearing the same pink sun dress she'd had on the day I met her, and she looked just as pretty. The prospect of us being apart was making me fall in love with her all over again. Thus began our long goodbye.

This was the first time I had ventured out on my own since the hurricane, and as we approached the entrance to the Thompson farm, I decided to turn in and see the damage that Camille had done. The first thing I noticed was the grain silo was gone and the barn was nothing but a heap of splintered wood. The smell of dead animals was heavy in the air.

Mary Alice put her hands to her face and said, "Where are we?"

"This is Frankie's dad's farm," I said. "It looks like the storm killed a lot of their cows." The few cows we had in our pasture had survived the storm, but so far we'd only found three goats. Daddy figured the 165 mile an hour winds had literally blown the rest of them away. For all we knew, if they survived the ride, most of our goats were over in Hancock county grazing in someone's yard.

Frankie's house looked like a bomb had gone off inside it. It was easy to see why anyone in there would have been seriously hurt. The remnants of the house, and all its contents, were scattered in a streak 50 yards long, filling most of the backyard. As I turned the car around in the front yard, I caught a glimpse of a colored man in my rear view mirror. He was waving for me to stop. I did and he ran up and asked me if I knew where Mr. Frank was. I recognized him as one of the men Frankie's dad had employed on the farm. I had to tell him that his boss was dead and I didn't know what was to become of the dairy farm where he worked. He told me Frankie's dad hadn't paid him last Friday and he needed money, that his house had been badly damaged by the storm. I knew if he lived in one of those dilapidated shanties in colored town, it was a miracle that his home had merely been "damaged" and not destroyed. I pulled out my wallet and gave him all the money I had, $14. He thanked me profusely and told me he'd pay me back.

"That was nice of you to help that man," Mary Alice said as we headed back down the drive to the road.

I didn't say anything, partly because I didn't believe I'd helped him all that much. What was $14 in the face of the destruction Camille had surely brought down on that man and his family? I wished I could have done more.

Main Street in Bells Ferry was busy. Most of the glass from the broken storefront windows that had not been boarded up was gone. And all the downed power lines that had littered the street had been removed. We'd seen the power crews working on that yesterday when we'd gone to Hattiesburg. Since I hadn't seen or heard from Dick in nearly a week, I stopped by the station. Dick was there, out at the pumps filling up a car with gas. It took a minute for that to sink in and I pulled up beside him and yelled, "You've got power!"

"Just came on about ten minutes ago," Dick said, looking over his shoulder at me. "Where the hell have you been? I was beginning to think the hurricane had blown you away."

"Trying to clean up the mess," I said. "How're things at your house?"

"Lost a few shingles and a bunch of trees. Nothin' major. You?"

"Aunt Charity's house is fine. Our house got moved off the foundation. Daddy says we're gonna have to tear it down and build a new one. And our barn is gone."

Dick frowned. "That's too bad. At least y'all are okay."

"Is it okay if I don't come back to work until next week? Daddy needs me to help him clean up the mess."

"Yeah, I think I can handle things."

I waved bye to Dick and we headed on out of town, taking 53 toward Poplarville, the very route I would be taking tomorrow to return Mary Alice to the Masonic home. When we got to the bridge over the Wolf River, I slowed and looked at the water. The level had receded, but was still up. I briefly thought about Peter Bong, but then pushed him out of my mind, trying to take to heart Sheriff Posey's admonition that this matter was closed.

Mary Alice and I spent the next hour riding around, me looking at the damage Camille had done, and her listening to me describe it. Her brother had called us late yesterday evening, when our phone service was first restored, frantic with worry. Up in Jackson, they were getting all the TV pictures of the destruction in Pass Christian and Gulfport, and we had to assure Beau that while the damage in Bells Ferry was considerable, it was nothing like what he was seeing on his TV of the coast. Aunt Charity had called the Masonic Home to make sure everything was fine, and it was. They had weathered the storm with little damage in Poplarville and were looking forward to having Mary Alice back.

When we got back to the house, Mary Alice and I spent the rest of the afternoon sitting on the front porch. Our power had come on back when Dick had told me he had power at the station, and Aunt Charity had her central air conditioning cranked up full blast. Daddy and Frankie had abandoned the front yard for the cool sanctuary of the den where they were now watching TV. Aunt Charity was preparing dinner and my sister was trying her best to annoy me by refusing to leave the front porch and give Mary Alice and me some privacy. I had a déjà vu moment, thinking back to that day I'd fought with Frankie in the front yard and broken his nose. Sachet was being a pill that day, too.

After dinner, Mary Alice and I went for a walk. We didn't talk, we just held hands. I found it curious that so much of this, our last full day together, had been spent just being together. Except for my descriptions of the hurricane damage during our ride, probably no more than two dozen words had been exchanged between us. I could sense that for the first time, the heartsoreness that had plagued me at times over the past several weeks whenever I contemplated this moment was now visiting Mary Alice. As such, we were both adrift in a sea of sadness where words seemed vapid and superfluous. A plaintive expression, a momentary gesture, a fleeting touch: these were all enough to convey thousands of words of emotion that crowded our hearts and rendered our eyes heavy with tears.

Late that night, long after Daddy had gone to bed since he had to work tomorrow and begin to help with the repairs at the plant, long after Sachet had ceased her annoyances and succumbed to the land of little girl dreams, long after

Aunt Charity had finished her evening routine and retired to the inner sanctum of her bedroom, long after Frankie had fallen asleep in the bed beside mine with a comic book still in his hand, I crept from my own bed in a restless fit of anxiety and went to the den. I had no idea what time it was. I walked over to the sliding glass doors and opened the draperies and looked out into the star-filled night sky. The moon was bright, nearly three quarters full, and its cool luminescence seemed to sooth my troubled spirit. I stepped over to the sofa and lay down and before long, with the moonlight streaming across the room and touching my face, I at last found sleep.

How long I slept, I didn't know. I was half awakened by someone lying down with me. In the fog of slumber, I assumed it was Sachet because she would often wake up in the middle of the night and either come to my bed or go to Daddy's. Once I put my arm around her and pulled her to me, I knew it wasn't Sachet. It was Mary Alice. Holding my arm, she turned over to face me. Before I could react, she had found my lips with hers. I had gone to bed in just my underwear and her hands were roaming, exploring the bare skin of my chest and my back as our tongues met. I touched her face and felt the tears. Her heart was breaking now. All the bravado she'd shown the many times she had chastised me for dwelling on our coming separation had vanished and the reality of it all was hitting her hard.

"I love you so much," she whispered in my ear as she held me tightly, our bodies pressing each other. She rolled on her side to face away from me and we assumed the spooning position we'd shared on her bed the night of Camille. Except this time neither of us was fully clothed. I was nearly naked, wearing only my briefs and Mary Alice

had on a thin summer nightgown. In the soft light of the setting moon, I could not discern the color but I knew it would
be pink. I put my arm around her and pulled her close to me,
and softly over her shoulder I said, "It hurts, doesn't it?" My
eyes were closed. I felt her nod and then felt her sobs.
"Don't cry, pretty girl," I whispered.

As Mary Alice had done with me, I let my hands roam
her body, though I could only wonder what the touch of her
bare skin would be like as she was shielded by her nightgown. Tentatively, I let my fingers explore the curvature of
her behind and then the length of her outer thigh. On the trip
back up, feeling the outline of her panties through the cotton
of her gown sent a jolt through me that nearly brought me to
climax.

Mary Alice was letting me have my way, and with my
hand resting on her hip just inches from the place I longed
to touch, I knew I could go no further. "You better go back
to your bed," I whispered in her ear.

"I want to stay here with you," she replied. Her sobs had
subsided, and I knew I could not press the issue and make
her leave my side, especially since more than anything, I
wanted her to stay.

I kissed her softly on the neck and said, "Let's go to
sleep." I felt her nod and locked together we lay like that
until sleep took us both away.

The next time I opened my eyes was to the smell of perco-
lating coffee. The faintest signs of dawn were visible
through the sliding glass doors. Mary Alice and I were still
lying in the exact same position when Daddy walked in the
den. He reached down and touched Mary Alice on the

shoulder. I had closed my eyes, so I don't think my father knew I was awake.

"Mary Alice? Honey..." Daddy said.

I felt Mary Alice stir beside me and then she went rigid as she realized where she was and who was calling her name. She bolted upright.

"It's all right, honey, don't be scared. You just need to go back to your room."

"I'm sorry, Mr. Gody," Mary Alice said, sounding groggy. "We didn't do anything," she added.

"I know that, sweetheart. I just don't want you to have to explain that to Charity. It'll be best if you're in your own bed when she gets up."

After Mary Alice went to her room, I got up and went to mine and got dressed. I found Daddy sitting at the bar in the kitchen having a cup of coffee. It was ten minutes to six.

"Good morning, sport," he said.

"Hey, Daddy. You woke me up when you woke Mary Alice up," I said.

"I figured I did."

"She was telling you the truth. We didn't do anything. We just slept."

Daddy took a sip of coffee and eyed me. "You don't have to tell me that, son. I know you wouldn't do anything."

"I sure wanted to," I said as I sat on the barstool beside him.

He chuckled and said, "You're sixteen. I'd think something was wrong with you if you didn't."

"Yeah," I said and laughed. I thought back to my thirteenth birthday when Daddy had given me the "birds and the bees" talk. Most of the physicality I'd already picked up from listening to older boys at school, but Daddy lectured me that day on the necessity for subduing my passions until marriage so that I could truly enjoy the physical act of making love in the spiritual sense that God intended. When I asked him about jerking off, Daddy just smiled and said he figured if God was against that he would not allow boys to get erections while at the same time giving them a pair of hands. As with all of my father's moral strictures, I took his lesson to heart. Earlier, as I'd held Mary Alice and almost allowed my hand to touch her in places I knew I shouldn't, I had approached that bright line of impropriety that had been written indelibly on the pages of my conscience that day, and no matter what, I knew I could not cross it. It would have been very easy for us to have made love right there on Aunt Charity's sofa, and I was sure had I initiated it, Mary Alice would have willingly submitted out of her love for me. But even setting the moral issues aside, I was nearly a man in stature and size, and I knew the full potential of my sexual prowess, inchoate as it was. Mary Alice was clearly much more sexually immature than the boy she loved and I would rather die than face the disastrous consequences that would surely come should I loose my unbridled passions on her. Physically, I was ready for it. But she wasn't. And neither of us was ready for it emotionally.

As if reading my thoughts, Daddy said, "I can tell you and Mary Alice are in love, son. What y'all have got…well, don't do anything to spoil it. If you're lucky, you find that one person who was meant for you. I was lucky with your mama. I think you've gotten lucky with Mary Alice."

"I'm sure gonna miss her," I said.

"I know. But Charity said you've got that all worked out. Mary Alice will be spending weekends with us, right?"

"Yeah, but it still won't be like having her living here."

"I know. But you have to remember, you're going to be in school and still working at Dick's. And we've got a house to build after we get the old one tore down. It's not going to be like this summer. The weekends will roll around before you can blink."

I attempted a smile at Daddy's assessment, and I knew he was right. Mary Alice's absence would not be the only difference. The summer of '69 was rapidly coming to a close.

Four hours later, Mary Alice and I were in each other's arms, standing beside Aunt Charity's Cadillac. All of Mary Alice's things were packed neatly in the trunk. My aunt would be taking her back to Poplarville. Mary Alice had said she preferred it that way. She wanted our long goodbye to end here, on the very spot where we'd first met just six weeks ago. Six weeks. So much had happened in such a seemingly short span of time.

I gave the girl I loved one last kiss as Aunt Charity came out the front door with Sachet in tow. My sister was going too. Frankie was sitting in the swing. I was fighting to hold back the tears as I got Mary Alice situated in the back seat. If she was battling to do the same, she wasn't having any success. I brushed the tears from her face and repeated my words from last night, "Don't cry, pretty girl." That just made her cry harder.

"I love you, Nelson Gody," she said as I leaned up and stepped back from the car.

"I love you, Mary Alice Hadley," I responded, and closed the car door.

Sachet got in the backseat on the other side and Aunt Charity got behind the wheel and started the engine. Even though I knew she could not see me, I waved to Mary Alice as Aunt Charity backed the car down the drive. But as if by some connection between us, where sight was unnecessary, Mary Alice raised her hand and waved back at me. And with that final wave, I lost my battle with the tears.

Frankie had come off the porch and was standing beside me. I turned and embraced him and he put his arms around me and held me. I cried like a baby on his shoulder. The summer that had changed all our lives forever was over.

Epilogue
August 22, 2009

It's been forty years to the day since I waved goodbye to Mary Alice in Aunt Charity's front yard and cried in my best friend's arms. After that summer, Frankie never did return to live with his family. When his mother and brother were released from the hospital, they moved back to Philadelphia where her family was from. A year later, Daddy talked to Preston Marks to see if there was anything further he needed to do to retain permanent legal custody of Frankie and Preston said no, the ex parte order stated that it would remain in effect "until further order of this court," which meant Daddy had custody until a new court order was issued saying otherwise.

Frankie thrived having Daddy as his surrogate father. And Aunt Charity's doting on him gave him a mother figure like he had never known at home. To the extent that any-thing good came from Frankie's encounter with Peter Bong, it squelched whatever nascent sexual adventurism had been growing within him. As we progressed through high school, Frankie developed a close circle of friends that he trusted enough to tell that he was gay (a term that was unknown to us back then). He had two brief and discrete relationships that I knew of, one with a boy in our school and one with a member of the football team of our archrival school. Once we were in college, Frankie had a steady relationship with a student from Scotland named Graham Sinclair that lasted from our sophomore year until we graduated and Graham returned to the U.K. I've often thanked God that Frankie never succumbed to the reckless sexual promiscuity that was rampant in the gay community of the late 70s and early 80s and which led to the death of so many from AIDS.

Frankie never mended his relationship with his mother, but he and Mark are still close to this day. In 1972, on his nineteenth birthday, as a freshman in his first semester at Ole Miss, Frankie got a card from his brother and they began to write to each other. Eventually, when Frankie was convinced that Mark's overtures were genuine, they arranged a meeting during spring break. It was the first time they'd seen each other in three years. Frankie and I are still best friends. He will tell anyone that will listen that whatever measure of success he has enjoyed he owes to the Gody family who took him in and loved him for who he was with all his flaws. And he has been quite successful. After graduating with his business degree from Ole Miss, he went to a culinary school in New York. Today he is a manager and the head chef at the Beau Rivage Resort and Casino in Biloxi.

My sister is married now with two children. My nephew is a rising senior in high school and my niece is about to graduate from Belhaven College in Jackson. Sachet and her husband live in the house that Daddy built on the spot where our house was destroyed by Camille.

As for me, I went to Ole Miss too. Frankie and I were classmates, both graduating with honors in 1976. I majored in English and when Frankie packed up and headed for New York to learn how to be a chef, I left for New Jersey to attend Princeton Theological Seminary to study for my Master of Divinity degree. Of course, I didn't go alone. My wife and 13-month-old son went too.

The promise that I made to Mary Alice, that I would drive to Poplarville every weekend and bring her back to Bells Ferry—well, I kept that promise. I kept it for the next five years, except during the summers, when, just as she'd done the summer of '69, she would come to live with us, staying at Aunt Charity's. We were married at Bells Ferry Presbyterian Church the summer before I started my junior year at Ole Miss. Frankie Thompson was my best man. Beau Hadley gave the bride away and Mary Alice asked Aunt Charity to be her matron of honor. Mary Alice and I have been married 35 years now and our only child, Nelson Patrick Gody, Jr., just turned 33. He is married, has a son and two daughters, lives in Jackson, and is a partner at the law firm where Mary Alice's brother was clerking in 1969. Beau has been a judge on the Mississippi Court of Appeals since 1995, being one of the first judges appointed to that court.

I finished my divinity degree at Princeton in 1979 and after pastoring several churches all over Mississippi, I finally wound up right back here at the church I'd grown up in, Bells Ferry Presbyterian Church, where I've been the pastor for nearly twenty years now. One of the hardest things I've ever had to do was to preach Aunt Charity's funeral not long after accepting the call to this pulpit.

Daddy is still going strong at 82 years old. He lives with Mary Alice and me in Aunt Charity's house, which she bequeathed to me and my sister when she passed away in 1990. By "going strong," I really do mean that literally. Daddy doesn't look his age and still rides his motorcycle regularly, and I ride with him whenever I can. And speaking of motorcycles, back in '69, when Frankie spent the night with me, the day when he'd almost made a fool of

himself with Beau, I was reading one of Daddy's motorcycle magazines after Frankie and I had gone to bed and I
noticed the road test on the new Honda 750 had been all
marked up by my father. Well, there was a reason Daddy
had marked it up. He had put down a deposit on a 1970
model that was scheduled to be delivered that September.
But after he assumed the responsibility of taking care of
Frankie, he knew he couldn't afford it so he canceled the
order and lost his deposit of $200. I found out all this at
Christmas that year and Daddy made me promise not to tell
Frankie. I kept that promise until just before Daddy's sixti-
eth birthday in 1987. When I told Frankie that story, he
broke down and cried. I had an ulterior motive for finally
revealing this secret to my best friend. I had located a fully
restored 1970 750 in candy red, the color that Daddy had
ordered, and I was planning to give it to him for his birthday.
But I got to thinking what a nice gesture it would be if it
came from both me and Frankie, especially if I could tell
Daddy that Frankie knew why he was getting this bike nearly twenty years after he'd first ordered it. I did not ask
Frankie about this joint gift with the intent of him helping
pay for the bike, but that's what he insisted on doing. He
wanted to pay for half of it, and he reminded me that was
what we had done when we were boys and got joint gifts for
Daddy or Aunt Charity at either Christmas or for birthdays.

Daddy still rides the old 750 on occasion, but the bike he
really enjoys getting out on is his 2007 Road King. I have a
new Super Glide, which has caused not a few tongues to
wag among the older members of the Bells Ferry community, for I'm the first preacher in Bells Ferry of any denomi-
nation that anyone can ever remember who rides a motorcy-

cle to the Wednesday night prayer meetings—or anywhere else, for that matter.

The Studebaker GT Hawk remained my trusted mode of transportation all the way through seminary and into my first pastorate. It finally gave up the ghost in 1981. I sold the car to a man in Nashville who later restored it, and for years it made the rounds to various car shows. It is now on permanent display at the Studebaker museum in South Bend, Indiana.

And, yes, I am a Freemason now. I joined O. D. Smith Lodge #33 in Oxford while a student at Ole Miss. When Mary Alice and I finally settled back here in Bells Ferry, I transferred my membership and for nearly two decades I've had the pleasure of sitting in Lodge with my father and working the Craft that did so much to shape his character, and consequently mine.

As for the white sand beach on the Wolf River, where, until the summer of '69, Frankie and I had spent many an hour swimming and playing, we never set foot down there again. We abandoned our cabin and never went back after that day because of the horrible memories associated with it. Whenever I'm driving that way and cross the river, I sometimes catch myself glancing over at the spot where the path Frankie and I cut into the woods once was. I sometimes wonder if our tiny cabin is still down there. I sometimes wonder if the only death on the Wolf that day was the death of my childhood or if the man I shot died there too.

MISSISSIPPI

Jackson

Natchez

Hattiesburg

Poplarville

Saucier

Wolf River

Picayune

Bells Ferry

MTF (NASA)

Bay St. Louis

Biloxi

Gulfport

Pascagoula

Pass Christian

AFTERWORD

It has been nearly two years since the summer of 2011 when I sat down and began writing the story that you have just read. Since its release in the fall of 2011, *A Death on the Wolf* has been downloaded or purchased in paperback by nearly 25,000 readers. It has garnered almost unanimous praise in reviews on Amazon and Goodreads and won the Kindle Book Review's award of "Best Indie Books of 2012" in the category of literary fiction. This updated version of the text has corrected some formatting issues and a few typos. I've also taken this opportunity to include some discussion questions that you may find useful in reflecting on the story, or discussing it with others.

If you would like to join all the readers who have taken the time to e-mail me and/or post reviews online sharing their thoughts about the story of Nelson, Mary Alice, and Frankie and their unforgettable summer, I would be most appreciative if you would post a review on Amazon or Goodreads, or feel free to drop me a note at gmfrazier@gmfrazier.com.

If you would like to keep abreast of my upcoming projects, just go to my web site at www.gmfrazier.com. There is a link there to my blog, which I update periodically.

G. M. Frazier
May 25, 2013

DISCUSSION QUESTIONS

1. Frankie is immersed in misfortune throughout most of the story. Can you imagine his life without Nelson's friendship? In what way does Nelson need or benefit from Frankie's friendship?

2. How important is the setting—semi-rural Mississippi, summer 1969?

3. Can you list some things that happen early in the story that show the Gody family may not harbor the stereotypical "Southern" beliefs about race, especially in 1960s Mississippi?

4. Two actual historical events, the Apollo 11 mission to the moon and Hurricane Camille, occupy an important place in the story. What if the story had taken place in a summer with no important, history-making events? Would it be as effective?

5. At least two other historically significant events took place during the summer of 1969: the Stonewall Riots in New York City and Woodstock. Given the subject matter of the story, why do you think these are not mentioned at all?

6. It's strongly hinted that Peter Bong represents pure evil incarnate. How does the description of this character tend to support that interpretation? Does the presence of what could be considered a "supernatural" or at least overblown, "larger-than-life" character contribute to or detract from the overall effectiveness of an otherwise realistic story? How and why?

7.   Mary Alice appears to be devoid of any bad qualities. Was she really that "perfect" or was Nelson just blind to any faults she may have?

8.   Which character did you most closely identify with? Why? What in the story helped you to achieve this sense of kinship?

9.   Charles Dickens allegedly said that a story should become almost, but not quite, sentimental. Are there examples of this fine-line approach to storytelling in *A Death on the Wolf*? If so, what are some of them?

10.   If you had to choose just one word to describe the overarching theme of this book, what would it be?

11.   Grandma Gody appears briefly in the story. Which character do you think her appearance shed's the most light on: Nelson or his father?

12.   Could this story be told as effectively from a third-person perspective? Why or why not?

13.   Frankie is often found reading a comic book. Does this have some special meaning?

14.   Is *A Death on the Wolf* a "pro gay" novel? Why or why not?

15.   Why do you think Frankie was so willing to go off with Peter Bong despite warnings from Nelson? Why do you think he was further willing to go to a motel with Bong?

16.   Do you believe Aunt Charity was playing "match-maker" and that was her real motive behind bringing Mary Alice to live with her for the summer?

17.   Were you surprised to learn that Nelson went to seminary after college and became a minister? Why or why not?

18.   Nelson seems confused by his father's assessment of Dick as a "good man." He later seems to understand what

his father meant. Why did Lem believe Dick to be a good man? Do you agree with him? Why or why not? Do you think Lem would have called Frankie's dad a "good man?"

19. What is the significance of Frank Thompson setting fire to all of his son's belongings in their front yard?

20. Nelson's mother was named "Hope" and her twin sister, "Charity," and their older sister, "Faith." What is the significance of these names in the story?

21. It seems clear in the story that Nelson's father probably suspected Frankie was gay even before he mentioned that possibility to Nelson. Why do you suppose Nelson had not suspected this about his best friend and yet his father had?

22. In the same vein, Nelson admits to being totally ignorant of Frank Thompson's alcoholism and the physical abuse Frankie endured at home. What does this say about the character of Nelson?

23. Give some examples of characters in this story that had the courage of their convictions. Can you name any characters that clearly didn't?